"*I do believe* in you, Lucia," he said, lightly stroking the underside of her jaw with his thumbs. "Have no doubt of that."

She didn't smile, or answer, her eyes wide and searching. She was holding her breath, and he didn't know why. Surely he'd said enough to reassure her, hadn't he?

Impulsively he leaned down and kissed her forehead, the slightest brush of his lips over her skin. He'd meant it as a gesture of fondness, of regard, nothing more. But instead of stopping there, that innocent kiss pushed his gallant resolve clear from his brain, and in the next instant his mouth was kissing hers, exactly as he'd been wanting to do.

By Isabella Bradford

When You Wish Upon a Duke
When the Duchess Said Yes
When the Duke Found Love
A Wicked Pursuit
A Sinful Deception
A Reckless Desire

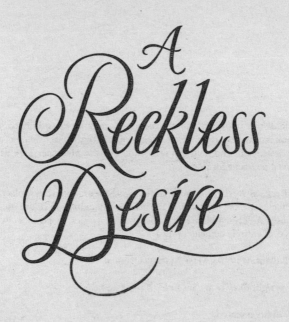

A Reckless Desire

A BRECONRIDGE BROTHERS NOVEL

Isabella Bradford

BALLANTINE BOOKS • NEW YORK

A Ballantine Books Mass Market Original

Copyright © 2016 by Susan Holloway Scott

Published in the United States by Ballantine Books, an imprint of Random House, a division of Penguin Random House LLC, New York.

BALLANTINE and the HOUSE colophon are registered trademarks of Penguin Random House LLC.

ISBN 978-0-345-54816-0
ebook ISBN 978-0-345-54817-7

Cover design: Lynn Andreozzi
Cover illustration: Gregg Gulbronson

Printed in the United States of America

randomhousebooks.com

9 8 7 6 5 4 3 2 1

Ballantine mass market edition: March 2016

For Junessa,

for always making my books better

Acknowledgments

As always, many thanks must go to the friends and colleagues who shared both their support and their expertise: Kimberly Alexander, Loretta Chase, Abby Cox, Mary Doering, Beth Dunn, Jay Howlett, Neal Hurst, Jenny Lynn, Mark Hutter, Michael McCarty, Annelise Robey, Mollie Smith, Janea Whitacre, and Sarah Woodyard.

A Reckless Desire

CHAPTER

1

"And I'm telling you the truth, Everett," said Lord Rivers Fitzroy. "The famous Madame Adelaide Mornay is the sorriest, most wretched excuse for a queen that I have ever witnessed."

"Speak it louder, Fitzroy," said his friend Sir Edward Everett as they squeezed through the narrow, noisy passage of King's Theatre. The leading actors and actresses had scarcely taken their final bows, yet already the cramped spaces backstage were crowded with friends and other well-wishers. "There may have been one or two people in Drury Lane who didn't hear you."

"Let them hear me," Rivers said as he maneuvered around a plaster statue of Charlemagne that had figured into the second act. "She was abominable, and you know it, too."

"What I know is that she's currently warming Mansfield's bed," Everett said, following close, "and I've no wish to make an enemy of a man like that. *He* doesn't seem to find fault with her, at least not when he's buried between her legs."

As the third son of the Duke of Breconridge, Rivers wasn't particularly intimidated by the Marquess of Mansfield or anyone else, unlike poor Everett, who as a lowly baronet lived in constant dread of offending one peer or another. "Damnation, but it's crowded here tonight. Who *are* all these rogues?"

The gentlemen around them had the overwrought, pop-eyed eagerness that marked men in the pursuit of beautiful women who'd welcome their advances. He recognized the signs in himself, for he'd never worked half this hard to reach a palace ball populated by aristocratic virgins.

The door of the dancers' dressing room stood open, and already Rivers could glimpse the intoxicating delights inside. Lovely, laughing young women, all in the process of shedding their gauzy, spangled costumes without a shred of modesty; what man with breath in his body could wish to be anywhere else? He loved how they darted confidently about in the crowded room, graceful and sleek, slipping teasingly among servants and well-wishers. He loved even their scent, a heady, sensual mixture of face-powder and pomatum, rosin and perfume and female exertion.

"Buona sera, innamorati!" he called from the doorway, cheerfully greeting them in the Italian that was the native language of so many of the dancers. "Good evening to you all!"

"Buona sera, Lord Rivers!" they chimed back, like schoolgirls with a recitation, and like schoolgirls, they collapsed into laughter afterward, while the other male visitors glowered unhappily.

Rivers was a favorite with the dancers, and not just because he was a duke's son with deep pockets, either. He was tall and he was handsome, with glinting gold hair and bright blue eyes, but most of all, he genuinely liked this company of dancers. He sent them punch and chocolate biscuits. He'd learned all their names, which none of the other gentlemen who prowled about the dressing room had bothered to do. He not only spoke Italian, but he spoke Italian with a Neapolitan accent on account of having spent much time in Naples with a cousin who'd a villa there.

He was also the only gentleman in London who'd managed last year to have a brief love affair—they called it a *poco amore,* or little love—with Magdalena di Rossi, the lead dancer of their troupe, and survive unscathed. Even more amazingly, he'd managed to emerge after those two months in her bed as her friend. He'd the rare gift of knowing the exact moment to end affairs to make such a transition possible (although a handsome diamond brooch had helped immeasurably). All of which was why now, as soon as he sat in the chair that was offered to him, Magdalena came to sit on his knee with territorial affection.

"*Il mio caro amico.*" She swept off his hat so she could kiss him loudly on each cheek without being poked in the eye. "Our evening is complete now that you are here, my lord."

"Hah, you say that to every gentleman who comes through the door," he said, and kissed her in return as he slipped his arm around her waist. Dancing had made her body firm and compact, and he'd always appreciated how her waist was narrow even without stays. "Truth has never been your strongest suit."

She pouted coyly. She still wore her stage paint, with blackened brows and dark rings around her eyes, and with her lips scarlet, it was a formidable pout indeed.

"I am not truthful like you, my lord, no," she admitted, trailing an idle finger along the collar of his silk coat. "But then, I am not English, with your English love of truth and, um, *franchezza.*"

"*Franchezza?*" repeated Everett, sitting nearby with another of the dancers on his knee. "I can only guess what manner of wickedness that may be."

"It's frankness," Rivers said. "Magdalena has always believed I am too frank for my own good."

"True enough," Everett said. "You *are* frank to a dangerous fault. Do you dare repeat what you told me about Madame Adelaide's performance?"

That instantly captured Magdalena's interest. There was neither love nor respect between the acting side of the playhouse's company and the dancers, with both groups claiming they were the real favorites with audiences.

"Oh, that lead-footed cow Adelaide," she scoffed. "*Vacca!* I wonder that you could keep sufficiently awake to judge her, my lord. What did you say to Sir Edward, eh? What did you say of the vile Adelaide?"

For a half a second, Rivers hesitated, considering not repeating the opinion he'd given to Everett earlier. Not only would it serve to inflate Magdalena's considerable pride further (an inflation that it did not need) to hear him criticize her rival, but the part about how he could do better smacked of boastfulness. He'd had a quantity of excellent smuggled wine with his dinner, enough to give him bravado, yet not quite enough to have him completely unaware of the peril of making a foolhardy statement. For as long as Rivers could recall, his father had always cautioned him against that, reminding him of the fine line between confidence and being a braggart.

But in that half second of reflection, he decided this was confidence, not boasting. More important, it was the truth, and so with a smile he answered her.

"I said that Madame Adelaide is the sorriest, most wretched excuse for a queen that I have ever witnessed," he declared, heedless of who overheard him. "There is not one iota of royalty to her or to her performance, and if it were not for the lord who's keeping her and paying for the production, she wouldn't have a place on this stage."

"Bah, that's nothing new," Magdalena said, disappointed. "Everyone knows that of her."

"But why doesn't she make a study of Her Majesty, so that she might better play queens?" he asked. He was serious, too, for willful ignorance was incomprehensible to him; with study and application, anything seemed possible. "If she'd rather not model herself on the queen, then there are plenty of regal duchesses about London. Why doesn't she observe them to perfect her art?"

"Because she has no art, that is why," Magdalena said with a dismissive sweep of her hand. "My dancers and I practice every day of our lives, hour after hour until we fall from weariness, but actresses like Adelaide are idle and useless—useless! They do not believe they need do more than display their breasts and mumble through their lines, and expect their suffering audience to be grateful for that."

"Madame Adelaide should take lessons from you, Fitzroy," Everett said. "Give her training in how to behave like a queen."

Rivers smiled, entertained by the idea of giving lessons in regal deportment. God knows he'd seen his share of haughty, queenly ladies, and those were just in his own family.

"I could do it," he said, "and do it well, too. Given the time to develop a proper course of study and a woman who is reasonably clever and willing to apply herself, anything would be possible."

Everett groaned. "Only if the poor thing didn't perish from boredom first. 'A proper course of study'! My God, Fitzroy, could you make it sound any more tedious?"

"It would be an education, Everett, not a seduction," Rivers said. "Not that you would know the difference. But it's only the most idle of speculation, since I doubt Madame would agree to become my student."

"No, she would not," Magdalena agreed, and heaved

a bosom-raising sigh directly beneath Rivers's nose. "More's the pity, *il mio caro*. It would be something to see, yes?"

A small tiring-girl—one of the servants who helped the dancers dress—hurried up to her, bobbing a quick curtsey. In her arms was an enormous bouquet of flowers, so large that it dwarfed the young woman holding it, a vibrant splash of floral color against her white apron and kerchief. Magdalena plucked the sender's note free, read it, and scowled, shoving it disdainfully back among the flowers.

"Such beautiful flowers from such a ridiculous man," she said derisively. "But it's not the fault of the poor blossoms to have been sent by a churlish oaf. *Allocco!*"

Rivers sympathized with the poor oaf. Any romantic attachment with Magdalena was fraught with such scenes. At first the drama was exciting, yes, but over time it became too exhausting to be pleasurable. He had to keep reminding himself of that as she sat on his leg, her bottom pressing against his thigh in a very enticing manner.

Magdalena's thoughts, however, had already gone elsewhere.

"Tell me, my lord," she said in the coaxing voice she employed to get what she wanted. "What if you attempted to train a lesser actress? One who was not as proud? One who, with your, ah, education, could knock the vile Adelaide from her post?"

"Do better than that, Fitzroy," Everett said with a bit of bravado of his own. "Take some ordinary hussy and turn her into your regal actress, the toast of London. Take this chit here. She'd do."

He caught the arm of the tiring-girl who had just presented the bouquet to Magdalena and pulled her back. The young woman caught her heel on the hem of her petticoats and stumbled, nearly dropping the flowers, and Magdalena rolled her eyes with disgust.

"So clumsy, Lucia," she scolded, bored, as if she couldn't really be bothered to say more. "Mind you don't drop my flowers."

"No, *signora*," the young woman murmured, her dark eyes enormous in her small face. Although she was obviously from Naples like Magdalena and the rest of the dancers, she lacked their lush figures as well as their voluptuous beauty. She was more delicate, her skin paler, and the dark linen clothes she wore were in stark contrast to the gaudy bright silks and ribbons around her. Rivers saw that, like too many young servants, she had a waifish quality to her that spoke of long hours and low wages.

Yet there was also an unmistakable spark in her eyes, a defiant fire that not even the somber clothes could completely douse, and Rivers guessed that she would like nothing better than to hurl the flowers into Magdalena's face. He sympathized. He'd often felt that way himself.

"Make it a true challenge, Fitzroy," Everett said, still grasping the tiring-girl's arm to keep her from escaping. "I'll wager fifty guineas you can't turn this little drab into your stage queen."

"Fifty guineas, my lord!" the girl exclaimed. "*Madre di Dio,* fifty blessed guineas!"

"A whole fifty *blessed* guineas!" Everett repeated, imitating her accent, lower-class London with a foreign flip. "Fancy!"

He laughed, and the dancer beside him tittered with him. The tiring-girl flushed, but with more of the same defiance Rivers had seen in her before; she did not look down, or apologize, either.

Nor did Rivers laugh along with Everett. He never enjoyed scenes like this one, when those with privilege and wealth made jests of those who didn't. The young woman had every right to find fifty guineas a staggering proposition. He doubted she earned even a fifth of that amount in an entire year.

"Enough," he said, a single word of warning.

Surprised, Everett nodded. Indulgently he winked at the girl.

"Very well, lass," he said, attempting an empty show of kindness. "If you feel you're worth more, then I'll raise my stake to a round one hundred guineas."

She gasped, her eyes even wider as she looked to Rivers. "I'd make you proud, my lord," she said eagerly. "I swear I would."

Rivers smiled, liking the young woman more by the moment. It took courage for her to speak up like this, especially after Everett had been such an ass. Her spirit intrigued him. She was a bold little thing, and he'd always had a weakness for women who weren't afraid to speak their minds.

"What do you say, Fitzroy?" Everett asked. "Will you take on this little scrap as your pupil?"

"Of course he will not, my lord," Magdalena said indignantly, sliding quickly from Rivers's knee to pull the girl's arm free of the baronet's grasp. "Lucia is a cousin and an orphan, entrusted to our care and keeping, and I won't have you ruining her usefulness for the sake of some foolish gentlemen's wager. Back to my room with those flowers, Lucia, *pronto, pronto*!"

She gave Lucia a light smack between the shoulder blades with the flat of her palm to urge her on, and the girl curtseyed and hurried away, the flowers held high in her arms for safekeeping. But as she'd curtseyed, Rivers had glimpsed regret in those large dark eyes, a genuine wish that things had gone otherwise. Could she truly want to be part of this, of what Magdalena had accurately described as a foolish gentlemen's wager? Would she really have wanted to cast away her lot on the whim of a man she didn't know, gambling that he could do what he'd grandly claimed?

As Rivers watched her slender figure weave among the others, he wondered, speculating as to whether he could have made so great a transformation. He tried to imagine her commanding both a stage and an audience as she played a queen.

Could he have done it? Could she?

Yet as soon as she disappeared from the room, she faded from his thoughts as well, and within minutes he'd forgotten both the girl and the wager entirely.

Lucia di Rossi dressed as quietly as she could, not wanting to wake the other two girls who shared the small room and its single bed with her. Because their room was in the attic, directly beneath the roof, the beams overhead slanted sharply from one wall to the other, and she was forced to crouch down before their tiny looking glass to make sure her hair was as smooth as possible, with no curling wisps slipping free of the tight knot at the back of her head. She knew she'd never be a beauty, but at least she could be tidy. Satisfied, she slipped her white linen cap over her hair, and tied her flat-brimmed hat on over that. For luck, she patted the strand of coral beads that had been her mother's, her fingers circling the little Neapolitan cameo that hung from it.

One of the other girls stirred and squinted at her.

"It's so early, Lucia," Giovanna said groggily. "Mother in Heaven, where must you go at this hour?"

"An errand," Lucia whispered, purposefully vague.

"You mean an errand for Magdalena," the other girl said. "Who else would be so cruel to send you out at this hour?"

For the rest of the world, the hour wasn't particularly early or cruel. Lucia had just counted eleven chimes of the church bell in the next street, and she prayed she wasn't already too late.

Now she merely shrugged and let Giovanna think the worst of Magdalena.

"I must leave," she whispered, wrapping her shawl over her shoulders. She looped her fingers through the latchets of her shoes, not wanting to put them on until she was downstairs. "You go back to sleep."

Giovanna grunted and pulled the coverlet over her head, and Lucia slipped through the door and closed it as gently as she could. She padded down the winding back stairs in her stocking feet, past the other closed doors, where the rest of the company remained soundly asleep. The lodging-house catered exclusively to foreign-born dancers, and the landlady respected their hours so long as they paid their reckoning on time.

Muffled sounds from the wide-awake London streets contrasted sharply with the sleeping house, and from the kitchen in the back of the house, Lucia heard the first crashings and thumpings of the cook beginning late breakfast. At the bottom of the staircase, she leaned against the door to buckle her shoes. Then, at last, she slipped outside, and she was free.

She walked swiftly, scarcely noticing how the neighborhoods changed from the crowded, narrow streets around Covent Garden, north and west toward Marylebone, where the houses were larger and more modern and their occupants more wealthy and more respectable. She knew the way, for Magdalena had sent her there before, carrying letters that she hadn't trusted to the lodging-house boy.

This time, however, Lucia was going on an errand of her own; one that, if things went as she hoped, could prove to be a thousand times more important than any of Magdalena's silly love-notes. With each step she rehearsed what she'd say. She so seldom was permitted to speak for herself that composing the proper words now wasn't easy, and she'd lain awake most of last night considering her speech.

All too soon she was standing on the immaculate white marble steps of the brick house on Cavendish Square. She knocked briskly, and because the butler who opened the door remembered her from other visits, he let her inside. After the bustle and dust of the streets, the front hall seemed cool and serene and impossibly beautiful, with its black-and-white stone checkered floor and the grand staircase rising up so gracefully that it might as well be ascending to Heaven itself.

The butler looked down his long nose and silently held out his hand to her, no doubt expecting another letter from Magdalena.

"I don't have nothing," she said. "The message's so private, it's not written. I must speak it to his lordship myself."

The butler frowned imperiously. "Careless girl," he said. "You lost it, didn't you?"

She raised her chin, refusing to be intimidated. He was only another servant. He wasn't any better than she, except that he wore fancy livery with gold lace.

"I didn't," she said, "and I'm not careless, not a bit. I told you before, it's a most private message, meant for his lordship's own ears alone."

The butler's frown deepened. "His lordship does not wish to be troubled with no reason. If this is an idle invention born of your wickedness—"

"It's not," she said doggedly. "It's born out of a private conversation with his lordship last night."

He gave her one long, final look of judgmental disapproval.

"Very well," he said. "You stay here whilst I see if his lordship is in. Touch nothing."

"Very well," she echoed, not to be impertinent, but because she thought it sounded like a grand and noble way of saying yes. "Although I'd think being his lordship's butler, you'd know whether he was in or not."

He glared at her, saying nothing more. As he headed up the stairs, he passed by a footman standing at attention like a sentry beside one of the doors.

"Watch her," he said.

It offended Lucia to be taken for a thief, simply because her clothes weren't as fine as his. But she'd come this far, and she didn't want to be pushed out the door now. She didn't dare sit on one of the straight-backed chairs along the wainscoting, fearing that it might be considered touching, so instead she simply stood where she was, her hands clasped at her waist where the footman would be sure to see she wasn't slipping anything of value into her pocket.

She did let herself look, though. There could be no harm in that, and she looked eagerly, searching for clues to the man whose grand house this was. Not that she found any. A large painting of a sunset over the ocean, a blank-eyed statue of a naked lady, an elaborate vase on a marble-topped table: what could any of that tell her of his lordship beyond that he was very wealthy, which she already knew?

She sighed restlessly, and touched her necklace again. She hoped he remembered his offer this morning, and she hoped he could do as he'd said. He'd smiled, not as if it were all a jest, but as if he truly believed it was possible. To be able to become a dramatic actress, to earn her own wages and have her own lodgings, and to be finally free of Magdalena and her endless demands—oh, it was beyond imagining!

She caught sight of her reflection in the looking glass that hung in a gold frame on the far wall. She appeared tiny and insignificant, a small, dark blot in a straw hat in the corner of these magnificent surroundings.

She sighed again, and steadfastly turned from the looking glass.

She hoped he remembered *her*.

The butler was coming back down the stairs, each step filled with disdain as he came closer to her. She'd no doubt he was going to send her away, and she'd a sickening dread in the bottom of her stomach. Her dream would be over before it had begun, and then—

"His lordship will receive you," the butler said, making it clear this was not his decision, but his master's. "This way."

Now dread of a different variety washed over her as she hurried after him up the stairs. The words that she'd so carefully composed last night had vanished from her head, with nothing to replace them but a babble of incoherent desperation.

The staircase didn't lead to Heaven, but to a short hallway with more heavy paneled doors. The butler stopped before one and knocked, and a muffled voice from within told him to enter. He did, standing to one side to announce Lucia, and she'd no choice but to enter, immediately dropping to a deep curtsey, her head bowed.

"The young person, my lord," the butler said wearily over her head.

It wasn't until then that she realized she hadn't given her name, nor had the butler bothered to ask it. Once again she'd been reduced to insignificance, one more example in a life full of similar indignities. But this time the slight didn't wound so much as it made her forget her nervousness. It *irritated* her. She was tired of being overlooked. She was after all a Di Rossi, and she longed for the attention of the center stage as much as anyone else in her family.

"I have a name, sir," she said, her head still bowed in her curtsey. "I am not merely a 'young person.' I am Lucia di Rossi."

To her chagrin, she heard his lordship make an odd,

snorting half laugh. She hadn't meant that as a jest, but as a declaration. Oh, already things were not going well!

"Come here to me, if you please, Lucia-Young-Person-di-Rossi," he said. "I must see this prodigiously brave woman who dares correct Mr. Crofton."

She rose as he'd asked, and crossed the room to where Lord Rivers sat in a leather armchair. Beside him was a small mahogany table laid with a white cloth, a silver coffeepot, and a large porcelain cup filled to the brim with lethal-smelling coffee. Although it was the middle of the day, only the curtains to one window had been drawn, and most of the room remained in a murky half-light.

It was, however, obvious that the room was being kept that way at his lordship's orders, and to Lucia the reason for those orders was clear enough, too. In the three years that she had been with Magdalena, she had become familiar with how a gentleman looked in the morning after a rich and eventful night, full of riotous company and strong drink.

Lord Rivers had that look. He was sprawled in the armchair, his long legs stretched before him and his head resting against the back of the chair. There was, she suspected, ample reason for that inky black coffee and nothing else for his breakfast. His golden hair was loose and rumpled around his face, and his jaw was dark with the beard he hadn't yet shaved. He wore a yellow silk dressing gown over dark linen breeches; he hadn't bothered to close the gown, and a wide stretch of his bare chest was on display. Rolling from his bed (or another's), he hadn't taken the time to locate either shoes or stockings, and his bare feet were thrust haphazardly into embroidered backless slippers.

"I know you," he said, squinting at her. "You're Magdalena's girl."

"Forgive me, my lord," she said. "But I'm not her girl. I'm her cousin."

He turned his head slightly to one side, considering her. "But she treats you as a servant."

"As a Di Rossi, I work for our company however I can," she said carefully. "All of us who are in London do the same. My uncle is our *maestro di balletto*—ballet-master—and it is for him to decide what roles each of us shall take for the good of the family. I am a tiring-girl, helping the dancers with their costumes and performing other errands for them."

She hoped that would suffice as an explanation. She'd no wish to have to describe exactly why she did what she did.

To her sorrow, it wasn't. He leaned forward in the chair, resting his elbows on the chair's arms to study her more closely. In the half-light, he apparently didn't see what he wished, and he waved his hand toward the butler, who was still standing by the open door.

"Crofton, the curtains," he said, not looking away from Lucia. Dutifully the butler drew them, and sunlight flooded the room. Lord Rivers winced and blinked, but still continued to look so intently at her that her cheeks warmed beneath his scrutiny.

Yet she met his gaze, refusing to give in and look down. If he studied her, then she could study him as well. She'd only seen him by the candlelight in the dressing room or by the lanterns in the street as he'd handed Magdalena into his carriage. He was more handsome than she'd realized—astonishingly, achingly handsome, with his golden shock of hair, his bright blue eyes (albeit bluer this morning for being a bit bloodshot), a jaw fit for a marble god, and a full, sensuous mouth that smiled easily. The glimpse of his bare chest, firmly muscled, was most distracting. He was the only gentleman that Magdalena welcomed back into her company once they'd ceased being lovers, and seeing him now like this, Lucia understood why.

"Why aren't you a dancer, too?" he asked bluntly, looking her up and down. "You're a little wisp of a girl, to be sure, but with a few good meals and the usual paint and spangles, you'd do well enough in the chorus."

Her blush deepened. "I am clumsy, my lord," she said, equally blunt. There was no reason why she shouldn't be, considering it was the truth. "They tried to make me a dancer, but no matter how hard I tried to follow the steps, I could not hear the music."

"You don't hear the tune?" he asked curiously.

"Not like the others, my lord, no," she said with long-standing resignation. "I hear the music, but I cannot sense the pattern or the rhythm of it like the others do, or figure out when or where to place my feet. I was the despair of my uncle, and he banished me from his classes, and from the corps."

His brows rose in skeptical disbelief. "A Di Rossi who cannot dance?"

"Yes, my lord," she said softly. It was a disgrace she always had with her, an agonizing defect that had kept her from ever being completely accepted into the sweeping embrace of her large family. Her uncle had called her willful, and beaten her with his maestro's baton when she'd stumbled. Her cousins had laughed at her, and called her a waddling goose and worse. Even her own father had been mortified, and when he drank too much he'd wept from the shame of siring such a daughter.

"A Di Rossi who cannot dance," he said again, marveling. "Who would have thought it possible?"

"But that is why I have come to you, my lord," she said fervently. "Last night you offered me the first chance I've ever had to change things, a chance to make them all see that I'm more than their chambermaid."

He leaned back against the chair. "I did?" he asked uneasily. "How in blazes could I have done that?"

Her heart sank. He didn't remember. But now that she'd come this far, she'd no choice but to continue.

"You did, my lord," she said, taking another step closer as she willed him to remember. "You said you could make me into a great actress who could play queens. You said you could teach me to be better than Madame Adelaide, that you could—"

"Everett's wager," he said slowly. "You're the girl he wanted me to transform, aren't you?"

Now that he'd remembered, she wished he'd show more enthusiasm.

"Yes, my lord, yes, yes," she said, eagerness and desperation making her talk too fast. "I would be the best student any teacher ever had. I'd make you so proud of me, my lord. You'd see. I'd make sure you'd win that wager from Lord Everett."

He sighed. "Do you truly believe I've the power to change you like that?"

"I do, my lord," she said promptly. "I must. Because if I don't, my lord, all I'll have ahead of me is an entire *life* of being ordered about by Magdalena, and that—oh, I do not think I would survive that."

"I know I couldn't," he agreed. "Given time, she'd make a turnip weep and beg for mercy."

He was obviously considering it, his expression thoughtful.

"Please, my lord." She pressed her palms together in dramatic supplication. "It might have seemed no more than a gentlemen's wager to you, but to me—to me it was the purest, rarest magic, like a gift from the very heavens."

He rose abruptly in a great swath of yellow silk and went to stand at one of the windows, his arms folded across his chest and his back toward her.

Was he dismissing her? Had her plea been too much, too impassioned? Even though she had lived in London for most of her life, she still forgot how much more reserved Englishmen were.

"Forgive me if I've spoken too much, my lord," she said sadly to that imposing back. "But it's only that—"

"Can you read?"

"Yes, I can read," she said, taken aback that he'd ask that. Just because the Di Rossis danced did not mean they were unlettered fools.

"Not just claptrap and nonsense, either," he said. "Can you read true English?"

"Of course I can," she said. "I have even read many of your English playwrights, too, so you needn't ask that."

He nodded toward the window. *"Ma sei più al tuo agio con la madrelingua, l'italiano di Napoli."*

Because he was still turned from her, she didn't bother to hide her dismay. He'd just declared that she was more at ease in her mother tongue, the Italian of Naples (which wasn't true), and he'd turned it into a self-righteous little statement that was designed more to display his own facility in that language than to test hers—hardly an auspicious sign of a sympathetic teacher. He wasn't alone, of course. Every other Englishman that she'd ever met who'd claimed to speak Italian was much the same. They might know the words, but they hadn't the heart or the passion to speak proper Italian, especially Neapolitan Italian. Living in the shadow of a volcano, as everyone in Naples did, changed everything.

Not that she could tell Lord Rivers that, not at all. She'd learned that much about male pride from observing how deftly Magdalena had managed that fragile article with her various lovers.

"You speak Neapolitan Italian as well as any Englishman, *il mio signore*," she answered sweetly instead, a bold-faced lie if ever there was one. Then she switched to French. *"Mais ma mère était française, pas Italienne."*

He turned around quickly with surprise, the dressing gown whipping about him. "You speak French, too? Ah, that is, *votre parlez*, ah, *parlent français?*"

"Oui, mon seigneur," she answered, and then returned to English, for the sake of sparing him. "My mother danced with the French Opera. I was born in Paris."

"Er, ah, so you were," he said uncomfortably, and in English, too. "I can hear it now."

She smiled, trying to be encouraging. He might be unnecessarily vain of his Italian, but at least he realized that his French was abysmal.

"I will learn in whichever language you care to teach, my lord," she said. "Though I should prefer English, for it is the English stage I wish to conquer."

"You must obey me in everything," he said, clearly relieved to once again be in unquestionable charge, "no matter how foolish it may seem to you. I will devise a plan of lessons that must be studied and followed. You will not be permitted to disagree."

"I won't, my lord," she said promptly.

He nodded. "If we are to do this properly, you must resign your position at the Royal, and devote yourself entirely to your studies with me."

Her eyes widened. "But I'll have no earnings, my lord. How shall I support myself if I cannot work?"

"You won't need earnings," he said, standing there like some great, golden, pagan god who could order the world to his liking. "Not while you're with me."

That made her uneasy. "I cannot simply disappear from the company, my lord. Who would take my place? Who would do my tasks?"

"I should think any maidservant from the street could do them," he said. "But I'll speak to Magdalena, and arrange to pay for another girl who'll take your place while—"

"No!" she cried, and instantly retreated. "That is, my lord, I should rather that my cousin and the others not know of this . . . experiment until it is complete."

"But they must know something," he reasoned, "because you'll no longer be in their midst. For you to make the most progress, I'll want you to stay here with me. If I am to devote all my waking hours to you, I expect you to do the same."

She ducked her chin, her cheeks hot. "Forgive me, my lord, but I . . . I cannot do that. I wish to be an actress, yes, but I don't want to share your bed."

He smiled, bemused. "You truly aren't a dancer, are you? You don't have the necessary wantonness, or the predatory heart that goes with it, either."

Her flush deepened. "No, my lord."

"I don't expect you to be my mistress," he said, smiling still. "You'll have a bed of your own in a room of your own, with a latch on the door if that makes you feel safer. I shall expect you to attend me throughout the day, and I should like it if you dined with me, but you have my word that your virtue shall be safe. *Entirely* safe."

"Thank you, my lord," she said softly. There couldn't be a better arrangement, and she was fortunate he felt this way. Yet even so, a small, perverse part of her wished he didn't find her so unbearably plain and undesirable that the very notion of it made him smile.

"I'll send word to Magdalena that you'll be in my care," he said, striding across the room to his desk. "I'll write it now, so you may deliver it to her yourself."

She shook her head swiftly. "If you please, my lord, she must not know anything. Truly. You heard her last night. She won't permit it."

"She will if I tell her to," he said, reaching for a fresh

sheet of a paper. "She won't be able to argue if I assume responsibility for you."

"Please, my lord," she begged. How could she explain to him that it wasn't well-meant concern for her welfare that would make her cousin object, but reluctance to part with a drudge that she could keep without wages? "I would rather tell Magdalena and my uncle myself that I'm leaving, and I'll contrive some sort of nonsense by way of explanation, too. They do not deserve the truth. I would rather amaze them than suffer the weight of their scorn."

He paused, perplexed, his pen in his hand.

"Scorn?" he repeated. "You wish to better yourself. What the devil could they scorn?"

"Me, my lord," she said succinctly. "They will not believe I can do this."

"Well, a pox on them," he said. "*I* believe you can. You wouldn't be permitted to fail, you know. You'll have no choice but to succeed."

"Truly, my lord?" she said, stunned that he'd finally agreed. "You . . . you mean that?"

"Of course," he said, regarding her curiously. "Why would I say anything that I did not mean?"

Yet she still couldn't quite believe it. "You believe in me, my lord? You meant that part, too?"

"I believe in you, yes," he repeated with satisfying clarity, "and even more, I believe in myself to teach you. There is no conceivable way that I intend to lose to Everett, not this wager."

That wasn't quite as good as having him believe in her abilities alone, but she'd accept it. In time she'd prove to him she could do it, just as she meant to prove it to so many others.

And if Lord Rivers did not intend to lose, well, then, he'd learn soon enough that neither did she.

CHAPTER
3

"What wager, Fitzroy?" Lord Everett said. He was comfortably ensconced in a large old wing chair near the front window of the club, a cheroot in one hand and a racing newspaper in the other. He was so comfortably ensconced that he had the perfect air of a gentleman who did not wish to be troubled except in the most dire of circumstance, and the faintly displeased expression on his face showed that he didn't believe Rivers's interruption could possibly fall into that category of extremity. "What in blazes are you talking about?"

"The wager over the girl," Rivers said, dropping into the empty chair beside Everett's. "Last night. Early in the evening. Come, you must remember it."

Everett screwed up his face with the exertion of thought, his cheeks hollowing as he drew deeply on the cheroot.

"I'm afraid I don't recall any wagers involving girls," he admitted. "Not last night anyway. What was the chit's name? Have I had her?"

"She's a Di Rossi," said Rivers, pulling his chair closer to Everett's. "And no, I can guarantee you haven't had her in your bed. You'd better remember the wager, because I'm going to accept your terms."

That earned Everett's attention, and he straightened in

the chair. "One of those delightfully slatternly Di Rossis? You should have said so in the beginning, you rogue."

"Not one of those," Rivers said with a wave of his hand, banishing all the slatterns in a single, dismissive sweep. "Her name is Lucia. Lucia di Rossi."

Everett frowned, considering. "Is she new to the litter?"

Rivers sighed impatiently. "You remember her, Everett. Fifty blessed guineas."

The other man's face lit with recognition. "The one you swore you could make over into the next Anne Bracegirdle! I recall her well enough now. A small, dreary, pinched creature. You say she's a Di Rossi, too?"

"So she swears." Rivers thought Everett's estimation was a little harsh. True, he himself had scarcely taken any notice of the girl in the past, but this morning, when she'd stood before him in his parlor and he'd had more time to study her properly, he'd been struck by her . . . her presence.

Yes, that's what it had been. Presence. It was all she had, really. She wasn't beautiful the way the rest of her family was, but there was a quickness, a lightness, to her that had made it impossible for him to look away. He was certain that with his guidance, education, and better clothes, audiences could be persuaded to feel the same about her, too. If Magdalena was the sun, blindingly brilliant and alluring, then her cousin Lucia was like a small, silvery star with a brilliance that was all her own.

Not, of course, that he'd ever dare speak such poetical gibberish to Everett.

"Another Di Rossi," Everett marveled. "She must dance, then. They all do. Yet I don't recall seeing her on the stage."

"She doesn't dance," Rivers said. "Which is why I intend to transform her into an actress. Or I will if you'll agree to our wager."

"The fifty blessed guineas?"

"No retreat, Everett," Rivers said firmly. "You increased the stake to a hundred, and that's what it shall be. One hundred guineas says I'll have that girl in a leading role on a stage in London by the end of the summer."

"That's three months," Everett protested. "You could make a horse recite Shakespeare in three months. I say you perform your miracle within six weeks, or there's no wager."

Rivers lowered his chin and frowned. If three months appeared an eternity to Everett, six weeks seemed the merest blink of an eye to Rivers for the task before him. It wasn't his own abilities as a teacher that he doubted. Far from it. While his friends and family might tease him about his scholarly habits, he'd always found that most anything really was possible through study and application. True, he'd never taught anyone else anything, but he was confident he would be successful, the same as he'd been with whatever he'd attempted, from learning ancient languages to jumping the stone walls at Breconridge Hall on horseback.

No, it was the girl herself that concerned him. Lucia di Rossi had impressed him with her eagerness to learn, but he still had no notion about how quickly she could shed her old self and adopt the new habits that would be necessary for her to succeed. If she truly wanted to play grand ladies, she was going to have to change nearly everything about herself, from the way she spoke to how she stood and walked. He would need to summon mantua-makers and hairdressers and every other kind of female-improver to help make her small, slight self palatable to an audience quick to criticize a lack of beauty. He didn't even know if she possessed the prodigious memory required to become a decent actress.

But because he did like a challenge, and perhaps because he'd had just enough to drink to believe that anything—anything!—was possible through application, he accepted.

"It shall be done," he declared, seizing his friend's hand to seal the wager. "Six weeks it is."

"How willingly you embrace the impossible!" Everett said, delighted. He held out his empty glass to a passing servant. "But no cheating, now. You must rely on your own genius to teach the girl. No bringing in Garrick or any of his professional ilk to help."

Rivers nodded. "I've a few terms of my own, Everett. You are not to see the girl again until she appears on the stage. I want no meddling from you, no interference. Nor do I wish you to speak of this to anyone else in town."

Everett's smile was smug as he settled back in the chair. "Why should I?" he asked. "I wouldn't dare risk lessening the exquisite surprise of seeing your plain little protégée make a fool of herself, and of you, too, my friend. I've never been more certain of a wager falling in my favor. You might as well give me the hundred guineas now and spare yourself the humiliation."

"What, and sacrifice the pleasure of seeing you humbled into submission by the divine Lucia di Rossi?" Rivers said, bravado making his confidence grow by the second. "You'll see in six weeks. I'll triumph, because she will."

Yet as certain as Rivers felt with Everett, he still saw no value in sharing the details about the bet when he visited his older brother's house later that afternoon.

"I'm going to the country for several weeks, Harry," he announced as they stood together in the library, waiting for the rest of the company to appear before they went in to dine. "Perhaps longer. I'm finding London quite tedious at present, and besides, I have a special new project in mind."

His brother regarded Rivers curiously. Harry was the Earl of Hargreave, and heir to the family dukedom. In

Rivers's opinion, Harry had always been as fine an older brother as could be imagined, as had Geoffrey, the middle brother. He'd no complaints. Oh, there had been the usual older-brother torments inflicted when they'd been boys, to which Rivers had always countered with his own brand of youngest-brother aggravation. But on the whole they had always been quite loyal to one another, and together had had their share of scrapes and adventures, especially on their Grand Tour.

Or at least they had until first Harry and then Geoffrey had fallen in love and married and fathered children. In Rivers's eyes, his brothers had become far too staid for their own good since then, and had ceased to be the raucous boon companions that he remembered so fondly, ones who could always drag him from his scholarly shell. They'd become *responsible*.

Which was exactly why he chose not to tell Harry about the bet, or the nature of his visit to the country, either. Harry would not have understood. He would have cautioned Rivers against rash wagers, against entanglements with Italian dance troupes, against devoting himself to a foolish experiment instead of finding a well-bred wife of his own.

"It's early in the season for you to leave town," Harry said, fortunately unable to read Rivers's thoughts. "I'm sure there will be many young ladies who will be unhappy to see you go so soon."

Rivers shrugged. "More likely their mothers will be the unhappy ones," he said. "Although I imagine both will find other more suitable quarry than I soon enough."

"You're suitable," Harry said, restlessly tapping his walking stick against the floor. A riding accident several years earlier had left him lame in one leg, and while in public he'd learned through sheer will to walk well enough with the aid of specially designed shoes and boots, at home and with family, he let himself rely upon the extra assistance of a walking stick. "Damned suitable. You need only ask Father. He'll explain it all to you."

Rivers sighed. "I've no more wish to hear that particular explanation than you do yourself."

"Then you know the remedy as well," Harry said, the sharpness in his voice unmistakable. "Marry, and give Father his heart's desire."

"Don't begin," Rivers said wearily. He'd always considered it his personal good fortune to be the third son of the Duke of Breconridge, free of the dutiful obligations of being his father's heir and permitted to do whatever else he desired. But his two brothers and their wives had thus far produced only daughters, five little girls who, despite their beauty and winsome charms, could never inherit the dukedom. Father's impatience with this lamentable situation had grown after each birth, and he'd lately begun to pressure Rivers to find a bride and attempt to sire a son himself. Rivers was only twenty-six, without the slightest inclination to wed just yet, as he'd told his father again and again. It did not make for pleasing family gatherings.

"Father's not coming here tonight, is he?" Rivers asked, glancing uneasily around the room.

"No, he is not," Harry said, glowering at the thought. "Fortunately he and Celia were expected elsewhere. But you are right. Let's not spoil the evening with any more of that particular subject, especially if you shall be leaving us for a while. Tell me instead of this new experiment of yours."

Rivers smiled again, relieved. It would be much easier to evade his brother's questions than to be forced to answer his father. Though Father was their father, he'd been a duke first, and he did not like to be denied in anything.

"The project's at such an early stage at present that I cannot tell you much," he said easily. "Once I'm in the country without distractions, I'll be better able to sort out my plan."

"You're not meddling with lightning again, are you?" Harry asked seriously. "I haven't forgotten the last time, you know. Standing on the Lodge's roof with the storm crashing around you, practically begging to be struck dead where you stood."

"I survived, with no harm done to me," Rivers said patiently. "I was merely attempting to replicate Monsieur Dalibard's 1752 experiment at Marly-la-Ville, wherein the electrical force of lightning would be transmitted through conductive rods into a Leyden jar. I'm sure I would have had true success, too, if only the storm had lasted another quarter hour."

"And for what purpose?" Harry asked, raising his voice so that the other guests at the far end of the room turned to look their way. "So that you might be roasted to a cinder? You're a gentleman, Rivers, not some fiendish philosopher determined to make his mark before the Royal Society."

"I'm a gentleman who likes to learn more of this world with the head that God gave me," Rivers said firmly. "There is no harm to that, and possibly a great deal of good to be gained."

Harry grumbled, unconvinced. "The harm could have come if you'd burned down the Lodge."

"I would never do that," Rivers said, "and you know it."

He meant it, too, for he loved the Lodge far too dearly to put it at risk. Breconridge Park Lodge, known within the family more simply as the Lodge, had first been built as a modest hunting box over a century and a half before. The dukes of Breconridge had absorbed the land on which it stood into their holdings, and over the years had improved the once-humble lodge with sufficient modern amenities and Palladian touches to make it comfortably livable for much more than hunting.

Father had given the Lodge to Rivers on his twenty-first birthday as a personal retreat, a generous gift indeed for a third son. As country houses went, it was decidedly eccentric, with old-fashioned mullioned windows and an ornate stone balcony across the entire front, but it had become home to Rivers in a way that his London house never would. The Lodge was the place where he conducted his various projects without worrying about interruptions. It was his private sanctuary, from the small library crowded with books to the flat roof with a telescope for stargazing, as well as the experiment with lightning that had so distressed Harry.

"Tell me at the very least that you're not taking some poor milliner's apprentice with you again as a companion," Harry said, looking serious and very older-brother-ish. "You frightened that last one nearly to death with the lightning. I heard that she was so convinced you were in league with the devil that she ran screaming all the way to the Hall."

"I assure you that it wasn't nearly so dramatic as that," Rivers said, striving to remember more about the girl. She'd been exceptionally beautiful, but also exceptionally foolish, as he'd soon come to realize during the week she'd been with him. What in London had seemed like an entertaining and amorous notion had turned woefully bad once they were alone together in the country. She had bored him to the quick, and if she hadn't run shrieking from the Lodge like a madwoman, he would likely have soon packed her back to town anyway. He thought her name had been Fanny. Or was it Annie?

"So no pretty milliner's apprentices will be accompanying you this time?" Harry asked, still suspicious. "No nymphs to chase beneath the ancient oaks and elders?"

"Not this time, no," Rivers said in perfect honesty.

Lucia di Rossi was neither a pretty milliner's apprentice nor a nymph, and he was certain there would be no chasing whatsoever. Thinking of her enormous eyes and pale face, her small body swathed in drab, dark clothing, he knew she'd offer no temptation of that variety. She might have spirit and presence, but those were not qualities he sought in a woman he wished to bed. Far from it. No, Lucia would be there for another purpose, one that would let her sleep entirely undisturbed in his single, small guest room. He was taking her to the Lodge only so he could transform her far away from any distractions— and from curious, interfering observers, especially Everett.

"No diversion of that sort," he continued. "Suffice to say that there is a small wager with Everett involved— a wager that I intend to win."

"A wager?" Harry repeated with fresh interest, cocking a single dark brow. "Now I am intrigued. I don't suppose you'll tell me more?"

Rivers shook his head, and smiled, relishing the mystery. His earlier misgivings had entirely vanished, and now he'd not a single doubt that he'd make the girl succeed.

"Not a word more," he said, stopping just short of ungentlemanly boasting. "But I can assure you, brother, when I am done in six weeks' time, you and the rest of London will be amazed—*astounded!*—by what I've achieved."

But the next morning, on the stage of the Prince's Theatre, the subject of Rivers's future brilliant achievement met with a much different reception to the news of the wager.

"Please, Uncle Lorenzo, I must speak with you," Lucia said, bravely stepping before him to block his path. She had been trying all morning to catch his attention and each time he had brushed her aside. She hated to interrupt her uncle here on the stage during the middle of a rehearsal, but Lord Rivers had told her to return to his house for the first lesson by noon, and if she waited any longer, she'd be late. "It's of great importance."

Clearly displeased, her uncle scowled down at her. Although he no longer performed himself, he took his role as the head of their family as well as the *maestro* of their troupe very seriously, and expected to be treated with the respect due to a great artist who had danced for kings and queens. Although he dressed like a macaroni, in an oversized frizzled wig, snug striped waistcoat, and gold hoops in his ears, he was still an imperious figure, and an impatient one as well.

"What is it, Lucia?" he said now, looking over her head toward someone or something else that he considered more important. "You know how important this dance will be for the benefit next week. There is nothing you can say to me now that will be worth your interruption of my thoughts."

Lucia flushed. When she'd failed at dancing, she had ceased to be of any value to her uncle, and this was how he always addressed her, as if she were the most insignificant and irritating creature imaginable.

"Forgive me for that lost moment, Uncle," she said. "But I must tell you that I am leaving the company."

His scowl deepened to thunderous proportions. "Do not be foolish, Lucia," he said. "You will not leave us. You are a Di Rossi. Where would you go? What would you do? You cannot leave."

She raised her chin, steeling herself against his temper.

"I am leaving," she repeated. "I have taken another . . . another position."

"'Another *position*'?" he repeated with booming incredulity. The dancers who had been rehearsing had also been pretending not to eavesdrop, but his exclamation was enough for them to drop the pretense. They stopped and shamelessly turned to watch and listen, their hands resting on the waists of the loose men's drawers that they wore for practice. "What *position* could that possibly be? You have no skills, no talents, no gifts, no beauty or graces. Holy Mother in Heaven! Who would ever employ you?"

But before Lucia could answer, Magdalena pushed her way forward, her dark eyes flashing.

"Some poisonous bawd has filled your head with nonsense, hasn't she?" she demanded heatedly. "She has promised you that you will be the queen of Covent Garden, surrounded by fine gentlemen who will cover you with jewels. Isn't that so, Lucia? Isn't that what you wish, you lazy slut?"

"It is not!" Lucia cried, shocked. "I would never sell myself like that."

Magdalena sniffed with disgust, and snapped her fingers in Lucia's face.

"Of course you would, you little jade," she said, each word sharp and scathing and meant to wound. "Every woman has her price, whether it is jewels or a wedding ring. But you—you have so little to sell on that market that you would do well to work in a stew by the India Docks, serving a dozen filthy sailors a night who will be too drunk to complain that they'd bought nothing but a little bag of raggedy bones to lie upon. Strumpet! Whore! Slat—"

"Enough of your venom, Magdalena," ordered Uncle Lorenzo, holding his arm outstretched to keep her away from Lucia. "Let the wretched chit speak for herself. Is this the truth, Lucia? That after all we have done for you these last six years, you would leave us like this?"

"You do not care for me," Lucia said, finally saying aloud the words she'd kept bottled within for so long. "You never have. Ever since Papa died, you've never considered me to be more than an imposition, an obligation, a slave you could force to do your meanest tasks for nothing. For *nothing*!"

"Nothing is more than what you are worth," he said angrily, his eyes bulging. "Impudent donkey! Ungrateful baggage! I see it now, the sins of your whoring French mother at last revealed in you."

Tears stung Lucia's eyes, tears not of suffering, but of fury. "You've no right to call my mother—or me—any such names. Papa swore she was an angel, both on the stage and in her life. He loved her and me with all his heart, something that you would never—"

"*Silenzio!*" Her uncle raised his stick, threatening to strike her. "You have disturbed my rehearsal long enough. Go back to your work."

"No," Lucia said, her hands clenched into tight little fists at her sides. "I am done with your work, and I am done with the company. *Done.*"

Before he could reply, she turned and walked swiftly across the stage. She kept her head high and her back straight, not looking at any of the faces of the others that she passed. Some had been friends who had treated her with kindness and affection, friends she would miss, but she did not dare to pause and say farewell. She knew she must leave now, before her uncle tried to stop her, and her steps quickened as she hurried down the theater's back passages to the stairs and the alley below, past the idlers who always gathered there, and finally into the street.

Yet it was only when she'd reached the cook shop on the corner that she slowed enough to wipe her face with her handkerchief, and blot away the last of her tears. She retrieved the box with her belongings that she'd left with the keep behind the counter—she hadn't wished to take the time to return to her lodgings—and resolutely turned to the north, away from the playhouse and toward Cavendish Square.

She'd once heard in a heroic play that great generals would burn the bridges their soldiers had crossed to keep any cowards from retreating or deserting. This morning, she'd as good as burned her own bridges with her family's company, and there'd be no returning now. Instead she'd cast her future entirely into the hands of Lord Rivers Fitzroy, and by so doing she had either made the wisest decision of her life or the worst, and—

No. She was determined not only to think the best, but to believe it as well. What other choice did she have now, really? With her box held tightly in her arms, she headed toward the fate she'd seized for herself with Lord Rivers.

CHAPTER
4

Rivers stood in his doorway and surveyed the traveling carriage waiting before him. He did not plan to return to London until the end of next month, when the wager was over, and he'd ordered a great many things brought with him. Several large trunks of books and other belongings had been lashed to the back of the carriage, with his coachman and two footmen still straining to secure the last. He'd trust most of his clothes to the baggage wagon that would follow, but not his books and journals.

Another footman appeared from the kitchen carrying a wicker hamper with provisions, followed by Rivers's ever-vigilant manservant, Rooke, to make certain no stray apples or pasties were removed from the hamper to disappear into one of the footmen's pockets.

Rivers smiled with anticipation. It wasn't a long journey to the Lodge, but exactly the right length to be enjoyable, not tedious. Driving through the night with the full moon to guide them, they should arrive early tomorrow morning. He intended to stop to dine tonight, but there would be many more hours on the road when he might wish the comfort of a glass of wine and whatever tasty little pleasantries his cook had tucked into the hamper for him.

At his feet, his favorite Dalmatian—ridiculously named

Spot by one of his young nieces—whined and paced back and forth, eager to be off.

"Almost ready, boy, almost ready," Rivers said absently, pulling out his watch once again to check the time. Hating to be late himself, he was habitually early, and expected others to do the same. By his reckoning, Lucia di Rossi should have been here by now. He'd told her noon, and it was a quarter to the hour. Until this moment, he hadn't considered the possibility that she might have changed her mind. He'd sealed the wager with Everett and told his brother about it; he'd feel like a damned fool if the girl had quit before they'd even begun.

He crouched down to ruffle the dog's ears, more to calm himself than the restless animal. With everything in readiness, he supposed he'd go on to the Lodge anyway, even if she didn't come.

But he couldn't deny that he'd be disappointed. He'd been thinking of the wager ever since the girl had left yesterday, and he'd spent much of last night choosing books of plays with her in mind. He'd already decided she was too solemn for the comic roles, and he was determined to concentrate on tragic parts for her, the kind that built a serious actress's reputation with theatergoers. He'd been looking forward to working with her, to seeing how much he'd be able to transform that determination of hers into something rare and special.

There was more, too, though he wouldn't admit it to anyone else. She amused him, and surprised him, in a way that most women didn't. He was *intrigued*. He'd never expected to feel that way about a plain little wren like Lucia, but as she'd stood before him yesterday morning, he'd realized how vastly entertaining these next weeks might prove to be with her for company.

He smiled again, remembering how she'd stood up to Crofton. If she could marshal that self-assurance into a performance, she'd have audiences falling at her feet.

Spot's ears pricked up with interest and he shifted sideways to look past Rivers, and Rivers turned, too, to see what had caught the dog's eye.

"Ahh, it's Lucia di Rossi at last," he said, smiling with relief and a bit of pleasure as well. They were nearly eye level, with him crouched beside the dog on the step, and she standing on pavement. "I am glad you are here. You're almost late."

Her cheeks pinked, and she dipped an awkward excuse for a curtsey while Spot sniffed and snuffled around her skirts, making things more awkward still. The curtsey wasn't awkward from the clumsiness that Magdalena had accused her of possessing, but from the more obvious fact that she was clutching a small, battered trunk in her arms.

"Forgive me, my lord," she said. "But I am not late. According to the clock on the tower I just passed, it still wants five minutes to twelve."

He hadn't expected that. It had been very amusing when she'd corrected Crofton, but much less so when she did it to him.

He rose, pointedly looking down at her. "I didn't say you were late. I said you were *almost* late. Which, in fact, you are."

She shifted the trunk in her arms. "Yes, my lord," she said evenly. "But if we are to speak of the future, then all the world is also almost dead and buried, and I cannot help that, either."

He paused, not sure how to reply. If she were his servant, he likely would have had her sacked for such impudent familiarity. But she wasn't a servant, although she was dressed like one, in some dreary linen petticoat and jacket with a little gimcrack necklace around her throat. She wasn't exactly a guest, either, and she certainly wasn't his equal. How was he to address her? He should have given this some thought earlier, to be better able to establish their relationship, and to have prevented this kind of . . . awkwardness.

Until he did, he had little choice but to overlook this little speech if he wished to win the wager. He cleared his throat, attempting to look properly lordly, and changed the subject.

"I see you have brought your, ah, your trunk," he said. "That was wise of you."

"I didn't have a choice, my lord," she said, shifting it again to the other arm. Whatever was in it must be heavy, and he fought the gentlemanly urge to take it from her. "Are you leaving town, my lord? Have you had a change of heart about the wager?"

Her glance darted toward the waiting carriage laden with his belongings and back to him, her mouth twisting anxiously. Of course she wouldn't know his plans. He'd decided to go to the Lodge after she'd left his house yesterday. Seeing the coach now, she'd every reason to believe that he'd changed his mind.

He grinned, delighted to be able to surprise her. "I am leaving town for the country, yes," he said, "and you are to join me. I have decided to continue your education at my country place, away from distraction."

Her eyes widened with distress. "How am I to travel there, my lord? I haven't the coin for a stage fare."

"I wouldn't expect you to take a stage," he explained patiently. "You'll be coming with me, in my carriage. We'll leave directly, stop to change horses and dine when necessary, and if all proceeds as it should, arrive early tomorrow morning. Now pray give your box to Walker so he can strap it on top with the others, and we may be off. *Finally.*"

Yet still she hesitated, studying the carriage and the horses and the trunks and boxes and making no move to hand her own to the waiting footman.

"If you please, my lord," she said, clutching her box to

her chest. "I'd rather not give it over, my lord, on account of the thieves."

"Thieves?" he repeated, mystified. The road his driver took through Hampshire was well traveled and generally uneventful, with the glory days of armed highwaymen long past. It would take a brave thief indeed—or one who couldn't read the crest painted on his door—to challenge a coach belonging to a Fitzroy, especially not when his driver kept a brace of loaded pistols in the box with him.

"I sincerely doubt we'll be plagued with thieves," he said. "Your box will be safe enough with my things."

Yet still she shook her head. "All I own is in here, my lord, and if some wicked rogues were to snatch it away as we passed, why, then I'd be left with nothing."

He glanced again at the humble little box, clutched so possessively in her arms. To think that it was all she owned in this world was sobering. He hadn't the heart to tell her that no thief would give her trunk a second thought, not with the much richer promise of his own costly leather cases, padlocked and studded with gleaming nail heads.

"There is always some peril to one's belongings whilst traveling," he agreed. "If these things were so precious to you, then why didn't you leave them behind in your lodgings?"

Her eyes widened, if such a thing were possible, considering how very wide her eyes already were.

"Because I don't have any lodgings anymore, my lord," she said. "I've quit the company, just as you told me to do, and my lodgings with it. If I'd left anything behind, my lord, Magdalena would've been sure to sell it to the old-frock sellers, just out of spite."

Now it was Rivers's eyes that widened. "She would do that to you?"

"She would indeed, my lord," she answered so firmly

that there was no doubt it was the truth. "From purest spite, and meanness, too."

"Hah," he said, taken aback. The other night, he'd believed that Magdalena had not wanted to part with her cousin from family devotion, but it seemed the truth was much less appealing. He'd already known Magdalena was greedy and supremely selfish; now it appeared she was jealous and vengeful toward her own kin. It was just as well that Lucia had left, but he felt a wave of unexpected responsibility for her welfare, too, for having blithely ordered her to leave her extended family behind.

"Exactly, my lord: *hah,*" she repeated grimly. "That would be the sum of it. If it does not offend you, my lord, I'd as soon keep my trunk with me."

"Of course you may," he said. "Keep it with you, if that pleases you. Now are we finally ready to depart?"

"Yes, my lord," she said with another curtsey. As she rose, she smiled, her eyes bright with excitement. "Forgive me for speaking plain, my lord, but I haven't left London since I was brought here as a tiny girl, and never in a coach like this one."

He smiled back, his humor improving by the second. He couldn't help it; like all women, she was prettier when she smiled. Not exactly pretty, but prettier. He had made this journey to the Lodge so many times that he generally spent it with his nose buried in a book to pass the time, but now he was beginning to see it through her eyes as a grand adventure.

She handed the box to the nearest footman, and shook her arms out. He couldn't imagine how stiff they must be if she'd been carrying it clear from her lodgings, but the way she was wiggling her arms and shoulders was making the rest of her body wiggle and jiggle, too. Before this he had not been aware of her breasts, but with all this shaking, he couldn't help but take notice of them, small but round and jostling there as her kerchief came loose.

It was a common sort of display, exactly the kind of thing he'd have to put an end to, but it was also unexpectedly fascinating to watch. Certainly he was watching her, and so were his footmen, and it was a relief to them all when she stopped, and swept him a grand curtsey, her eyes sparkling.

"I am most very grateful to you for all this, my lord," she said, raising her voice more than was necessary. "Most very blessed grateful for everything, and that's a fact."

How in blazes had she passed beneath his notice when he was with Magdalena? How could he ever have believed her meek? At least he knew now she'd the personality for the stage; Everett might as well concede the wager right now. The proof was right here on the pavement. Every one of his footmen plus his driver and Rooke (who generally had the most professional of blind eyes regarding women, as every gentleman's manservant should) had stopped what they were doing to watch and listen to her, and even the passersby—generally a jaded group in this neighborhood—had halted in their tracks to gawk without shame.

"Into the coach," he said brusquely. "Now. We've squandered enough time."

She nodded, and clambered up the carriage steps, giving Rivers and all the other men who were ogling her a quick flash of neat little ankles in darned gray stockings. He pretended not to notice as he followed her, and whistled for Spot to jump into the carriage as well. The footman closed the door and latched it shut before he climbed onto the box with the others, the driver flicked his whip and the horses pulled at their traces, and finally—*finally*—they were on their way.

Rivers checked his watch one more time. It was only noon, the time he'd said they'd leave, but he couldn't help feeling that somehow he'd already fallen behind.

His traveling coach was an older model that had originally belonged to his father, refurbished and improved but still grand enough in size for a full ducal party. Rivers settled comfortably in one corner, as was his usual habit, while Lucia sat primly on the opposite seat, square in the middle of the wide tufted bench. She was holding that infernal box again, this time balanced on her knees with her hands folded on top of it.

At least she'd tucked her kerchief back into place over those distracting breasts, so he could think other, more useful thoughts. It would have been a damnably long journey if she hadn't.

"Put the trunk at your feet," he said, no longer a suggestion and closer to an order. "I promise you I have no interest in stealing it or its contents."

"No, my lord." With a sigh that could have been from relief or doubt (he didn't care to know which), she carefully set the trunk beside her feet on the floor of the carriage, shooing Spot away when he approached for an exploratory sniff.

"Spot won't hurt it," Rivers said. "On the contrary. He's an excellent guard dog."

"'Spot'?" She looked up at him over the dog's head, her voice ripe with amusement. "How long did it take you to think of that, my lord?"

"He came to me with the name," Rivers said defensively. "He was a gift from my brother, and my niece had already named him."

"As you say, my lord," she said, grinning.

"I had no choice in the matter," he said, striving to explain. "If I'd changed the name to something more suitable, then my niece would have been terribly disappointed. She's only three, you see. She would not have understood."

"Yes, my lord." Her smile softened. No doubt she was thinking him a weak-hearted fool for bowing to the whims of a three-year-old—not that her opinion should matter. Not at all. She was here to help him win a wager, nothing more. He couldn't forget that. Resolutely composing himself, he looked down on the round, flat brim of her straw hat as she bent over the dog.

At least she didn't venture her opinions aloud, concentrating instead on rubbing Spot's boney forehead until he closed his eyes and groaned with happiness.

"Better to call him Punto, my lord," she said, her face still hidden by the hat. "Isn't that so, Punto?"

" 'Punto'?" repeated Rivers indignantly. Spot might be unimaginative, but at least it wasn't thumpingly awkward and foreign. And what right did she have to rename his dog? *"Punto?"*

"Punto," she said again, decisively. "It's Italian for Spot, my lord."

"I know that," he said. "But that's not his name."

"Oh, but I can tell he's a clever boy, my lord." She patted the seat beside her. "He'll know it. Up, up, Punto! Here, here!"

Eagerly the dog scrambled up onto the leather cushion, swaying stiff-legged with the carriage's motion as he leaned against her shoulder.

Rivers stared, aghast. It was bad enough for her to invent another name for his dog, but then to have the audacity to invite the beast to jump onto the carriage seat—an indulgence no canine was ever permitted in any Fitzroy coach, by the unimpeachable decree of various Fitzroy wives—that was beyond bearing.

"Down, Spot," he ordered sharply. "Damnation, *down*!"

With a fretful little whimper and his head hanging in shame, Spot slid from the seat to the floor and lay guiltily across the toes of Rivers's booted feet, his rightful place.

Lucia, however, shared none of Spot's remorse. "How could you do that to him, my lord? Poor Punto! I didn't mind him sitting beside me."

"But I did," Rivers said sternly. "Once we are in the country, it is Spot's habit to run alongside the carriage, on the road and beside it, and root through whatever foulness he pleases. At some point in our journey, he'll return to ride with us, and I've no wish for him to drag muck, dust, and the scraps of dead squirrels onto the cushions. He knows he shouldn't do it, and you should, too."

She lowered her chin a fraction, gazing up from beneath the curving straw brim of her hat. It wasn't coquettish, either. It was out-and-out rebellious.

"That is very *tidy* of you, my lord," she said. "But I cannot help but feel pity for poor Punto, to be kept not only from these soft cushions, but also from his master's bed, the favored place of every other English dog."

"His name is Spot, not Punto," Rivers insisted, his exasperation growing. "And he is indeed permitted to lie on my bed at night. Once we arrive at the Lodge, the stable boys will wash him, and make him presentable for the house."

She looked down at the dog. "He would appear presentable enough now, my lord."

"Lucia, I do not wish the dog on the carriage seat," he said crossly, his temper finally fraying. "You may not care if Spot sits beside you with dirty paws, but I can assure you that the ladies who sit on these seats do."

Too late he realized how pointedly that simple statement had excluded her as not being a lady. She understood. How could she not? Her cheeks flushed and her shoulders drew together, and as he watched, she seemed to shrink into herself, shuttering that rebellion tightly inside.

"Forgive me, my lord," she said, her expression guarded and her voice reduced to the sad little whisper of perfect servitude. "I did not mean to give offense."

This was how she had been with Magdalena, and the

reason she'd always escaped his notice before this week. Frowning, he studied her closely, wishing she hadn't retreated from him like this. Her head was bowed, her hands meekly folded in her lap, her eyes downcast and revealing nothing. He remembered how she'd said she'd been forced to act as a servant for her own family, how she'd been made to feel worthless by her uncle and the others because she couldn't dance.

But he couldn't deny that his unthinking comment just now had accomplished much the same thing. He felt uncomfortably as if he should apologize for offending her, something that he knew he'd no obligation to do. He'd simply made his own wishes rightly known, that was all. He *was* the master here, a gentleman, and the son of a duke, while she was his social inferior in every way. In this carriage, his word should be law, especially if he was to transform her as he hoped.

So why, then, did that apology still sit stuck in his throat, unspoken yet unable to be swallowed?

He sighed irritably, eager for a distraction from this . . . this uneasiness. He reached into the leather bag of books on the seat beside him, and pulled out a slender, elegantly bound edition of Shakespeare's *Hamlet*. He slid his thumb beside the slip of paper that marked the page with the passage he'd chosen last night, a soliloquy spoken by Ophelia. He intended it as Lucia's first test, so that he might judge her memory, her reading skills, and her feeling for the magnificent words that were such a staple of the theater.

Yet as he glanced over the short passage again, he wondered whether he'd been too ambitious. What seemed an easy task to him might prove too difficult for her, and discourage her from their experiment before it had fairly begun.

Still, better to know now than later, and smoothing the pages open, he held the book out to Lucia.

"Here," he said, pointing to the beginning of the passage. "This will be your first lesson. Read and memorize the twelve lines beginning with O, *what a noble mind is here o'erthrown*. Take as long as you require, and when you are ready, I'll ask you to recite the passage to me."

Her expression did not change as she took the book.

"Very well, my lord," she said in the well-practiced drone of every servant. "Will that be all?"

He nodded, perversely longing for the return of the girl who'd challenged him about Spot. "Do you have any questions for me?"

"No, my lord," she said. "I'm to read these twelve lines, learn them by rote, and then speak them back to you."

"Exactly," he said, nodding. "And the word is pronounced 'sp-EE-k,' not 'sp-AA-k.' We shall have to work a great deal on your vowels to make them acceptable."

Her brows rose. "My vowels, my lord?"

"Your vowels," he repeated. "The letters *a, e, i, o,* and *u.* If you are to play queens and noblewomen, you must learn to pronounce them as such ladies would, and not like—well, not like a dresser from Drury Lane. You can hear the difference, can't you?"

She nodded. "Sp-EEEEEE-k."

"Well, yes," he said. "Though you needn't draw it out as if you'd seen a mouse."

"Sp-EE-k," she said proudly. "This is how I must sp-EE-k if I wish to sound like a lady."

"Yes," he said. Of course she didn't sound like a lady at all, but this was only the first day, and he knew this would take time—a great deal of time, apparently. "Now attend to the passage, and pray tell me when you are done."

He took up another book, this one featuring the witty reflections of a French philosopher, opened it, and set himself to reading. He resolved not to look up at her until either he'd finished the chapter or she declared herself ready to recite the passage. She said nothing and neither did he as the carriage traveled through the outskirts of London and into the countryside.

Ordinarily the French philosopher's ideas amused Rivers, but today he found them slow going indeed, and instead his thoughts kept returning again and again to the young woman across from him. How was she faring with her first assignment? The way she'd responded, he'd felt more as if he'd asked her to dust the front parlor than to memorize Shakespeare, but at least she'd find the Shakespeare a more pleasant task.

Or at least he hoped she would. Damnation, what if she didn't care for Shakespeare? He hadn't considered that possibility until now. She was being quiet.

Very quiet.

But that could be a good sign as well, the mark of a diligent scholar, and with pleasure he imagined her applying herself to the passage, the book clutched in her small hands, her brows drawn solemnly together, and her mouth pursed as she read the words over and over to learn them.

It took all his will not to sneak a furtive glance at her over the edge of his book, and when at last he reached his own designated finishing line at the end of the chapter, he made a contented little grunt of anticipation, closed the book, and finally raised his gaze to look at Lucia.

The slender volume with the play lay closed on the seat beside her. Her head was tipped back against the leather squabs, her straw hat knocked askew and the narrow ribbon that had held it in place half untied. Her hands were once again clasped in her lap, but her lips were slightly parted and her eyes were closed, her thick dark lashes feathering over her cheeks.

She was sound asleep.

Oh, it was going to be a long, *long* six weeks.

* * *

"Lucia," *the* man's voice said from a great and echoing distance in her dream. "Lucia, it's time you woke. Past time, really."

She frowned, not willing to give up her rather splendid dream just yet, a dream that involved eating clotted cream and strawberries while sitting on a bench in Hyde Park beside a handsome prince with a crown studded with strawberry-sized rubies. The prince's face was a bit hazy, but in the way of dreams she was still certain he was handsome, and wonderfully attentive to her, offering her more berries from a large silver bowl.

"For God's sake, Lucia," the man's voice said again, more irritably this time. "I can't leave you here in the carriage. You must wake."

The bowl full of ripe strawberries faded away like mist, and with it the handsome prince. Reluctantly she dragged her eyes open, squinting a bit at the late-afternoon light that was slanting directly into her eyes. In the place of the prince was Lord Rivers, while his footmen were also peering at her curiously through the open carriage door.

"Finally," Rivers said, his voice rumbling ominously. "I was beginning to believe you'd completely forsaken me for Morpheus."

"Forgive me, my lord," Lucia said, quickly sitting upright and shoving her hat back from her forehead. With the sun behind his lordship, she couldn't see his face well enough to judge his humor, but it was hardly a good omen for him to be speaking of her in connection with some unknown man named Morpheus. "I, ah, I must have fallen asleep."

"Indeed," he said drily. "You fell asleep before we'd reached the Holborn gate, and you've stayed asleep ever since, until this very moment."

She looked at him uncertainly, her heart racing, not quite sure how to proceed. "How long, my lord?"

"Four hours," he said, "and twelve minutes."

Madre di Dio, four *hours*! She'd no doubt that he'd kept track of every minute with that enormous gold watch of his, too.

Was she supposed to have stayed awake for the entire journey? Is that how she'd erred? He'd been reading and paying her little attention, but perhaps he'd expected her to converse with him to pass the time. Did he expect an apology now? She'd found that apologies usually corrected most any error, whether they were merited or not.

"Forgive me, my lord," she murmured. She slipped from the seat to curtsey awkwardly in the carriage's narrow foot space, her skirts brushing against his legs in a way that was uncomfortably intimate. "I did not intend to disturb you by sleeping."

"Well, you didn't," he said. She could see his face now, disgruntled in spite of his efforts to remain impassive. "But I had set you a task—a very small task indeed—to learn a passage for me. Instead you chose to sleep."

"But I *did* learn it!" she protested. "Forgive me, my lord, but I know it perfectly! *Perfettamente!*"

He made a skeptical, gruff sound in his throat that as much as declared that he didn't believe her.

"You're keeping me from my dinner, Lucia," he said, waving his hand impatiently to show he wished her to move aside. "I don't intend to stop here more than an hour, only long enough to change horses and dine, and you've already squandered a good ten minutes of that time before we've even left the carriage."

Mortified, she hopped down from the carriage and ducked to one side of the tall footman holding the door while his lordship quickly stepped from the carriage after her.

They were in the yard of a country inn, with all around

them a noisy, confusing muddle of other travelers and their carriages and horses, as well as servants and stable boys from the inn itself. Lord Rivers's spotted dog was dancing about two other dogs, their tails wagging furiously as they barked and bounced back and forth under the carriage's wheels. Clearly the Fitzroy crest on the carriage door was the most impressive in the yard that afternoon, for the innkeeper himself was standing before them, beaming with his hands clasped over his green apron.

His lordship stopped before the innkeeper, giving the man only a moment to bow before he addressed him.

"Good day to you, Hollins," he said, or rather announced, as his voice boomed heartily across the yard. "I trust your good wife is well?"

"Very well, my lord," the innkeeper declared, "and already in the kitchen overseeing your dinner, just as you like. The same fare as you always order, my lord, with the same table in the back parlor set and ready for your pleasure."

His lordship laughed, and clapped the innkeeper on the shoulder. Whatever testiness he'd felt with Lucia seemed to have been forgotten, and had passed clear away.

"Add a tankard of your excellent ale, Hollins," he said, "and I shall be a happy man indeed," he declared.

He whistled for Spot to join him, and went striding off toward the inn's door with the keeper bobbing along at his side.

Still standing to one side of the footman, Lucia watched Lord Rivers go. She'd a fleeting image of him that became instantly frozen in her memory, of his broad shoulders in the dark blue coat, framed by the inn's doorway, the length and confidence of his stride in his polished black boots, how the skirts of his coat flapped around his legs and how the afternoon sun gilded his blond queue, tied with a black ribbon.

Then he was gone, and she was left with the much more pressing question of what she herself was supposed to do next. She'd been abandoned for now, that was clear enough, and she felt both irritated and a little wounded by it. She'd ridden in his carriage with him almost as an equal—which of course she wasn't—but then he'd scolded her as if she remained a servant, which she wasn't, either, or at least not his servant. As a woman, she couldn't very well remain with the carriage while the horses were changed by the stable boys, nor could she stand by herself about here in the yard and wait for his lordship to return.

What she wished most was to eat. Lord Rivers's insistence on his own dinner had served to remind her that she'd had only a cup of watery tea and a slice of buttered bread early this morning and nothing since, and as if to remind her further, her empty stomach rumbled loudly.

"You can dine with us, miss," the tall footman said beside her as if reading her thoughts. "Won't be as fancy as the fare in the back parlor, but his lordship always sees that his people are well looked after, and you won't go hungry."

She flushed, sure that he must have heard her rumbling stomach. She didn't want to be pitied, but sometimes it was better to be practical than proud.

"I'm not sure I *am* one of his people," she said. "At least not to eat."

"Fah, of course you are, miss," the footman said. "You wouldn't be here in this place if you weren't, would you?"

She couldn't argue with that. She wasn't sure where she'd be, but it definitely wouldn't be here.

"Thank you, yes," she said, grateful. "I'd like that.

And you needn't call me 'miss.' *Lucia* serves me well enough."

The footman nodded. "I'm Tom Walker, and this is Ned Johnston," he said, cocking his head toward the other footman. "Stay with us, and we'll watch after you. But we'd best hurry if we want to eat. His lordship keeps powerfully strict hours."

Slowly she nodded in agreement, remembering how his lordship's watch seemed to pop from his waistcoat with ridiculous frequency.

"Come with us, lass," Walker urged again. "We can't very well leave you here with those rascals from the stable."

He wasn't handsome like his master, but his plain face had a kind smile, and right now to Lucia that seemed of much greater value than all the world's gold watches and their titled owners. With a sigh of relief (or perhaps resignation) she fell in with the footmen, following them through the inn's second door, to the parlor meant for servants and other lesser folk. At least here she'd know her place, which was more—*much* more—than she'd have in the company of Lord Rivers Fitzroy.

CHAPTER
5

There was a set pattern of things that Rivers always did whenever he stopped at the Red Hart Inn on his way to the Lodge. He would solemnly taste and judge the latest batch of ale that Mr. Hollins brought him, and offer an opinion that he suspected was repeated over and over throughout the county. Then Mrs. Hollins would appear with the first plate of her excellent ham with leeks, which he would praise as it deserved. Next a younger Hollins child would be brought and pushed toward him to sing a warbly song in his manner, which Rivers would also praise, and which it usually did not deserve. Only then would he be left alone with his dinner and his book in the little private parlor.

But today when he was left alone, he abruptly realized that he shouldn't be, and called again for Hollins to join him.

"There was a young woman accompanying me today," he said, feeling both mystified that Lucia was missing and a little careless that he'd only now noticed her absence. "She was to dine with me."

"Yes, my lord," Hollins said. "The small dark lass with the straw hat?"

"That's the one," Rivers said, relieved. "If she's out there in the hall, pray show her in here."

Hollins screwed up his mouth, clearly unhappy to be

unable to oblige. "She's not in the hall, my lord. She's dining with your other servants, in the long room off the kitchen."

"She is?" Rivers paused, his fork in the air with surprise. He thought he'd made it clear that he wished her to dine with him, both here and during her stay at the Lodge. "With the servants?"

"Yes, my lord," Hollins said. "Shall I fetch her here?"

Rivers considered, his fork still poised in the air with the ham steaming faintly before him. Although Lucia had said she'd memorized the passage as he'd asked, he'd seen her sleep so long that he suspected her claim wasn't true. It couldn't be. No doubt she'd chosen to eat with his footmen to avoid having to confess the truth about the passage.

He was sorry she'd made that choice, and sorry that she'd felt it necessary to avoid him, but in a way he didn't blame her. She'd clearly been exhausted when she'd joined him, and then he'd expected too much of her so soon. Besides, if the other Di Rossis he knew were any indication, swearing to untruths to save their skins was as natural as breathing. Of course he must deal with that, but not now.

"No, Hollins, that will not be necessary," he said. "Let her dine where she pleases."

At last he brought the forkful of stew to his mouth, striving to show that Lucia's choice was inconsequential to him. With great deliberation, he once again opened the French philosopher's book that he'd brought with him from the carriage. He smoothed the pages open with the heel of his hand and rested a clean pewter spoon across the top to hold them open while he ate. As a bachelor, this was often how he dined at home, alone with a book, and perfectly happy that way, too.

But this evening he wasn't happy, and the book that should have provided ideal company failed again to hold his interest. Instead his thoughts kept wandering to the Red Hart's long room off the kitchen, a place where he'd never been, nor had ever considered.

He imagined long tables with benches, with the diners sitting close-packed together. There would be much laughter and jesting and shouting over one another, the way it always was among servants, and not a word about any French philosophers. He pictured Lucia sitting squeezed between his two tallest footmen, Walker and Johnston, with her looking almost dainty between them in their elegant livery coats. Or maybe they'd shed their coats to preserve them while they ate, so she'd look even smaller, a tiny figure in dark blue against the white linen of their shirtsleeves. He wondered if they'd made her laugh, and then she'd laugh, too, her cheeks rosy and her eyes bright and—

"Mrs. Hollins has just taken an apple pie from the oven, my lord," Hollins said, his round face appearing at the door. "With a wedge of fine cheddar, there's few things more tasty."

"Thank you, no, Hollins, I believe I am done." Rivers rose abruptly and stuffed the book into the pocket of his greatcoat. "Pray send word to my driver that I wish to depart."

The word was swiftly sent, and by the time he'd returned to the yard, his carriage was waiting with his footmen at the ready. Walker opened the carriage door, revealing that it was empty, with no sign of Lucia except for that wretched box of hers. Rivers frowned, glancing about the yard for her. She couldn't dare be late again, could she?

Then he looked up, and there she was, sitting on the bench between his driver and Rooke.

"Please, Lucia," he said. He told himself he wasn't begging; he was simply being patiently agreeable. "Come down at once. I wish you to ride inside with me."

Her eyes widened. "Very well, my lord," she said, and as she gathered her skirts in one hand to climb down both his footmen rushed to help her. Rivers whistled for Spot, who had wandered off during the delay, and at last they were all in the carriage again and on their way.

At last: that, he thought, seemed to be the best way to describe this entire day.

She was sitting squarely in the middle of the seat across from him, her back straight, her hands clasped, and her expression a little wary. That was wise. She should be wary after what she'd just done to him at the Red Hart.

He took a deep breath to compose himself.

"Lucia," he said. "It would appear that we have certain matters to discuss between us."

"We do indeed, my lord," she said with startling indignation. "Yes, we do have our agreement and the wager and all, but there's many other things that need saying now, else I *will* be going back to London and that wager of yours is over and done."

"'Things'?" he repeated, taken aback. "I would say there are things. You didn't follow my wishes at the Red Hart, but went off with my servants. Then you virtually scolded me before the entire inn yard, pretending that I'd somehow wronged you."

"Which you *did,* my lord," she said vehemently. "You woke me to call me a liar, and then swept me away so I wouldn't keep you from your dinner. What was I supposed to make of that?"

He frowned. He was not accustomed to being addressed with such . . . such *directness*.

"I woke you because we had stopped," he said. "I expected you to join me when I dined, as I had specifically requested earlier. Nor did I accuse you of lying. You maintained that you had learned the passage, whilst I had observed you sleeping instead. I chose not to believe you. That is not the same thing."

"It amounts to the same thing by my lights, my lord!" she exclaimed. "Why would I have claimed to have learned your lesson if I hadn't? What would I have gained by lying?"

"Perhaps you were uneasy about having to make such an admission," he said, growing a bit uneasy himself. "Perhaps it was easier to, ah, exaggerate."

"Bah!" she said with determination. "I'll show you how I exaggerate, my lord."

She leaned back against the squabs with her palms pressed down flat on the cushions, one either side of her, and closed her eyes. She took a deep breath, and in a loud, singsong voice, she recited the twelve lines he'd given her.

> O, *what a noble mind is here o'erthrown!*
> *The Courtier's, soldier's, scholar's, eye, tongue, sword,*
> *Th' expectancy and rose of the fair state,*
> *The glass of fashion and the mould of form,*
> *Th' observ'd of all observers, quite, quite down!*
> *And I, of ladies most deject and wretched,*
> *That suck'd the honey of his music vows,*
> *Now see that noble and most sovereign reason*
> *Like sweet bells jangled out of tune and harsh,*
> *That unmatch'd form and feature of blown youth*
> *Blasted with ecstasy. O, woe is me*
> *T'have seen what I have seen, see what I see.*

Cautiously she opened her eyes, unsure of what his reaction would be.

Speechless, Rivers stared at her, stunned by what he'd just heard. She'd learned every word of the passage, exactly as she'd said she had, and without a single error, too. True, there was much about her recitation that would require work. It was perhaps the strangest reading of Shakespeare that he'd ever heard, turning the golden

words into a kind of droning street vendor's cry—
or worse, into the very twin of the dreadful Madame
Adelaide—but he'd take it. He'd take it, but he'd something else to do first.

He needed to apologize.

He swept his hat from his head and held it to one side,
and bowed his head.

"Madam, you have my heartfelt apology," he said solemnly. "I didn't believe you, even as you professed the
truth. You did indeed do as I asked, without error."

Her cheeks grew red, and she ducked her chin, unable
to meet his eye. "You shouldn't say that, my lord, not to
me."

He settled his hat back on his head. "Why not, when it
was true? I was wrong."

"Because of who you are, my lord, and who I am," she
said, her hands twisting restlessly together in her lap.
"It's not right. I did what you told me to do. It was no
great task, either."

"But it was," he insisted. "I was in the wrong, and
I'm not above admitting it. Most people have the devil of
a time memorizing much of anything, let alone Shakespeare. Yet you did it with apparent ease. That's a
necessary gift for an aspiring actress."

She looked up at him uncertainly, her chin still lowered. "You do believe that is so? That I have a gift?"

"I do," he said, and he would have said it even if her
thick dark lashes weren't fluttering over her cheeks. They
were very beguiling, those lashes, especially in the dusk
of early evening, and because of them he let his compliment stand as it was, without the qualifications that
would make it more honest. There would be time enough
tomorrow for a true critique. "It will without doubt
make my—our—task far easier."

"Oh, I am *glad*," she said fervently. "You cannot know
how I feared you'd changed your mind, my lord, that

you'd wanted no more of me, that I'd somehow made you unhappy and that you'd leave me behind, there at that inn."

"I wouldn't do that," he said, appalled that she'd think so low of him. "What made you think such a thing?"

"What else *was* I to think, my lord, when you spoke to me all stern as you did?" she asked, spreading her fingers open over her lap. "My life with the company was not so fine, my lord, but it was what I had, and I gave it up for what you offered me. With you I had a chance to better myself, but if you're going to take that chance back from me, well, then, I wish to know now, so I can make other plans for myself."

Rivers made a noncommittal grunt. She'd spoken so plainly that it stung Rivers's conscience, and perhaps his pride as well. He knew he must answer her just as plainly, or both conscience and pride would give him no peace tonight.

"You're a direct little creature, aren't you?" he said at last. "What manner of assurance do you wish from me? Must I ask a solicitor to draw up papers for signature? Would that be enough?"

He wasn't entirely jesting. She, however, wasn't jesting at all, and she frowned thoughtfully.

"Like some sort of apprenticeship papers, my lord?" she asked. "Binding me to you, but making you promise to look after me?"

He grimaced, deeply regretting having begun this particular line of conversation. "Somehow I doubt any respectable court would agree to that," he said. "Besides, they'd question why my word as a gentleman wasn't sufficient assurance for you."

"Forgive me, my lord," she said solemnly, "but your word as a gentleman won't hold much water considering I'm not a lady."

He grunted again. "*Touché*," he said. "Not only is your memory exceptional, but your argument as well."

Clearly perplexed, she leaned closer toward him, swaying gently with the carriage's motion. "But that's the problem, my lord, isn't it? It's all about *words*. I don't know who or how or even what I am to be with you."

"That's easy enough," he said, for to him it did seem so. "Who you are is Lucia di Rossi, and what you are is rather what you will become, which is to say an actress."

"That is what I hope to become, yes, my lord," she agreed earnestly. "But that's later, and it's now that confuses me. One moment you treat me as your—your guest, having me ride here in your carriage with you and all, and then the next you order me about as if I'm your servant, except that you don't want me going about with your other servants. I'm all turned about trying to make sense of it, my lord, and I fear I'll displease you if I can't."

Rivers sighed, and crossed his arms over his chest. He understood what she was saying, and he understood, too, how it had come about. When he planned his course of study for how to create the model dramatic actress, he'd overlooked the fact that Lucia wasn't a wad of clay for him to mold; she was a living, breathing woman with the sort of feelings and notions that plagued every woman. He'd left her in the dark about her exact position, because it hadn't mattered to him. But it did matter to her, and now it must matter to him, too. He sighed again, mightily, as he tried to determine a solution.

"See now, my lord, I've displeased you again," she said. Dramatically she pulled off her hat and threw herself back against the squabs with a sigh that rivaled his own. "Nothing I do is right."

"Not at all," he murmured, an easy way of buying more time for himself to think. This was entirely his fault, of course, and though he'd admit that to himself, he wasn't sure it would be wise to admit it to her as well.

He'd already apologized to her once this evening, and if he did it again, he'd feel as if he were groveling, and that would be an end to any sort of proper balance between them as teacher and student. It didn't help, either, having her flung back against the squabs like that, with her hair coming down from beneath her cap, and her breasts pushed up by her stays and—

No. He needed a way to think of her with distance, with propriety. And in a flash the idea came to him, in the manner that great ideas usually took.

He clapped his hands once in triumph, startling her. "I have solved our dilemma, Lucia," he announced proudly. "What is required is more formality between us."

She shook her head, not understanding, and perhaps not wanting to. "You make no sense to me, my lord."

"No, no, it makes perfect sense," he insisted. "The problem here is that I do not know how to address you, and you do not know how to behave. As you are, Lucia di Rossi, formerly of the Di Rossi Ballet Company, you have no acceptable place in my household."

"*Rifiuti,*" she muttered, openly skeptical. "What solution is there in that, my lord?"

"Because we shall put Lucia aside, and instead create a new persona for you," he said. "You weren't going to launch yourself onto the stage as a Di Rossi anyway. We'll simply accelerate the process, so there will no longer be any question of you being a servant."

"I'll need a grand new name, my lord," she said eagerly. "Every actress has another for the stage. Madame Adelaide's really Moll Dunn."

"Cassandra," he declared, the name coming to him in another of those flashes of brilliance. "That's who'll you'll be, because you'll speak the truth about your character. Although I do hope you'll have more people heed your words than that poor lady in ancient Troy."

"Cassandra," she repeated, testing the sound of it. "I like that, my lord. It's very grand. Madame Cassandra!"

"I think you shall be Mrs., rather than Madame," he said. "Audiences don't always take to foreign actresses, Madame Adelaide notwithstanding. You shall be an English lady who has lived abroad most of her life. That will make you mysterious, but still English. You'll need a surname."

She nodded with excitement, glancing out the window as if searching for inspiration in the passing landscape. Apparently she found it.

"Willow," she said suddenly. "That's who I'll be, my lord. Mrs. Cassandra Willow. Because I'll bow when the audience cheers, but I'll never be broken by the critics."

"Mrs. Cassandra Willow." He considered it, imagining how the name would look on playbills and in papers. "It's simple enough for those in the pit to recall, but sufficiently elegant for those in the boxes, too. I like it, Mrs. Willow. When you step from the carriage, I'll introduce you by your new name, and so you shall be called by my household and everyone else."

She laughed, and he laughed, too, and the journey was suddenly much more pleasurable again. They were sitting here together in a carriage that was rapidly growing dark except for the light of the moon, and the bumpy misunderstandings that had sprung up between them this afternoon had been smoothed over and corrected. Their shared adventure was just beginning. Ahead of them lay a little more than a month where they'd attempt something grand and glorious together, something that was far beyond the initial wager with Everett.

Yes, that was the main difference from earlier. By making her Mrs. Willow, he'd also after a fashion made her his partner in this endeavor—a realization that pleased him as much as it seemed to be pleasing her. Together they were going to change her life. Damn, he might even be *saving* her life, considering how wretched it had been before. How could he not be pleased by that?

He reached down and unfastened the compartment beneath the seat where the hamper had been tucked, and pulled it out, setting it on the cushion beside him before he opened it.

"We must drink a toast to Mrs. Willow," he said with relish, pulling out a crystal decanter of wine and two glasses. "To the good lady, and her success."

Her laughter now sounded a bit uneasy as he opened the wine and poured the first glass. He held the glass out to her, and she hesitated, looking first at the wine and then at him.

"Forgive me, my lord, but I—I do not drink wine with gentlemen," she said primly. "It can only bring trouble and sorrow."

"Hah, now, that's a lecture from a pulpit." Still he offered her the glass, the ruby liquid shimmering in the crystal. "I'd wager a guinea you've never before drunk wine with any gentleman, have you?"

The primness continued, and with it now was a steadfastness he hadn't expected.

"I do not have to commit murder to know that it's a sin," she said. "I've seen enough to learn that strong drink and men can lead to—to things that will later be regretted."

Well, *that* was true. He'd seen such raucous, regrettable behavior himself behind the scenes in the theaters—and participated in it, too—to know what she'd likely witnessed, and to understand the wisdom of her reluctance. Prim or not, if he pressured her further, he'd be a bully.

"Fair enough," he said, staring down at the suddenly forlorn and rejected glass. "But that doesn't mean I cannot drink to Mrs. Willow, and her success. To the lady!"

He raised the glass in her direction and drank it down.

When he set the empty glass on his knee, she was watching him thoughtfully.

"Thank you, my lord," she said, now more wistful than prim. "And Mrs. Willow thanks you, too."

"Yes, yes," he said expansively, refilling the glass. Just because she chose not to drink didn't mean he couldn't. "Mrs. Willow *would* thank me, even if she didn't approve of me in general on account of the glass in my hand."

"Oh, but she would," she said quickly. "Approve of you, I mean. All gentlemen drink. So how could Mrs. Willow not approve of you?"

"You tell me, Mrs. Willow," he said, stretching his legs out more comfortably, Spot settling beneath them. "She is your creation now, and you must speak as she would speak."

"You mean that I should lie?" she asked uncertainly.

"It's as much a lie as any story or play is a lie," he said easily. "Consider Mrs. Willow a character, a role to be played, and tell me everything about the dear lady. Where she was born, how she came to the theater, even how she escaped that ne'er-do-well husband of hers."

"I have a husband, my lord?" she asked, incredulous.

"Most actresses have one tucked away somewhere or another," Rivers said blithely. "You should know that. I'd wager even your Madame Adelaide has an unfortunate monsieur in her past. Playhouse husbands generally are rascals and rogues, on account of actresses being so tenderhearted. But I wish to know more of the roguish Mr. Willow."

"I don't know where to begin, my lord," she admitted sheepishly. "What should I say?"

"It's for you to decide, not I," he said. "Go on. Think of how you'd describe your life to a friend you hadn't seen for a long while. Surely you must have done that."

"No, my lord, because everyone I know in London

stays together," she said. "Or rather, they did stay together. Now I'm the one who's left."

"For the better," he said firmly, not wanting her to
have any misgivings. Her life already sounded bleak
enough without that. "Entirely for the better."

"Yes, my lord, it is," she said, clearly striving to convince herself as well. "It *is*. And . . . and I have told stories before. While the dancers were onstage, I'd make up
tales for the others in the tiring room to pass the time.
They liked my stories better than anyone else's, too."

"Well, then, there you are," he said, relieved. Of
course, it remained to be heard what manner of stories
those were, but they would be sufficient for now. "Pretend you're with them again, and tell us all about that
wicked, wicked Mr. Willow."

More confident now, she chuckled, a husky little laugh
that charmed him to no end. "Very well, my lord. This
will be about my husband, Mr. Willow. He was an older
gentleman when we first met."

"Deceitful old bastard," Rivers said to encourage her.
"Go on."

She chuckled again. "He wasn't so very old," she said.
"Only older than I, and I was very young."

"You must have been," he said, reaching again for the
decanter. "You're not exactly an ancient old crone now."

"I suppose he must have been nearly as old as you, my
lord," she said sweetly, which made him laugh outright.
"He was from—oh, from Birmingham, though he'd often
pretend he was from Paris to impress ladies. A macaroni
with gaudy waistcoats and gold rings in his ears. He was
a comely man to see, my lord, and clever as blazes, too."

"Was he now, the dog!" Rivers exclaimed, delighted by
her invention. He'd let her mangled vowels go untram-
meled for now; who'd want to interrupt a tale like this
for the sake of pronunciation?

"Pray tell me more," he said, encouraging. "Pretend

I'm writing your story for the *Gentleman's Magazine,* so make it as lurid as you wish. If you don't, you know the scribes will."

"Recall that I am a Di Rossi, my lord," she said. "I know how to be lurid. And life with Mr. Willow—*dio buono,* it was *wicked.*"

She paused, making him wait, and then lowered her voice to a more confidential level. The girl knew how to tell a story, he'd grant her that.

"He stole my heart, Mr. Willow did," she continued, "and then I let him have his way with me. Oh, he was such a pretty rogue, and his kisses were so sweet! My father was a wealthy merchant esteemed by all and I his only treasured daughter, yet still I ran from that happy home to wed Mr. Willow. I loved him too well to question him in anything, and when we'd spent all the money I'd taken from my father's strongbox before I'd run away, Mr. Willow put me on the stage to earn a living for us both."

"Now, that *is* wicked," Rivers said, fascinated. He guessed that much of this standard tale of ruin was based upon third-rate plays she'd seen at the theater or songs she'd heard from ballad-singers—the predictable pattern of the words and story betrayed as much—but it didn't matter.

Here in the shadowy carriage, where all she had to give life to her tale was her voice, she was doing a first rate job of entertaining him. She might not realize it, but they'd just begun another lesson, and she was performing so well that she'd made him forget completely her earlier singsong recitation.

In fact, she'd made him forget everything except what would come next in her hackneyed little fiction. She'd made him believe it was absolute truth, and he could not wait to hear more.

"Where did Mr. Willow take you to perform?" he asked. "A playhouse in some distant county?"

"Oh, no," she said. "It wasn't nearly so grand as that. We'd fallen in with a small circus, with rope-dancers and all, that played in little towns and villages on market days. We'd set up a stage in the back of a wagon, and I'd wear a pink silk gown and say sad poetry to make the ladies weep, and Mr. Willow would pass the hat. I could be most piteous, my lord, and as the tears fell, their purses would open."

He hadn't expected that. But then, he hadn't expected any of this, and he was almost convinced that she was telling him the true story of her life.

"You must have been accomplished," he said, "to support both you and Mr. Willow like that."

"I was, my lord, I was," she said confidently, and then let her voice slide toward melancholy. "They called me an angel, stepped down from the very heavens to our humble stage. But alas, it did not last between me and Mr. Willow."

"It never does with rascals like that," Rivers said, commiserating. There was something very intimate about sitting here in the darkened carriage with her while she told him her life's story, albeit an invented one. Intimate, and unexpectedly seductive, too. He hadn't noticed that about her voice before, how it had a rich, velvety quality that made him want to listen to it all night. "Did he leave you for another lady, then?"

"Not at all," she said, and paused again. She'd a knack for those pauses, sensing exactly how long to hold them to make him crave to hear more.

"It was much more tragic than that," she continued. "You see, the circus also had wild beasts for show, and one night, the tiger—a great, huge, ravening cat he was, my lord, straight from the jungle and striped all over—

this savage beast broke free from his cage and dragged off poor Mr. Willow as he returned from the privy."

"No!" exclaimed Rivers, with exactly the right amount of feigned horror and shock—although to be honest he hadn't expected poor Mr. Willow to meet with such an exotic fate. At his feet, Spot groaned in his sleep, likely in sympathy with the tiger. "Did no one come to his rescue?"

"No, my lord, they did not," she said succinctly, "for no one knew that he'd been taken. All that was ever found of him were the rings from his ears, golden rings that I wear to this day on a ribbon about my neck to remember him by. Shall I tell you another tale, my lord?"

"Yes, Mrs. Willow, if you please," he said, smiling though he doubted she'd see it, or him, in the darkened carriage. Here was another useful gift he hadn't known she possessed, and from the way she'd begun, he guessed her store of tales might well be inexhaustible. It was a good thing, too, since they'd still hours of travel before them, and he'd every intention of letting her continue amusing him until they reached the Lodge. "Pray tell me what happened to you after the lamentable demise of Mr. Willow."

"I shall be honored, my lord," she said, clearly pleased. "*Most* honored."

He settled back to listen, smiling still. Not only was his wager with Everett all but won, but he'd also bet this was going to be the most entertaining journey he'd ever undertaken.

She took a deep breath, as if launching into a river instead of a story. "It all begins after I parted ways with the circus . . ."

CHAPTER

6

Lucia woke with the sun full in her face, and not the slightest notion of where she was. That was enough to wake her fully, and with a start she sat upright in the bed.

It wasn't her bed, that was certain. Instead of the narrow little cot beneath the slanting eaves, she was sitting in a wide, high, luxurious bed with tall carved posts, a pleated canopy and curtains, and a veritable sea of snowy linen around her. The bed took up much of the space in the room, a curious square chamber with windows on three sides and a ceiling swirling with ornamental plasterwork. She'd a vague memory of drawing the velvet curtains to one set of windows so she could see the view last night, or, more truly, very early this morning, with the setting moon and the first gray light of dawn making shadowy ghosts of the trees and meadows. For that was what she'd seen: trees and meadows and gardens, as far as was possible from her usual morning view of chimney pots, slates, and sooty skies.

Those curtains were still drawn open, which accounted for the midday sun that had awakened her. Her clothes were still folded neatly over the back of a chair where she'd left them last night, with her little trunk open on the floor beside it. She remembered now, and smiled.

She was at Breconridge Lodge, somewhere far, far away from her old lodgings in Whitechapel, both in miles and in manner. She'd come here with Lord Rivers in his coach, and she'd kept them both awake nearly all the night through by telling him stories, fancies she'd made up as she'd gone along. To her amazement, he'd listened, every bit as rapt as the girls and hangers-on in the tiring room. She couldn't believe that he had, any more than she could really believe that she was in this room, in this place, in a bed grander than any she'd ever seen, let alone slept in.

She'd been so weary by the time they'd arrived that she'd only the sleepiest of recollections of it, of how Lord Rivers had bowed and bid her good night in the front hall, how a footman had carried her box upstairs to this room for her, and a maidservant had pulled back the coverlet and plumped her pillows for her.

And all because somewhere on that long carriage ride, she'd ceased to be Lucia di Rossi, and had instead become Mrs. Cassandra Willow.

She chuckled to herself, and slipped from the bed to go to the window. Her room seemed to be in some sort of square tower at the end of the Lodge, which accounted for the windows on three sides, and on the top story. Green lawns and trees were spread before her, divided by the long, straight drive to the gates, beyond her sight, that had marked the entry to the property.

It seemed impossible that one person should own the house in Cavendish Square and all this as well, and yet she recalled Magdalena saying how Lord Rivers was the poorest of his family, on account of being the third son and not the first. He himself had jested last night about how humble his country place was, a tiny corner of land carved from his father's enormous estate, and yet to see this now by day made his jest beyond her comprehension.

Lightly she tapped her fingers on the glass, thinking. From the height of the sun—and the emptiness of her stomach—she guessed it was already afternoon. His lordship had promised that they'd continue her lessons today, but he'd set no time for beginning. She hoped she wouldn't be late on account of sleeping too long; he'd already made it very clear that sleeping seemed a special irritant to him.

She washed and dressed herself swiftly, wearing the only other clean linen petticoat and jacket she'd brought with her. She'd have to ask if there was a laundry in the house, where she could wash her clothes; she'd so few things of her own, she couldn't go for more than a few days without laundering. She knew from Magdalena's lady's maid that the gentry judged people by the cleanliness of their linen, and she'd no wish to offend Lord Rivers because the cuffs of her shift were grubby. She plaited and pinned her hair into a neat knot, covered it with a fresh linen cap, and then tucked her trunk beneath the bed. Despite what his lordship had told her about thieves, in her experience it was always better not to leave temptation in plain sight.

She opened her door cautiously, not quite sure who or what she'd find on the other side. There was a hall paneled in dark wood with more of the same busy plasterwork overhead that was in her room, plus several enormous paintings and gilt-framed looking glasses on the walls and a few chairs and benches beneath them. But she saw no servants or anyone else, and with a thumping heart she began down the hallway toward the main staircase she'd been led up the night before. She realized she was tiptoeing, as if she were an interloper who didn't belong amidst such grandeur, and with a conscious effort she made herself walk more firmly. She'd every right to be here; she was his lordship's guest, as he'd assured her again and again.

Yet when she passed a low arched doorway that led to

a much more humble set of stairs, used by servants, she quickly ducked inside it. She told herself that this would be the fastest way to the kitchen, and to something to eat and drink, pretending that this wasn't an excuse. The truth, of course, was that she felt much more comfortable here, slipping down these back stairs as she had all her life, and in the kitchen and servants' hall she might meet with her newfound friends among the footmen.

She had enjoyed last night's journey with his lordship, enjoyed his attention and his praise, but she still did not feel at ease with him. True, he'd tried to set things to rights after that unpleasantness about her memorizing his precious passage, but she hadn't forgotten it. He could declare her to be Mrs. Cassandra Willow all he wanted, but she didn't yet *believe* herself to be Mrs. Willow, and she wasn't sure he did, either. Inside—and outside, too—she was still Lucia di Rossi, running down the back stairs to beg a cup of tea or coffee and a slice of bread from the cook.

She followed the stairs to the basement floor, and then followed her nose down a short hallway to the kitchen. Preparations were already under way for dinner, and the smell of roasting meats and onions made her mouth water. In her experience, cooks were jolly and generous, and eagerly she opened the door, anticipating being offered a taste or two of whatever was simmering on the hearth.

But as soon as she opened the door, she realized the warm welcome she'd anticipated would not be forthcoming. Lord Rivers's cook was a thin, brittle-looking woman with an oversized ruffled cap and red-checkered apron. Standing over a large copper kettle with a long ladle in one hand, she made a sharp little bark of displeasure when she saw Lucia over her shoulder. With the ladle still in her hand, she turned and made a perfunctory bob of a curtsey, and didn't wait for Lucia to acknowledge it before she spoke, either.

"My stars, Mrs. Willow!" she exclaimed crossly. "Creeping about, startling a body like that! What are you doing downstairs, eh? You belong upstairs with his lordship, not down here spying an' prying where you've no place to be."

"For-forgive me, please," Lucia stammered, stunned by this reception. "I'd no intention of spying on you, Mrs., ah, Mrs.—"

"Mrs. Barber," the cook said, brandishing before her the ladle with ominous efficiency, "not, ma'am, that it's any affair of yours. You'd best know that I take my orders direct from his lordship, not any of his *guests*."

"I'd no intention of giving any orders, to you or anyone else," Lucia said, only now noticing the pair of cowering scullery girls peeling apples. The way she'd said *guests* made it clear that his lordship had brought other women here before her, and it was easy enough to guess that they hadn't been aspiring actresses.

She smiled bravely, determined to appease the cook. "I can see that you're busy, Mrs. Barber, but all I wish for is a cup of tea and perhaps a slice of bread, and—"

"Then why did you not ring for it properly, ma'am, instead of coming here?" Mrs. Barber demanded. "Why come here to vex me?"

"I'd no intention of vexing you, Mrs. Barber," Lucia said. "I only wished—"

"'Only wished, only wished,'" repeated Mrs. Barber sourly, waving the ladle in Lucia's direction. "Upstairs with you now, ma'am, to the green parlor in the back, and I'll see that one of the girls brings you tea. Unless you *wish* to explain to his lordship as to why his meal's not ready when he'll be wanting it."

That was enough for Lucia. She fled back up the stairs, to the first floor of the house, and found the front hall where they'd entered last night. In comparison to Lord Rivers's house in town, where there'd been servants hovering all over the place, the Lodge seemed curiously understaffed, and without anyone to ask, she followed the passage beneath the front stairs. If the stairs were in the front of the house, then the green parlor must be on the opposite side.

The first room she peeked inside was some sort of office, filled with books and a large table covered with papers, which obviously served as a desk. She couldn't be expected to take her tea here. But the room across the passage had a small dining table with chairs before the open windows, which made it much more likely to be the parlor in the back, and the parrot-green wallpaper made it a certainty.

Dutifully she sat in one of the chairs, smoothing her skirts over her knees. The snowy linen cloth on the table was so immaculate, the pressed creases so sharp and perfect, that she didn't dare touch it, and so she carefully folded her hands in her own lap, and waited. She'd no idea how long she was expected to do so, and given Mrs. Barber's bad temper, she'd no idea what she'd be brought when the waiting was finally done.

Yet still she sat, gazing out the open window to the flower garden below. It *was* a beautiful garden, filled with bright flowers nodding gently in the sunshine, the perfect view for anyone dining. Having lived all her life in cities, her only experience with flowers was the cut variety that attentive gentlemen had had sent to Magdalena. She'd always wondered what it would be like to pick flowers for herself, to choose one blossom over another and make a posy exactly to her own tastes. Perhaps she'd muster the courage to ask Lord Rivers if flower picking could be included in her lessons.

She sniffed impatiently, swinging her legs under her skirts. Right now she'd be content if Lord Rivers simply *appeared.* He'd told her repeatedly that they had much work to do in six weeks' time. Well, here she was, ready to begin, and he was nowhere to be seen.

Three quick raps on the door behind her, then it swung open. At once Lucia slipped from her chair, hoping that her grumbling thoughts had somehow summoned his lordship. But instead of Lord Rivers, it was the same maidservant who'd shown her upstairs last night, a woman of middling age with a broad, determined face with full cheeks. In her hands was a large silver tea tray, heavily laden with all manner of tea things.

Automatically Lucia hurried forward to help her, but the maid held the tray from her reach, her expression scandalized.

"If you please, Mrs. Willow, I can manage well enough," she said, brusque and a little out of breath. "Please sit, ma'am, please, and let me tend to you."

Self-consciously Lucia sat back in her chair, and the maid placed the large tray down on the table. No matter how sharp Mrs. Barber had been earlier, she'd sent up a splendid assortment of good things to eat. In addition to a steaming pot of tea, there were also two plates of neatly trimmed sandwiches, a bowl of oranges, and small dishes of sweet biscuits and candied nuts.

"Shall I pour, ma'am?" the maid asked.

"Thank you, yes," Lucia said, overwhelmed by the sheer amount of food before her. As part of the company, she'd been given lodgings and board, but those meals, like her wages and the room she shared with the other girls, had been meager indeed. Even before, when her father had been alive, most of his money had gone to drink, and for food they'd made do with what had been left. As such, she could never remember having so many good things to eat presented to her like this, and she could only stare as the maid poured her tea.

"What is inside the bread?" she asked at last as the

maid handed her her cup. The white porcelain, painted with orange and gold dragons, was so fine that the sunlight shined through the rim, and Lucia held it with infinite care, half-afraid it would shatter in her hand. The tea itself was sweet and fragrant and redolent of mysterious places she'd never see, and far, far better than the watery gray stuff she drank at the lodging house.

"Sliced roasted beef in the first tray, ma'am," the maid answered, "and sliced breast of duck in the other, both with cress. Mustard on one slice of the bread, and butter on the other, as his lordship prefers."

"Where is Lord Rivers?" Lucia asked eagerly. "I haven't seen him yet today."

"I do not know, ma'am," she said with the merest hint of rebuff. "I do his lordship's bidding, not ask his business. Will there be anything else, ma'am?"

Lucia shook her head, and the maid withdrew, the door closing after her with the click of the latch. Lucia sighed; while Lord Rivers's male servants had liked her well enough, the female ones were making it abundantly clear that they regarded her as only one more of his lordship's doxies, brought down from London for his passing amusement. Which of course she wasn't, but she doubted anything she could say would persuade them otherwise. At least they'd brought her splendid things to eat, and with resignation—and anticipation—she set the teacup down and pulled her chair closer to the table.

She reached first for one of the beef sandwiches, marveling at the pillowy white bread cut into neat triangles with the darker crusts cut away. What a spendthrift thing to do, she marveled, even if it made for a much more dainty morsel. Then she bit into the sandwich and instantly forgot those discarded crusts. The tenderness of the beef, the spiciness of the mustard, and the peppery crunch of the cress, all wrapped within the featherlight fresh bread—ah, she'd never had anything to compare.

In three bites the sandwich was gone. She wondered whether it would be unseemly to have another, and then reminded herself that the tray had been brought to her alone. She wiped the mustard from her fingers on the overhanging edge of the cloth, and reached for another sandwich, and then another, and another after that. Before she'd quite realized it, she'd eaten nearly all the sandwiches on both plates, the crumbs on the cloth before her the only proof she'd left.

Yet still she wasn't full, and she reached for one of the oranges, digging her thumb under the dimpled peel. This orange wasn't at all like the oranges that were sold at the playhouse: sorry, wizened fruit that the orange-girls plumped by dropping in boiling water the afternoon before a performance. This orange was sweet and delectable, with juice that dribbled down her chin and left her fingers pale and sticky, and made her smile from the pure, delicious joy of it.

And it was at that point, of course, when she was covered with crumbs and orange juice, that the door opened once again, this time without a warning knock. First Spot came bounding into the room, followed—inevitably—by Lord Rivers. She gulped and slid from her chair, dropping into a hasty, sticky-fingered curtsey. Spot came to her at once, snuffling at the crumbs on her skirt, his tail whipping furiously.

"Good afternoon, Mrs. Willow," Lord Rivers said. "Spot, leave her alone. Here, here, you wicked devil-dog. Please, Mrs. Willow, take your seat again. No ceremony on my account, I beg you."

She did as he'd bidden, took her chair, and finally lifted her gaze to meet his. His voice was loud and hearty in the parlor, booming away as if he were roaring across open fields.

Which, from the look of him, was exactly what he'd been doing. His riding boots were comfortably worn and caked with mud, making her remember how he'd been so stern about Spot's muddy paws—a rule that apparently did not apply to his own feet.

He'd shed his coat and his hat somewhere else, for now he was bareheaded, with the sleeves of his shirt rolled carelessly over his elbows. She was not accustomed to seeing the forearms of a gentleman, which were usually tucked away beneath silk coats and lace cuffs. Lord Rivers's forearms, however, were worthy of any laboring man, strong and well muscled and dusted with golden hair, and exceptionally . . . pleasant to gaze upon. The collar of that shirt was unbuttoned and open, too, with a blue printed cotton scarf knotted loosely around his bare throat.

And his breeches: leather breeches were common enough for men, but not like these, closely cut of such soft buckskin that they clung to every muscle and sinew and everything else in a way that was thoroughly distracting. She forced herself to look away, to keep her gaze on his face alone, but that wasn't much easier to do. He was like an extension of the country day itself, his face browned from riding, his eyes blue as the sky and his hair golden like the sun. For Lucia, who had lived nearly all of her life in the most crowded parts of cities, and whose days had been turned around into most people's nights by the playhouse's schedule, he was almost blindingly brilliant.

Not that he was aware of any of this. Instead he dropped into the chair opposite hers, his legs stretched out before him as he reached down to ruffle Spot's head.

"So," he said. "Are you feeling quite restored now?"

She nodded, still tongue-tied by having all his manly magnificence dropped here before her. That tongue-tiedness made no sense, she told herself fiercely. Hadn't she just spent hours and hours with this same man in a carriage? What was the difference now? If he hadn't attempted to dishonor her when they'd been alone together on an empty highway at night, then surely she'd nothing to fear from him now.

But then, perhaps the risk wasn't with him, but with herself. She was the one who'd been reduced to tongue-tied silence simply by his presence, not him by hers.

"Are you sure you've had enough to eat?" he asked, surveying what little remained on the tray. "You certainly didn't leave much for me."

She gasped with horror. Why hadn't the maid told her that the tray was intended for his lordship? "Forgive me, my lord, I did not know! I thought it was for me!"

"All for tiny little you?" he asked, and laughed. "No, Mrs. Willow, I'm afraid not. Mrs. Barber always sees that there's tea waiting for me here when I return from riding. She might have added a bit more knowing you'd likely join me."

Now she realized there were two teacups and saucers, and her mortification grew. "Oh, my lord, I am so—"

"Hush," he said gently. "You were hungry, and now you're not. There's no sin to that. Adam, here!"

Instantly a footman entered, so instantly that Lucia was certain he'd been listening on the other side of the door. Not that his lordship appeared to care as he sent for another tray of food and a fresh pot of tea.

"So tell me, Mrs. Willow," he said when the footman left them. "You're a tiny creature for having such a prodigious appetite. Didn't your family ever feed you?"

"The company looked after me, my lord," she said carefully, unsure whether he was teasing or not. "I took my meals with the others, in my lodgings."

He studied her, appraising. "From the look of you, I'd guess that Magdalena and her lot must have reached the table first."

She flushed, unwilling to admit that was very close to the truth. They weren't treated equally in the company;

and she didn't need him to point it out to her. It was an unwavering hierarchy determined by Uncle Lorenzo. Because the first dancers like Magdalena earned the money that supported everyone else connected to the company, they were the ones rewarded with the best lodgings and plenty of food and drink so they'd dance their best. The tiring-girls like Lucia brought no income to the company, and therefore were expected to content themselves with watered tea and gruel for breakfast; and pease porridge, coarse bread, and gristly stew for supper; and rooms beneath the roof. According to Uncle Lorenzo, they received what they were worth, and they weren't worth much.

"We were looked after, my lord," she said carefully. "Everyone in the company was. I did not want."

He frowned, skeptical. "I don't believe it," he said. "You're far too thin. I want you to eat as much as you please. You could do with a bit of plumping. You want the people in the last rows of the playhouse to be able to see you, don't you?"

"They'll hear me, my lord," she said, eager to turn the conversation away from her size and appetite. She knew she was too thin, especially compared to Magdalena and the others, and it stung to have him remind her of it. Purposefully she raised her voice as if she were in fact projecting to those last rows. "I won't let them overlook me."

"No, I doubt you will," he said drily. "They wouldn't overlook a yowling fishwife anyway."

She scowled. "I am not a fishwife, my lord, and I don't sound like one, either."

"Nor do you sound like a queen, a princess, or even a duchess, which are the parts I wish you to make your own," he said, thoughtfully rubbing his left temple. "It would be easy enough to turn you loose on broad humor and drollery, and let you bellow and flounce your way around the stage where the audience would no doubt adore you. But that's not the wager. You're to become the next Madame Adelaide, which means I must make you fit for the exalted roles."

"I know that, my lord," she said, inching forward on her chair with excitement. *This* was the reason she'd agreed to the wager. "That's what I was born to do!"

"Rather, you were not born to play the frivolous parts, since they require dancing and singing as well," he said. "I am assuming that if you cannot dance, you also cannot sing, yes?"

"No, my lord," Lucia admitted, adding a huge sigh of regret. She'd thought he'd seen some genius for tragedy in her, not simply a lack of the dancing and singing required for comedy. "Not at all."

"I thought as much. Ah, more reinforcements from the kitchen," he said as the same maid as before returned with another tray and even more plates and saucers. This time, she was all smiles for his lordship, fussing about him and cooing at Spot and generally pretending that Lucia did not exist.

Fortunately Lord Rivers did not feel the same. "Set the tray there, Sally, where Mrs. Willow can reach it," he said, smiling so wickedly at Lucia that her cheeks grew hot. "I wouldn't wish to stand in her way where a biscuit was concerned."

Sally cleared her throat to make sure they knew how much she disapproved, and left them alone.

"You shouldn't have said that, my lord," Lucia said as soon as the door closed after the maid. "She and Mrs. Barber already hate me, and now you've only made it worse."

Lord Rivers laughed, taking one of the sandwiches and feeding it to Spot.

"They don't hate you," he said. "More likely, they do not trust you, and that's not the same thing. You're younger than they are, and considerably more attractive, and you're sitting here with me. That's reason enough for them."

Lucia remained unconvinced, especially the part about her being attractive. He was teasing; he couldn't mean that at all. She could well imagine the sorts of women he ordinarily brought here for his amusement, and they'd all look much more like Magdalena than her.

"They think I'm another of your London doxies," she said darkly. "They think I'm stupid and foolish and not worth their time."

"Then they're mistaken on every count." He chose a sandwich, studied it briefly, and then popped the entire thing into his mouth. "Especially the stupid and foolish part. I wouldn't have agreed to this wager otherwise. Here, help yourself to another morsel or two."

"I'm not hungry any longer, my lord," she said impatiently. "When will we begin my lessons? We've only six weeks—forty-two days, and we've already wasted three of them. Four, if you count today, too. When will we *begin*?"

"We already have," he said, smiling with irritating smugness as he leaned back in his chair.

"We have not, my lord." At least for now she'd stopped noticing his alarmingly male person, distracted by his equally male smugness. "All you have done is given me that one short, silly passage to remember, and now you sit here stuffing food into your mouth while we could be *working*!"

Deliberately he reached for another sandwich and poured himself a cup of tea. "Forgive me, but I'm rather late to arrive for the food-stuffing. I'm trying my best to catch up with you."

She lowered her chin and glowered, angry and disappointed. "I thought you'd wished to help me, my lord, and that you wanted to win that foolish wager. I thought you'd keep your *word* as a gentleman."

His eyes narrowed, enough to make her wonder that she'd said too much. Wonder, yes, but not apologize. He was the one who wasn't doing what he'd promised.

"That one 'silly passage,' Mrs. Willow, is from perhaps the greatest play ever written in the English language," he said, each word clipped. "It's from *The Tragedy of Hamlet, Prince of Denmark,* which was written by William Shakespeare. I trust you have heard of him?"

She nodded, a quick little nod with her anger still simmering. She had heard of this Shakespeare, barely, from playbills and from the cover of the book he'd handed her last night, but he couldn't possibly be the great playwright that Lord Rivers claimed he was. The passage he'd given her *was* silly, and old-dated, too, and besides, if he was such an important fellow, then why didn't his plays have ballets, and why weren't they being performed at the King's Theatre, where she would have seen them?

Her cursory nod clearly didn't please him, and he set his cup down with a saucer-rattling thump.

"The passage I gave to you belongs to the character you will learn whilst we are here," he continued curtly. "She is a young noblewoman about your age, tragically in love with Prince Hamlet, heir to the Danish throne. You say you like to make others weep. If you learn this part well, you will make all London weep, and love you for it."

"A lovesick, tragic noblewoman, my lord?" she asked, her anger fading before this intriguing possibility. She'd like to make all London weep; she'd enjoy nothing more. "How was I to know that from what you gave me last night?"

"I didn't wish to overburden you with too much at once," he said. "But now that I know that your memory is equal to the challenge, I shall give you the entire play to read and learn."

"Yes, my lord, yes," she said, now eager. "You heard how I learned the passage perfect. You heard how I gave it the right tragic manner, too, all solemn and gloomy."

"Oh, it was solemn and gloomy, all right," he agreed. "Solemn and gloomy enough to make a man queasy from the thump of it."

She frowned uncertainly. "I read the lines exactly as Madame Adelaide would have done it, my lord. With *awe*."

"But I don't wish you to emulate Madame Adelaide," he said. "Madame Adelaide's tragic ways were old in the reign of good Queen Anne. Have you seen Mr. Garrick perform?"

She shook her head. "Not if he hasn't played the Royal, I haven't."

"I already guessed as much from your . . . your interpretation." He took another sandwich and rose to pace back and forth across the room, waving the sandwich in his hand for emphasis. "You say we haven't begun your training, but we have. Last night I learned that you have a quick memory, an ear for mimicry, and a facility with the language. I learned that you can improvise and invent at will, and that you can be thoroughly entertaining. I also learned that you are not nearly as timid as you pretended to be with your cousin."

Lucia sighed. "Those are no mysteries, my lord," she said. "I could've told you the same if you'd but asked."

He nodded, agreeing as he bit the sandwich. "But what I have also learned is that you have acquired dreadful habits of what you believe an actress should be from Madame Adelaide and her ilk. There is a world of theater beyond the doddering old King's, which is much better known for its dancers than its actors. You deliver your lines like a canting peddler, and you believe that shouting is the same as speaking loudly with authority."

"I do not," she said indignantly. "That is, my lord, I know what makes a proper actress."

"If you wish to be a proper actress who is not a hack, you will follow Mr. Garrick's more modern ways, and not Madame Adelaide's." He motioned for her to stand. "Go to the door, and when you turn back to me, I want you to make your entrance as if you are a noble lady, betrothed to a prince."

Eagerly Lucia slipped from her chair and hurried toward the door, smoothing her hair back beneath her cap. This was the chance she'd been waiting for, her opportunity to show him exactly how much she'd already learned about acting from observing all the actresses (and not just Madame Adelaide, either) who'd played the King's Theatre. She took a deep breath and raised her chin so high that she was looking down her nose. With another deep breath to swallow her nervousness, she spread her arms out on either side with her palms turned up, and turned her body sideways.

It was exactly the posture that Madame Adelaide took for entrances, and Lucia saw no reason to abandon it. Even if his lordship dismissed Madame as a hack— a *hack*!—Lucia had witnessed how audiences worshipped her, and she'd also seen the handsome carriage that Madame was able to keep because of her success.

Imagining those audiences as her own, Lucia turned and began to walk slowly across the patterned carpet to where his lordship stood. While Spot bounded along beside her, convinced this was a game of some sort, Lord Rivers had his arms folded over his chest and an awestruck expression on his face as he watched her draw closer, an expression that made her proud of the impact she was creating as a noble personage. She stopped before Lord Rivers, grandly circling her wrists with her nose still pointed toward the ceiling.

"What in blazes are you doing?" he demanded, his eyes widening with bewilderment. "You don't look noble. You look utterly deranged."

Disappointment swept over her, and she dropped her hands to settle them squarely at her waist. She had wanted so much to earn his praise!

"I am not deranged, my lord," she said. "You asked me to portray a noble lady, and that's how it is done."

He shook his head, more in disbelief than in contradiction. "I cannot fathom why you should think such a thing. You have your head bent back as if your neck is broken, your hands fluttering like wings, and your body all twisted around."

"I'm walking that way to display my costume to the audience, my lord," she said, wounded that he hadn't recognized her purpose. "So my hoops are crossways. You must pretend I'm wearing a rich costume, my lord, with spangles and ribbons and hoops, the kind of costume an audience pays to see. As for holding my head back—that's to show I'm high-born, and superior to everyone else, my lord."

"No noble lady would dare appear at Court in such a fashion," he said flatly. "If she did, she'd be removed directly."

"How do you know?" she demanded, her apparent failure making her turn defensive.

He tipped his head to one side, and too late she realized she'd forgotten his title.

"How do you know, *my lord*?" she repeated.

"Because of exactly that," he said with irrefutable logic. "I'm the son of a duke, and my entire family is riddled with titled ladies. I know how they behave, because that's what I've seen all my life. Even the duchesses don't walk about believing they're superior to everyone else at Court, because they're not. There's always His Majesty above us all. Apparently Madame Adelaide and her ilk forget that."

"I still do not see how—"

"You agreed to trust me, Mrs. Willow, and to do as I say," he said firmly. "That was our understanding."

Lucia didn't answer, considering how best to salvage her tattered pride. Of course he was right, or at least partly right. She had agreed to follow his instruction, and he would know better than she about how a true noble lady would enter a room. But she still wasn't convinced that was what audiences would be willing to pay to see.

Bored, Spot yawned, and settled on the carpet behind his master, his head on his legs.

"Have you ever been to Court with His Majesty, my lord?" she asked, stalling. "Inside the palace, I mean?"

"More times than I can count," he said with a nonchalant shrug that proved it was the truth. "My father began hauling us there when I was barely in breeches."

"Truly, my lord?" she asked, impressed. "I've seen Their Majesties in their carriage on holidays, but only from far away. To think you've been in the same room with them!"

"I assure you, it's not very exciting," he said. "Now, are you willing to try your entrance again?"

She sighed deeply, letting her shoulders sag with resignation. "Very well, my lord. What do you wish me to be instead of Madame Adelaide?"

"I don't wish you to be anyone other than yourself," he said firmly. "That is what Garrick advises. Aspire not to 'act,' but to capture reality. You needn't play so obviously to the audience; rather, let them come to you."

"How shall that work, my lord?" she asked incredulously.

"You must trust me that it does," he said. "Now think

of the most confident woman you know, and imagine
how she would enter a room."

"That would be Magdalena," she said, thinking of
how her cousin made every man in any room look her
way without even trying. "But I do not believe any noble
lady walks like Magdalena."

He sighed, doubtless remembering her cousin's commanding entrances.

"That is true," he agreed reluctantly. "No noble lady
would ever *undulate* like Magdalena. Perhaps instead
you should imagine Magdalena entering a church—
a church filled with nuns, and no men. A penitent Magdalena, if such a thing exists."

"Oh, it does, my lord, it does," Lucia said thoughtfully. "Magdalena has done many, many things to be
penitent for. I shall try my best."

She crossed the room and again faced the door. She
remembered Magdalena on her way to confession, of
how her cousin still walked with her usual confidence,
but with her head lightly bowed beneath her shawl, as if
the burden of her sins somehow made her temporarily
demure. Lucia could copy that, even if it was the furthest
thing imaginable from Madame Adelaide's grand dramatic entrances. If nothing else, she'd demonstrate to his
lordship how wrong he was.

Composed, she turned back to face him. This time she
thought of Magdalena and walked toward him with her
spine straight, her shoulders drawn back, and her hands
clasped at her waist. It felt much different from her own
usual self-effacing walk, the walk of a servant whose role
was to be invisible, and with each step she felt her confidence was her own, and not borrowed from her cousin.

She stopped directly before his lordship, her head
bowed just enough that her chin was dipped toward her
chest, and she ignored the imaginary audience, as he'd
directed.

He watched her critically, one hand beneath his chin and his arm resting in his other hand. He wasn't exactly frowning, but he was concentrating hard upon her, which was disconcerting, and made her in turn concentrate harder on how she was standing and holding her shoulders.

If only his eyes weren't so very blue . . .

"Much improved," he said finally. "Now do it again, but this time, do not clench your hands together. They should be gentle, like resting doves."

" 'Resting doves'?" she repeated, stunned by the description. Automatically she looked down at her hands, chapped and rough from work and cold water, and without so much as a feather of the elegance or purity of white doves. She blushed, ashamed by how unladylike they were, and tried to hide her fingers in the folds of her skirts. "Forgive me, my lord, but not my hands."

"Show me," he said, and slowly, self-consciously, she held her hands out for him to see.

He took her hands in his own and held them lightly with his thumbs, turning the palms upward to study as if they were some rare curiosity worthy of his scholarly attention. His were gentleman's hands, with long, strong fingers accustomed to holding a pen, a crystal goblet, or the reins of a fine horse; on his right hand he wore a heavy ring with a carnelian signet, the gold gleaming against his skin. In comparison, her hands looked small and rough, and the only birds they'd be likened to would be the scruffy little starlings that scratched out their living around the rooftops of Whitechapel.

"It's from the laundering, my lord," she blurted out, uncomfortable beneath his scrutiny. "My uncle doesn't trust the costumes to be sent out for washing, so the other tiring-girls and I had to wash all the dancers' things for them."

"It doesn't matter now," he said, his thumbs lightly

tracing little arcs across her palms, as if to prove he didn't care how rough they were. "That time is done. Your hands will improve while you're here, since you won't be working. I'll send for some manner of unguent that will heal them."

Tears stung her eyes at the unexpected kindness. "Thank you, my lord," she said, grateful for more than the promised unguent. "But they'll still never be white doves."

He smiled wryly. "I know it does sound foolish, but doves are the conventional allusion for noble ladies' hands. You have small, slender hands with delicate fingers that many ladies would envy. I'm certain they will improve, and be a graceful asset to you on the stage— a stage I am certain you'll claim as your own. Now, as we were. Keep your hands folded before you, but relaxed and easy."

"Shall I curtsey this time, my lord?" she said. The breathlessness of her words surprised her. "A proper entrance for a noble lady should end that way, shouldn't it?"

He nodded, his gaze finally leaving her hands to settle on her face, and make her blush all over again.

"A curtsey isn't necessary now," he said, clearly believing she'd no idea of how to perform one. "Concentrate on the rest instead."

"Yes, my lord," she said, intending to add the curtsey regardless of what he said. "But I swear to you I can do one."

"Then show me," he said. At last he released her hands, and she quickly pulled them free and hurried back across the room to the now-familiar door.

She needed these few moments to herself. He'd had good reason to hold her hands, and yet the simple gesture had left her heart racing. She was sure he hadn't intended anything flirtatious by it—why should he, given who and what she was?—but she also couldn't deny the impact that his touch had had upon her. No man had ever held her hands in such a way, and she couldn't have predicted the intimacy of it. By sharing his confidence in her, in turn he'd somehow made her own confidence blossom.

She gave her head a little shake, preparing herself yet again. But this time when she turned and crossed the room, she wasn't trying to copy her cousin, nor was she rattled by nervousness. Because she wasn't, the role she was playing became a seamless, effortless extension of herself, and when she swept across the carpet toward his lordship, she felt every bit the noble lady she was supposed to be.

She didn't look ahead to see his reaction. She didn't have to, for instinctively she knew that what she was doing was *right*. When she came within a few feet of him, she paused, and sank into a sweeping curtsey, her head nearly touching her knee, and stayed there, waiting for him to respond.

Over her head she heard him swear, in the quiet way that men did when they were caught by surprise. Then he reached down and took her hand, and raised her up to stand close before him.

"Where in blazes did you learn that?" he demanded.

"My uncle Lorenzo taught every woman in the company how to present honors and make a curtsey like that in case any royalty ever came backstage, my lord," she said, unable to tell if he was pleased or not as she looked up and searched his face. The way he'd pulled her had left her standing close to him, with little space between them. Yet she didn't step back, nor did he, and she didn't pull her hand free, either, relishing the warmth of his fingers around hers.

"My uncle Lorenzo learned what was proper when he was a member of the Ballet de l'Opéra de Paris, my lord," she said, hating herself for babbling like this but unable to stop. "He said a quick, common bob-curtsey was well enough for every day, but for a prince or higher, we must do—"

"That's not what I meant," he said abruptly, cutting her off. "I meant how you walked, how you crossed the room, how you *were*. Where did you learn that?"

"I did what you said, my lord," she said, bewildered. "I put aside Madame Adelaide, and instead only thought of how I should be as the noble lady you described. Did I misunderstand, my lord? Was I wrong?"

"Not at all," he said slowly. "You were very nearly perfect."

She gasped with delight and at last slipped free of him, stepping back to clap her hands together in amazement.

"Oh, my lord, I am so pleased!" she exclaimed happily. "Now you'll believe that I'll do whatever you say, whatever you want, to be the actress I know I can be."

But to her confusion, he didn't smile in return.

"That will be enough lessons for today, Mrs. Willow," he said, looking past her. "I do not wish to tire you."

"But I'm not tired, my lord, not at all," she pleaded, disappointed. "We have so little time to accomplish so much, and I—"

"I said that will be all," he repeated, an unmistakable distance to his voice that hadn't been there earlier. "I have made arrangements to dine with a friend. Request whatever you wish for your own dinner. I shall leave word with Mrs. Barber to oblige you and send a tray to your room."

"Yes, my lord," she said wistfully, the prospect of a solitary dinner and evening alone yawning before her. She supposed she should be grateful for his hospitality, but she'd much rather continue to work. "As you wish."

"Yes," he said, and cleared his throat. "I will have the copy of *Hamlet* brought to your room, so you may begin reading it in its entirety."

"Yes, yes, my lord," she said eagerly. "The sooner I can begin to learn my role, the better."

He nodded, still avoiding her gaze as if her enthusiasm made him uncomfortable. He whistled low, and Spot rose, sleepily wagging his tail.

"Well, then," he said, retreating. "Until tomorrow morning. Good day, Mrs. Willow."

And just like that, he—and his dog—were gone.

CHAPTER
7

In Rivers's experience, there was no better place for composing an apology than on the back of a horse, preferably alone and by moonlight, or so he told himself that night as he made his way home from the Four Chimneys, an inn not far from the Lodge. Which was just as well, considering that he once again owed Lucia an apology, and he hadn't the faintest notion of how to begin.

It was late, very late, or perhaps very early, as he finally turned his horse through the stone gates to the Lodge. When he had met Squire Ralston while riding earlier in the day (or was that now yesterday?), he had politely declined the squire's enthusiastic invitation to join the Breconridge Hunt for a turtle feast at Four Chimneys. While he often rode with them (he was always welcome, considering how the hunt had borrowed its name from his family) when he was in residence at the Lodge, he'd no desire to spend a long evening in a low, smoky room watching country gentlemen consume more turtle soup and strong drink than was good for any mortal.

But that had been before he'd met with Lucia—or rather, Mrs. Willow—in the parlor. Not that renaming her had made any difference in how he'd behaved, the way he'd convinced himself it would.

It was entirely his own fault, of course, every bit of it. Lucia had done everything he'd asked of her and done it splendidly, too. She hadn't once tried to entice him or beguile him, the way her cousin most certainly would have done. Instead she'd made it clear as could be that her only purpose in being here was to become the actress he'd promised. When he'd made that wager, he'd thought that was his only purpose, too, believing everything would be businesslike between them. How could it not, given what a plain and untempting little thing she was?

Yet the more time he'd spent in her company, the less plain and untempting she'd become. He couldn't fathom it. He'd concede that she could amuse him; she was surprisingly clever with words, and her inventive storytelling last night had kept him so enthralled that he'd regretted their journey's end.

But she still dressed like a drab lower servant with her hair scraped back beneath that dreadful white cap. Her eyes were still too big for her face, and her body too slight for her clothes. She still scurried rather than walked, and this afternoon she'd devoured his entire tea.

Yet that last time when she'd walked across the carpet toward him she'd been so delicately graceful that all he'd been able to do was stare, as if she were some sort of ethereal sprite dropped into his green parlor. Her dark eyes were like magic, drawing him in, and when she'd sunk into a curtsey at his feet, he'd nearly gulped aloud at the grace and vulnerability of the pale nape of her neck.

Her *neck*. Damnation, what kind of fool was he?

He swore crossly at himself, remembering exactly what kind of fool he had been. He'd told her how to make herself irresistible to audiences, and she'd listened, and done it. He simply hadn't expected it to work on him the same way.

As a result, he'd blustered and stammered and then fled to the dubious blandishments of the Hunt's turtle feast, abruptly leaving her in a confusion that she hadn't deserved.

Now he half-expected to learn that she'd disappeared, too, gone back to London instead of being trapped here with him. He could hardly blame her if she had.

Glumly he left his horse at the stable with a sleepy groom, and headed into the house, where he was greeted by an equally sleepy footman. Only the night lantern was lit in the front hall, casting angular shadows across the old portraits that were gloomy enough by daylight. In their stiff ruffs and pointed beards, the portraits were never good company, but as Rivers climbed the stairs, he decided they were likely no better than he deserved.

Perhaps in the morning he'd know what to say to Lucia.

Perhaps with a good night's sleep, the right words would come to him, and they could begin afresh.

The hall to his bedchamber was even more murky and shadowed, lit only by the moonlight through the diamond-paned windows. He should have stopped for a candlestick, but hadn't bothered, and now he'd have to rely on his familiarity with the old place to find his way. He smiled, remembering how as a boy he'd been convinced the Lodge was haunted by those old Elizabethans in their fussy ruffs.

He heard a door open behind him, and turned swiftly at the sound. A figure in white with long trailing hair raced toward him through the shadows, and instinctively he drew back, too startled to reply.

"Lord Rivers!" Lucia called breathlessly as she hurried toward him. "At last you are returned, my lord. I've been waiting and *waiting* to speak with you, and I'm so glad you're finally here."

Candlelight from her open bedroom door sliced into the hall, and by it he could see that she wore only her shift, with the coverlet from the bed wrapped haphazardly around her shoulders. Her hair was combed out, falling like a dark cloak nearly to her waist, and if he'd thought her eyes seemed too large for her face by daylight, now in the near-darkness they truly belonged to another world.

"It's very late, Mrs. Willow," he said, striving to regain some semblance of propriety. "Whatever you wish to discuss can surely wait until the morning."

"Forgive me, my lord, but it cannot," she said with dramatic conviction. "There are things that I must say to you, things that cannot wait."

Damnation, here it was. Of course she wanted to speak to him after he'd left her with such awkward haste. He couldn't avoid it, or her, any longer. He was going to have to apologize now whether his apology was composed or not.

"Very well, then," he said reluctantly, pushing the door to his rooms open. "This way."

Gathering her coverlet-shawl more tightly about her shoulders, she swept ahead of him, her bare feet making no sound on the floorboards and her dark hair streaming behind her. The first of his rooms was a small chamber where he often took his breakfast and read his mail, and there close to the banked fire sat his manservant, Rooke, asleep and slumped to one side in a chair, his mouth open and his wig askew.

"Rooke!" he said sharply, more irritated at himself for forgetting Rooke would be here waiting to help him undress. "Rooke, wake yourself."

The manservant jolted awake and rose immediately, unperturbed as he straightened his wig.

"My lord," he murmured, his glance flicking past Rivers to Lucia. So much for discretion, thought Rivers with dismay; the rest of the household would know by morning that Mrs. Willow had been in his rooms in a state of undress in the middle of the night.

"You may retire for the night, Rooke," Rivers said. "I'll look after myself."

The servant bowed and backed from the room, closing the door quietly after himself. At the same time, Rivers hurried to close the other door, the one to his adjoining bedchamber. The last thing he needed now for a difficult conversation with a young woman was to have his bedstead looming in view as an unwelcome intruder.

But then, he had to recall that was what Lucia was: a young woman of a dubious foreign family with equally dubious morals. She wasn't a lady, which was why she thought nothing of coming alone to the country with him, and standing here in his room wrapped in a bedcover, and why, too, she hadn't seemed distressed by having Rooke see her. When she'd complained about her reception by Mrs. Barber, her reason had been because the cook hadn't liked her, not because the woman had believed Lucia to be his mistress. If she didn't care, then he shouldn't, either. Her virtue didn't need protecting by him, if her virtue even still existed—a possibility that he realized he'd never considered until this moment.

It was also a possibility that his conscience now heard in his father's voice. Father would understand none of this. Of course it would come as a warning, sternly admonishing Rivers to take care not to put himself in a difficult situation with a vulgar creature like this, to stop squandering his time on cunning playhouse doxies and instead consider a suitable young lady as a wife.

Irritated more than was reasonable, Rivers jabbed at the banked fire with the poker to bring the coals back to life, and lit one of the candles from the flame. He was twenty-six years old. He could do as he damned well pleased. He set the candlestick on the table between a pair of chairs, and motioned for Lucia to sit.

"No thank you, my lord," she said, shaking her head for extra emphasis. She seemed to be vibrating with inexplicable energy, unable to keep still. "I needn't sit, not for this. I don't believe I could sit now anyway, I'm that on edge and turned about."

"Then it's up to me to begin," he said, not sitting, either. If she insisted on standing, then he would, too. It was already disconcerting enough standing here in the middle of the night, still in his riding boots and spurs, while she had clearly tumbled directly from her bed. If he weren't feeling so guilty about disappearing this afternoon, he would never have agreed to anything as inappropriate as having her here at this hour.

"I can only imagine what you must think of me, Mrs. Willow," he continued, "after my, ah, hasty departure earlier this afternoon. It was an, ah, a very low thing of me to do."

"Oh, but it wasn't!" she exclaimed breathlessly. "That is, at first I thought so, and I felt sure you'd left because you were angry with me for having eaten your tea."

"Not at all," he said, surprised. "You could have consumed every last crumb in Mrs. Barber's larder and I wouldn't have objected. You're my guest here, and I do not wish you to be hungry."

"Thank you, my lord," she said, and he could tell by the slight tremor in her voice that at last she'd blushed; strange how he'd already learned that of her. "I waited for you for a bit in the parlor, hoping you'd return, and when you didn't I went upstairs to pack my trunk, because I thought you'd send word that you wanted me gone."

How could she be so mistaken? "I would never do that," he said. "We had—have—an agreement, and I gave you my word."

She smiled wistfully, making it obvious without words that she believed a gentleman's word to be an untrustworthy thing where she was concerned.

"It doesn't matter now, my lord," she said, so swiftly

that it clearly wasn't of any consequence to her. "Because now I understand. I understand *everything*."

"Do you?" he said, taken aback. Again he had to remind himself that she wasn't a lady, but a young woman whose life had been spent in the tiring room of a theater. She might well understand more than he did himself.

She nodded, taking a step closer to him in her excitement. "While I was packing my trunk, one of the footmen brought me your book with the *Hamlet* play, as you wished. And I read it, my lord, I read it all the way through and I did not stop until I was done. And, oh, my lord, it was *glorious,* just as you said it was!"

"Ahh," he said with guilty relief. "You mean you understood the play."

"Yes, my lord, yes, yes," she said. She reached up to tuck her hair behind one ear, the coverlet slipping to reveal her bare collarbone and the slightest swell of her breast. By the candlelight her skin was like polished ivory, and with effort he made himself look once again to her face. "It's perfect and sad and tragic and filled with swords and knives and death, and the crowd will *love* it."

"They already do," he said. "It was written over a century and a half ago, and it's been vastly popular ever since."

"It should be, my lord," she said eagerly. "And now that I've read it all, I understand why you left as you did, and what you wanted me to learn."

He frowned, again not following her. He'd always considered himself a clever man, but she could make him feel like the most ignorant fool. Fortunately in her excitement, she continued, so he didn't have to admit it.

"Oh, yes, my lord, I can see exactly why you did it," she said, nodding sagely. "It was wicked clever of you, too. First you made me act like a fine noble lady, such as

Ophelia was, and then you scorned me, same as the prince did to her, so I'd feel like her."

He stared, stunned. He'd inappropriately lusted after her, fled in cowardly fashion without any explanation, and *this* was how she'd interpreted it? That he'd intended it all along as another acting lesson?

"O-FEEL-i-ah," he said, correcting her pronunciation to avoid confessing why he'd truly left. "That's how you say it. Not Opp-HEL-yay. O-FEEL-i-ah."

"O-FEEL-i-ah," she repeated carefully, and nodded with satisfaction. "It's a peculiar name, one I've not heard before. Ophelia. But now I understand, my lord. I understand *her*, and what that passage you gave me to learn means."

"What does it mean, Lucia?" he said, intrigued, and forgetting to use the name he'd concocted for her. "What do the words say to you?"

She tipped her head to one side, unconsciously making her eyes glow in the flickering light as her hair rippled over one shoulder. He couldn't fathom how he'd once judged her to be plain, not after he saw her like this.

"It's what the words mean to Lady Ophelia, my lord," she said firmly. "She's so in love with the prince that she can't believe he'd be this hateful to her. Instead she thinks he's lost his wits. She loves him so much that it makes her sad for him, and breaks her heart to see."

He nodded. She had, in fact, deciphered the meaning of the passage on her own, without any assistance from him. He was proud of her cleverness, very proud, though a small part of him regretted that there'd be no chance for him to be her attentive tutor—at least not for this.

"You're entirely right," he said. "Not even Garrick himself could explain Ophelia's lines here any more clearly."

She grinned shyly, and the last of those harsh cautionary thoughts in his father's voice vanished. How could they possibly survive in the face of a smile like hers?

"I can speak it much better now, too, my lord," she said. "I can recite it for you here, if you please."

Without waiting for his consent, she turned her back to him, all shining dark hair and lumpy coverlet. He wondered where she'd acquired this habit of turning away to compose herself, like a conjurer who didn't wish to reveal the secret behind a trick.

Except that she *was* the conjurer, and the trick was how she'd transformed herself so completely. When she turned around again to face him, she'd become the image of Ophelia's heartfelt sorrow: her shoulders were hunched by the weight of her distress, her features pinched by it, and her eyes seemed filled with the horror of what she'd just witnessed.

> O, *what a noble mind is here o'erthrown!*
> *The Courtier's, soldier's, scholar's, eye, tongue, sword,*
> *Th' expectancy and rose of the fair state,*
> *The glass of fashion and the mould of form,*
> *Th' observ'd of all observers, quite, quite down!*
> *And I, of ladies most deject and wretched,*
> *That suck'd the honey of his music vows,*
> *Now see that noble and most sovereign reason*
> *Like sweet bells jangled out of tune and harsh,*
> *That unmatch'd form and feature of blown youth*
> *Blasted with ecstasy. O, woe is me*
> *T'have seen what I have seen, see what I see.*

She buried her face in her hands, a fitting close to the passage, and stayed that way. She wore no fancy costume, and her cheeks were free of stage paint, and yet by the light of the single candle and the embers in the hearth, she'd managed to create a more convincing show of loss and suffering than he'd ever seen on the stage. He was amazed, and proud, and pleased as well, to think she'd taken his advice yesterday so thoroughly to heart.

But most of all, he was touched by the raw emotion that she'd dared to display, here, just for him. It was something he'd never forget. When he'd begun this experiment, all he'd considered was the wager. Now he realized that Fortune had granted him something much richer. This wasn't a game any longer. Lucia di Rossi possessed all the natural gifts to become a true leading actress, and he felt privileged to have just seen her, in twelve lines, *become* Ophelia.

He raised his hands and slowly began to clap, giving her the applause she so richly deserved. Her head jerked up, and instead of the elegant curtsey of acknowledgment that he expected, her infectious grin returned, accompanied by a joyful little hop that reminded him of just how inexperienced she truly was.

"It *was* better, wasn't it, my lord?" she asked proudly. "I had to read the rest of the play to learn why Lady Ophelia was so upset, and then it made sense how I was to speak her lines."

That made sense to him—too much sense, really.

"Why do you say that?" he asked. "About how you needed to know the character before you could recite her part."

"You told me to do so, my lord," she said promptly. "In the green parlor. You said I should act the way Mr. Garrick advises, and forget Madame Adelaide."

"That's very flattering, but I'm not so sure it's the truth," he said, walking back and forth before her. "You've already proved you learn quickly, and I trust that I am an adept tutor, but for you to make such progress in a single day would be prodigious indeed."

"Ahh," she said, a single syllable of wariness. "Is it good to be prodigious, my lord?"

"Oh, yes," he said evenly. "Very good. Remarkable.

Extraordinary. All of which your performance was. But I don't believe I can claim it was all my teaching. Rather, I think you've had a bit more experience to make you so . . . so prodigious."

In three quick steps she was standing directly before him, blocking his path.

"But how could that be, my lord?" she demanded defensively, her hands bunched into two knots beneath the coverlet. "You know my family's company as well as I. The Di Rossis are dancers."

He shook his head, unconvinced. "That tale you spun for me last night in the carriage," he said. "The part about how the famous Mrs. Willow began her career standing on the back of a wagon, reciting poetry to make the women weep. That wasn't an invention, was it?"

"But there's never been a Mr. Willow, my lord, because I've never had a husband, not then nor now," she said with a frantic edge to her voice that hinted at a half truth. "I vow I wasn't lying, my lord, not to you. I'll swear to it, whatever way you wish of me!"

Oh, hell, he hadn't even considered some ne'er-do-well playhouse-husband lurking in the shadows of her past. He hoped she was telling the truth about that much.

But a blasted *husband*. No, he didn't want to imagine her with a husband, or any other man, either.

"Hush, Lucia, please," he said, striving to sound more calm and measured than he actually felt. "I never accused you of lying. All I wish to know is this: have you ever before given a performance before a crowd?"

She went very still, so quiet that the pop and hiss of the fire was the only sound between them.

"Lucia," he said softly. "The truth."

"You will not be angry, my lord?" she asked in a small voice. "You will not claim I have spoiled your wager, and turn me away?"

"How in blazes could you spoil the wager?" he asked, his misgivings increasing by the moment.

"If I were not the inexperienced actress that Sir Edward believed me to be when he chose me," she said. "If that no longer made your wager fair."

"What, because Everett unwittingly gave me an advantage?" he said, relieved, and hoping against hope that this was all. "He chose you, not I, and if I benefit from his choice, so much the better. I intend to win this wager, and I require your presence to do so. So I have guessed correctly?"

She sighed forlornly. "Yes, my lord, in a way," she said. "One summer I did do what I said. When I was younger, I did travel about with a circus company, speaking pieces from a wagon while the hat was passed. And I did wear a pink silk gown, too, and though it wasn't new, it was the best I've ever worn."

"You weren't alone, were you?" he said, picturing all the dangers to a young girl in such a situation. "Who was passing that hat?"

"Not Mr. Willow," she said with a sad attempt at a smile. "It was my papa."

"Your father," Rivers repeated carefully. He was relieved more than he should have been that it wasn't the phantom husband, but a father—an irate, outraged father . . . who could raise an entirely different set of problems. "You've never mentioned him before. Does he know you're here at the Lodge?"

"He's dead," she said, the words brittle with old sorrow. "He died three years ago December. My mother died so long ago that I can only just remember her. I'm all that's left."

"I'm sorry, Lucia," Rivers said. No wonder she'd seemed so vulnerable to him. She was. He'd always been surrounded and protected by his brothers, his father, and the rest of his extended family of cousins and wives and their children, and at first he'd assumed that she'd enjoyed the same security in that den of Di Rossis. But she'd let enough slip about how little they regarded her, he now realized that parting with them had been a relief, even if it meant she was every bit as solitary as she appeared now: a small, brave figure who was achingly alone in the world.

"Thank you, my lord," she said, her voice reduced to little more than a whisper. "It was consumption that took him in the end, but it was strong drink that broke him. That summer when we were with the circus, after he'd quarreled with Uncle Antonio, he'd sworn he'd stop drinking, and he nearly did. He'd do comic dances between the acrobats' tricks while I said my pieces before the show, and the circus folk were kind to us. It was the best time of my life, doing that with him. But then the cold weather came and the circus stopped, and Papa took to drinking again, and that—that was all."

She raised her hands and let them drop, as final a gesture as Rivers had ever seen. But now he understood why she'd refused to drink with him in the carriage, and inwardly he winced to recall how he'd unwittingly tried to tease her from it, even when she'd claimed then that liquor only brought "trouble and sorrow." For her that was undeniably true, and for her sake he resolved not to drink in her company as long as she was here with him at the Lodge.

"I am sorry," he said again, painfully aware of the inadequacy of the words.

"You needn't be, my lord," she said, a quick refusal of his sympathy. "None of it was your fault or concern. When Papa died, I wasn't left to fend for myself like most orphans would've been. I'd a place and lodgings with the company."

"I should think so, given that they are your family," he said. He had been very young when his own mother had died, but he recalled how as bereft as his father had been, he had done his best to ease the grief and suffering for Rivers and his brothers. They had all supported one another, as a family was supposed to do. "Whether you're part of the same dancing company or not is inconsequential. You're related by blood, and it was their duty to look after you."

"Yes, my lord," she said, hedging. "But it would have been a much easier duty for my uncle if I hadn't been so—so disappointing to him."

"An inability to dance should hardly qualify as a disappointment," Rivers insisted, unable to imagine how anyone could feel this way about her. She didn't deserve it, not one bit. "I cannot begin to understand why your uncle and Magdalena don't show you more kindness."

"I understand completely, my lord," she said with a resignation that chilled him. "Ballet must be perfect. Each dancer, each step must be in harmony, or the whole is destroyed. My uncle danced for kings and queens. He was such a great dancer that on the night of his last benefit, the House of Lords canceled their debates so that the lords could attend."

"But that has nothing to do with you!"

"It has everything to do with me, my lord," she said firmly, bunching the coverlet around her shoulders like woolen armor against her fate. "Uncle Lorenzo was perfect, and he expects perfection from everyone in the company. I could not give it to him. I was like the one broken wheel that keeps the entire clockwork from working, and he could not help but loathe me for it."

He fought the almost irresistible urge to wrap his arms around her, to hold her and tell her how that damnable uncle was an ignorant bully without the brains to appreciate her. It would be easy enough, natural enough, and she was less than an arm's length away from him. But it would not be *right*, even if he'd never wanted to do anything more in his life. Instead he simply stood, his arms folded across his chest in order to keep them where they belonged.

"But your father never felt that way, did he?" he asked, striving to say only what he should. "He looked after you while he lived, didn't he?"

"As much as he could, my lord," she said sadly. "*Santo cielo,* the fights he had with my uncle over me! Of course it grieved Papa that I could not dance like either him or Mama, but he never faulted me for it. Instead he believed that one day I'd be a great actress."

"A wise man," Rivers said. "It's a pity he didn't live to see you make your debut as Ophelia."

She smiled wistfully, her eyes luminous as she looked up at him.

"He would have liked that," she said softly. "He was the only one who ever believed I'd the talent to act. The only one, my lord, until you."

He could think of nothing to say to that, and any words that could be formed into a sensible reply had fled his brain. She had never seemed so achingly alone, and he longed to prove to her that he did, in fact, believe in her, as she'd just said. He just wasn't sure how to do it, because jumbled together with that was the distinct and ungentlemanly awareness of how, at this moment, she was also achingly desirable. He'd always thought himself to be a rational man, a man ruled by his head and not his passions, yet there was nothing rational about what he was feeling right now as she gazed up at him.

And so with a little grunt of capitulation, he stopped trying, and did what he'd been working so hard not to do. He took the last step that remained between them and cupped her face in his hands, turning it up toward his.

"I do believe in you, Lucia," he said, lightly stroking

the underside of her jaw with his thumbs. "Have no doubt of that."

She didn't smile, or answer, her eyes wide and searching. She was holding her breath, and he didn't know why. Surely he'd said enough to reassure her, hadn't he?

Impulsively he leaned down and kissed her forehead, the slightest brush of his lips over her skin. He'd meant it as a gesture of fondness, of regard, nothing more. But instead of stopping there, that innocent kiss pushed his gallant resolve clear from his brain, and in the next instant his mouth was kissing hers, exactly as he'd been wanting to do.

But until their lips touched, he hadn't realized how much he'd been holding back. If he was honest, he'd wanted to kiss her when she'd appeared at his doorstep with her belongings in her arms, her face filled with such eagerness and life that he'd been instantly drawn to her. That was when he'd first (and belatedly) realized that it was her spirit that made her beautiful to him, and desirable as well.

It was no wonder, really, that now he kissed her hungrily, possessively, as if she'd some special secret that he wanted to taste. He thrust his fingers into her hair, the heavy waves falling over his wrists like a silken caress. He slanted his mouth over hers, coaxing her lips to part so he could deepen the kiss. She swayed toward him, as delicate as an angel, and with one hand he cradled the small of her back to draw her closer.

He was acutely aware of how warm and soft her uncorseted body was beneath the coverlet, of how yielding she would be in his arms, in his bed. The bed that was beckoning in the next room, only a few steps away. It seemed like such an old story, the stuff of bad novels and plays. How many other young women had been swept off to similar convenient havens by other gentlemen— young women who, like Lucia, were of such inconsequential stations in life that their virtue, or lack thereof, wasn't really an issue?

And yet she wasn't like them, not at all. In her kiss he tasted not wantonness, but eager inexperience, the same eagerness with which she'd greeted every other challenge he'd set before her. She had courage. *That* was Lucia, and what separated her from all the other dancers and milliner's apprentices and lady's maids in London, and it only made him desire her more.

She made a small, shuddering gasp of surprise when his tongue pushed into her mouth, and he took his time to let her grow accustomed to the heady new sensations. He wanted her to want him as well, and not be frightened. While she didn't fight him or try to break free, she'd let the coverlet slip forgotten from her shoulders to a woolen puddle around her feet, leaving her clad only in the rough white linen shift she slept in. With her hands slightly raised at her sides, the full sleeves hung around her arms like wings, and her fingers fluttered uncertainly beneath the drawstring cuffs like little birds.

He tried to keep his eyes closed and his conscience at bay, and focus instead on the endless pleasure of kissing her. But he couldn't quite forget those little fluttering hands, nor those last words she'd said about how he was the only one besides her father who believed in her.

Because she trusted him.

With a muttered oath aimed at himself, he tore his mouth away from hers and stepped back from her, dropping his arms to his sides.

"Forgive me, Mrs. Willow," he said, his voice harsh from the exertion of breaking away from her, and staying away when all he wanted to do was haul her back into his arms. "I regret that I have, ah—"

"No, my lord, do not say it!" she cried. He wasn't sure how he'd expected her to behave after he'd taken such patent advantage of her—a tear or two of calculated shame, perhaps, or a bowed head to hide a mortified blush—but the fire he now saw in her dark eyes wasn't it. Her cheeks were flushed, her lips ruddy and full from kissing, and her hair was tangled around her face. She snatched the fallen coverlet back over her shoulders, and those fluttering hands were now clasped around the edges in determined fists.

"You were going to say you regretted kissing me, my lord," she continued with fierce indignation. "I *know* you were, because you apologize about *everything,* and—and I won't hear it!"

"You'll hear it if I say it," he said, taking another step back from her. "I shouldn't have kissed you, and I regret it."

"Why, my lord?" Her small chin rose defensively, and she shook her hair back from her face. "If you will not speak the truth, then I shall. Am I too common for the son of a duke to kiss? Am I too plain, too small, too slight in my figure?"

"Lucia, I have never once so much as thought any of those things of you." He was determined to control his temper; of course, as was always the case when he tried to employ reason over passion, he failed. "Damnation, not *once.* I regretted kissing you only because you trusted me to behave as an honorable gentleman should, and instead I behaved like a selfish, arrogant boor, and if I wish to apologize to you for that, then I will."

She studied him with guarded eyes, unwilling to give up her assumption.

"You're a gentleman, my lord," she said warily. "You needn't be honorable with me, because I'm not a lady."

"Your station has nothing to do with this, Lucia," he said. "You deserved better from me, just as you deserve my apology, if only you'd be agreeable enough to accept it."

Abruptly her face lost its wariness and softened, and

her eyes glowed too brightly. She tried to smile, and instead her mouth trembled and crumpled. He knew what that meant. Blast, he'd made her cry.

"Here now, Lucia," he said gruffly. "No tears, or I'll have to apologize all over again."

She lowered her gaze and shook her head, and then, before he quite knew what was happening, she threw herself at him. Small she might be, but she hurled herself forward with such force that he staggered back, catching her around the waist to steady them both before they crashed to the floor.

Not that she cared. She was kissing him, kissing him with the same fervor (if not the same experience) that he'd employed whilst kissing her earlier. She'd once again lost the coverlet that had given her a semblance of modesty, and with it she seemed to have lost her reluctance to touch him. Those once-fluttering hands were now firmly locked around his shoulders and her body was pressed so close against his that he felt the curve of her breasts through his coat and waistcoat and shirt.

She kissed him eagerly, ardently, and as soon as the shock had worn off—a quick process—he realized that, because it had been so unexpected, being kissed by her was perhaps even better than when he'd been the one kissing her.

Finally she slipped free and retreated, her gaze never leaving his as she caught up the coverlet and wrapped it tightly about her body.

"I—we—should not have done that, my lord," she said breathlessly, shoving her hair back from her forehead with one hand. "It wasn't right, not for either of us, and—and I must go."

"You can't go now." He reached for her, but she slipped away.

"I must, my lord," she said, hurrying toward the door. "Good night, my lord."

He stared at the closed door after she'd left, perplexed. He hadn't meant to kiss her, but he had, and she hadn't meant to kiss him, but she had, too.

Yet she was perfectly correct about none of it being right. It wasn't because of the usual reasons against falling into bed with a particular woman: she wasn't a lady, or the sister of a close friend. Being a Di Rossi and also clearly of a passionate nature would have been reason enough. But she *was* beneath his roof for the sake of the wager, not for a dalliance. What the devil would they say to each other tomorrow morning? Could they return to *Hamlet* as if this hadn't just happened between them?

He ran his hand along his jaw, thinking of all she'd told him this night, of her father and her aspirations of becoming an actress, and of how much she'd endured from her wretched family. He'd never have guessed any of that, and yet still she'd said he was the only one to believe in her, the only chance she had to make her dreams become real.

To him this was only a frivolous wager with a friend; to her it was her life. He sighed, thinking of how she'd felt pressed against his chest, and how warm and wet and sweet her mouth had been when they'd kissed. He couldn't simply forget that, nor was he entirely sure he wanted to.

And he'd still five and a half weeks with her to figure it out.

8

It was one of the worst nights that Lucia could ever recall. Guilt could do that, and as she'd raced down the hall from Rivers's rooms to her own, she'd never felt more guilty, or more confused, in her life. Her heart racing, she'd locked her bedchamber door in case he tried to follow her, and then a quarter hour later, she'd unlocked it again for the same reason. She didn't know what she wanted or what she expected, beyond that kissing Lord Rivers Fitzroy had been at once glorious, and thoroughly, hopelessly disastrous.

In one impulsive, foolish moment, she could have ruined everything. She should never have gone to his rooms in her nightclothes in the first place. What was he to think? What more obvious invitation could there be than that? Surely he must judge her to be exactly like her cousin Magdalena, available to any wealthy man who could purchase her fancy.

But she wasn't, not at all. He'd likely never believe it, but that kiss had been her first. She was twenty-three years old, old enough to qualify as a spinster, and she'd never had a sweetheart, let alone a noble lover. She remained a virgin not so much by choice, but because she'd never known a man worthy of her surrender. Surrounded by the more brilliant beauties at the playhouse, she'd always gone unnoticed, an undistinguished and lowly weed among so many exotic blossoms.

But here in the country, Rivers (for in her head she'd abandoned his title) hadn't overlooked her. Although the wager had brought them together into a kind of partnership, she hadn't expected the intimacy that would come with it. He did believe in her, in her talent and her ambition, but there was more to it than that.

When she was with him, she felt a kind of spark, an energy she couldn't find words to explain. It wasn't just that he was clever, and charming, and as handsome as sin itself. He made her feel as if her life were richer, more vibrant, more filled with possibilities. He made her feel more *alive*, if such a thing were possible, as if the rest of her life had been spent in a dreary, gloomy sleep, and he alone had the power to wake her. No one else could do that, and knowing she'd little more than a month with him had only served to make the time in his company more precious.

All of which was why she'd run to join him last night as soon as she'd heard him return home. All she'd wanted was the pleasure, the excitement, of sharing her understanding of the play with him, and instead she'd unwittingly destroyed what they had together.

One kiss, and they'd ceased being simply partners in the wager. Two kisses, and they'd become something else entirely: a wealthy lord and a common little girl from the playhouse, a passing amusement for his entertainment and nothing more.

No wonder she'd spent the night tossing and turning and burying her face in the pillows in despair. She would try to explain to him that what mattered most to her was her chance to act, but the damage was done. She might not be experienced with men herself, but she'd seen enough at the playhouse to know that once men were granted a favor by a woman, they'd expect it again, and more besides.

That, really, was her choice after last night. For the sake of becoming the actress he'd promised, she could let him continue what last night had begun, and be his mistress until he tired of her. There'd be no shame in it for her. In the eyes of the public, such an alliance with a high-placed nobleman was to be expected, even envied, and would likely be advantageous in creating her allure as a popular actress. Even bearing his illegitimate child could bring certain advantages, and no stigma in the theatrical world. She was sure Rivers was the kind of honorable gentleman who would acknowledge and support a bastard child, which would in turn bind him closer long after his love for her was spent.

But she knew herself well enough, and she knew the personal consequences of such a path. A mistress would never be the same as a wife. When she left here, she'd have the training and chance to succeed on the stage that he'd promised, but she'd also have a broken heart.

Now she sat alone in the back parlor where Rivers took breakfast and waited for him to come downstairs. On the cloth beside her teacup was the copy of *Hamlet* that he'd given her, with the ribbon marking the passage she'd already learned. She'd been sitting here nearly an hour, not wanting to miss him. Over and over, she'd rehearsed what she'd say, a carefully chosen speech that had nothing to do with Ophelia. All she could do while she waited was sip at her tea, and pray he'd listen, and understand.

She started when at last the parlor door opened and he joined her. She slipped from her chair and curtseyed silently, waiting for him to speak first. He was dressed for morning in the country—a red waistcoat, fawn-colored buckskin breeches, and a blue frock coat—and not for riding, so at least he'd no intention of escaping from her on horseback. But he looked every bit as uneasy as she did herself as he motioned for her to return to her chair.

"Good day, Mrs. Willow," he said, using the false name he'd concocted for her. "I've told you before that you needn't curtsey to me whilst we're here. The Lodge is not so formal a house as that."

"Thank you, my lord," she murmured as she perched on the edge of her chair, her hands folded in her lap. Her rehearsed little speech hung awkwardly unspoken as she waited for the proper opportunity to begin.

He poured his own tea—another example of the Lodge's informality—dumped two spoonfuls of sugar into the cup as well, and stirred it with a clatter of silver against porcelain.

"I trust you slept well," he said, concentrating on the steaming tea to avoid meeting her eye. "No, you needn't answer that. If you slept even half as badly as I, then you passed a most miserable night."

"Yes, my lord," she said. "That is, I likewise passed a most miserable, horrible night."

He sighed and sipped at his tea, grimacing from its heat.

"Then that makes two of us," he said. "We both know the reason why, too, so I suppose there's no use in ignoring it any further."

"No, my lord," she said faintly. Now would be the time to begin her speech, now, *now*, yet her usual gift for memorization had fled.

"No." He cleared his throat. "Given your, ah, unusual upbringing in the theatrical world, I suspect you do not have the usual, ah, delicacy regarding men and women, and what occurred last night between us."

"I'm not like Magdalena," she blurted out, and flushed. "That is, I'm not as . . . as . . . ."

"As much a mercenary?" he suggested, and smiled wryly. "I don't believe any other woman could rival your cousin in that arena. But while they say that blood binds kin together, I've never once thought of you and Magdalena in the same light."

She nodded cautiously, but said nothing more. That remark could cut two ways. Her heart was racing with uncertainty, and for another precious moment she wanted to cling to the hope that he'd meant to flatter her, not Magdalena.

"Indeed, indeed," he said, the kind of empty, meaningless word that gentlemen said when they were at a loss for something of more substance. Could his thoughts be as unsettled as her own?

"Yes, my lord," she said softly. "Indeed it is a tangle."

He let out his breath with relief. "A tangle, yes. I know you've forbidden me any further apologies, which is a complication. But when I say that you differ from Magdalena, I mean to say that you are a better, more honorable woman than she will ever be. What happened between us last night—"

"It should never have happened, my lord, not at all," she said as firmly as she could, even as her heart fluttered with the great compliment that he had just paid her. "The hour was late, and at that hour things will happen that will be regretted by day."

He placed his teacup deliberately on its saucer, tapping the rim lightly with his finger. "I don't regret kissing you, Lucia. Not one bit."

Sharply she drew in her breath, taken aback. "You don't, my lord?"

"I don't," he said evenly, looking up at her. "What I do regret, however, are the circumstances that make it both unwise and unacceptable for me to kiss you again, as I would like."

This was very nearly what she'd planned to say herself. Relief swept over her, but mixed with her own regret, too.

"That is very true, my lord." She was glad he sat on the other side of the table, where he couldn't see how her hands were twisting together in her lap. "If I am to become the actress I wish to be, I must make certain—certain sacrifices. I don't want things to be the way you said, unwise and unacceptable."

"Indeed," he said solemnly, that empty, hollow word again. "Then we are agreed, yes?"

"Another agreement," she said wistfully. "We're good at that, aren't we?"

"It's for the best," he said, even though he wasn't sure it was. "We shall proceed this morning as if last night had not happened."

"Because it didn't, my lord," she said, though she could not quite keep the sadness from her voice. "Leastways, not that I recall."

"Nor I," he said, a shade too heartily. "Which is just as well, considering how much work we have before us. What you did with the passage last night was first-rate, but there's an entire play for you to learn, and we've less than six weeks in which to do it."

"Yes, my lord," she said. "I am ready to begin whenever you please."

He didn't answer, his blue eyes studying her so intently that she felt her cheeks grow warm. He'd looked at her like this last night as well, when she'd told him he was the only one who believed in her, and just before he'd kissed her.

"It cannot be otherwise, my lord," she said softly. "No matter what we might wish, it cannot."

He sighed, and looked down, and whatever spell had been cast between them was broken. He pulled another copy of the play from inside his coat and opened it on the table, pressing the pages flat. "Then let us begin with the first scene."

Dutifully she opened her own copy, and bowed her

head over the pages even if her eyes failed to make out the words. She'd gotten exactly what she'd wished, and what was undeniably for the best.

So why, then, did she feel as if she'd lost?

For Rivers, the next two weeks were simultaneously the most rewarding of his life, and the most frustrating. The rewarding part came from all he was able to accomplish with Lucia. Although he'd entered this wager assuming that he could be a most excellent tutor, he hadn't realized how much more important it was to have an excellent student.

Lucia was every teacher's dream: she was clever and quick, as ready to ask a thoughtful question as she was to give an answer to his. She was acutely aware of how much she had to accomplish in a limited number of days, and she worked feverishly hard on whatever he assigned. He wondered if she ever slept, for she always seemed both to have been long awake before he rose and after he'd said good night and retired to his own rooms. He knew because there were some nights when his thoughts were too busy for sleep, and he would go walking with Spot, and while every other window in the Lodge might be dark, there would still be candlelight shining from her corner of the house.

She learned her lines without flaw, and she'd improved her diction, her mannerisms, her posture. As her confidence grew, she stood straighter, with more and more presence when she entered a room. She'd outdone Garrick's instructions for a natural approach to the point that she'd practically *become* Ophelia, and he was almost as proud of her as she was of herself.

There were, however, several grave areas that needed improvement. While she was very good at playing scenes in the drawing room, she had difficulty projecting her voice and making her gestures grand enough to carry to the farthest seats of a playhouse. She occasionally became so enraptured by her lines that she stood immobile, and forgot to add the gestures that would bring her part to life. The hint of her Neapolitan accent was charming, but the working-class-London accent that accompanied it remained a sizable challenge, and though Rivers continued to correct the most egregious and broad-voweled examples, she still would not convince anyone that she'd been born a lady in the royal court of Denmark.

But of course the single greatest challenge had nothing to do with her acting, and simply everything to do with her. Ever since they'd agreed—and wisely, too—that what had happened that night in his room must never happen again, he had perversely thought of doing exactly that, and much more besides.

It didn't matter that she had behaved in a manner that was completely without fault, a model of propriety. The smallest things about her enticed him: a tiny wisp of hair, escaped from her cap and dancing free against the nape of her neck, the huskiness of her laugh over some canine foolishness by Spot, the way she'd tip back her head to watch the swallows wheel in the sky above the stable, or how her eyes would brighten whenever she smiled at him. She might not have been born with a dancer's rhythm, but the grace was effortlessly there in every beguiling twist and turn of her neatly curving figure. If her hand or arm grazed his by accident, he felt as if he'd touched a burning coal.

He knew she felt the tension, too. He'd seen the unabashed longing in her eyes when she looked at him, and heard the little catch in her breathing whenever they touched, and the small bursts of temper that she'd show during a difficult session he guessed were due more to the frustration of their situation than to any mere words— even words by Shakespeare.

It all combined to make working closely with her day and night the greatest delight and the greatest torment. And then, on the Tuesday morning of the third week, came the lesson that changed everything.

They were in the green parlor as usual. Most of the breakfast things had been cleared away, but both his coffee and her tea remained in case of necessary fortification. Likely they would need it, too, for once again her vowels were presenting their mutual torment.

"Cake, not 'cyke,'" he corrected for what seemed like the millionth time. "Can you truly not hear the difference?"

"Ca-a-a-yke," she said, beginning well but sliding backward into the murkiness, her face screwed up with the effort.

His expression darkened. He would not see this entire project destroyed by a piece of cake.

"Cake, Lucia," he said. "C-a-a-ake."

"Ca-a-a-yke," she said.

He sighed. "C-A-A-AKE."

"Oh, blast your infernal cake!" she cried, sweeping dramatically from her chair to stalk across the room. She stopped at the window, arms flailing dramatically toward the flowers, while Spot rose and left Rivers's side to go stand by her in sympathy. "Not one person in all the playhouses in London will be as picky as you are, my lord, nor so provoking, either."

At least she had her grand gestures correct this morning. "Lucia, please. Histrionics such as these accomplish nothing."

"Vowels be th' very trial, don't they, Spot?" she said to Spot and pointedly not to Rivers, crouching down beside the dog. "We don't care nawt for them, an' t'the very divil they may go."

"What was that, Lucia?" Rivers said, startled. It wasn't *what* she'd said that surprised him, but the way she'd said it. She'd spoken exactly as the Yorkshire stable boy who was responsible for washing Spot did, imitating his accent flawlessly and without a hint of her own.

"Did y'hear something, Spot?" she said to the dog, whose tail whipped happily at the attention, and perhaps the accent as well. "I dinna, did you?"

"Lucia, look at me," Rivers said. "Why is it you can copy Ned's accent so perfectly, and yet cannot grasp the proper voice for Ophelia?"

She rose, and slowly turned as he'd bidden.

"Why, my lord?" she said, still cross. "Perhaps it's because I can hear Ned every day, which isn't the way with noble Danish ladies, least not that I've seen."

"That is not the point," he said, refusing to let her distract him. "If you spoke like a lady from the Danish royal court, no one in London would understand you, either."

"Now *there's* the problem, isn't it, my lord." She grandly flung her arms open. "And isn't it what I've said all along? If they don't know, how can they care?"

"Because they'll want you to sound like a lady," he insisted. "And you do so have an example to copy. Forget the vowels and everything else. Just imitate me."

"You, my lord?" That surprised her, and her eyes widened. "Oh, my lord, I couldn't do that. It would be wicked rude of me."

"No, it wouldn't." He joined her at the window, determined to discover if the key to correcting her speech could really be this simple. "I've spent my entire life around the royal court and amongst the people there. Copy me, and you'll have Ophelia's accent exactly right."

She gazed up at him, doubtful. "You are certain of this, my lord? You will not be angry, or take insult?"

"I give you my word that I shall not," he said. "Go on. Prove to me you can do it."

"Very well, my lord." She took a deep breath and

turned her back to him, the way she always did when composing herself to perform.

While she did, he realized he was holding his breath, and pointedly let it out. He really didn't know what to expect, given that it was Lucia.

He hadn't long to wait. When she turned around, she'd squared her shoulders and made her chin jut up. She'd puffed out her chest, which was made all the more noticeable by how she clasped her hands behind her waist, and somehow she looked down her nose at him, a rare feat considering how much taller he was than she.

"Do it," she said, pitching her voice gruff and low. "I expect nothing less from you. Come along, come along, don't tarry."

He stared at her. The effect was uncanny, and also disturbing. What was he to make of this miniature female version of himself?

She raked one hand back through her hair, ignoring how the gesture pulled her hair half-free and scattered hairpins, and scowled darkly.

"Don't make me wait any further," she said. "What do you wish of me in return? Damnation, I've already given you my word as a gentleman."

"I can't possibly sound as pompous as that," he exclaimed. "Am I really so vastly righteous?"

"*Vastly* righteous," she repeated with the exact same inflections.

He grunted. "You're grumbling and growling like a wild beast."

"That's how you sound, my lord," she protested, reverting to her own voice and accent. "You promised you wouldn't—"

He could see the uncertainty flash across her face, for deep down she understood the importance of this. It was one thing to make a jest of him, but quite another to do this seriously.

"I shall try, my lord," she said slowly and carefully. "Is this better? Do I sound as you wish me to be?"

"More," he said, barely containing his excitement. "'O, *what a noble mind is here o'erthrown!*'"

"'*O, what a noble mind is here o'erthrown!*'" she said, and grinned. "That's it, my lord, isn't it? I can tell by how you're looking at me. That's what you wanted?"

"I believe it is, Lucia." Gone were the flattened vowels of Whitechapel, and in their place were the fulsome, rounded ones of St. James's Square. It wasn't quite perfect, but close, very close, and with another week's worth of practice, she'd be able to fool any playhouse audience. "It is."

She yelped with joy and impulsively threw her arms around his shoulders to hug him. Automatically he pulled her close, unable to resist holding her the way he'd been so desperately longing to. Her breasts crushed against his chest, exactly as he'd remembered, and her waist was small and her hips rounded and her mouth was only inches away from his and *damnation he must not do this.*

Reluctantly he disentangled himself from her and set her down, and apart from himself.

"You are, ah, to be congratulated, Mrs. Willow," he said deliberately. "You have succeeded beyond my highest expectations."

"I'm sorry, my lord, I didn't mean to do that," she said in a breathless fluster as she smoothed her hair. "Our arrangement and all."

"The arrangement." He cleared his throat momentously, and felt like a fool for doing so. "Of course."

"Oh, of course, my lord," she said, making no more sense than he had. "I was—I was *overcome.*"

Overcome: well, that summed it up, didn't it? Knowing she felt the same as he did wasn't helping his composure one bit. Her cheeks were flushed and her kerchief had slipped just enough that he could see how rapidly her breasts were rising and falling above the stiffened edge of her bodice, and *he must not think of this.*

"Let us take the lessons out-of-doors," he said abruptly. "A brisk walk through the garden will do us both a world of good."

"Yes, my lord," she murmured. She was well aware of how much her eyes betrayed her emotions, and she bowed her head to hide them from him now as they stepped through the door and into the garden.

The morning was perfect for June, with brilliant blue skies overhead and a soft breeze in the air. Spot bounded ahead, equally glad to be outside, and clumsily flushed several indignant birds from the hedges. In weighty silence, they walked around the perimeter of the rose garden twice before at last he spoke.

"We shall be traveling to Newbury this afternoon," he said. They were walking side by side, with him purposefully keeping his hands clasped behind him to keep them from the temptation she represented. "You and I shall have business there."

She glanced at him sharply. "Business, my lord?"

"Yes." What with all the overcoming, he'd nearly forgotten the surprise he'd planned for her for this day. "It's high time that Mrs. Willow had some clothes more befitting her station. Mrs. Currie is an accomplished mantuamaker whom even my stepmother has employed on occasion. She will be expecting us."

She stopped walking, her expression wary. "A mantuamaker is to make new clothes for me, my lord?"

He stopped, too. "Yes, she is," he said. "Consider it a small celebration in honor of your achievement this morning."

"That is most kind of you, my lord," she said slowly, "but I do not believe I should go."

"Why shouldn't you go?" he asked, surprised and disappointed that she wasn't as pleased as he'd expected.

"What woman doesn't enjoy such a shop? I will, of course, take care of the reckoning. You will not be accountable for whatever fripperies you choose, if that is your concern."

"It is, my lord, but not how you think," she said darkly, folding her arms over her chest. "It's one thing for me to be here at the Lodge as your guest, but another altogether if I were to accept costly clothes made by a mantua-maker that you have paid for. I'd be no better than every other doxie you've had here, wouldn't I?"

"No, you would not," he said testily. He knew her well enough to understand that when she folded her arms like that, she meant it as a kind of self-protection, a way of reassuring herself when she was upset. Usually he found the gesture poignant, and it reminded him of how difficult her life had been until now.

But today his obstreperous male brain could only focus on how those folded arms were pressing her breasts upward, in a fashion that he couldn't avoid noticing.

He cleared his throat again, as if that would help. "I should hope that you would realize by now that there has never been the veritable parade of doxies through the Lodge—or through my bed—that you believe. Not even your cousin came here."

She frowned, unconvinced. "Forgive me, my lord, but the way Mrs. Barber and Sally treat me says I'm not the first woman to have been brought here."

"There have been one or two," he admitted. "Most recently there was a most unfortunate mistake with a young woman who behaved more like a ninny than a doxie. Most likely that's what Mrs. Barber recalls. But that does not constitute the raging flock of doxies that you imply."

She didn't say anything, which was far worse than if she'd raged at him the way Magdalena would have. Why the devil didn't she realize that she was as far removed from that ninny of an apprentice as the moon was from the sun? Behaving honorably in the face of constant temptation to do otherwise had not been easy, and he would have appreciated a bit of acknowledgment for it, especially this morning. Her suspicion had stung his pride, and he was sorry, very sorry that she still didn't trust him despite his best, manful efforts.

"I am purchasing clothes for Mrs. Willow as part of the wager," he continued, "and not because I expect you—or her—to behave in a doxie-like fashion. Why must you think otherwise?"

She ignored his question. "No obligations at all?" she asked warily. "I know you paid my cousin's mantua-maker's bills for a time, and the lace-maker's, and the stay-maker's, and even her plume-maker's, and I know what you received in return."

He kicked his boot at the graveled path in frustration, and Spot skittered ahead, ready to chase the flying small rocks.

"What I expect to receive in return for buying you clothes, and stays, and laces, and even plumes, if you desire them, is the sum of the winning wager, payable by Everett," he said with excruciating patience. "I consider the purchases part and parcel of creating the actress known as Mrs. Willow. She requires the proper costuming for her role. You can't very well present yourself to a stage manager dressed as you are."

He had wanted to sound patient; instead he realized he was sounding merely disgruntled and a little petulant, neither of which were agreeable qualities, and he kicked the gravel again.

He heard her sigh beside him, doubtless at how pathetically unmanly he was being.

"Forgive me, my lord," she said at last, her voice small and contrite. "You are right, and I am wrong. If you had merely wished to seduce me, then you would have done it by now. You would have done it just now, in the parlor. You could have ravished me then and there, yet you didn't. If that was all you wanted from me, you wouldn't have bothered with correcting my vowels."

"That is true," he said quickly, wishing with both his heart and his cock that she hadn't mentioned ravishing. "I gave you my word, and I will not break it. We shall put aside that last little, ah, transgression, and continue to abide by our agreement."

"Yes, my lord, your word, and our agreement," she said, and sighed again. "You truly are a gentleman. Please forgive me for doubting you."

He grunted. He didn't like her apologizing to him any more than she liked it when he did it, and it didn't help that while she wasn't doubting him, he was noticing how the breeze was teasing at the kerchief tucked into her bodice and over those maddening breasts, threatening to pull it free.

"There's nothing to forgive," he said gruffly. "Now come, let us walk through the gardens."

He stalked off ahead of her, determined to leave this conversation behind. She followed, but brought the conversation with her.

"Thank you, my lord, for understanding," she said, a little breathless from keeping pace with him. "You've always been so kind to me, and so generous, even when I didn't deserve it. It's only because this wager has been so . . . so difficult. I don't wish to be quarrelsome, especially not to you, but *santo cielo,* these weeks have been a trial to me. A regular trial."

"I can imagine." They'd been a trial for him as well, though likely not in the same way she was intending. "I have not always been an easy tutor to you. But you have been so apt a pupil, and have made such spectacular progress in your studies, that surely you must believe the trials have been worth their trouble."

She nodded, leaving him to decide whether she agreed, or was simply being distracted by the flowers. Either was possible, especially once they entered the rose garden.

She gasped with wonder as soon as he opened the gate. "Oh, my lord!" she exclaimed. "Look at the roses! *Look* at them!"

Nodding obediently, Rivers tried to do as she asked. The first red roses were already in bloom, and the air was heady with their scent. He'd always taken them for granted. The precisely tended bushes, each in their perfectly squared beds, had been designed to make a pretty show for guests taking breakfast in the back parlor, and he'd always found their beauty a bit too lush, a bit too predictable, to be genuine.

Lucia, however, had no such reservations. She stopped directly in the middle of the raked gravel path and flung out her arms as if to embrace the entire garden. She tipped back her head so the sun washed over her face beneath the curving brim of her flat straw hat, closed her eyes, and inhaled deeply.

"*Such* a beautiful smell, my lord," she exclaimed without opening her eyes. "I know poets write of lying in a bed of roses, but I should rather have this, to be surrounded by this smell, without any of the prickly thorns."

"It's not just any old poet who wrote that," he said. "It was Christopher Marlowe."

With her eyes closed, he could unabashedly study her face. She'd blossomed like a flower herself here in the country, with enough to eat and no more of the unappreciated physical toil for others that destroyed the soul. The circles beneath her eyes were gone and the sickly pallor replaced by a charmingly plump rosiness. No one would overlook her now, not when she looked like this.

"Christopher Marlowe, my lord?" she asked without opening her eyes. "Should I know of him? Has he written plays, too, or only poems?"

"A few," he said. *Hamlet* was enough for her to consider at present without tossing Marlowe into the mix as well. "His plays are not the fashion now."

She opened her eyes and lowered her chin. "Then why speak of him at all, my lord?"

"Because he wrote quite splendid verse," Rivers said, reciting for her.

And I will make thee beds of roses
And a thousand fragrant posies,
A cap of flowers, and a kirtle,
Embroidered all with leaves of myrtle.

Lucia smiled, her joy in the words and images lighting her face as surely as the sun had, and sending a little lurch to his chest.

"Oh, my lord, that is splendid," she declared. "Is there more to it?"

Of course there was more. There was an entire poem. But he'd be damned, doubly damned, if he recited all of *The Passionate Shepherd* to her now. *Come live with me and be my love* indeed. What kind of infernal mischief in his brain had made him think, after all that had happened earlier, standing in the middle of a rose garden and quoting Marlowe to her would be a wise idea.

"There is more, but it's mostly about sheep," he said quickly, hoping to distract her. "Come, there's another garden here you haven't seen. This way, through this gate."

"Oh," she said, clearly disappointed, even as she followed him. "But will you answer me one question about Mr. Marlowe's poem, my lord?"

"Mr. Mar-*loh*," he corrected almost without thinking. "Mar-*loh*."

She sighed with dutiful frustration. "Will you answer me one question about Mr. Mar-*loh's* poem, my lord?"

"If I can," he said, albeit reluctantly. The last thing he wished to do was discuss all the swoony, erotic overtones of the poem.

"It's the kirtle, my lord," she said. "What exactly might that be?"

He wanted to laugh with relief. "It's only a gown of some sort," he said. "An old-fashioned garment, much enhanced by the flowers. Here's the other garden I wish you to see."

He held the old oak door open for her to step inside, and she laughed as Spot ungallantly pushed ahead of her. He was glad that she'd laughed, and glad, too, that he'd decided to lead her here.

Later he'd think back to this decision, and wonder why and how he'd made it, and consider all that had occurred because of it.

But not yet. Now all he did was follow her inside the garden, and let the heavy oak door fall shut after them.

CHAPTER

9

This garden was small and square, with unruly beds
filled with every color of wildflower and herbs mixed in
for fragrance's sake, and as far from the neatly groomed
garden of French roses as could be. The walls enclosing
this garden were the same gray stone as the Lodge itself,
but rough-hewn and haphazard, and settled into place by
time. Twisting, gnarled crabapple trees grew in each corner, their boughs bright with new green leaves and filled
with the chirps of the songbirds who'd wisely chosen this
haven in which to build their nests. In the center of the
garden stood a small bronze sundial, and sitting beneath
it on a stone was a flat pan of water for birds to bathe in.
No matter whether Rivers was here or in London, his
orders were that that pan be filled freshly each day, as it
had been for all his life and more.

"No roses here, I fear," he said, wanting to defend this
humble garden, and hoping she wouldn't find it lacking
by comparison. "But I much prefer the exuberance of
these wildflowers."

"I do, too, my lord," she said, sunlight filtering through
the straw brim of her hat to dapple her face with tiny
freckles of brightness. "I'm more a wildflower than a
rose myself."

"That was what my mother said, too." The long stems
and spreading leaves brushed against the hems of her

skirts, reaching out to her as he himself longed to do. "She loved the roses too, of course, but this garden was hers. She'd little interest in the hunting, and this was her private retreat while Father rode off with their friends and guests. Father kept this garden in her honor, and I do the same now that the Lodge is mine."

She tipped her head to one side. "Your mother is dead?"

"She is," he said, the sorrow in his voice more for what he'd never had rather than for what he'd remembered and lost. "So long ago that my father has had time to grieve her and remarry, to a lovely, gracious lady who is a joy to have in our family. But she will never replace my mother. She can't. I was so young when she died that I have only the vaguest of memories of her."

"I am sorry, my lord," she said softly, reaching out to touch the tall daisies nodding on their stems beside her. "It's much the same with me. I can only just recall my mother's face, but it's the other things—her laughter, her gentleness, the way she brushed my hair and sang silly songs to me in French—that's what I remember most. That's why I wear her necklace, too, to help with my remembering."

He watched how she touched the little cameo pendant that rested in the hollow of her throat, a pendant she always wore and that, before now, he'd dismissed in his head as some little bit of poor rubbish. Now he understood how the humble necklace must be more valuable to her than any diamonds, because of who had worn it before.

He understood, and her words rang true to him as well. He'd always tried to remember his mother as the beautiful lady in the portrait in Father's library, dressed in jewels and ermine and red velvet for Court, and not the frighteningly fragile woman, wasted by her final illness, that he'd been forced to kiss on her deathbed.

He looked up at the trees, striving to clear away that last melancholy thought.

"I fear that most of the memories I have of my own mother are based upon what others have told me rather than what I recall for myself," he said carefully. "She was especially close to my brother Geoffrey."

"Yet you were her son, too, my lord," she said. The breeze was toying with the ribbons on her hat, blowing them up into her face, and impatiently she brushed them away. "You *are* her son."

"Of course," he said, agreeing to the obvious. He envied those ribbons, dancing across the curve of her cheek.

"That is why you've kept this garden as she left it, my lord," she said, a statement rather than a question. "Even if you can't remember her, you can still be with her in a way when you're here."

He frowned, taken aback by the notion that the Duchess of Breconridge would be laid to rest beneath an informal garden of wildflowers.

"My mother isn't buried here," he said brusquely. "She's with the rest of my ancestors, in our family's crypt in St. Andrew's."

"But if she loved this place and these flowers so much, my lord, then part of her is still here," she reasoned. She bent and plucked a deep purple pansy, one of the last of the spring, and traced her fingertips across the velvety black-and-purple petals. " '*There's rosemary, that's for remembrance; pray, love, remember. And there is pansies; that's for—*' "

"For thought." He smiled with relief, glad she'd turned their conversation back to *Hamlet* and away from his family. "Knowing the actual flowers in that scene will add richness to your interpretation. They won't have real ones in any playhouse, of course—they'll doubtless be some sort of imitation trumpery—but if you can recall the flowers here, you'll be able to convince your audience that the false ones are every bit as real."

"That's my last scene in the play, my lord," she said

softly, twirling the flower's stem gently in her fingers. "If audiences do not believe in my Ophelia by then, and if they cannot feel for her plight and be ready to weep for her, then it will not matter a whit whether my flowers are real or false."

"But they will care for you, Lucia, I am sure of it," he said. He was sure of it because *he* cared about her—though he hadn't realized until this moment exactly how much. "In a way it's a shame that your death is offstage, and only related to the audience. Of course not even the most clever of stage wizards could contrive a drowning death on the stage, but even if there were some way you could be seen on the farthest branch of the willow, over the deep currents, so that the audience could share the trepidation of Ophelia's danger."

"No, my lord," she said firmly. "To do that would be to meddle too much with Master Shakespeare's play. You've said yourself his words are sacred."

"Yes, yes," he said hurriedly, chagrined that she'd recall that, and chagrined, too, because she was right to remind him. "It's a shame that it cannot be done. But you must admit how poignant such a scene would be, and how affecting to every sensibility."

"I will be carried out on my bier," she said. "That will be sorrowful, or it shall be if I can manage to lie still as death."

"I trust you will," he said. "The crowds on the benches like nothing better than to shed a tear for a doomed lady, not a restless corpse. As I have explained before, my studies have discovered that every expert in theatrics declares that it's the task of the entire playhouse, from the lowest stage-sweeper to the highest actor, to indulge the crowd's pleasure."

He'd expected her to smile and nod and agree with him, the way she usually did. But today she wasn't smiling, and he suspected she wasn't going to agree with him, either, and he wasn't sure which was more unsettling. Instead she continued to study the pansy's fierce little face as if it were the most fascinating thing in nature, and certainly more fascinating than him.

"Surely you agree with what those experts have written," he said doggedly. He'd grown so accustomed to her usual attentiveness and conversation that now, when they were absent, he missed them more than he'd like to admit. "Surely you must think similarly, that the desires and entertainment of the audience must always come first. Surely you can't think otherwise, after all we've discussed."

She turned to stand directly before him and reached up to tuck the pansy into the top buttonhole of his coat.

"'*Pansies for thoughts,*'" she said, quoting the play again as she snugged the little blossom into place. "That's what matters most to you, my lord, isn't it? Banish that idle, sentimental rosemary! Thinking this, thinking that, and what's been written in a book is always better than everything else."

"That's not true," he said defensively, looking down at the purple flower and with it her little hand still lingering on his chest. "Not of me anyway."

"Forgive me for speaking plain, my lord," she said, taking back her hand, "but it is true. As true as can be, and being in this place only makes it truer."

He was sorry she'd taken her hand away, and somehow he felt as if the imprint of her palm remained on his chest like a subtle brand. She'd said much the same thing earlier, when she'd accused him of relying too much on reason. Books had always been his comfort, their knowledge the one sure thing in an often uncertain world. He'd always believed he could learn anything he desired from the right book, and prove whatever he wanted as well. He'd been proud of it, too.

But what if Lucia was right? What if he'd been using

his library not as a sanctuary, but to keep the rest of the world at bay? Perhaps he had relied too much on the words and thoughts of others, and hadn't dared to trust his own.

And ever since that night when they'd kissed, perhaps he'd been trying so hard not to say too much that instead he'd said too little.

"I'm most grateful for what you've taught me, my lord," she continued, "and I'd never wish not to know all I've learned from you, about acting and history and life among grand folk like yours. But there's still so many things in life that cannot be learned from books and scholars, things that must be enjoyed and remembered for their own sakes."

"I know that," he said, unsettled by how close she'd come to reading his thoughts. Damnation, how could she? Spot dropped a stick on the toes of his boots, and Rivers snatched it up and hurled it so hard it struck the garden's far wall. "I *know* that."

She gazed up at him, her face solemn but clearly not believing him.

"Very well, my lord," she said with maddening evenness. "It is as you say. You know it. You know everything."

She turned away to follow the dog, but Rivers grabbed her arm to pull her back toward him.

"My lord!" she gasped, startled and struggling to pull her arm free. "My lord, please, let me go!"

"How can you call me unfeeling, Lucia?" he demanded, emotion turning his voice rougher than he'd intended. "How can you say I care for nothing in life beyond what I've learned in books? That's not a fair judgment, and you of all others must be aware of it."

She stopped struggling, her eyes wide. "What are you saying, my lord?"

"I'm saying what you must know for yourself," he

said. "That these last weeks here with you have been among the best and most enjoyable of my life. That I regret how swiftly the days have passed, and dread the time when the last of them will be done. That I have enjoyed your company more than I would ever have imagined. So do *not* tell me that I care for nothing beyond books, Lucia, because damnation, it is not true."

He hadn't intended to say so much or to say it so freely, and he could tell from the expression on Lucia's face that she clearly thought him to be a madman for it. He couldn't blame her if she did. He was raving like a lunatic, and he could not help himself.

And then, like a lunatic, he drew her closer, and into his arms, and kissed her.

She didn't fight, but melted against him as warm as the sun, her hands sliding over his shoulders and along his arms. The tiny part of his brain that was still capable of thought was vaguely aware of the songbirds in the trees around them and the breeze still blowing the ribbons on her hat, and of how there really couldn't be anything he'd rather be doing than kissing Lucia here among his mother's wildflowers.

The brim of his hat knocked hers back off her head and to the path and she didn't seem to notice and neither did he, and when he deepened the kiss, she instantly parted her own lips and drew him deeper into her warmth. She'd accused him of not feeling, yet he'd never felt anything more certainly than the desire he was feeling for her now. He kissed her with feverish intensity, and with a certain desperation, too.

How could she not understand what she'd become to him? What would he do if she didn't feel the same?

He pulled her closer, one arm tight around her waist while his other hand found that temptingly round bottom that had so tormented him this morning, and his fingers spread to cup her and pull her more closely against him. She not only yielded, but pressed shamelessly to him so that he was sure she must have realized how aroused he'd become. His cock was hard as iron, and because she wore no hoops, there was only the linen of his breeches and her petticoats between them. She wore no hoops because she wasn't a lady—a tiny, sharp dagger to niggle at his conscience.

She wasn't a lady, but she was Lucia, yet instead of that being a balm to his irritated conscience, it only served to remind him again of how she trusted him not to behave like this. He'd sworn not to dishonor her, not to take advantage of her station, not to do anything beyond what they'd both agreed.

And because she *was* Lucia, he couldn't bend that agreement to suit the other argument raging in his breeches. He couldn't. He'd given her his word. Because she trusted him, she deserved better from him, and reluctantly he broke his mouth away from hers, his heart drumming in his chest. Yet he couldn't part with her entirely, not yet, and he kept his arms still linked around her waist.

"Oh, my lord," she said softly, pushing back but remaining in the circle of his arms. She looked up at him without raising her chin, her eyes filled with uncertainty and her breathing rapid. "This wasn't part of our agreement, not at all."

"No, it wasn't," he said. Loose strands of hair were tossing across her forehead in the breeze, and he lightly smoothed them away, not wanting even a single hair to hide her face from him. "But when you called me unfeeling—"

"Forgive me, my lord," she said, and eased herself free of his arms. She didn't go far—only a step away—but she made it clear that she wished to be apart from him. He felt her separation keenly, a blow he hadn't expected nor wanted.

"There's nothing to forgive," he said gruffly, wondering what in blazes he was supposed to do now. His arms hung at his sides, empty and useless. "At least not for you."

"But there is, my lord," she insisted. She bent to retrieve her hat from where it had fallen on the path and settled it on her head, reaching to tie the ribbons at the back of her neck: small, brisk, ordinary gestures that seemed only to emphasize how awkward he now felt, and how great a fool he'd made of himself.

It was at once the most wonderful, and the most awful, moment of Lucia's life. To have Rivers say such things to her, such beautiful, important things about what she meant to him, and then to kiss her in a way that proved he believed those things, was more than she'd ever dreamed.

But that was exactly why it had been so awful as well. Even asleep, she knew better than to dream something as impossible as this. She'd never met another man who came as close to perfection as Rivers, or another who could leave her breathless and quivering like this with a single kiss. Despite how hard she tried to pretend that everything was as it should be, fussing with her hat and retying her ribbons, she was sure he must see what he'd done to her. No, what he *did* to her, because the effects wouldn't end, her heart beating far too swiftly and her lips still burning from his, and her entire being yearning to return once again to his embrace.

Yet how could any of it matter? Along with being nearly perfect, Rivers was also the son of a duke, while she was far, far less in every possible way. She didn't doubt that he'd meant those lovely words when he'd spoken them, but she doubted very much that he'd mean them even next week. He couldn't, not when he'd spoken them to a woman of her station. Words like those could only mean misery to her if she believed them, and now it was up to her to remind him of that fact.

Unsure of where to begin, she gazed up at him with tears in her eyes. She'd never wish to hurt him, but the confused and wounded expression now on his face was undeniably her doing.

Tell him, her conscience ordered sternly as the silence stretched longer and longer between them. *You've told him before. Tell him again, now, so he understands how it must be between you. Remind him of your agreement, and of the wager. Remind him of who he is, and who you are.*

Unaware of her thoughts, he nodded curtly. "I am sorry to have inconvenienced you, Mrs. Willow. Rest assured that I will not bother you further, nor—"

"No!" she cried, and every good intention vanished. "Do not say that, my lord, I beg of you! What you've said—how you feel about these last weeks together—it is the same for me as well, only more."

He stared at her warily, not trusting. "I do not believe that is possible."

"Not possible, my lord?" She stepped forward, closing the short distance between them to stare up into his face. "How could it not be possible when it is the truth? I cannot begin to explain what you have come to mean to me, my lord, and the very thought of parting from your company when this wager is done grieves me beyond measure. How could that not be possible?"

"You do not say this from a sense of obligation?" he asked slowly, his expression unchanged. "Mind that you owe me nothing. I have never forced my attentions on any woman, and by God, I would not begin now with you."

"But you haven't, my lord, not a bit," she said fervently, searching his face. "When you gave me your word, you kept it, even to me."

"Because you deserved that from me, Lucia," he said, and finally smiled. "Because of who and what you are to me, I could do nothing less."

Something squeezed tight in her chest. "Oh, my lord," she whispered. "My lord!"

"Rivers," he said, cupping her jaw in the palm of his hand. "I wish you to call me by my name, not my title."

"Yes, Rivers," she said shyly, realizing what an enormous freedom that was. Not even her cousin had been permitted to be so informal. "Rivers."

His smiled warmed, and he rubbed his thumb lightly over her cheek. "How fine that sounds to me."

"Rivers," she repeated, her own smile tremulous with emotion. "You even left my vowels alone."

"My name contains only short vowels, which you pronounce without difficulty," he said. "It's the long vowels that tax you so. What will be next for us, Lucia?"

"Next?" she echoed. Part of her wished she could stop time and keep this moment forever as it was, but a man like Rivers would not be satisfied with that, nor would she. What better definition of temptation could there be than this man before her?

Lightly she laid her hands on his chest, her hands pale against the soft woolen superfine of his coat. He'd been right; without the rough toil that she'd been accustomed to and with the sweet-smelling balm that he'd ordered from the apothecary for her, her hands had become as smooth as any lady's. Only three weeks, and yet in how many ways she'd changed!

"Next," he said more firmly. "What do you wish it to be?"

What she truly wished, she could never have. She was sure of that. But there was another possibility that, until this moment and this temptation, she hadn't allowed herself to consider. Even if Rivers could never be hers for life, she could still be his for a day, a week, a month. Joy, and pleasure, and love that she would never forget would become a memory that would be hers forever: *that* was what she could have, if she dared. The pain when he inevitably left—like every other gentleman had left every other woman like her—would be agonizing, but she would survive, and she would have the memory of his love always.

That was her choice. She wasn't a fine lady, expecting an offer of marriage. She was a Di Rossi, and Di Rossis knew how to seize whatever chance was offered to them, whether in Naples or Paris or London, or here at Breconridge Lodge. Fate had already brought her to Lord Rivers Fitzroy, and this moment. The rest was up to her.

She took a deep breath.

"I wish for things to fall as they will between us," she said with fierce determination, her fingers spreading over his chest. "No plans, no regrets, for whatever time we have together. If you say you can care for more than books, Rivers, then show me. Be less a Fitzroy, and more a Di Rossi. Show me you can simply *live* instead."

He turned his head slightly to one side, intrigued. "Live," he said, "and love?"

She nodded, her cheeks hot with excitement. "Minute by minute, day by day, whatever fate and the stars decree."

"Trusting to fate can be full of risk, Lucia," he said, his voice seductively low. "Most women wouldn't wish it."

"I am no ordinary woman," she declared with a little flip of her wrist. "But you know that of me by now."

"Indeed," he said, touching his thumb to her lower lip. "You are most *extraordinary*. Have you the courage for such a course?"

"You know that I do," she said fervently. " '*My fate cries out, / And makes each petty artery in this body / As hardy as the Nemean lion's nerve.*' "

He chuckled. "That's not your line, Ophelia. It's Hamlet's."

She turned her mouth against his hand and playfully nipped at his palm. "It is mine now."

He laughed, and finally kissed her, a kiss that was both rough and sweet, mingled with promise and desire.

"Lucia," he said. "*My* Lucia."

"And now?" she asked, her voice a breathless whisper. For all her bold talk, she was still a virgin, and unsure of exactly how these things transpired. "What now?"

He smiled, all mysterious. Perhaps he was already being more like a Di Rossi, just as she'd hoped he could be.

"We'll go to Newbury, Mrs. Willow."

"And after that?" she asked, her anticipation growing.

"Minute by minute, madam," he said, kissing her again. "Minute by minute."

Since Newbury was the nearest town of any size to both Breconridge Hall and Breconridge Lodge, Rivers had traveled the way to it countless times since he'd been a boy. The road had not changed in that time, either, remaining a seldom-journeyed path through green fields and a few small woods, all of it belonging to the Fitzroy family. Despite this lack of traffic, the road itself was in excellent condition, due to his father having invested a sizable amount in its annual upkeep. True, it made for an easier ride for the Fitzroys and their guests, but his father also believed firmly that his position as the highest-ranking landowner (and the only duke) in the county meant that he'd a duty to the others who lived there as well. His father had made improvements to the local roads, arranged for a new roof for the small parish church, supported the local charity school for young children and orphans, and allocated a substantial sum each

Christmas to the largest public house in Newbury for the express purpose of having Newburians raise a seasonal tankard to His Grace's health.

It all contributed to the Fitzroys being regarded with great favor in the town, and as Rivers's carriage with its Fitzroy crest painted on the side rolled through the streets, townspeople bowed and curtseyed and raised their hats, and he nodded and smiled in return through the open window. He was accustomed to the attention, but for Lucia, nestled beside him, it was a stunning experience.

"I cannot believe it, Rivers," she said, staring past him out the window. "I know your father's His Grace the Duke of Breconridge, but *dio buono,* the folk in this town treat you as if you were His Majesty himself!"

He laughed, his arm comfortably around her shoulder. If he'd been the true rake she'd accused him of being, he would have hurried her off to his bed this morning, as soon as they'd agreed that their agreement was to be no more, or perhaps even tossed up her petticoats and tumbled her there in his mother's garden.

But because he wasn't that rake, he wanted to seduce her properly so that it would be as enjoyable for her as it would be for him. Even though he'd said he'd live minute by minute, he wanted to make plans for a memorable evening, one that neither of them would forget, and so in the meantime he'd brought her here to Newbury. Not that the anticipation wasn't pleasurable in itself, because it was. He was so happy this afternoon that she could have said the sky was black with horned toads descending from the heavens, and he would have laughed, too.

"We do have royal blood, you know," he said. "My great-great-great-grandfather was in fact the King of England."

"No!" she gasped in awe. "You don't mean it, not truly."

"I do so mean it, because it's true," he said, relishing her response. "Of course, my great-great-great-grandmother was only his mistress, not his queen or his wife, but he did give her a dukedom for their bastard son, and declared the boy legitimate so he could inherit the title and the lands and estates with it."

She fell back against the squabs with an extravagant show of shock. "Royal blood, Rivers! Oh, I cannot fathom it, even if you're only your father's third son. Don't you wish you'd been born first, so you'd be the duke, too?"

"Not in the least," he said without hesitation. Many people had asked him that throughout his life, and the answer he now gave her had always been the same. "If I were to inherit the dukedom, it would mean that my father and both my brothers were dead before me, and no title under Heaven is worth that price. Their wives would also need to have borne no sons, which thus far is sadly the case. Three daughters for Harry and Gus, and one for Geoffrey and Serena, and though they are lovely little creatures, every one of them, the fact that none of them is male has distressed my father no end."

She twisted around to face him, as fascinated as if he'd been telling her a fairy story.

"Daughters are always welcome among the Di Rossis, because daughters will always earn more than sons as dancers," she said. "Unless they're me. But what if your wife has a son? Could he become Duke of Breconridge?"

"He would," Rivers said. "As heir, he'd jump right over all those little lady cousins of his, and claim the coronet for himself. But since I have neither a wife nor a son, it is all moot for me."

"Doesn't your father press you to marry?" she asked. "I'd think he would, just to better his odds of a grandson."

Rivers sighed, some of his enjoyment in the afternoon

fading at that unwelcome reminder. "Oh, he does, he does. That mythical parade of doxies is nothing compared to the very real legion of eligible and presumably fertile young ladies of good families that are trotted beneath my nose on a regular basis. I am a long odds ever to be a duke, but there's plenty of mamas ready to roll the dice that I will, and push their darlings toward me for a match."

"But you won't be pushed, will you?" she asked, with more than a tinge of hope in her voice that was very much in sympathy with his own wishes.

"No, Mrs. Willow, I shall not," he said, "no matter how firmly my father pushes his hands upon my back. Besides, I've perfect faith in my brothers and sisters-in-law that they will eventually produce the heir between them. Gus is with child again, and by every law of nature and averages she must be carrying a boy."

"Poor lady!" she said, sighing in commiseration for the unfortunate Countess of Hargreave. "That would be dreadful, having everyone staring at your belly and laying wagers about whether it would be another daughter."

He nodded, not really wanting to discuss this further. Lucia was right: the lack of a male heir was a great stress within his family, leading to short tempers, raised voices, and general ill-feeling whenever they gathered together.

He glanced from the window, noting that they were only a few streets away from Mrs. Currie's shop. "Are you willing to carry our lessons into the mantua-maker's?"

"How?" she asked curiously. "So you wish me to play at Ophelia there for the seamstresses?"

"Not quite," he said. "But I do want you to be Mrs. Willow in all her glory whilst you are being served and fitted."

She nodded eagerly, ready for the challenge. "Oh, yes, Rivers," she said. "If the mantua-maker asks who I am, might I tell her my story of Mrs. Willow's adventures?"

"What, with the tiger and all?" He couldn't begin to imagine what Mrs. Currie would make of that. "Perhaps a less, ah, dramatic tale. You are a longtime friend of mine whose coach was attacked by a highwayman. Your trunks were stolen, and you lost all your belongings, reducing you to wearing clothes borrowed from one of my servants."

"I like that!" she exclaimed with relish. "I was stripped naked by a rapacious highwayman, and left to wander, naked as Eve, on the public road until you in your great kindness rescued me from my peril."

"You needn't go into such detail," he said quickly. Perhaps they'd been better off with the man-eating tiger after all. "If you spin too lurid a tale, then it's sure to sound false."

"Oh," she said, crestfallen. "Could not the highwayman at least be a handsome rogue?"

"Let us do away with the highwayman altogether," Rivers said. "We'll say you were returning to Dover from Calais, and your trunks were mislaid by the boatmen."

She sighed mightily. "How boring," she said. "But if that is what you believe they will believe, then I shall give up my dashing highwayman."

"It is for the best," he said, thinking of how narrowly they'd again avoided her overreaching imagination. "But there's one other thing. No one is a better judge of a lady's true rank than her milliner and her mantua-maker."

"That is true," she said quickly. "It vexed Magdalena no end that they always knew what she was, no matter how she tried to impress them."

That *was* true enough; even when he'd escorted her cousin to one of the London shops, the women had smirked and simpered, recognizing Magdalena as his mistress.

"Well, then, you will understand," he said. "I want

you to speak as you did this morning, copying me, and see if you can convince Mrs. Currie into believing you are as we wish you to be: a genteel young lady, tossed cruelly about by the vagaries of life, who has turned to the stage to earn her living. There cannot be so much as a breath of Madame Adelaide, or of your cousin, either. Can you do that?"

She nodded so eagerly her hat nearly slipped from her head. "You'll see, Rivers. I can do this. I'll trick them all, the cullies."

"Act, don't trick," he said firmly, trying to ignore his misgivings. "And don't you dare call anyone in the shop a cully."

He wouldn't have suggested this if they'd been in London, where the mantua-makers were as sharp as the needles they wielded when it came to appraising their customers. But here in Newbury, he was counting on the favor his family and the occasional custom that his stepmother brought to Mrs. Currie to help convince her to see Lucia as a member of the gentry of the middling sort who'd fallen on unlucky times.

Unless she began calling the shop women cant names.

"I shall prove it to you, my lord," she promised. She'd already adapted his accent, and she was also sitting straighter, her shoulders back and pressed inward in the manner of a true lady's posture, her ankles neatly together, and her hands folded, not clasped, on her lap. "You shall be *amazed*."

Even those long AYs were perfect. Damnation, perhaps she really was going to amaze him, and the rest of the world besides.

"Then come, Mrs. Willow," he said as the carriage came to a stop before the mantua-maker's shop. He smiled, and offered her his hand. "Amaze me."

CHAPTER
10

The footman opened the carriage door and folded down the steps, and Rivers stepped out first. Lucia leaned forward to look past his broad shoulders and black cocked hat to the mantua-maker's shop. Mrs. Currie must have prospered in her trade, for her shop was elegantly presented, with a curving bow window picked out with glossy black paint, a signboard with gold letters, and a green door with a shining brass plaque engraved with the proprietor's name. To keep all this from being too sober, a ribbon-tied bouquet of silk flowers hung from the plaque, beckoning customers to the feminine delights within.

Lucia had never so much as looked in the window of such a shop. Now she was not only to enter and be served as a customer, but in the process make her first true performance as an actress, before an audience (albeit an unknowing one) that wasn't Rivers. She must remember everything he'd told her about being a lady, and make every gesture, every word count to convince the tradeswomen that she was whom she claimed. Anything less and she'd instantly fall to the status of those infamous doxies, and though because of Rivers the women would treat her well enough, she knew that as soon as she left they'd be laughing and ridiculing her.

She didn't want to fail at this first real test as an actress, and she didn't want to fail Rivers, either. The enormity of this moment was daunting, and despite her excitement, she hung back in the carriage. She told herself sternly that she *could* do this and wasn't a coward, that she *was* ready, and yet her heart was racing and her palms were damp as she sat riveted to the carriage seat.

"Mrs. Willow?" Rivers had turned and was holding his hand out to help her down. "I know this establishment is not of the quality to which you are accustomed, but there is no need for reluctance. I'm certain you shall be treated with the utmost civility and will find many items to your taste."

She realized he was speaking loudly for the benefit of the curious passersby, and offering a reasonable explanation for her reluctance. She couldn't keep him waiting any longer. Her performance had to begin *now*.

She glanced down at his offered hand, and then back to his face.

"Amaze me, madam," he said again, softly and so only she could hear. "Take your place, and let the curtain rise."

And then he winked.

That was enough. She lifted her chin, striving to be an imposing, even regal, Mrs. Willow, took his hand, and swept down the steps and into the shop. A round-faced older woman in a ruffled cap with many ribbons stepped from behind the counter to greet them, with two fashionably dressed younger women in ruffled caps and sheer aprons, pin-balls and scissors hanging from their waists, following closely behind.

"Good day, Mrs. Currie," Rivers said. "As I wrote, I have brought to you a dear friend, a lady who is in need of a new wardrobe. Mrs. Willow, Mrs. Currie."

All three of the tradeswomen curtseyed in unison. It was the first time Lucia had ever been honored this way, and she had to fight the automatic impulse to curtsey back in return.

"Good day, Mrs. Currie," she murmured, taking special care to round her vowels. "Lord Rivers speaks only the highest praise in regard to your work."

The mantua-maker nodded graciously, and to Lucia's relief there wasn't so much of a hint of suspicion or scorn. She'd tricked them royally—or as Rivers would say, she was winning them with her performance.

"Thank you, ma'am," Mrs. Currie said. "We are most grateful for your custom. How may we serve you? What would it please you to see first?"

"She needs everything, because she has nothing," Rivers declared. "A half-dozen gowns for day, two for evening, a habit or Brunswick for travel, hats, stays, hoops, stockings, muffs, and all the rest. You know better than I what is required, Mrs. Currie."

"Oh, indeed, my lord," the mantua-maker said, her smile warm at the potential of such a sizable sale. "We will be honored to oblige Mrs. Willow in every way. Shall this be on your account, my lord?"

Rivers waved his hand with studied nonchalance. "Of course, of course, send the reckoning to me," he said. "What matters most is that this dear lady be clothed as befits her, and swiftly, too. I should like everything delivered to Breconridge Lodge the day after tomorrow."

Mrs. Currie gulped. "It can be done, of course, my lord—anything for his lordship!—but pray be aware that such speed must come at a price."

"I understand completely," Rivers said, smiling. "All that concerns me is that this lady is accommodated as she requires."

But Lucia understood, too, and his nonchalance stunned her. From her work among the costumes, she knew that anything made as quickly as he was requesting came at a dear price indeed. Extra seamstresses—likely every skilled one in Newbury—would need to be hired and set to working by the expensive light of candles instead of the free light of day.

"Very well, my lord, very well." Mrs. Currie exchanged a few meaningful glances with her assistants, who at once began producing lengths of fabric and trimmings. "If you please, Mrs. Willow, let us begin with one of the gowns for day, so that I may learn your tastes. May I suggest a round gown, or one gathered up in the Polish manner?"

She swept a length of shimmering green silk—lustring, she called it—over her arm while one of the assistants held up a fashion plate of the Polish-style gown, with a close-fitting, pointed bodice, skirts looped up over contrasting petticoats, and pert small bows at the gathers and along the stomacher for accents. Forgetting to act, Lucia made a wordless sigh of admiration, for she'd never seen such a deliciously charming gown.

"It is a very cunning choice, ma'am," the mantua-maker said, noting Lucia's reaction. "A *très belle robe à la mode,* as the ladies say in Paris."

Lucia smiled, automatically shifting to French. *"Les dames françaises savent tout sur la mode, non?"*

"As you say, ma'am." Mrs. Currie flushed and looked down at the silk over her arm, smoothing it with her palm to hide her confusion. Too late Lucia realized she'd gone beyond the limits of the mantua-maker's grasp of French, and that her single sentence of French had unwittingly made the other woman feel foolish and discomfited.

"The French ladies do know everything about fashion, don't they?" she repeated in English, not wanting the other woman to feel ill at ease on her account. She'd been ridiculed often enough herself never to wish to inflict the same misery on anyone else. "If you say a *Parisienne* would wear this gown, then surely it's as fashionable as it is lovely."

"Oh, yes, ma'am," Mrs. Currie said quickly, nodding in eager agreement. "The Paris ladies are most wise in setting the fashions. I can tell you have traveled widely, ma'am, and recognize quality and style. You possess such a dainty figure, ma'am, very much like the ladies at the French court, that you would wear such a gown to perfection."

But Rivers was not nearly as impressed, or susceptible to the mantua-maker's flattery.

"I suppose that will do for one of the day dresses," he said with a shrug as he sat on one of the leather-covered benches for customers. "But first I would like you to provide a gown for this evening, when Mrs. Willow shall be dining with me."

"But it is already two, my lord," Mrs. Currie protested. "Not even my girls could make a gown—a gown worthy of this lady's beauty—in so short a time."

"Surely something can be arranged," Lucia said, wondering if he truly had planned some special dinner that required a new gown, or if this was only another part of Mrs. Willow's role. "His lordship has been so kind to me that I could not disappoint him and appear again in *this*."

She held her worn skirts out to one side and looked beseechingly at the mantua-maker, and tried to focus on being Mrs. Willow, and not think of whatever it was Rivers was planning for her this evening.

Mrs. Currie dolefully shook her head. "I am sorry, madam, but as much as I regret disappointing you, I do not wish to promise what I cannot deliver."

"Then perhaps there is another gown, nearly complete, here in your shop that could be made to fit my form?" she asked with her most winning smile. From her own experience as a tiring-girl, she knew that an even-tempered request would work much better for a favor than imperiously raging about like Magdalena would have done. "I know it shall be a great inconvenience to you, Mrs. Currie, but if there is any possibility, I shall be very grateful, and so shall his lordship."

The mantua-maker hesitated, studying Lucia so closely that Lucia feared the worst. She must have somehow given herself away, and the woman had seen she was an imposter, and the whole thing a ruse. Perhaps it was the lapse into French, or perhaps some intangible droop to her posture that betrayed her humble, unladylike origins. And oh, if only she'd paid closer attention to her infernal vowels!

"I may be able to oblige you, Mrs. Willow," Mrs. Currie said at last, and thoughtfully, too. "You are such a pleasant lady, I only desire to please you."

"Thank you, Mrs. Currie," Lucia said as graciously as she could, somehow managing to keep her relief from showing. She hadn't failed, or given herself away. She'd played the lady, and won her audience.

"It is my pleasure, ma'am," Mrs. Currie said, beaming. "There is a gown in the workroom at present—a splendid gown of silk taffeta in the deepest shade of scarlet that would be most becoming to you—that could be made to suit. Miss Jenny, fetch the scarlet gown for Mrs. Willow's consideration."

"I like a lady in red," Rivers said, which as much as sealed the scarlet gown's fate as far as Lucia was concerned. If he liked it, then she would, too.

But when Miss Jenny reappeared with the gown, there was no need for compromise, no need to be obliging. It was simply beautiful, the silk taffeta rich and the color subtly changing with the light. There was ruching trim around the neck and down the front, and more in serpentine borders along the edges of the open petticoat. Tiny gold silk flowers were scattered over it, as if they'd grown there of their own accord, and the entire effect was both charming and elegant.

The most difficult part for Lucia of playing Mrs. Willow was pretending, as grateful as she was, that she'd already owned gowns like this one by the score. She let herself be whisked to a dressing room behind the shop, where Mrs. Currie herself fitted the gown to her small figure, smoothing and pinning and taking a pleat here and narrowing a seam there before the gown was taken off to the seamstresses for finishing.

What followed was a whirlwind of choices and purchases made, of Italian silks and Indian cottons spread across the counter, of ribbons unfurled, and trimmings considered. Dimities and dresdens, camlets and calamancos and cherryderrys, laylocks and broglios and siamoises: even the names of the fabrics were like an exotic foreign language to Lucia. While Rivers would occasionally offer his opinion, for the most part he retreated into the book he'd brought along for the purpose of diversion, and left the decisions to Lucia herself in what was for her a heaven of unimaginable, indulgent beauty and luxury.

Yet by the time the last ribbon had been chosen and the final fitting made, the afternoon had begun to fade into evening, and Lucia was thoroughly exhausted. It was not simply the challenge of being Mrs. Willow, but also the stress of choosing so many new things for herself in an elegant lady's shop. She had never purchased so much as a length of ribbon from a place such as this. Instead she'd always worn jackets and petticoats that had been passed down from others in the company, plus the rare plain linen gown that she'd bought for herself from one of the peddlers and small shops that sold secondhand (or third-, or fourth-, or fifth-hand) clothing in Whitechapel.

She'd no experience with costly silks and precious lace and other trims, or having a small flock of seamstresses and apprentices hovering about her, ready to obey her every suggestion or whim. While she knew Rivers had meant this as a treat, a pleasurable indulgence, she'd been unable to shake the uneasy feeling that she didn't quite deserve such luxury, and beneath the smiling façade of Mrs. Willow, her inexperience had made her uncertain and anxious. If only she'd had written lines to memorize so she'd be certain to say the right thing!

With each decision that Mrs. Currie presented to her to make, she feared she'd choose a color or cloth that was somehow wrong, and she'd be eternally grateful for how the mantua-maker tactfully had guided her as to what was not only fashionable, but flattering as well. The red gown would be finished so that they might bring it back to the Lodge with them today, and Mrs. Currie herself would come out with the rest of the things in two days for more fittings.

It was all more than Lucia could keep straight herself, and when at last Rivers handed her back into the carriage, she was too exhausted and overwhelmed to take pride in what she'd accomplished, or pleasure in her new wardrobe.

"You were brilliant," Rivers said proudly as the footman latched the carriage door shut. "Not only did you convince Mrs. Currie that you truly were Mrs. Willow, but you were also so endearing that she went out of her way to please you."

"Do you think so?" she asked with a sigh, sinking wearily into one corner of the seat. "I hoped I'd done well, but I could not tell for certain whether I'd succeeded, or if she was simply being nice to me because of you."

"When we first arrived, I would guess she was being agreeable in deference to my family name," he said, settling beside her. "But it didn't take long for you to win her over in your own right."

"I shouldn't have spoken French," she said, wincing a

bit at the memory. "That was wrong. I did it without thinking, and I shouldn't have."

"No, it was exactly right," he said. "Every English lady speaks French, or at least the clever ones do. Clearly Mrs. Currie does not, but the way you salvaged her pride for her showed both kindness and understanding. That's why she gave you the red gown, not because of me. You played a lady to perfection."

That was exactly it: she had *played* a lady. She must remind herself of that. Mrs. Willow was a role, improvised without lines to memorize, but only a role, a character, a part to be learned. She'd welcomed the chance to put aside her old life for a better one, but she hadn't realized that by becoming Mrs. Willow, she'd lose so much of Lucia di Rossi. Instead of feeling proud of what she'd done, she felt confused and unsettled, and having Rivers praise her like this somehow only made it worse.

"It didn't seem perfect to me," she said, shifting back to her old way of speaking. She untied her hat and placed it on her lap so she could lean her head back against the squabs. "If I did, then it was your doing, Rivers, not mine."

"No, it wasn't," he said firmly. "It was all yours, and your serious study and work. I merely led the way."

He patted the seat beside him and with a sigh she slid across the cushion to join him. He slipped his arm around her shoulders and pulled her close, and with another sigh she nestled into his side, finding comfort in the warmth and strength of his body.

"Thank you so much, Rivers," she said softly. "For—for everything."

"I knew you'd enjoy choosing some new clothes," he said, clearly enjoying having given her such a gift. "I know how much you ladies do love your finery."

She smiled wistfully at how he'd unconsciously included her among the ranks of ladies of his acquaintance, a place where she never would belong.

"It was not easy for me, Rivers," she confessed, gazing across the carriage to where the new scarlet gown, swathed in protective linen, had been carefully laid on the other bench for the drive back to the Lodge. "I do not know how ladies make such choices every day when they dress."

"*'The lady doth protest too much, methinks,'*" he said, teasing by quoting more from *Hamlet*. "It's true that Mrs. Currie had a veritable bazaar of temptations for you, but what lady doesn't relish making such decisions?"

"I didn't," she insisted, twisting around to face him. "And that line of Queen Gertrude's makes no sense at all here."

He smiled indulgently. "I only meant it as a jest, sweetheart."

"And I meant it as the truth." She sank back against him, her head pillowed against his shoulder, and thought of the significance of the new dress, pale and ghostly in its linen wrapping. "I've never had bespoke clothes, Rivers, not so much as a single petticoat. This gown is my first. With so many things to choose from, it was hard for me to know what was right to pick."

"What was right was what you wanted, and what gave you pleasure," he said, his voice growing more gentle and losing the edge of teasing. "But how did you come by your clothes before, if not from a shop?"

She shook her head, reluctant to explain exactly how very different their circumstances were. Most times he understood, but there were others, like now, when the distance between them felt yawning and insurmountable. He'd been born to enormous wealth and position, and she had not, and she'd no wish to emphasize the difference between them any further, especially not today.

"It doesn't matter," she said, evasive. "Not at all."

"Everything about you matters to me," he said, with

such conviction that she wanted very much to believe him. "There must have been one special gown in your life. Every woman has one."

"There was one," she confessed slowly, remembering. Although she'd worked among the bright and glittering dancers' costumes in the tiring room and wardrobe, only one dress had been special in the way he meant. "The pink silk gown that Papa bought for me in an old-frock shop in Lancaster. I wore it as my costume the summer we toured with the circus-folk."

"What was the gown like?" he asked, his interest genuine. She'd always loved that about him: he wished to learn *everything,* not to make light of it, but because that knowledge made him wiser, and better, too.

"I remember the dress as being vastly beautiful," she began slowly. In the fading light of day, here in the carriage, it was easy for her to imagine that long-ago dress, and easy to trust him with the memory of it. "It had a damask pattern of swirling pomegranates, and it was unlike anything else I'd ever worn."

"You must have looked beautiful in it," he said gently, falling into the reverie with her. "If I'd known, I would have asked that Mrs. Currie bring out every pink silk damask in her stock for you today."

She smiled at his enthusiasm, and his generosity, too.

"It would not have been the same," she said wistfully, "nor could it have been. Although I believed that gown was magical, it had been worn by so many others before me that the damask was soft and nearly in tatters, with a large blotchy stain on the side of the skirts."

He chuckled fondly. "I doubt anyone noticed," he said. "Not on you."

"No, they didn't," she agreed, also remembering how undiscerning her audiences had been, and how often half-drunk, too, at the end of a fair-day. "We were in the country, and the audiences believed the dress was every bit as beautiful as I did. They wouldn't notice that the cut was years out of date, and the silver thread that had once outlined the pomegranates—there were still a few traces of it left—had been picked out to be resold, leaving hundreds of little holes in the faded pink silk. Even so, every time I wore it I'd felt like a princess, standing in the lantern's light on the back of the wagon to recite my pieces."

"Do you have the gown still?" he asked.

"Oh, no," she said, knowing how foolish such a memento would have been in her life. One day after they'd returned to London, the gown had simply disappeared; most likely Papa had sold it away to another old-frock dealer. "By the end of the summer, I'd outgrown it, and I do not know what became of it after that."

"No doubt your father was proud of having such an accomplished daughter," Rivers said. "Rightly so, too."

"He was," she said sadly, a memory that was not quite so fair. She'd often thought how differently their lives would have turned out if she and Papa had been able to stay with the circus-folk in the green fields and wandering roads in the country, and had not returned to London, and the company. Papa might not have fallen so deeply into despair and strong drink, and she herself would never have had her final hopes of becoming a dancer beaten from her by Uncle Lorenzo.

But then she would not have landed here, either, with Rivers's arm protectively around her shoulders. For now, with him, she felt safe, and she settled a little more closely against him, her hand curling lightly on his chest.

"When I was with Mrs. Currie in the shop, I felt wrong as Mrs. Willow, as if I were hollow and empty and false," she confessed, her words coming out in an anxious rush. "I felt as if I was forgetting who *I* was and where I'd come from, that all I had left was the lie of being Mrs.

Willow, and . . . and it frightened me, Rivers. I feared that I had—that I *have*—lost myself."

He drew her closer. "That won't happen, Lucia," he said. "You're far too strong a woman for that. Besides, I like you too much as you are to let that happen."

She looked up at him, startled. "You do?"

"I do," he said solemnly. "I'm vastly proud of how much you've accomplished, and how as an actress you've learned to transform yourself so completely into another. But it's Lucia di Rossi who has become dear to me, not Mrs. Willow, and I'm far too selfish to let her vanish."

"Oh, Rivers," she said, tears stinging her eyes. "I do not wish to go away."

"Then we shall both be content, yes?" With his fingers on her jaw, he turned her face the fraction more that was necessary for him to kiss her, his lips finding hers in a way that felt like a sensual pledge, a promise that he would do exactly as he said, and keep her safe and with him. She closed her eyes, relishing the kiss. In that moment, she trusted him completely, more than she'd ever trusted another, and whatever fears she'd held before slipped away, forgotten. He'd done that for her, and she felt strangely at peace.

"I am content," she whispered against his cheek, her eyes still closed. "I *am*."

The moon had risen and the stars with it when at last the carriage turned into the long drive that led to the Lodge. Rivers glanced down at Lucia, asleep in his arms, and smiled. She was soft and warm against him, her long, dark lashes feathering her cheek and her lips parted as if frozen in a kiss in her dreams.

He had not expected her to fall asleep like this; he supposed he should feel slighted that she had, even insulted. If any other woman had drifted off like that after he'd kissed her, he would have been. But Lucia wasn't like other women, and what he was feeling toward her now was far, far from insulting.

He hadn't expected her to completely *become* Mrs. Willow in the mantua-maker's shop, or to so thoroughly project the essence of a well-bred lady that Mrs. Currie and her assistants never doubted her for even an instant. There had been not so much as a breath of a rapacious highwayman and no tigers. Instead she'd played her part to near-perfection, from her accent to her posture to the smattering of French, and how she'd been the one to smooth over Mrs. Currie's gaffe had been pure gracious genius worthy of any duchess, including his own impeccable stepmother.

She'd every right to crow after such a triumph, and savor the success she'd earned. But again she'd done what he hadn't expected, and instead of crowing in the carriage, she'd wilted in a way that had reminded him of her old days in the tiring room, when she'd been nearly invisible. Her explanation had touched him deeply, and he couldn't imagine how the brave little woman he saw each day could fear she'd disappear like an insubstantial wisp of smoke.

He'd grant that she had changed in these last weeks. She now walked with confidence, and spoke with assurance. The shadows were gone from around her eyes, and the hollows from her cheeks. She'd learned how to hold a teacup, and not to wipe her fingers on the tablecloth. Not only had her accent changed, but her vocabulary had blossomed as well. The young woman who'd only read broadsides and the Bible now stayed awake at night to devour the books she borrowed from his library.

So yes, she'd changed, but to his mind these changes were only little improvements to the woman she already was. He'd done his best to reassure her, hoping to ease her anxieties, and he'd hoped, too, that the spree of free spending he'd granted her in the shop would have cheered her. Every other woman he'd known would have wallowed happily in a greedy sea of silk.

Yet she'd surprised him there as well. Instead of finding joy amongst the taffetas and dimities, she'd been overwhelmed and miserable, and convinced she didn't deserve such largesse. He was so accustomed to her usual confidence that he hadn't quite believed her, not until she'd confided that heartbreaking story of the stained and holey pink gown. Only Lucia could have infused a raggedy secondhand dress with enough of herself to make it sound magical and fit for a princess. He hoped the new gown he'd bought her today would come to hold even more of her magic.

He glanced across at the gown and smiled, trying to picture her wearing it. He hadn't gone back to the shop's dressing room with her for the fitting—they weren't yet on the terms that would permit that kind of intimacy— but in a way he was glad, because it meant he'd have the great pleasure of seeing her wear it for the first time tonight, just for him.

Tonight would be special in many ways, or so he hoped. For any other woman, he would have arranged the obligatory small supper in his dressing room, the sort of small supper that every young nobleman of means was expected to order for fair young creatures. There would be much wine and a Frenchified meal that might or might not be eaten before they moved on to his conveniently nearby bedchamber. In the course of the night, there would also be many declarations of passion and affection that neither party would believe, and after a small parting gift in the morning, there would be mutual satisfaction with the arrangement, which would soon be forgotten.

But Lucia deserved more from him than that. Her words this morning about how he lived too much through his books had struck home. He wanted to prove to her that he could be as impetuous and romantic as any Neapolitan. He was determined to put aside his customary British reserve, and share with her a side of himself that no one else had ever seen, and prove to her that he knew how to experience the very best that life had to offer firsthand, not through words written by another.

Lightly he kissed the top of her head, her dark hair mussed like a child's from her hat, and she stirred, but did not wake. He hoped she'd understand. No, he *knew* she would, because she was Lucia.

There was one more thing he intended to share with her tonight, something he would have already revealed if she hadn't fallen asleep. Tucked inside his coat was the letter from Mr. McGraw, the manager of the Russell Street Theatre. The letter had arrived shortly before he and Lucia had left for Newbury, and though Rivers had had time to read it only once, the significance of its contents had been running through his mind all afternoon.

When he'd first made his wager with Everett, he'd envisioned training Lucia to perform a single scene for Everett and a small circle of other acquaintances in the drawing room of his house in Cavendish Square. If there were interest enough, he might even have hired the ballroom of a local inn, and offered a subscription for tickets, so she'd have some kind of payment for her performance that didn't come from him.

That would have been sufficient to win the wager, and it was how he'd described to her his plans for a performance when she'd asked, early in their time together. She had trusted him to make whatever arrangements were necessary, and had asked nothing more, concentrating instead on perfecting her role.

But as Rivers had discovered the depth of Lucia's talent and witnessed the progress she'd made, his own ambitions for her had grown. He'd no longer be content with an amateur performance for an invited audience. He wanted her to have the opportunity to become a true actress, able to make her living on the stage, the way that she wanted. She'd said he believed in her and he did, and to prove it, he'd written to McGraw to request an audition for Lucia to play Ophelia in a staged production of *Hamlet* at the Russell Street Theatre.

It would be considered a benefit, a single, pared-down performance on a single night, the kind of thing that was often done in the theater, but it would also become a public audition for her as an actress. In that night, she'd also become a professional, for while McGraw would take his share of the ticket sales, Rivers intended to make sure that she herself would receive the lion's share of the benefit's profits, a surprise reward.

Russell Street was second only to Garrick's own Theatre Royal in Drury Lane—the two playhouses were in fact within sight of each other—and a very grand place indeed for an aspiring actress to make her debut before the notoriously critical London crowds. Now the manager would present himself at the Lodge in three days for an impromptu audition, and Lucia would take her first step toward being the actress she'd always wanted to be.

It was the greatest gift that Rivers could give her, one that would make an entire shop of clothes pale in comparison. Yet as much as he wished her to have her dream, he did not want her to think there was any obligation to him in return. If they became lovers—which he now hoped very much that they would—he wanted her to come to his bed freely. He wanted her to love him for himself, and not because she felt she owed him for this very sizable opportunity.

It was foolish of him to be so sentimental, he knew, and he could only imagine how his brothers and friends would howl with laughter if they ever learned. She'd earned this chance, and she deserved it. From the very difference in their rank, his relationship with Lucia would always have an inescapable mercenary air to it. But for tonight at least, he could pretend otherwise. He could simply enjoy her company for who she was, and pray she did the same with him.

Of course he'd tell her when the time was right, and he reminded himself again of how much he wanted her to have it. Because he did, didn't he?

For now, McGraw's letter and its news would keep for another day or two, buried deep in his pocket and away from his heart.

"Almost ready, ma'am," Sally said, critically arranging the gathers at the back of Lucia's skirts. The maid had had experience dressing ladies, and was on occasion called up to Breconridge Hall to help with the guests for balls. "His lordship wanted everything perfect before he sees you."

Obediently Lucia stood without moving, even as her heart raced with anticipation. She had dressed countless other women at the playhouse, but she'd never before been the one being dressed, and it was an odd experience. She sat still as a statue while Sally had brushed out her long hair and skillfully curled and pinned it into a fashionably tall pouf with trailing curls down the back. She lifted one foot and then the other for Sally to roll on her yellow silk stockings with the red embroidered clocks at the ankles, tie her red silk ribbon garters, and slip on her heeled shoes with buckles of glittering paste stones. Then she stood with her back to the looking glass to have her shift adjusted, her stays laced, and her red silk gown slipped over her shoulders and pinned into place.

For the first time in her life, everything was new, and while all the newness was exciting in itself, it was also a bit disorienting as well. The new linen and silk sat differently against her skin, slightly apart and crisp, unlike her old familiar linen petticoats and shifts that were so worn and soft that they'd become almost a part of her. The pins that held her hair in place jabbed against her scalp, and the unfamiliar weight of her hair piled high made her hold her head up straighter. The hoops tied around her waist held her petticoats away from her hips, giving her the sensation that they were floating away, and she with them.

Unconsciously she touched her mother's cameo for comfort and reassurance. Not everything was new; not everything could be bought and replaced. She hadn't lost herself, not at all—it would take more than new clothes to do that. Hadn't Rivers told her exactly the same thing in the carriage?

"There, ma'am, you're finished," Sally said, clearly taking no pleasure in what she'd done. "Turn about and see yourself in the glass."

Lucia was almost afraid of what she'd see. She'd never been one to spend time admiring herself in the glass, not possessing that kind of vanity. She knew perfectly well what she looked like, and there had never been that much to admire. The looking glass in this dressing room was large, nearly pier-sized, and would show her from head to toe. There'd be no hiding. Slowly, very slowly, she turned, and forced herself to look.

And gasped.

The reflection before her was unlike any that had ever stared back at her. The *robe à la Polonaise* was every bit as beautiful as she'd expected, the scarlet silk shimmering and catching the candlelight like an ever-changing jewel. It didn't need gold thread or spangles: the color, the rich fabric, and the exquisite style were what would make it impossible to ignore in any gathering. The bodice was cut low over her breasts and sleekly fitted to her body, with narrow sleeves, lavish flounces at the elbows, and petticoats looped into extravagant poufs on either side, which served to make her waist look even smaller. This was the kind of gown that most women would only dream of owning, and she could scarcely believe it was now hers.

But the gown alone wasn't what had made Lucia gasp. It was how she herself looked that did that. She *glowed*. Her hair, her skin, her eyes: there was a vibrancy that she couldn't recall having seen in herself for a long while, if at all. It was as if she'd a candle lit inside of her.

"You're not the same as when you came here, are you?" Sally observed, shrewdly watching Lucia's reaction. "Even the lowest stray from the streets would improve with Mrs. Barber's cooking."

True, her cheeks were more plump and the ribs that she'd once been able to feel through her skin had disappeared, but she knew the change wasn't entirely due to Mrs. Barber's cooking. Rivers could make much more of the claim. His lessons and her time here with him at the Lodge had worn away the dull, self-effacing mask of unhappiness and frustration that she'd unconsciously assumed while in the playhouse. The self-confidence and accomplishment that she'd discovered thanks to him showed in her face and even how she stood, for gone were the hunched, defensive shoulders and the tightly clasped hands. She was happy, happier than she'd ever been, and it showed.

And, though she didn't wish to admit it, she was also more than a little in love with him.

The thought alone made her blush, her cheeks a guilty red that nearly matched her gown. She'd heard the gossip from the other women in the tiring room, and she knew in great detail what men expected once they'd gotten beneath a woman's petticoats. To some, it had sounded like a tedious chore to be endured for the sake of a reward afterward, but to others it was a magical, earth-shattering experience with the right man.

Lucia was certain that lovemaking with Rivers would be magic. Certainly kissing him was, and that was only the beginning. But no matter whether or not she ended this night in his bed, she must remember that he could never be hers, not entirely. She could have his friendship and his kindness as well as a hundred other little things that they'd shared and laughed over together, and if she dared, she might claim his passion, too, but she'd never have his heart, not to keep.

Perhaps that was what she thought most as she studied her reflection. Dressed like this, she could now have held her own among the other Di Rossi women, and been every bit as attractive, even seductive, as Magdalena. But because of Rivers, she was different from her cousin and the others, and always would be.

Because of him, she was *better*. Most likely he believed he'd only improved her as an actress, but in the process he'd also helped her become a more thoughtful, more polished, and more honorable woman that any other Di Rossi had ever been. He'd never know how much he'd done for her, just as she knew she'd never be able to repay him. Whatever happened tonight they could share a memory that would become endlessly special to her no matter what happened a week, a month, a year from now.

"See now, there's a smile," Sally said, not bothering to hide her contempt. "High time you did, too. When you first came here with his lordship, none of us could figure what he'd seen in you. Now there's no doubt to it. I suppose his lordship knew it from the beginning. Looking as you do now, ma'am, there's no doubt at all."

"I must join his lordship now," Lucia said hurriedly, glancing away from the looking glass to the little porcelain clock on the mantelpiece. It was already eight, long past their customary time for dining, and although Rivers had told her to take as long as she required to dress, she knew how much he hated to be kept waiting. "Has he gone downstairs yet?"

Sally shrugged and stepped back, leaving a clear path for Lucia to the door. "I do not know, ma'am."

"Then I shall go discover for myself." Lucia ran her palm along the front of her bodice, smoothing silk that did not need smoothing, then turned away from her reflection and toward the doorway and the staircase beyond. Everything was in play now; everything would happen as fate would have it.

Yet still she took the time to pause before Sally, placing her hand on the other woman's upper arm.

"I thank you, Sally," she said. "I know that you have done this for me from an order, not an inclination, but still I am most grateful for the care you have taken with my dress tonight."

Sally flushed. She looked down, avoiding Lucia's gaze, and bobbed a quick, noncommittal curtsey.

Given any encouragement, Lucia would have said more, but she recognized a purposeful slight when she saw one, and she knew, too, the best way to respond was to ignore it. The Lodge's female servants had disliked her from the first day she'd arrived, and nothing she'd done had changed their minds. Perhaps they'd resented how their master had favored her, a low, common woman from London who they all looked down upon; or perhaps it was simply because they knew she'd be gone from their lives in another week, they figured she wasn't worth their trouble.

Yet still their scorn stung because it was unfamiliar. Lucia had always been so invisible that no one else had bothered to be jealous or envious of her. Still, if she was going to make her way in the London theater she'd have to weather much worse than this, and with as pleasant a smile as she could muster, she turned away from Sally and walked through the doorway.

It was all one more lesson to learn, she told herself fiercely. One more reason to be strong so that she might succeed.

As much as she longed to join Rivers, she didn't run, but walked deliberately with the grace that he had urged her to find in herself. The silk petticoats rustled around her legs with each step, as if whispering more encouragement, and by the time she reached the parlor, her smile was genuine with eagerness to join him again, and her heart was racing with anticipation.

For once a footman—Tom, her first acquaintance amongst the staff—was stationed beside the parlor door in full livery, ready to bow and open it as soon as she approached. That made her smile, too, for life at the Lodge wasn't generally so formal. Having Tom there was much like having Sally dress her, both servants signifying the special importance that Rivers had placed upon this evening. As Tom held the door open for her she took one final deep breath to calm herself, and swept into the room with her head high, making the entrance that Rivers—and her new gown—deserved.

But instead of the blaze of candles and the impeccably set table that she'd expected, the room was nearly dark except for the moonlight. There were only two candles lit on the mantel, and the table where they usually ate was not only not set, but at rest against the wall with the leaves folded down.

And Rivers wasn't even looking at her. Instead he stood at the open door to the garden, gazing out at the night sky with his hands clasped behind his back. He was dressed for evening, too, and the moonlight glinted on the silver threads in his embroidered front and cuffs of his dark silk coat, just as it gilded on his golden hair, and reminded her once again how glad she was that he didn't powder it, or wear a wig. His long shadow stretched out behind him, away from the door and across the flowered carpet. She'd often before seen him lost in his thoughts like this, but not when he was supposed to be waiting to welcome her.

Panic and disappointment rose within her. Had she completely misjudged his intentions for this evening? Was he planning not to make love to her as she'd imagined, but to send her packing and bid her farewell, with the clothes purchased today no more than a lavish parting gift? She swallowed hard, wondering what she was to say and do under such circumstances, and how she would ever live with the disappointment.

But then he turned, and the way his face lit with pleasure when he saw her swept aside all her doubts, all her fears. She sank gracefully into a curtsey, her skirts crushing around her in a soft, silken pillow, and smiled up at him. It was a curtsey meant for the stage, not for Court—according to Rivers, smiling up at His Majesty would have been considered a terrible impropriety—but now she found, and charmed, her audience.

"My God, Lucia, but you're beautiful," Rivers said. He stepped forward and bent to raise her up, taking her by both her hands and keeping them. Without breaking his gaze from hers, he lifted one of her hands to his lips and kissed her open palm, and then the other.

"It's entirely the gown that you bought for me," she said, breathless from what he'd said and the touch of his lips on her palms and everything else about being here alone with him. "You're dazzled by the scarlet silk."

"I'm dazzled by the woman inside the silk," he said, more solemnly than she'd expected. "You are more dazzling than the stars and the moon in the sky."

She was thankful for the half-light that would hide how she blushed. She still was not accustomed to compliments from him, nor to the great rush of pleasure that she felt when he gave them. Compliments were not idle, empty things with him, the way they were with most men, who saw them only as a means toward a kiss or other favor. To Rivers a compliment was purest truth, or not said aloud, and to hear him speak such things of her was glorious indeed.

"Such fancies, Rivers," she said shyly, betraying her blush even if he couldn't see it. "The stars *and* the moon?"

"Every one of them," he said. "Come, and I'll show you."

Still holding her hands, he began to lead her from the room. He meant to take her upstairs already, to his bed, without supper or any other preliminary. There could be no other explanation. Though she'd thought she was eager for that, she hung back, suddenly uneasy, or perhaps only disappointed. She'd thought Rivers would be different from other men, and take his time to win her. She'd thought he would woo her, enchant her, seduce her in every sense of the word.

"I—I thought we were to dine," she said hesitantly, unable to say what she was thinking. "That is why I am dressed like this, yes?"

He frowned, confused. "Of course we shall dine," he said. "I would never deprive you of a meal, Lucia."

Under any other circumstances, his literal answer would have made her laugh, but not now.

"But when you said you'd show me the stars . . ." she began, faltering.

"When I said it, that was exactly what I intended," he said firmly. "This morning you accused me of relying too much upon knowledge gleaned from books, and not enough from life itself. I wish to prove you wrong, Lucia. No, that's not right. Rather, I wish to *show* you, so you may judge for yourself. Trust me. That is all I ask. Trust me, and see."

How could she not trust him after that?

She took a deep breath, her smile wobbly with emotion. "Then show me, Rivers," she said. "Show me."

CHAPTER
11

The stars and the moon.

It had sounded foolish the instant Rivers had spoken the words, and yet he could think of no other words that would have done the job any better. Lucia *was* more beautiful than all the heavens combined, and he'd every intention of showing her, too.

He'd left detailed orders for how everything should be arranged while they were away this afternoon in Newbury, and as soon as Lucia had gone off to dress, he'd gone racing upstairs to make sure those orders had been followed exactly as he'd intended. For the most part, they had, but he still had not been able to refrain from making a few adjustments, final changes here and there, to be certain that everything was perfect for her.

There was, of course, a certain risk involved in bringing Lucia up to his rooftop retreat. He'd never trusted any of his family with the secret of its existence, and the only other outsider who'd visited it—uninvited—had been the terrified milliner's apprentice, and with hysterical results, too. But he'd come to know Lucia well enough to feel certain she wouldn't behave as that wretched young woman had done, and besides, there was no lightning predicted for tonight's weather. Instead there was only a slip of a new moon in a midnight-blue sky, plus more stars than the eye could count, all of which he intended to offer to her.

He led her up the main staircase, past the first floor, and then up the smaller, twisting stairs that led to the roof. He noticed how her trepidation eased when they passed by his bedchamber, which chagrined him. Did she really believe he'd ravish her with such boorish haste?

Not that he didn't want to, of course. From the moment she'd appeared in that red dress, he'd been thinking of nothing else, even as he'd asked her to trust him. How the devil was he supposed to trust himself when she looked as fiery as the silk itself, her small, delectable figure barely contained by her tightly laced stays and her breasts thrust upward into his face without her usual kerchief for modesty's sake? Really, as a man, how was he to contend with that—except in the most obvious way?

It was taking all his effort to keep his gaze on her face. Later, he told himself sternly, later, after he'd proved to her—and to himself—that he deserved that trust, and her with it.

He paused at the top of the twisting stairs, his hand on the latch of the arched door. He prayed he was doing the right thing by bringing her here, and he hoped she didn't think he was a madman, the kind of eccentric that belonged in Bedlam.

"Go on, Rivers," she urged, her eyes wide with curiosity. "You cannot stop here. You've made such a great, precious secret of this that I'm guessing all kinds of things lie on the other side of that door. Perhaps you keep a menagerie, with wild beasts like the tiger that devoured poor Mr. Willow, or—"

"There's no tiger," he said quickly. "I can promise you that."

She smiled up at him in a way that squeezed his heart. "I didn't really believe there was."

"I've never brought anyone else here, Lucia, not even my brothers," he said. "You'll be the first."

Her smile softened, for she recognized the significance of that. If he'd come to know her over these last weeks, then she'd done the same with him, knowing now how important his brothers were to him.

"Then I'm honored, Rivers," she said, "whatever it may be that you've squirreled away behind this door."

He felt like an ass for dragging this out so long, and instead of making things any more ridiculous, he threw open the door and stepped aside to let her pass first.

She pulled her skirts to one side and slipped through the narrow doorway, and stopped still, pressing her palms over her mouth in wonder.

It was exactly the response he'd hoped to have from her. He'd been coming here for years, even before the Lodge had been his, yet he still felt that same sense of wonder and awe each time he stepped through the door.

They were standing on the flat roof of the Lodge, far above the rest of the county. The house stood on a slight rise, and with no trees immediately around it, the unimpeded view was sweeping and vast. By day, he could see most of the county from here, and to the west, when the sun was setting, the golden marble of Breconridge Hall, his family's grand country house, gleamed like a polished trophy in the far distance. On a clear night, as it was now, the sky was limitless, an overarching canopy of deep blue velvet scattered with stars.

But as breathtaking as the view was, that wasn't all that made the Lodge's roof so special to him. Over the years, Rivers had transformed the roof into his most private space, and when the weather permitted, it served as an outdoor room. There was a large telescope that he used to study the sky, plus a sextant and a compass for more calculations, and baskets filled with books and journals in which he recorded his observations.

A canvas canopy was slung between the towering square chimneys, shielding the Spartan space that was made more comfortable with a bright Turkish carpet, a desk, an oversized armchair, and a folding camp-bed with another small bed beneath it for Spot (who had, for this night, been banished below into Rooke's keeping). Everything, in fact, had been made along the lines of a military officer's kit, and could be quickly taken down and packed away by the servants into the heavy, weather-proof chests that remained on the roof year-round.

But on this summer evening, the outdoor room had been dressed for entertaining. Beneath the shelter of the canopy, a small dining table had been brought upstairs and was elegantly set with fine linens and gold-edged French porcelain. Red and white roses from the garden were arranged in a crystal bowl, flanked by small lanterns that protected the candles within from the breeze. Two chairs were set beside each other at the table, each cushioned with bright silken pillows, while more pillows were strewn across the bed, giving the space the exotic feel of a sultan's tent.

"Oh, Rivers, this is—this is *perfect,*" she said, gazing around with unabashed pleasure as she walked slowly across the roof to the stone parapets. "I feel like a most fortunate bird with a perch on the tallest of trees."

He laughed, both from relief and delight in her reaction. "It rather is like that," he said. "This is my favorite place on earth, and I suppose in the heavens, too."

"We *are* in the heavens," she said, resting her hands on the carved stone rail. "From here I can see the rose garden, and your mother's wildflowers, and in the distance is the lake. All the times we've walked below, and I never once knew any of this was here."

"You wouldn't," he said, joining her. "Because of the lines of the roof and the parapets, no one on the ground can see any of this. It is completely open, yet completely enclosed as well."

"So it is your own private aerie," she marveled. "No wonder you have kept it your secret. If I'd created such a magic place, I wouldn't share it with anyone else, either."

He'd told her earlier that she was beautiful, but that was nothing to how she looked now in the moonlight, with the warm summer breeze tossing the tiny loose wisps of hair against her forehead and along the nape of her neck. He knew that her formally arranged hair, tortured and pinned into place, was all the fashion, but it was the disarray that he found far more beguiling, how her heavy locks were already beginning to rebel and slip free of the pins.

It was the same with her gown. He much preferred it now with the red silk fluttering about her legs than when it had been static and flawless. He always thought of her as being constantly in motion, of darting here and there and twisting and turning with unconscious grace, and he supposed that was how he liked her dress to be as well.

She turned now to look over her shoulder at him, her expression expectant, and he realized he'd been staring at her too long instead of answering.

"I didn't create this place," he said, somehow managing to recall the thread of their conversation. "The roof has always been open like this. Stag-hunting was the fashion when the Lodge was first built, back in the days of Queen Bess, and those who chose not to ride to the hunt could still watch its progress from here on the roof. Then later, when the huntsmen returned, there would be banquets and dancing held here as well. My father claims that that's the reason for the size of these stone parapets, to keep the guests who were deep in their cups from toppling from the roof."

She peered over the rail as if imagining some luckless reveler lying broken on the ground below.

"Dancing and drinking and mad from hunting," she mused. "At least one of them must have gone over the side. Have you ever had a ghost for company?"

"Not one, Lucia," he said. "If a guest had died with such violence, then it would be remembered, even after a hundred and seventy years. It would have been an unforgettable tragedy."

"I suppose so," she admitted. "But it could have been purposefully forgotten, to hide a scandal. There *could* be a ghost here even now."

Abruptly she drew herself up, holding her arms out as if beseeching some phantom specter as she began to quote from *Hamlet,* her voice ringing out over the railing and into the night.

> *"What art thou that usurp'st this time of night,*
> *Together with that fair and warlike form*
> *In which the majesty of buried Denmark*
> *Did sometimes march? by Heaven I charge thee,*
>   *speak!"*

He laughed. Now that she knew the play so well, she often did this, hauling scraps of dialogue out of context to amuse him. It did, too, even as it impressed him to see just how far she'd come as an actress, and he thought again of the upcoming audition he'd arranged for her with McGraw. That first raw magic that he'd glimpsed on the street before his house still remained, but even these impromptu recitations—exaggerated for effect— showed how she'd learned to command both her lines and an audience, and he dared anyone to look away from her when she was speaking a part.

"Pray deliver me from the ghost of Hamlet's father," he said, chuckling. This was one of the best parts of being with her, laughing together over some bit of shared foolishness. "That's not the company I wish to keep, any more than those are your lines to learn."

"Well, no," she said, laughing with him as she slipped back into herself. "You've told me that boys played women's roles in Master Shakespeare's time, but I don't believe it would work the other way around."

He snorted, thinking how no matter how much of an actress she became, there would never be a way to mistake her for a male. "Nor do I believe that Horatio would ever present himself before the castle in red silk. Whatever would Prince Hamlet say?"

"But since Horatio is the only major character to survive the entire play, he can likely dress himself however he pleases." Her laughter fading, she turned away from the rail, and rubbed her bare forearms below the flounces. "I'd no notion we'd be out-of-doors, or I would have brought a shawl with me."

"Forgive me." Swiftly he began to pull his arms free of his sleeves. To him the air was agreeably warm, but ladies did feel things differently, and he regretted not thinking of that before. "Here, take my coat."

"No, no, that's not necessary," she said, gliding away from him and his offered coat to the camp-bed. She shook out one of the light wool coverlets that was folded at the foot of the bed and wrapped it over her shoulders. "There now. Mrs. Currie would be horrified, but I'll be quite snug."

He was sorry to see the red gown hidden, yet also relieved that the temptation it offered was now out of sight.

"I can send for Sally to fetch a proper shawl for you if you wish," he said, following her across the roof. "They'll begin bringing up dinner anyway as soon as I ring for it."

"I'm not hungry yet," she said, perplexed as she looked down at the pillow-strewn bed. "I thought this was a settee, but it's—do you *sleep* here, Rivers?"

"On a night as warm as this one, I might, yes," he said.

Her confusion was understandable, for the bed was not neatly made up like more ordinary beds meant for rest. Instead he'd made this one a respite for inspiration, indulgently piled with striped silk Turkish pillows and soft wool coverlets and bright silk quilts, all on an embroidered blue velvet counterpane. "But mainly I lie upon it and gaze up at the sky. By day I watch the clouds, and by night the stars, and let my thoughts wander where they will."

As soon as he'd spoken, he realized what an astonishing confession that was for him to make. An English gentleman was supposed to proceed through life with purpose and forethought, and not while away his hours and thoughts lying on his back and staring idly up into nothingness. He had wanted to share the roof with Lucia, but perhaps he'd shared too much.

"That is, I read whilst I am here," he said, hedging. "I consider it my outdoor library."

She smiled, her arms folded inside the coverlet. "Liar," she said softly. "You know it, too."

He shook his head doggedly. "I'm not lying. I do read here."

"I'm sure you do, Rivers, because you read *everywhere,* but that's not why you brought me up to this rooftop," she said. "Earlier you said that you wanted to prove to me that you didn't live through your books. Yet here, now, when the proof is all around us, you're denying it."

He made a low grumbling sound deep in his throat, feeling completely abandoned by the words that were usually his facile friends. Why was it now, when he'd so much he longed to tell her, he could say nothing?

She, however, didn't seem disturbed in the least. She tipped her head, gazing up at the gauzy wisps of clouds drifting over the silver moon.

"In our Whitechapel lodgings, I'd always take the outside place in the bed," she began, her throat pearly pale and vulnerable in the moonlight. "Three of us shared the bed, you know, and being on the outside isn't as warm as taking the middle or the wall, but from there, if I lay on my side, I could see the sky from the little window up near the eaves."

He nodded, letting her continue uninterrupted. He hated the thought of her living in such a place, yet she had simply accepted it as her lot, no doubt the way countless other young women in her situation were forced to do. But she wasn't one of them: she was special, and he would make sure that she'd never go back to that kind of life again.

"It was only a little scrap of sky," she was saying, "squeezed by roofs and chimney pots, but I still could see the stars. On some nights, I'd even see the moon glide by, and I'd think of all the great places and grand folk that same moon had smiled upon. It made me forget what had happened during the day, and gave me the freedom to dream."

"That's it exactly," he said, though he was looking at her, not at the stars. "The same moon, those same stars, shone on Cleopatra and Marc Antony, on Eloise and Abelard, on Petrach and Laura."

She glanced at him uncertainly. "Cleopatra I know, but not the others. Are they all grand folk, too?"

"In their way." He didn't want to explain that they'd all been famous lovers; not because he was reluctant to mention lovers, but because tonight he didn't want her to think of him as her tutor, endlessly explaining what she did not know. "But I've always thought that of the moon as well."

She smiled wistfully. "From now on, whenever I see the moon, I'll think of it shining down on you."

He didn't want to be reminded of a future without her in it. "But tonight that moon is shining on us together."

"Yes," she said softly, a single word, then turned away from him.

He wondered if she felt the same sadness about their future, or more accurately, their lack of a future together. He almost hoped she did, even as he could not think of what to say to ease her regrets, or his own—especially as that faceless specter of the bland, proper young lady who would one day be his wife rose, unbidden and unwelcome, in his thoughts, only to be quickly banished.

"Can you see the stars better with your spyglass?" asked Lucia, fortunately unaware of his thoughts. She ran the fingers of one hand lightly along the telescope, a large and costly instrument of mahogany and polished brass that he kept here on its tripod stand, pointed to the heavens.

"It's not a spyglass," he said. "It's a telescope."

She nodded solemnly, the way she did when she'd learned some new piece of information and was storing it away. Ordinarily it pleased him to see her learn something new like this, but now he winced inwardly, realizing too late that he must be lecturing once again.

"A telescope, then," she said, looking down at her reflection distorted on the polished brass tube. "What is the difference between the two?"

He barely refrained from a discourse on the variety of lenses, of curvatures and spherical and chromatic aberrations and corrections.

"Spyglasses are used at sea by mariners to plot their voyages and adventures," he said instead. "Telescopes are employed by astronomers and other learned gentlemen in their studies and observations."

She glanced up, and smiled wryly. "I need not ask which you are."

"You might be wrong." He stepped closer to stand with the telescope between them. "When I am here, Lucia, I can imagine whatever I please, with the stars I see through this as inspiration. My thoughts can take me on adventures that no sailor in his right mind would dare ever choose."

"Will you show them to me, too?" She gazed up at him, her eyes brighter with excitement than any of the stars above. "The way you promised?"

"Of course." Quickly he unscrewed the brass dust cap that protected the lens, made several small adjustments, and turned the telescope toward her.

"Place one eye to this place, here, shut the other one," he said, guiding her to stand behind the eyepiece. "Now with your hand here, slowly turn this and scan the sky until you find a star."

She did as he'd said, letting the coverlet fall from her shoulders. She shoved her hair impatiently back from her face as she concentrated and peered through the telescope.

"You needn't hold your breath," he said. "The sky is filled with—"

"Oh, Rivers, I found one!" she cried. "Oh, and it's so blessed beautiful I can't bear it, so pure and white. Look, Rivers, see it there, brighter than a hundred silver spangles all together. No, a *thousand* spangles!"

She stepped aside for him to look, unable to keep from hopping up and down with excitement. "Can you see it, Rivers? Can you?"

"I couldn't miss it, could I?" he said, sharing her excitement. "That one's not really a star, but a planet, one of the brightest in the entire sky. Most appropriately, it's the planet Venus."

"Venus?" she repeated, smiling, and clearly not sure whether to believe him or not.

"Venus," he said firmly. "I would not toy with the heavens."

"Let me see it again," she begged, squeezing in between him and the telescope. It was natural enough for him to put his arms around her waist, and natural, too, to pull her close against his chest, her body fitting neatly against his.

"Can you see it now?" he asked, his lips close to her ear.

"Oh, yes," she said, her voice dropping to a husky whisper. "That star's so beautiful, Rivers. I know it's still so far, far away from us, yet looking at it this way, I feel as if I could reach up and pluck it from the sky."

"If I could do that, Lucia, then I would," he said. She was so small and feminine in his arms, and he felt the warmth of her skin through the red silk, felt the vibrancy that was always in her. "I'd claim that star for you to have so you'd never forget this night."

Swiftly she turned around to face him, still within the circle of his arms.

"But I won't forget it, star or not," she said wistfully. "Because I won't forget you, Rivers, not ever."

"Lucia," he said softly, brushing those tossing curls away from her face. He could have lost himself in those luminous dark eyes, even before he'd had a chance to kiss her again. Instead all he did was lose what he'd meant to say next, and in his muddle he fell back on more lines from the play—lines that were nearly appropriate, because they'd been said by Hamlet to Ophelia, but not quite, since they were being repeated as a mark of the Danish prince's careless seduction.

> *"Doubt thou the stars are fire,*
> *Doubt that the sun doth move,*
> *Doubt truth to be a liar,*
> *But never doubt I love."*

There, he'd said that he loved her, even if it came by way of Hamlet. And he *did* love her, loved her in a way that he'd never loved any other woman.

She caught her breath, drawing back. "Do not taunt me like that, Rivers. I—I cannot bear it, not from you."

"It wasn't intended as taunting," he said, surprised by her reaction. "Not at all."

Her eyes swam with unshed tears, and her slender throat convulsed with emotion. "Then don't say it as wretched, faithless Prince Hamlet, for I've no intention of falling from a tree and drowning myself. Say it for yourself."

"I love you, Lucia," he said, the words so simple and yet meaning so much. "I love you."

"You are certain?" she asked, her voice no more than a breathless, broken whisper. "That you love me?"

"Never more certain of anything in my life," he said firmly, not wanting to leave any doubt. "I love you, Lucia."

She tried to smile as a single tear escaped to slide down her cheek and along her jaw. "And I love you, Rivers, I'm daft, I'm mad, I'm a fool to speak such a thing aloud, but—"

"You're not," he said. "Not at all."

Before she could speak again, he tipped her back into the crook of his arm and kissed her, a kiss blistering with all the passion he'd been keeping bottled up within himself for these last weeks. He had his answer. He loved her, yes, but better, infinitely better, to learn that she loved him. It was all that mattered to him now, and all he'd left to do was to show her how much she meant to him, and how much he wanted her.

But with that handful of words, she was his now. Her full, ripe mouth was his to kiss and taste and relish as much as he wanted. Her round, full breasts would finally fill his hands as he'd so often imagined, her lithe legs would part for him, her body would rejoice with his as they truly made the love they'd just declared.

He couldn't mistake her hunger as she kissed him, her

little tongue darting against his as she made small happy moans of excitement that he felt rather than heard, vibrating between their mouths. Her hands were everywhere, blindly sliding under his coat and waistcoat and up along his back to his shoulders and down again over his spine, as if striving to learn every bit of his body.

It excited him, knowing her desire matched his. What little restraint he still possessed was rapidly fraying as she began to open the long row of buttons on his waistcoat, her fingers brushing against his chest. Impatiently he growled, and brushed one of her hands aside and cupped her breast, her flesh warm above the scarlet silk. Deftly he pulled the already-low neckline down farther, freeing both her breasts from the stiff boning of her stays, and immediately her nipples tightened against his palms. She shuddered, arching into his caress with a hissing small sigh of pleasure, and he kissed her again with unapologetic hunger, marking her as his.

He had to get her to the bed, only a few steps away. His thoughts had narrowed to one goal, desire pounding through his blood and more especially in his cock. She was so small that it was nothing for him to sweep her from her feet and into his arms and across the carpet.

But before he could set her down again, she had wriggled free of his embrace, stronger than he'd guessed. Now she was backing away, determined to separate herself from him. She stopped just out of his reach, tantalizing him, her lips parted and swollen from his kisses, her eyes wild. Although she pulled her shift back over her breasts, her aroused nipples showed through the thin linen in a way that was almost more enticing than if they'd still been bared.

"What the devil?" he asked roughly, stunned. She could not change her mind, not now, not after they'd come this far, yet the gentleman that he'd been bred to be knew that he could not force her against her will. "Lucia, please, you can't mean—"

"Are you certain no one can see us from here?" she asked breathlessly, tossing her hair back from her forehead. "Are you sure of it?"

"It's impossible," he said, breathing hard. "No one can, and no one will."

"Very well." She raised her chin, almost defiantly, and yanked the carefully arranged pins from her hair. She raked her fingers through the heavy waves, breaking the stiffened curls that Sally had labored so to create, and shook her now-freed hair back over her shoulders like a wild, tousled mane.

"I love you, Rivers," she said, her voice shaking, "and *will* love you, here, with only the heavens as witness. But I'll come to you without shame, without artifice, without acting, without these fine things that you've bought me."

"There's no shame between us," he said firmly. "Whatever I've bought for you was meant as a gift, not an obligation."

"That's not what I mean, Rivers." She pulled the pins that closed her bodice from the silk and shoved the gown from her shoulders, leaving her standing before him in her stays, shift, and petticoats.

"Lucia, please." He reached out his hand to her and she backed away, shaking her head.

She kicked off her slippers as she quickly untied the knot on her petticoats and her hoops as well. She let them fall around her ankles and stepped free in her stockinged feet, her gaze never leaving Rivers's face. Finally she reached behind her and undid the knot that closed her stays, pulling apart the lacings until she could work the stays over her head and cast them aside as well.

In silence, she now stood shamelessly, even proudly, before him in only her shift and stockings, her head held high and her hair streaming behind her. Her breathing was rapid from both the exertion of undressing and, as he watched her breasts rise and fall, excitement as well. Her knee-length linen shift was so fine as to be nearly translucent, with the dark triangle of hair at the top of her thighs a shadowy temptation. There in the moonlight, she'd never been more beautiful to him, nor more desirable.

Yet still she purposefully stayed out of his reach, and something about her expression warned him not to cross the invisible barrier she'd put up between them.

"Love me as I am, Rivers," she said, her voice raw with emotion. "Here, now. Love me and want me as Lucia Maria di Rossi, and nothing else."

He nodded, accepting, and understanding, too. He thought of how she'd worried that she'd lose herself through acting, that somehow the Mrs. Willow that they'd created together had come to mean more to him than she herself. She was wrong, achingly wrong, but words alone wouldn't prove it to her.

She'd said she wished to come to him free of any artifice, and she could not have chosen a braver way to make her point, standing here before him in only her shift. If this was some kind of challenge, some kind of dare to prove he truly loved her, then by God he would match it. He would not fail her now.

With his gaze still locked with hers, he pulled his arms from his coat and tossed it aside, followed in rapid succession by his waistcoat, his neck cloth and shirt, his buckled shoes and stockings. All that was left now was his breeches. He liked the feel of the warm evening breeze across his bare skin, the freedom of it shared with her. In all the times he'd come here, he'd never once stood on the roof this close to naked; perhaps all this time he'd been waiting to share the experience with Lucia. She'd asked him to feel, not to think, and there couldn't be anything less intellectual than standing bare-chested here beneath the moon.

Briefly her gaze flicked downward, over that bare chest to the undeniable bulge in his breeches. She didn't regard him with the coy appraisal that her cousin would have shown, but rather looked with unabashed interest, with eagerness, with desire, which only made his cock swell harder still.

"I'll take you as you are, Lucia." He raised his voice to proclaim to the world, not caring who heard him so long as she did. "I'll take you if you'll do the same, and take me as you see me. Forget everything else, and take me only as a man. Your man tonight, Lucia, if you'll have me."

She didn't answer, and for an appallingly long moment he wondered if he'd misread her. Then she swept her hair back over one shoulder, lowering her chin and granting him the merest beginning of a smile, and he knew he hadn't.

"You know I will," she said softly. "Now untie your hair."

"My hair," he repeated, mystified. He wore his hair in a tidy queue, the way most gentlemen did, wrapped and tied with black ribbon by Rooke each morning; he was never seen without it. He'd be more comfortable without his shirt than with his hair untied, but if she wished it that way, then he'd do it. He reached up to the back of his neck and fumbled with the knot, silently cursing Rooke for being so thorough. Finally he undid the ribbon and raked his fingers through his hair.

"There," he said. "Is that what you wished?"

"It *is*," she said, her voice husky. "Your hair is like a mane of gold. *Il mio grande leone d'oro!* You *are* like a great golden lion, the fiercest, bravest king of all the wild beasts."

He smiled, thinking of how this was odd and yet how

very Lucia, and ridiculously arousing, too. Because of her, he did feel like a wild beast, barely able to keep himself in check. "If I am a lion, does that make you my lioness?"

She didn't answer, but reached down and seized the hem of her shift, and in one swift motion swept it over her head, leaving her only in her stockings and garters. With her body bathed in moonlight, she was more beautiful, more perfect, more enticing than he'd ever imagined.

She'd tormented him long enough. She might not be able to dance, but she certainly was a devilishly seductive Di Rossi, through and through. He tore away the buttons on his fall and shoved his breeches down and kicked them aside. Two could play this game—it was, in fact, much better if two did—and he was glad to see how her eyes widened at the sight of how flagrantly hard she'd made him.

This time when he lifted her from her feet and caught her in his arms, she didn't struggle, but instead melted against him with a willingness that inflamed him further. To have her naked against him like this, her velvety skin impossibly soft and as heated as his own, sharpened his lust even more.

Swiftly he carried her to the bed, and with one arm shoved aside the pillows. Not bothering to turn back the counterpane, he dropped her onto the bed. She stretched sensually with her dark hair fanned around her face, her body ivory-pale against the dark blue, and obviously delighting in the feel of the silk velvet beneath her. She smiled up at him, her eyes heavy-lidded and her white teeth pressing lightly into her lower lip, and held her arms up to him.

He lay beside her, and instantly rolled on top of her, kissing her hungrily. Mindful of how much larger he was than she, he braced most of his weight on his arms, but let himself glory in the feel of her body against his, how her breasts crushed softly against his chest and how at once she'd parted her legs for him to settle more comfortably between them. She'd called him her lion, and it was taking all his willpower not to ravage and devour her.

He slipped down to find one of her breasts, her nipples already hard from the evening air and from arousal. Her breasts enchanted him, not large in size, yet irresistibly lush to touch. Gently he sucked on the tender flesh, laving and teasing the tight little berry with his tongue, and she murmured wordless sounds of rising excitement as she arched wantonly beneath him, clearly wanting more.

Her hands roamed freely across his back, from his shoulders to his buttocks and back again. He suckled harder on her breast, grazing the nipple with the edges of his teeth, and in response she purred against his shoulder. Her fingers dug into his upper back, her nails sharp enough to make him grunt.

"Wicked," he growled, coming up to kiss her again, and she chuckled into his mouth. Why in blazes had he waited so long, he wondered as he delved deep into the wet sweetness of her kiss. What possible, ridiculous scruple could have been worth them waiting for this?

Her legs were shifting restlessly beneath him, rubbing against his cock to tantalize him, and driving him past the point of restraint. His blood was pounding in his ears, driving him on, and he breathed deep of the heady scent of her arousal. He reached down between her parted legs and stroked her lightly and she tensed and arched against him, her hips bobbing in the air and wordlessly begging for more. He understood that tension, because he was feeling it, too, where the fever of desire made even the slightest caress almost unbearable. His cock was heavy and engorged with it. Yet she was soft where he was hard, her sex wet and swollen against his hand and her honey-sweet juices slick on his fingers—enough to drive him mad with lust.

Easing his finger between her nether lips, he rubbed and pressed the little bud at the top of her opening to build her need. She was moaning now in rhythm with his strokes, and he loved how she wasn't shy about the primal sounds she made, without any missishness. He dipped lower, deeper, easing a single finger within her to press deeply into her slick passage and tease her from within. In turn she clenched tight around his finger even as her nails clawed over his back at the delicious intrusion, even as her hips rose greedily to seek more.

"Shush, shush," he whispered hoarsely. "My wild little lioness. You're so hot, you'll scorch me."

She was panting now in breathy little catches, and she clutched at his shoulders as if she'd never let go. Her body was taut and feverish against him, and even in the moonlight he could see the flush that stained her cheeks and chest.

He pushed his finger deeper, curling against the front of her passage, and she rewarded him with a soft cry that nearly undid him. She was so tight, so small, so hot that all he could think of was how much he wanted to bury himself deep inside her.

"Please, Rivers," Lucia begged in a ragged whisper. "Oh, please, *please.*"

And yet as she writhed beneath him, Lucia was too overwhelmed to be certain what it was she begged for. For more of the unbelievable pleasure he was drawing from her body, for more of the intimacy that came with his touch, for more of this passion: oh, yes, she wanted more of all that. But she sensed there was more than that, an intangible, glorious *more* that was maddeningly just beyond her reach.

"Please, Rivers," she gasped again, her breath tight in her chest and her entire body on edge.

"Yes," he said, as if he'd been waiting to grant her wish. His face was strained with concentration as he shifted over her, settling between her legs, and impatiently he shook his untied hair back from his face. With his palms on her knees, he pushed her legs apart to open her farther. He stroked her again, and she shuddered and arched against him, seeking more of his marvelous touch.

But this time it wasn't his finger pushing into her, but something blunter and larger, much larger. She looked down between her knees and saw his cock in his hand, so much larger and more rigid than it had appeared earlier, with the head an angry purple-red. She could not possibly take such a thing into her body, and frantically she tried to pull back and away, up against the mounded pillows.

"You're so small," he said, gritting his teeth as he stated the obvious, and she whimpered with agreement. He drew back and wetted the head of his cock with his spittle to ease his way. He held her steady and lodged the head between her lips, and flexed his hips. He pushed, and pushed again. He was stretching her wide and it hurt, forcing her to accommodate him in a way she'd never imagined.

"Relax, Lucia," he said. "Be easy, love, and let me in."

She wasn't relaxed. She was holding her breath, every muscle tense, and trembling from the effort.

"Here," he said, hooking his arms beneath her knees. "That should help."

He nipped the inside of her knee, right above her garter, and stupidly she focused on how the red silk ribbon had come untied, the crumpled end trailing along the side of her leg.

He pushed again, and again, relentlessly making way until suddenly he was buried deep inside her, their bodies touching. He paused, breathing hard. She gasped at the unfamiliar pressure and the fullness of him inside her, and yet the first sharp pain was already fading. It was curious to hold him like this inside her and feel him pulsing within her passage. She'd feared she could not accommodate him, and yet it seemed somehow they were exactly the right size for each other. She'd always heard how a man possessed a woman, but she felt as if she'd possessed him instead, taking him so intimately deep inside her body.

Above her his handsome face sheened with sweat as he leaned down to kiss her, and once again he began to move his hips, slowly pulling back and then shoving into her again.

She liked having the fullness of him inside her, of how he could stroke her even more deeply with his shaft than with his finger. Instinctively she began to move with him, rocking her hips to meet his, and the tension she'd felt before began to return, coiling deep in her belly.

"Damnation, Lucia, but you're good," he growled, his head bowed over hers and his eyes squeezed shut. "I should go slower, but I can't stop, you're that good."

"I don't want you to stop," she whispered, her hands roaming along the length of his back. "*This* is what I want, Rivers."

"Then you'll have all of it, love." He released her knees, and she curled her legs over his back to take him deeper, giving an extra wriggle to her hips as she did. He swore some sort of dark, muddled oath, and kissed her again.

"I won't last much longer if you keep doing that," he said raggedly. "Are you close?"

She wasn't sure what he meant. They were as close as two people could be, joined together as they were, and instead of answering she kissed him again.

He was moving more forcefully now, his breathing harsh and his expression fixed. He thrust with a determined purpose and power that sent waves of sensation rippling through her, clear to the soles of her feet, and she felt her belly grow unbearably tight around him.

She struggled to breathe, her heart drumming in her ears. He lifted himself slightly and stroked her again where they were joined, relentless. She was so sensitive there that she cried out, but he did not back away, and in a rush she felt all the tension crash apart, convulsing around him in breaking waves that were so sublime she cried out again with the wonder and joy of it.

Rivers continued to drive into her, his thrusts frenzied with urgency and so hard that he shoved her across the bed. As her own pleasure began to subside, she watched him find his, contracting and jerking with the power of it, and his guttural shout when he spent truly was worthy of the lion she'd called him. Gasping, he collapsed over her, and let the last shudders vibrate between them.

As he lay against her shoulder, she held him close, not wanting to let him go. She was grateful that he was silent. Words would spoil everything, because no words could say enough. Exhausted, she was limp and spent and filled with contentment, and she felt closer to him than she'd ever felt to anyone. She had no regrets, none. He was hers for now, and she was his. No wonder she wished the moment would never end.

And it had been magic, she thought, pure, perfect magic, and as she gazed up into the sky overhead, she saw all the stars that he'd promised her.

CHAPTER
12

∾

It was, Rivers decided, the best sex he'd ever had in his life.

He lay with his cheek pillowed on Lucia's breast, which was likely the best place he'd ever laid it. In fact, everything at this moment was about the best in his entire life. He was agreeably exhausted and drowsy and supremely content, lying inside the body and in the arms of a woman he loved, beneath a cloudless summer sky. How, really, could anything be improved?

"Love you, Lucia," he mumbled into her hair, as many words as he could muster. "Love you."

"I love you, too," she whispered, sweetly, as if a secret meant for his ears alone, and he smiled. How could he not love her?

With a sigh, she struggled to shift beneath him. Of course, he must be a weighty, thoughtless, male lump, crushing her as he was, and with a grunt of regret he withdrew and rolled over on his back. He pulled her with him so that she'd curl beside him, her head nestled in the crook of his arm and her warm little body against his. Fondly he kissed her forehead, and thought of how well she fit with him.

"Oh!" she said, that small, familiar sound of uncomfortable distress that women often made under these circumstances. He understood. Usually he'd offer a convenient handkerchief to swab away the sticky embarrassment of their spendings, and the distress would be resolved.

But his handkerchief was well out of reach, being elsewhere on the roof, with his coat and breeches. He considered himself to be gallant and all, but right now he felt so bonelessly relaxed that the thought of having to leave her and the bed to fumble about for a handkerchief seemed beyond his ability. Fortunately Lucia seemed to feel the same, saying nothing further. He kissed her again, and let himself drift back into that charmed, hazy state of nonthinking bliss.

But the bliss was soon to be shattered, and nonthinking with it. In fact he was going to be forced to think quite a bit, whether he wanted to or not.

"Forgive me, Rivers," Lucia said, her voice filled with dismay. "But I fear I've—I've ruined your counterpane."

"Oh, I doubt it," he said, unconcerned. "I'm sure the laundress can cope with whatever we've left."

"It wasn't you, Rivers," she said, her dismay shifting to mortification. She disentangled herself from Rivers and slipped from the bed. "It was me. On silk *velvet.*"

Missing her already, Rivers sighed again and reluctantly rolled on his side to survey the damage that so disturbed her.

She was standing beside the bed, her hands pressed to her mouth. As far as he was concerned, there was no reason to feel any shame, not over something as inevitable as a wet place on the bed.

Then he looked lower. Her thighs were daubed with blood, with more on the counterpane. Quickly he looked down at his shaft, and saw that he hadn't escaped, either.

He took a deep breath, reminding himself once again that these things happened.

"It's nothing to fuss over, Lucia," he said. "Unfortunate, yes, to happen now, but I understand that a woman's monthly—"

"It's not from that." She raised her chin, bravely striving to rise above her dismay even as she flushed. "This was my first time, Rivers, and I—"

"You were a maid?" he blurted out in disbelief. "A virgin?"

The stain to her cheeks deepened as she nodded.

"A virgin." Abruptly he sat upright, swinging his legs over the side of the bed, and pulled one edge of the counterpane over his cock. He wasn't ordinarily so modest, but under the circumstances, his naked parts didn't seem appropriate. "Damnation, Lucia, why didn't you tell me?"

"Because I didn't." She grabbed another of the coverlets from the end of the bed and wrapped it around herself. "Would you have believed me if I had?"

He took another deep breath, fighting the uncomfortable realization that she was right. Most likely he wouldn't have believed her. She was a Di Rossi, and Di Rossis weren't virgins, at least not at her age. He'd known that she wasn't promiscuous, that she didn't have any protectors or admirers, but he'd assumed that somewhere, at some time, she'd had at least one lover.

"You still should have told me," he insisted, not answering her question, to avoid wounding her further. "Had I known, I would have, ah, done things differently."

Disappointment flickered across her eyes.

"And that is why I didn't tell you, my lord," she said, biting out each word with bitterness. "Because I have no regrets at all, and I would not have changed a single thing. Not *one*."

"Lucia, please," he began, hating how she'd begun using his title again. The last thing he wanted to do was hurt her, and yet it seemed with every word he was doing exactly that.

"No," she said firmly, in the same tone that she used when Spot misbehaved: a single word that was as sharp and definitive as a slammed door. "If you are done with me, my lord, I will return to my room."

"Don't leave," he said quickly, before she could do exactly that. "Please. Damnation, Lucia, that's not what either of us wants."

To his relief she didn't go, but her expression—wounded and guarded and trying to be neither—didn't change as she waited for him to say more. He'd no idea exactly what that should be, what to say to put things back to rights between them. Still, he had to say something, and so he said what came first to his head.

"I don't want you to go," he said. "Not at all. Instead I want you to stay here with me all the night through, and I want to watch the sun rise, there to the east, with you in my arms."

"Why?" she asked, the most direct and disarming question she could have asked.

"Because I love you," he said, the simplest answer, and the truest as well. "I love you, Lucia, and I want you to stay so I can tell you again and again until you listen and believe me."

Still her expression didn't change. She touched the cameo around her neck, rubbing it lightly between her thumb and forefinger, and then sighed. "I must wash."

"Behind that screen is a washstand," he said quickly, pointing across the roof to the other side of one of the chimneys. "There's water and soap and a chamber pot. Everything you could need."

At once she turned and headed to where he'd pointed, her long hair wafting behind her. He had wanted this night to be special, not the disaster it had turned into, and he'd only have a few minutes before she rejoined him to try to redeem it.

As soon as she'd gone behind the screen, he jumped from the bed. He wiped himself as clean as he could with the counterpane, then wadded it up and shoved it from sight beneath the bed, where she wouldn't be reminded of it, and neither would he. He retrieved his breeches and pulled them on, hopping across the floor in his haste, and threw his shirt on over his head. He turned again to the bed and smoothed the sheets as best he could, plumping the pillows and generally trying to make it look inviting and not like the scene of a ravishment.

A *virgin*. He'd no experience with virgins and maidenheads. None. What he'd interpreted to be a charming boldness on her part had really been innocent ignorance, and he cursed himself for not realizing it. That was what he'd meant about doing things differently. He still wouldn't have been able to resist taking her to his bed. But if he'd known it was her first time, he would have been much more gentle, more careful, instead of roaring ahead like the village bull in rut.

At least he knew he'd given her pleasure. There'd been no mistaking that. But he hoped she'd give him the chance to show her how he could make things even better for them both, and to really, truly make love to her.

He did love her. He'd meant it when he'd said it, and love wasn't something he took lightly. He wasn't one of those gentlemen who professed heartfelt love to every pretty face that crossed his path.

In fact he couldn't recall ever feeling as much in love with a woman as he was with Lucia, nor could he think of another woman whose company he enjoyed more. She made him laugh and she made him think, and she kept him guessing because he never quite knew what she'd say or do next. He liked her intelligence and her wit and her breasts, though the order of those likes could change depending on what she was wearing.

But most of all, she made him happy, which was why he'd already been trying to think of a way to continue seeing her once this time at the Lodge was done and they were back in London. He wasn't ready to give her up, especially after tonight.

If only her father had been an earl instead of some drunken Neapolitan dancer . . .

Would he find her as fascinating if she'd been born a lady? Would he still find her as beautiful, as seductive, as endlessly intriguing? What if she were that earl's daughter, the kind of suitable young woman who would earn his father's approval as a future wife?

But she wasn't, he argued firmly, turning back those questions with logic. Logic and reason said that the lessons in etiquette and speech could transform her into an actress, not a lady. Logic said that they were the gloss of appearances, not reality. Because if she truly were a lady and he'd just taken her maidenhead and ruined her, there'd be no question of what came next. He'd marry her, as soon as could be decently arranged.

Logic said—loudly—that a young woman from the theatrical world like Lucia wouldn't be considered ruined, and no one would be demanding a wedding. Instead he should offer to put her into keeping, with a small house, a servant or two, and an allowance. Even that would be considered generous of him.

That was the logical, intellectual argument, with the full force of reason to support it.

But when had logic anything to do with Lucia? He looked up at the stars, heartily wishing the evening were back at the beginning again.

"Rivers?"

Startled, he turned around quickly. He hadn't heard her come up behind him, her stockinged feet quiet on the carpet. She had replaced the coverlet with the silk dressing gown that he'd hung from a hook on the screen. The dressing gown was cut from an extravagant striped yellow silk and sized for him, and she'd tied it close to her body with the sash wrapped tight, twice around her narrow waist. Although the sleeves were still too long and the hem trailed behind her like a train, it was surprisingly becoming with her long, dark hair, and as sensuous as hell.

"Are you better now?" he asked, and immediately could have kicked himself for asking such an inane question. "That is, I trust you are, ah, recovering."

"Recovered, and restored." She smiled shyly, smoothing her hair behind her ears, and instantly the world seemed more back to rights. " *'The chariest maid is prodigal enough, / If she unmask her beauty to the moon.'* "

He frowned, not expecting her to quote the play now. "That's Ophelia, not you," he said. "I should hardly call you prodigal and extravagant, Lucia, even if you are beautiful by moonlight."

She gave a little shrug, unconsciously making the silk dressing gown slide farther from one shoulder. "Very well, then," she said. "I was unsettled."

"Entirely understandable, given the, ah, circumstances," he said, restlessly tapping his hand against one of the canopy posts. The oversized dressing gown kept gliding open at the neck, giving him a distracting glimpse of her naked body beneath it. Even after her sobering revelation, he still wanted her again, wanted her now.

"But the circumstances could not have been more splendid," she said wistfully. She looked around at the elegantly set but neglected table, where candles in two of the lanterns had already guttered out. "You went to such trouble for me."

"I could have gone to a great deal more," he said, his regret tinged with guilt. "Lucia, when I said I wished I'd known of your innocence so that I could have done things differently, I meant that, had I known, I could have shown more kindness toward you. I would have been more gentle, more—"

"You were exactly as I wanted you to be," she said, coming to stand in front of him. "I wanted to be as much a part of you as I could, Rivers, to join with you not just with our hearts, but in every way, and so I trusted you, and it was . . . it was magic. Oh, I know you must think that a foolish way to describe it, but that's how it was to me. Magic."

"I don't think you're a fool," he said. "I think you're entirely right. It was magic, the purest, most passionate magic of all."

"*Most* passionate magic," she repeated, clearly delighting in the phrase. "I didn't understand at first, but later, after you told me you wished to watch the sun rise with me, I did. I knew you wouldn't wish to undo what we'd done, not after you said that."

"Of course I wouldn't," he said. "Why should I wish to undo something I'll never forget?"

"Oh, Rivers," she said, dipping her chin and smiling with pleasure in a thoroughly disarming way. "But you see, that's why I didn't tell you I was still a maid, or even that you are the only man I've ever kissed."

"Ever?" he repeated, stunned, and aroused as well by the thought that he was the first man in her life.

"Ever," she said with unimpeachable finality. "But you are so noble and gentlemanly that I didn't want to risk having you refuse me if you knew."

He smiled ruefully. "I do not believe I'm half as noble as that, Lucia. Not with you."

"But you are," she insisted. She reached up to cradle his jaw against her palm, and he could have sworn there were tears in her eyes. "*Il mio caro, dolce, leone d'oro!*

You have given me so much already, and yet I wanted this, too. For this night, I wanted to be yours."

Gently he took her hand and turned it toward his lips so he could kiss her palm, then ran his lips down to the inside of her wrist, to where he felt her pulse quicken beneath his kiss.

"For this evening, and many more besides," he murmured. "Do you believe I'd be content with only tonight?"

Swiftly she turned her hand and covered his mouth.

"Don't say that," she said. "You mustn't. We cannot count on anything beyond this, here. Minute by minute, day by day. That is what we have together."

"And whatever fate and the stars decree," he said, repeating what she'd told him in the garden. "I haven't forgotten."

"Then you understand," she said, her voice husky yet achingly bittersweet with unshed tears. "Oh, Rivers, I did not intend to be so weak and weepy!"

"You're hardly that," he said. "You are so many things to me, but weak and weepy are not among them."

She shook her head and turned away from him, looking up at the sky, fighting both her emotions and the tears. He slipped his arm around her waist and drew her close, her back to his chest. It was warm and familiar, holding her like this, and with a sigh she leaned against him, resting her head against his shoulder.

"Would you like me to send for our supper?" he asked, hoping such a bland subject would help her to collect herself. "That is, if Mrs. Barber hasn't given us up completely by now."

"Hah, one more reason for her to fault me," Lucia said with a sigh. "But I find I'm not hungry just yet. Later, perhaps."

"Then what is your wish?" he said. "For this minute."

"*This* minute." She twisted, her face turned toward

his. She circled her arms around his waist and teasingly slipped her hands up inside his shirt to find the bare skin of his back. "I want to love you, Rivers, lie beside you and gaze up at the stars, and I want you to show me every one, and then the sunrise besides."

"Then you shall have it," he said, unwrapping the sash on the dressing gown as if he were unwrapping a gift. "All the stars, and Venus and Jupiter besides."

Ever since she'd been a child, Lucia had believed in magic. It wasn't the kind of petty magic that conjurers performed in the park, making coins appear from behind their ears. Instead it was a private, personal, and hazy definition of the word, an indefinable force that would come and somehow transform her life for the better. Through all the bad times and unhappy days—and she suffered through many of both she had steadfastly clung to this notion of magic, certain that it would come.

And in this balmy month of June, the magic had indeed come: first in the form of Rivers himself, whisking her away to the country, and then in the opportunity he'd offered her to become an actress, and finally, now, the love that they'd found together, a love that blazed hot and bright with the desire they'd discovered there on the roof of Breconridge Lodge.

Under the stars, the magic was everywhere.

They had spent the entire first night beneath the crescent moon, exactly as he'd promised, and they'd exhausted themselves making glorious, shameless love. Lying together with their arms and legs intimately tangled, they had watched the night sky fade beneath the morning star and the dawn turn the east a golden rose with the new day.

They had spent the next two days in each other's company, eating in the garden, walking in the woods and beside the lake, and in his bed and hers and always ending up in the one they shared on the roof. Not once did he fault her accent, nor did she accuse him of living too much in his books, and the only time that *Hamlet* was ever mentioned was in inappropriate passages quoted and chosen to make the other laugh.

That is, until the morning of the third day, when Rivers told her that they were expecting a visitor later that morning.

"A visitor," she repeated. They had awakened to a sky that was a dull pewter gray this morning, the air heavy and chill with a coming storm that would surely mark the end of their sunny June days. Sudden gusts of wind ruffled the tops of the trees and made the canopy overhead puff and blow like the sails of a ship. Yet still they lingered in their rooftop bed, snug beneath a pile of striped coverlets and unwilling to be driven into the house just yet. Lucia was lying lazily half-across Rivers, her breasts crushed against his chest and her chin resting on her folded hands, while he kept one arm possessively flung over her hips.

"A pox on your visitor, Rivers," she said. "Who would come to call upon you here?"

"He's not calling to see me, Lucia," he said, shoving a pillow behind his head so he could better see her. "He's coming to call upon you."

"Oh, no, he's not," she scoffed. "In all my days, not one person has called anywhere to see me."

"Then today's visitor shall be the first," he said, and yawned extravagantly—and, suspected Lucia, purposefully as well. "I hope you'll manage to be civil to the poor fellow, considering he will have come all this way from London for the express purpose of calling upon you."

Swiftly she ran through any possible men who might make the long ride from London for her sake. Among her acquaintance, only Uncle Lorenzo possessed the where-withal to make such a journey, but she doubted very much he would so much as cross the lane to see her, especially given their last conversation.

No, she was certain that Rivers was teasing her about having a caller, and she glowered at him.

"You are filled with rubbish, Rivers," she said, thumping his chest to make her point. "I don't know anyone who would come here for me. You have invented this phantom caller entirely to plague me."

He yowled dramatically and clutched at his chest before shoving her aside.

"Very well, then, madam," he said, pretending to be wounded. "You may believe what you choose. I shall simply have Mr. McGraw turned away when he arrives, and told that you are not at home."

"*McGraw?*" she exclaimed, sitting upright. In the world of London playhouses, there was only one Mr. McGraw, but she couldn't dare hope that this was the one that Rivers meant. "Which McGraw?"

Rivers screwed up his face as if to think deeply. "I believe he is *the* Mr. McGraw, the manager of the Russell Street Theatre. But since you have no knowledge of any such—"

"What have you done, Rivers?" she demanded, her heart racing with anticipation, and a bit of dread as well. "When last we spoke of it, I was to perform in a public room for an invited audience. You have never said a *word* to me of Mr. McGraw!"

Smiling serenely, Rivers sat up against the pillows and linked his hands behind his head.

"Then I shall say them now," he said. "When first we made our agreement, I believed that a performance in a public room would suffice to silence Everett and secure the wager, and also display your accomplishments to a select audience."

"Yes, yes," she said impatiently. "That is what we agreed, without any mention of Mr. McGraw. You must tell me, Rivers. What have you *done*?"

"What I have done, Lucia, is to reward your talent and hard work." His expression lost its teasing edge, and his smile faded. "I realized that you deserved a far better audience than the circle of my friends. Therefore I wrote to Mr. McGraw, and invited him here for a private audition with my dear friend Mrs. Willow. If he is suitably impressed—which I do not doubt he will be—then he will consider staging a single-night benefit performance of *Hamlet* featuring the actors of his company, and you as Ophelia."

She gasped, and pressed her hands over her mouth. It was more than she'd dreamed, and far more than she'd expected. She knew from her family's company that most theatrical benefits lasted only a single night, but if the performance was well received, then the house's manager could extend it into a regular run of a week, a month, or even longer, if the play became a sensation—and the actors and actresses with it.

"Richard McGraw is coming all this way to audition me?" she asked, wanting to make absolutely certain she hadn't misheard. "Me, here?"

Rivers laughed, and nodded. "Your reputation precedes you, sweetheart."

"Only because you told him," she said, letting the wonder of what he'd said sink in. An audition for Russell Street! There would be no better way to become a celebrated actress, and to have the career she'd always wanted. She knew she could win audiences. She *knew* it. The chance was waiting for her. All she'd need do would be to seize it, and impress Mr. McGraw the way she knew she could.

"I've so much to do if he's arriving this morning," she

said, her mind racing ahead. "How shall I prepare for him? How can I know which scene he'll wish to hear?"

"You *are* prepared," Rivers said. "He can ask you to speak any scene, and you'll know it."

"But managers try to trick actors during auditions," she said. Too excited to remain still, she slipped from the bed and reached for the striped silk dressing gown that had become hers. "I saw it at King's. Mr. Lane is the manager there, and he'd interrupt actors during their auditions and toss out lines from other plays, just to fuddle them."

"That doesn't mean McGraw will do the same," Rivers said, watching her pull the sash snug around her waist. "Russell Street is a few rungs above King's."

"Which only means Mr. McGraw will have more cunning ways to try to confuse me," she said, her agitation growing as she began to pace alongside the bed. "What shall I wear? Should I try to contrive a costume fit for Ophelia?"

"He'll be expecting Mrs. Willow, not Ophelia," Rivers said. "Any one of your new gowns will do."

Lucia shook her head, not really listening. "I must review my lines again, so they'll be perfect. We haven't done anything these last two days."

"I would hardly say we've done nothing, sweetheart," Rivers said drily. "Besides, you already know your lines perfectly."

"But this is my one chance," she said, more to her pacing feet than to him. "What if I forget the words, what if I—"

"Lucia, please." Rivers caught her by the arm to stop her pacing, and pulled her onto his lap. "You will not forget your lines. You will choose the perfect gown. You will stun McGraw with your brilliance, and he will fall at your feet in amazement at your talent."

She pursed her mouth, unconvinced. "I wish I were as certain as you."

He kissed her lightly, a kiss of reassurance rather than passion.

"You should be certain," he said. "I would not have asked the man to come here to the Lodge if I didn't believe you were ready."

An unsettling doubt, perilously close to suspicion suddenly clouded her thoughts. "When did you invite him?"

Rivers shrugged, tracing his fingers along her collarbone as he eased the dressing gown aside. "I do not recall the exact day that I wrote to him. Sometime last week. Why does it matter?"

She pulled the gown back into place. "When did you receive a letter in reply from him?"

He frowned at her once-again covered chest. "His letter was delivered to me before we left for Newbury. A sorry, scribbled thing it was, too, for all that it contained such excellent news."

She would not be distracted by McGraw's penmanship, and she twisted around on Rivers's lap so she was facing him directly.

"So you knew of this when we drove to Newbury," she said softly, "and in Mrs. Currie's shop, and on the ride back to the Lodge, and then when we came here to the roof?"

His expression didn't change. He was the same irresistibly handsome Rivers that she loved, tousled and with a night's worth of beard glistening on his jaw. Yet she couldn't help but sense that he was holding something back from her, and that there was an unfamiliar air of distance in those blue eyes.

"I did," he said simply. "I did."

"And all through these last two days?" she asked, incredulous. "You knew, yet you did not choose to tell me until this morning? Until now?"

He sighed, and leaned back against the pillows and away from her. "I judged it best for you, Lucia. I didn't want you fussing and worrying for the two days before McGraw's arrival. By the way you're behaving now, I was right to do so, too."

"Perhaps you were, and perhaps you weren't." She scrambled from his lap and stood looking down at him, her arms folded across her chest. She couldn't believe that he'd kept something this important from her. It stung that he'd been so high-handed in his decision, too, as if she were an overeager child unable to withstand the excitement of anticipation.

"I appreciate that you wrote to Mr. McGraw, Rivers, but I would have liked to have known about it before this," she said, unable to keep the disappointment from her voice.

He lowered his chin defensively, a bad sign for a reasonable conversation. "Why? What difference could those two days possibly have made?"

"Because this audition could change the rest of my life," she said. "Because having you write to Mr. McGraw without telling me makes me feel as if I am simply another of your possessions, to be ordered about however you please."

"That's not true," he said irritably. "I'd never think that of you."

"But Mr. McGraw will," she said, unable to keep the unhappiness from her voice. "I'm sure he already does. As soon as he read your letter, I'm sure he decided that I must be your mistress, for you to take such a proprietary interest in me."

He held his hands out, indicating the rumpled sheets of the bed. "It's a bit late to consider that, isn't it?"

She flushed. She wouldn't deny that she'd willingly shared this bed with him, but in her mind she'd been his lover, not his mistress. Apparently he thought otherwise.

She'd known it would be like this. Because of the distance between their ranks, he would always think of himself as better, higher, than she. He might love her, but he'd never think of her as his equal. He couldn't help it. It had been that way for him since the day he'd been born. He'd always be the one who would unconsciously make decisions like this one. She'd known from the moment she'd agreed to the wager, but she'd let her heart overrule her common sense, and now it had come to this, and she was no better than Magdalena.

"It wasn't too late when you first wrote to Mr. McGraw last week," she insisted. "You made the decision for me when all that was between us was the wager. I would like to have been the one to decide if I was ready for an audition or not."

"But you are," he said with his own maddening logic. "I've no doubt of it. Have you forgotten that you promised to trust me in all things, Lucia? Don't you recall that was part of our initial agreement?"

She looked down, away from him. There was nothing to be gained from this conversation. She had agreed then, but many things had changed between them since that agreement—some that she hadn't even realized.

"The question is not whether I trust you, Rivers," she said quietly. "Rather it seems that it's you who doesn't trust me."

She turned away quickly, not giving him time to answer, and headed for the door to the stairs.

"*Lucia.*"

She stopped, and took a deep breath. Would he explain? Would he apologize?

She looked back over her shoulder. He'd left the bed, and was pulling on his breeches, the sight of his taut, ridged abdomen and well-muscled thighs enough to make her pause.

Ahh, her *grande leone d'oro,* her own great golden lion!

"I'll come with you," he said. "We can review your lines if you'd like."

That wasn't either an explanation or an apology, and her heart sank a fraction.

She shook her head. "You told me that wasn't necessary. You just said I was ready for an audition."

"I did," he said, buttoning the fall on his breeches. "But if it will give you more confidence, then I am willing."

"No," she said. "Thank you, no. I'm going to dress."

"Ahh," he said with an awkward shrug. "If that is what you wish. I expect McGraw later this morning, before dinner. I will receive him first, and then send for you to join us, if that is agreeable to you."

"Very well," she said. "I shall be ready, and waiting in my room for you to send for me."

And then she turned away and left him, her bare feet making little sound on the stone steps. He did not follow, and she was so unhappy that she didn't know if she wished he had.

For a long while afterward, she stood at the window of her room, and watched the first raindrops blow and splatter against the diamond-shaped panes. It was the first time she had been alone, without Rivers, for nearly three days, and she missed him. No matter how infuriating he was, that wouldn't change.

She missed him.

Finally, with a deep sigh, she called for Sally to help her dress. Before long Mr. McGraw would arrive, and if she did her best, then her future would begin as well—either with Rivers in it, or not.

CHAPTER
13

~~~~~~~~~~~~~~~~~~

Rivers sat in the drawing room at the back of the Lodge, and pretended to read. As the most formal room in the house, this drawing room was also the one he used the least. It remained most true to the Lodge's original use for hunting, with heavy, dark oak furniture from the last century and dark paneling on the walls. There were a handful of paintings of long-ago hunts and hunters, and a pair of stuffed stag heads with many-pointed antlers, one on either end of the room. He'd found those stags forbidding when he'd been a boy, convinced their glass eyes were watching him wherever he stood in the room. He didn't find them much more welcoming now, either, nor did Spot, who always lowered his head and growled on principle at the doorway before he entered.

But Rivers had decided that the room would make an excellent place for receiving the theater manager. He expected the man to be cocky and full of bluster, the way his letter had been, and if ever there was a room that had a gloomy, aristocratic omnipotence to it, this was it. Without a word, the room would remind the man that he was dealing with the Fitzroy family, whose ducal crest was carved into the stone mantelpiece, and that Lucia was a Fitzroy protégée. This was also the reason why Rivers had chosen this chair, an imposing throne-like monstrosity fashioned of antlers with red leather cushions beneath the arched window. McGraw might be from the world of playhouses and actors, but Rivers knew a bit about theatrics as well.

But the best reason for choosing this room was how it would flatter Lucia. The acoustics were splendid, and would amplify every word she spoke. All the dark wood and masculine hunting memorabilia would serve to make her appear more feminine, more delicate, more beautiful, by comparison. The gloominess, too, seemed appropriate for the dark drama of *Hamlet*. Even the weather was cooperating. He had never traveled to Denmark, but he imagined it as a dank and melancholy place, and the rain driving against the windows outside only contributed to a suitable setting for a play filled with tragic mayhem. He'd even ordered a fire lit in the huge fireplace, something he seldom did in June, but felt was necessary for this day. What better setting could there be for Shakespeare than this?

Yet as Rivers sat near the window, Spot sleeping on the floor beside him, his thoughts were not on Shakespeare or Denmark, or even McGraw's impending arrival. All he could think of was Lucia, and how badly he'd botched their earlier conversation. He had wanted to make a great, generous revelation of McGraw's visit. He'd envisioned her excitement and joy, and how fondly she'd display her gratitude toward him.

But he'd made a mess out of the whole affair. Instead of being generous, he'd sounded selfish and controlling and uncaring, and the more he'd tried to unsay what he'd said, the worse he'd made things. He should have told her as soon as he'd received the letter from McGraw. No, further back than that: he should have told her he was writing to McGraw in the first place. He shouldn't have kept the audition from her until now, and she'd every right to be upset with him.

He knew the reasons why he hadn't, too, which didn't

make it any easier to bear. He had wanted the dinner he'd planned for her on the roof to be entirely about love, without any distractions. He hadn't wanted to think about the future, which would inevitably pull them apart. Most of all, he hadn't wanted her to think she was obligated to love him on account of the audition. He had wanted her to feel the same unconditional love and desire, friendship, and trust he felt for her, and now it seemed that all he'd accomplished was the exact opposite.

She'd said he didn't trust her, which couldn't be further from the truth. He'd trusted her with his home, his books, his thoughts, and his past, and most of all his heart, and yet clearly there was something more that was missing. How could he win her trust? How could he win *her*?

And why, why, when he'd had the chance, hadn't he told her again that he loved her?

She'd called herself his mistress. That wasn't how he thought of her, not at all. Her cousin Magdalena had been his mistress. Lucia wasn't. The difference seemed clear enough to him. A mistress was for pleasure, for amusement. Lucia was that, of course, but more important she was his lover in the best sense of the word, his friend, his partner in the wager, even his inspiration. But he hadn't corrected her, and now it was likely too late to do so.

He swore softly to himself, making Spot groan in sleepy sympathy beside him as he stared out at the garden. It was raining hard now. The rain beat down the heavy heads of the open roses, scattering their petals on the dark soil, and filled the garden paths with dappled puddles. He could only imagine what the roads must be like. At this rate, McGraw couldn't—or wouldn't— be able to come, and this morning's misunderstandings would have been for nothing.

He wondered what Lucia was doing now. He'd always been a man comfortable with his own company, but he'd grown so accustomed to the pleasure of having her beside him that he felt lost now without her. She'd been right. Books really weren't the same, and chagrined, he gave up the pretense of reading and closed the book on his lap. Was she dressed and waiting for his summons? Was she studying the play one more time, making certain she knew every word? Or was she, too, watching the rain?

He was so lost in his thoughts that he started when the footman knocked to announce McGraw's arrival. Quickly he glanced at his watch: to his surprise, the manager was right on time, and Rivers called for them to enter.

"Good day, Mr. McGraw," he said as the manager came forward and bowed more grandly than was necessary. Sleepily Spot rose, wagging his tail and stretching his head forward to sniff at the newcomer. "I hope your journey was not too arduous. Who expects so much rain in June?"

"It was nothing, my lord, nothing at all," McGraw declared, his smile broad in his round, ruddy face as he glanced about the room in swift appraisal. During McGraw's few steps from his hired carriage to the door, raindrops had speckled his serviceable gray suit and florid orange waistcoat, but clearly had not dampened his personality one whit. Only a hint of the good looks that had once led him to acting himself remained in his face, but in their place was an unabashed shrewdness that likely served him much better as a manager than any actor's perfect profile.

"I am honored, most honored," he continued effusively, "to be invited here by your lordship, and for such an exciting reason, too. I am always on the hunt for new faces and novelty to cast before the ever-ravenous public."

"Mrs. Willow shall be entirely new to London, that is true," Rivers said, motioning for McGraw to sit in the straight-backed chair across from his. Spot, too, resettled; having decided McGraw passed muster, he promptly fell back asleep. "She is most eager to perform for you as well."

McGraw flipped the skirts of his coat up and deposited himself heavily on the chair.

"She must be new, my lord," he said, leaning forward with his elbows on his knees. "Her name is entirely unknown to me, and I am not merely flattering myself when I claim that I am aware of every young actress, good, bad, and indifferent, traipsing upon the London stage."

"Mrs. Willow's performances have been limited in the past to the north and on the Continent," Rivers said, falling back on the final version of Mrs. Willow's biography that he and Lucia had agreed upon. "She had in fact retired from the stage with her marriage."

"Most ladies do," McGraw agreed sagely. "Husbands don't care to have wives on the stage."

Rivers nodded in agreement, hoping that he was relaying Mrs. Willow's fictional past convincingly. It was impossible to tell if McGraw was trustworthy or not, given the general blather with which all theatrical people swathed themselves. Spot had the best method, deciding worthiness with a brisk sniff, but that would not work for Rivers. Instead he forced himself to look somber, and plowed on ahead.

"Mrs. Willow herself would not have agreed to the notion of this benefit were it not for the unfortunate death of Mr. Willow, and the change in her circumstances," he said, omitting all references to tigers. "I need not say more."

"A lady should always be able to rely upon her closest

friends in times of need, my lord," said McGraw with a knowing smile. "What gentleman wants to see a poor delicate creature suffer, I ask you?"

"Indeed," Rivers said coolly, determined to offer no more details about his friendship with Lucia. He didn't like how McGraw said the word *lady,* emphasizing it in a way to show that Lucia must be anything but a lady, and more likely a whore—exactly as she'd predicted. "That is why I have convinced Mrs. Willow of the wisdom of a benefit performance of *Hamlet.*"

"Oh, yes, yes, my lord, it's a wise plan indeed for any lady in her circumstances." Pointedly McGraw looked about the room as if hoping to spy Lucia hiding beneath one of the stag heads. "Mrs. Willow herself is present today, my lord, isn't she?"

"She is." Rivers lowered his voice for emphasis. "But I wished to speak with you alone first, Mr. McGraw, before she joins us."

McGraw smiled again, that sly and knowing smile that Rivers did not like.

"Oh, I know how important it is to keep a lady content, my lord," he said, "especially where money's concerned. *Most* especially, my lord. They get greedy, don't they, my lord? I vow I won't reveal a word to her about your, ah, support of the production, if that's what concerns you."

"It is not," Rivers said, his displeasure gathering into anger. The man was damnably presumptuous, and insulting as well. Money had never been an issue between him and Lucia, nor had she even once displayed a hint of greed. "Not in the least."

"Ahh." McGraw lowered his head toward his chest, with the same demeanor as a man who'd inadvertently poked a stick into a large nest of snakes. "I intended no offense, my lord."

"I am glad of that," Rivers said, each word clipped.

"Because I expect you to show only the greatest respect to Mrs. Willow, and treat her with the regard due a lady, and an artist."

"Oh, of course, my lord, of course," McGraw said, attempting a recovery, and failing. "Clearly she is a special, ah, lady to you."

"She is my *friend*, Mr. McGraw," Rivers said, "and I hold her in the highest regard, and with the greatest respect possible. And if I ever learn that she has suffered any insult or slander whilst in your company or elsewhere, then you will answer directly to me. To *me*. Is that clear?"

"Entirely, my lord." McGraw nodded vigorously. "You have my every assurance, my lord, that I shall offer the lady every opportunity for her gifts to shine, with no offense whatsoever."

"As it should be," Rivers said, only a little mollified. "As she deserves."

He could tell exactly what McGraw was thinking: that Lucia was a talentless and inconsequential bit of fluff, and that Rivers himself was blinded by desire into believing she was more than that.

But Rivers had had enough, and briskly he waved for the footman to summon Lucia. He was confident—more than confident—that Lucia herself would prove to McGraw exactly how wrong his assumptions about her were; he could not wait to see it.

The footman reappeared so quickly that he suspected Lucia must have been waiting not far from the door. He would have been surprised if she'd been late. Not only was she as prompt as he was himself, but he knew how eager she was for this audition.

"My lord, Mrs. Willow," the footman droned, holding the door open wide for her to enter.

And enter she did.

Gone forever were the awkward dramatics that she'd

shown three weeks ago, and gone, too, was the self-effacing maidservant who'd begged for his attention. Instead she entered the parlor with the exact mixture of confidence, grace, and elegance that many noble-born women spent their entire lives striving to achieve. Her gown was the palest blue silk, painted with scattered wildflowers, and she'd tucked some manner of filmy lace kerchief around her shoulders and into the front of the bodice. The neckline was cut very low, yet the lace kerchief was more tantalizing than modest, with the fullness of her breasts only faintly veiled. Resting against the hollow of her throat was the only jewel she ever wore, her mother's necklace with the little cameo.

The pale silk of her gown floated around her as she walked, or perhaps she truly was floating. Rivers couldn't say for certain; she was so achingly desirable that he couldn't say much of anything, and beside him Spot thumped his tail on the floor with approval of his own.

Her dark hair was swept up and away from her face, with glossy curls falling at her nape. She wore no powder nor other paint, for she didn't need them. Her cheeks glowed with a natural vivacity, and her large, dark eyes with their thick lashes and arching brows were filled with the kind of intelligence and beguiling amusement that could make a man forget everything else.

At least that was the effect she had on Rivers as he automatically rose to his feet to hold his hand out to her. She didn't take it at first, but curtseyed instead, exactly as Mrs. Willow should have done to the son of the Duke of Breconridge, and exactly the degree of curtsey that was proper for a third son. Then, finally, she took his hand, letting him guide her back to a standing position with a smile that seemed to have forgotten their earlier disagreements.

Happiness surged in his chest as his fingers gently pressed hers, only to be tamped down once again as she slipped her hand free. She might have thought that one touch was enough to show she'd forgiven him, or she might have been behaving as Mrs. Willow would, politely accepting his support as she rose and no more. Damnation, he could not *tell*. How much was acting, he wondered, and how much was the truth?

She turned toward McGraw, and at once the man seized her hand, not bothering to wait for Rivers to present her.

"Mrs. Willow, your servant," he said, bowing and kissing the air over the back of her hand. "I am enchanted to make your acquaintance at last. I have heard so much about you."

"This is Mr. McGraw of the Russell Street Theatre, madam," Rivers said brusquely, introducing them even though it was now unnecessary. "Mr. McGraw, Mrs. Cassandra Willow."

"I am honored, Mr. McGraw," Lucia murmured. Her accent was impeccable in those few words, and even Rivers would have sworn she'd been raised in Portman Square. "You are most kind to come so far from London on my account."

"Not at all, Mrs. Willow," McGraw said. He was freely ogling Lucia's breasts, and it took every last scrap of Rivers's willpower not to strike the man senseless. "The honor and the pleasure are entirely mine."

"Indeed," said Rivers curtly. "Pray do not forget our earlier discussion, McGraw."

At once the manager released Lucia's hand, and he smiled blandly at Rivers. "I recall it, my lord. My memory for such things is surpassingly good."

"I trust it shall continue that way," Rivers grumbled. McGraw had no right to stare at Lucia like that, and yet Rivers himself had no real right to regard her as his to defend, either.

He should be concentrating on her audition, looking

for any little ways he could assist her and letting her show herself off to the best advantage. He'd anticipated this moment as one more important step in her education and the culmination of his teaching, as well as the wager. He'd expected it would be a triumph they'd share. He'd expected to enjoy it, too, and celebrate like any proud tutor would with a prize student.

Yet instead he was behaving like a bad-tempered, defensive, selfish boor, out of sorts and possessive and generally miserable. He'd always prided himself on doing and saying the right thing, but today, where Lucia was concerned, he couldn't seem to do anything right.

Frustrated and disgusted with himself, he looked down, and felt her hand lightly on his arm. Swiftly he glanced at her, her dark eyes bright with the familiar anticipation and eagerness that was hers alone.

"Shall we begin, my lord?" she asked softly, the flicker of uncertainty in her voice unmistakable, and enough to melt his own misgivings. "That is, if it pleases you."

"It does," he said, and it did. If he loved her, he could do nothing less. He forced himself to smile, the warmth of her gaze making everything better. "Begin whenever you please, Mrs. Willow."

Lucia smiled in return, her heart racing. For a few awful moments, she'd felt sure Rivers had intended to stop her audition before it had begun. After they'd parted earlier this morning, she'd worried that he might lose interest in this part of the wager and not bother to welcome McGraw when he arrived.

What she hadn't expected, however, was that he'd suddenly become so overprotective, even territorial; her thoughtful, genial golden lion had shown his teeth when McGraw appeared, and the transformation shocked her. In the tiring room she'd seen what happened when men became like this, blustering and posturing over a woman, and it never ended well. It made no sense to her for him to behave like this now, especially when so much was at stake, and his tight-lipped smile did not comfort her.

"You are certain, my lord?" she asked, striving to keep the anxiety from her voice as she pressed her hand lightly on his arm. She had planned to keep physically apart from Rivers in McGraw's company, wanting things as formal as possible between them for the sake of the audition, but she couldn't help herself now. She wanted to reassure him as best she could, and herself, too. "You are ready for the audition to proceed?"

He covered her hand with his own, and his smile thawed a fraction. "Whenever you are ready, Mrs. Willow, and the best of luck to you."

"Yes, Mrs. Willow, let us begin," McGraw said, impatiently clapping his hands together. "According to his lordship's letter, you have prepared the tragic role of Ophelia, from *Hamlet*. I assume you know both the monologues and the dialogues for the part, yes?"

"Oh, yes," Lucia said. She slipped her hand away from Rivers's arm and turned toward the manager. She must focus on her audition now, and concentrate on everything McGraw said to her. "I have learned the entire play by heart, sir, and not just my own lines."

"Very well." McGraw pulled a battered, unbound copy of the play—the antithesis of Rivers's elegantly bound edition—from inside his coat and smoothed the curled edges flat over his knee. "A small test of your memory. I'll say one line, and you say the one that follows."

"That's hardly a useful test," Rivers protested. "She'd never be called upon to speak lines that were not hers."

"I can do it, my lord," Lucia said quickly, determined to prove it not only to McGraw, but to Rivers as well. "You know I can. Try me, Mr. McGraw."

McGraw nodded, flipping through the pages. "'How

can that be, when you have the voice of the king / himself for your succession in Denmark?' "

" '*Ay, sir, but, While the grass grows,—the proverb / is something musty,'* " Lucia said without hesitation.

McGraw grunted. "Here's another, then. '*What act / That roars so loud, and thunders in the index?'* "

Lucia smiled, recognizing the line in an instant, and knowing what followed, too. " '*Look here, upon this picture, and on this, / The counterfeit presentment of two brothers.'* Shall I continue, Mr. McGraw?"

"That shall do, Mrs. Willow." McGraw nodded with approval. "I wish all my company could do as well, but most, particularly the actresses, are too idle to bother."

Lucia dipped a small curtsey in acknowledgment, grateful that the first test had been so easy—or at least easy for her.

"Now let us see how you fare with your own lines," McGraw continued. "Pray go stand a distance away, by that window, if you please, and speak Ophelia's speech beginning '*O, what a noble mind is here o'erthrown!*' "

She made a small curtsey to the two men, and walked slowly across the room to the window, as McGraw had requested, using the time to compose herself. She didn't miss the irony of the speech the manager had chosen, for it was the same one that Rivers had first given her to learn in the carriage from London. That had been less than a month ago, and how much she'd learned since then.

It hadn't been just the tricks of acting and accents and standing properly, but of the magic of poetry, of drama, of passion. Only Rivers could have taught her those, and only she could have learned them so well from him. Now when she took a final breath, raised her head, and turned toward the two seated men, the familiar words reverberated with that same poetry, drama, and passion, and, as

Ophelia would have done, her entire small frame trembled with the meaning.

> "O, what a noble mind is here o'erthrown!
> The Courtier's, soldier's, scholar's, eye, tongue, sword,
> Th' expectancy and rose of the fair state,
> The glass of fashion and the mould of form,
> Th' observ'd of all observers, quite, quite down!
> And I, of ladies most deject and wretched,
> That suck'd the honey of his music vows,
> Now see that noble and most sovereign reason
> Like sweet bells jangled out of tune and harsh,
> That unmatch'd form and feature of blown youth
> Blasted with ecstasy. O, woe is me
> T'have seen what I have seen, see what I see."

She finished the last line, and forcibly returned to being Mrs. Willow. The speech ended the scene for Ophelia; there was nothing more she could or should say, and so she waited for McGraw's reaction. She didn't dare look at Rivers, fearing the emotions of the role could spill over into her own.

"Impressive," McGraw said blandly. "Another. 'How now, Ophelia!'"

It was the prompt for Ophelia's most challenging scene, and her last in the play. Lucia had guessed McGraw would request it, which was why she'd chosen to wear this gown scattered with wildflowers, as much a costume as she'd have.

In the scene, Ophelia had lost her wits from grief and had become mad, which as Lucia had quickly learned, was not nearly so easy to do as it would seem. Raving like a lunatic Bedlamite wouldn't do. She had to be poignantly mad, as Rivers had explained, with the kind of madness that makes audiences weep, not wriggle with discomfort.

The hardest part for Lucia were the lines that Ophelia was supposed to sing. The same affliction that made it impossible to dance likewise made her hopeless at following a tune, but she and Rivers had devised a kind of singsong way of speaking the lines that he assured her was far more affecting than if she'd sung them perfectly. Now all she could do was pray that Rivers had been right, and that she wouldn't make a fool of herself.

She spread her hands open, tipped her head to one side, and began the first song.

> *"How should I your true love know*
> *From another one?*
> *By his cockle hat and staff,*
> *And his sandle shoon."*

To her relief, McGraw didn't laugh, but read the next lines that belonged to Queen Gertrude, and then, further along, to King Claudius, too. As the scene continued, she forgot her first nervousness, forgot McGraw, and forgot the importance of this audition. Instead she became the pitiful Ophelia, grieving her much-loved father and scorned by the prince who had seduced and abandoned her. The further she went along, the more the old-fashioned words seemed to describe her own situation with Rivers.

> *"Alack, and fie for shame!*
> *Young men will do't, if they come to't;*
> *By cock, they are to blame."*
> *Quoth she, "Before you tumbled me,*
> *You promised me to wed."*
> *"So would I ha'done, by younder sun,*
> *An thou hadst not come to my bed."*

Of course she was no noblewoman and Rivers would never have promised to marry her, but she now keenly understood the loss and betrayal that Ophelia must have felt. By the time she spoke the last lines of her scene and made her exit in a melancholy daze as the part required, she felt both drained and overwhelmed. With a shudder of emotion, she closed her eyes for a long moment to recover, and then turned back toward the two men who were her audience.

Without thinking she sought Rivers's reaction first. She hoped for a nod or a smile of approval, the judgment she'd come to expect. The smile was there, but in his eyes she saw her own emotions reflected: pain, loss, confusion, and love.

Love.

"Mrs. Willow, you were marvelous," McGraw was saying, the sharp crack of his applause enough to make Lucia finally look away from Rivers. "If you can repeat that on my stage, I shall have crowds weeping in the stalls."

His praise was far more than she'd dared hope for, and she pressed her hands to her cheeks with amazement.

"Thank—thank you, Mr. McGraw," she stammered, crossing the room to join the men. "That is, I am most grateful for this opportunity."

"Nonsense," the manager said, tucking his playbook back into one pocket of his coat, and pulling a well-thumbed almanac from another. "It's I who must be grateful to his lordship for recommending you to me. I'll admit that I was skeptical, my lord, but this lady has made fools of all my doubts."

"I did not exaggerate," Rivers said, his gaze not leaving Lucia. "Mrs. Willow's gifts are worthy of the highest of praise."

"That they are," McGraw said absently, flipping through the pages of his almanac. "I do not ordinarily approve a full staging of a play for a single-night benefit, but under the circumstances, I will have the costumes and scenes from our last *Hamlet* brought from storage. Mr. Lambert will be your Danish prince; he could speak the role in his sleep. Will Thursday next be an agreeable date to you, my lord?"

Lucia gasped. Next Thursday seemed so soon.

"Thursday next," Rivers repeated, the earlier edge that had been in his voice gone, and replaced by his usual well-bred reserve. "That's six days from today."

"It is, my lord," McGraw said, frowning down at the almanac. "Thursday evening for the benefit, with rehearsals on Tuesday and Wednesday. In your letter you had mentioned that you wished the performance to take place before the end of the month."

Of course Rivers had wanted the benefit then, for the sake of the wager. However could she have forgotten the purpose behind all of this? But in six days, he'd no longer have a reason to be with her. Everything would be done, finished, exactly as they'd both agreed from the beginning.

"Thank you, Mr. McGraw," Rivers said evenly. "If the date is acceptable to Mrs. Willow, then we shall agree upon Thursday."

"It is acceptable," Lucia said, for what else could she say?

"Excellent." McGraw made a final note in the almanac, then tucked it away. "I shall send word of the details to you when I return to London, which I fear I must do directly. My lord, I remain your servant. Mrs. Willow, it has been my pleasure."

He bowed his way from the room, and the footman closed the door gently after him, leaving Lucia and Rivers alone with the sound of the rain and the awkwardness of the silence yawning between them.

She hadn't seen this room before. It was chilly, even in June, and forbiddingly filled with the dead, preserved trophies of long-ago hunts and long-ago Fitzroys, too.

Unlike the rest of the Lodge, there didn't seem to be so much as a trace of Rivers in this room—except, of course, he himself, standing there before her. He was impeccably dressed in subdued clothes fit for the country, the model of an English nobleman, and yet she was far more conscious of what simmered beneath all that expensive elegance. He stood coiled and tense, his shoulders bunched beneath the tailoring and his jaw tight.

Now it wasn't the furious possessiveness that he'd shown toward McGraw that had him on edge, but the same wariness she herself was feeling. Uncertainty did that. She didn't know if he was considering sending her back to London today, or tumbling her here on the carpet. Neither would surprise her.

Yet still she stood before him, letting him break the silence first.

At last he cleared his throat. "You were magnificent, Lucia," he said. "No, you *are* magnificent."

Her smile blossomed with relief. At least for now he seemed willing to move beyond their uneasy parting earlier this morning. "Truly?"

"You were, without question or doubt," he said. "Now all your talent and hard work will most certainly be rewarded."

"Truly?" she said again, wincing inwardly at her repetition. She'd imagined this moment as being filled with wild elation and joy, and yet because of the awkwardness hovering between them, it didn't feel that way at all. "That is, I hope Mr. McGraw will continue to be pleased with me after the benefit."

"He will," Rivers predicted. "You have captured him, and you'd have to be very bad indeed for him to turn against you now. I would not be surprised if he offered you a more lasting place in the company."

"That is my dream, isn't it?" Her smile faded and turned bittersweet. That *had* been her dream—to become a primary actress on the London stage, applauded by all, celebrated and independent—but much of the luster of it had dulled because going to London in a handful of days meant the end of her idyll here at the Lodge with Rivers. She knew from the beginning that this day would come, knew she shouldn't mourn over it, yet here she was, granted the one thing she'd claimed she desired most and unable to take any joy in her achievement.

"Lucia, what is wrong?" Rivers said when she didn't continue. "Tell me."

"There's nothing wrong," she answered automatically. "Nothing."

"Don't lie," he said, then sighed, raking his fingers back through his hair. "Please. When I listened to you just now I felt as if you were not reciting lines, but speaking directly to me. Your sorrow, your grief, your loss—have I done that to you?"

She shook her head, startled. How could he have guessed what she'd been thinking? What had she done to betray her thoughts so easily?

"It was the play," she said quickly. Her aristocratic accent slipped away with her uneasiness, and she paused to recover it. "My lines. That was Ophelia speaking to you, not me."

"No, it wasn't," he insisted, "because I saw the same look in your eyes this morning before you spoke a word, and earlier, when you left me on the roof."

"I am concerned about the rehearsals," she said, avoiding the truth. "Working with the other actors and actresses on a true stage as their equal. What if they resent me? What if they believe I've no place among them?"

"The only complaint they shall have of you is that the audience will see only your glory, and be blind to their pitiful efforts." He was trying too hard, his manner forced. "You'll see, Lucia. After next week, the world shall be your oyster, to open as you please."

She shook her head, not so much denying the compliment as being unable to trust it. She wished he wouldn't speak of next week. Of course she was excited about the rehearsals and the benefit, but at the same time she didn't want to think of how swiftly her time with Rivers was coming to an end. The more he spoke of London, the more she couldn't help but think he was eager to leave the Lodge, and be done with her as well.

It was painful for her even to look at him now, and she shifted her gaze away from him, up to the glass-eyed buck's head looming overhead.

He sighed again, his frustration clearly growing. "Don't retreat from me, Lucia. What have I done to upset you? What have I said? What can I do to make things right?"

Hastily she looked down at her clasped hands, hiding the eyes that had betrayed her.

"You've done so much for me already," she said. "My training, this audition, the benefit next week. I owe you everything, and have no right to expect more."

"There's nothing owed," he said firmly. "Nothing. It's all been given to you freely, with no obligations. I'd give you so much more if only you'd let me."

Silently she shook her head, too aware of how every last thread and stitch on her body had been his gift. She'd already resolved that, if Mr. McGraw did offer her a place, that she'd put every farthing toward paying Rivers back. She had to do it. She could never have what she truly wished from him, which was to be with him always. She'd known that from the beginning, and there was no point in arguing over things that could not be changed. She knew, too, what he was offering her now: more clothes, jewels, perhaps even a house and a carriage, the gifts men like him lavished on women like her in exchange for warming their beds.

She wanted none of it.

"No more, Rivers," she said, unable to keep the sadness from her voice. "You've been more than generous to me this last month, but I can't accept anything else."

"You've only to say what you want, Lucia," he said slowly, as if that alone could change her mind, "and it will be yours."

"I told you, Rivers," she said. "No more *things.*"

He frowned, clearly not understanding. "My love isn't a thing."

She hadn't expected that, and it made her catch her breath. It was so easy for him to make statements like that, devastatingly lovely statements, as if they truly had a future to share. How could he know how they tore at her heart?

He took a step toward her, his hand outstretched as if she were a wild animal to be coaxed. "I promise you, Lucia, once we're in London—"

"I beg you, Rivers, do not speak of London!" she cried unhappily. "Whatever became of us living minute by minute and day by day, instead of making endless, empty plans for the future?"

He let his hand drop. "I have not forgotten," he said. "What fate and the stars decree, yes?"

She nodded, short, quick jerks of her chin. "It's what makes us who we are, not what we might become, with no guarantees of certainty."

"Very well," he said slowly. "If that is what you desire, then I'll do my best to oblige."

He called for the footman. "Grant, have the carriage readied, and have Mrs. Willow's maidservant bring her a cloak against the weather."

"Where am I going?" No matter how brave she tried to be, her voice rose with trepidation, and she hurried toward him with her hands pressed together. "Rivers? Are you sending me away?"

He raised his brows with disbelief. "Why in blazes should I do that?"

"Because—because you have tired of me," she said, faltering before the truth. "Because you wish me returned to London. Because—"

"Hush," he said softly, taking her by the arm and drawing her close. "I wish no such thing. I'm taking you with me, not sending you away."

She settled close to his chest, comforted by the rightness of it. They had been apart for less than three hours, and yet it had felt like an eternity. "We're not going to London?"

"Not at all," he said, curling his arm around her waist. "You want my trust. I'll give it to you now, in this minute. We're going to my father's house. I'm taking you to Breconridge Hall."

CHAPTER
14

It had come to Rivers suddenly, this notion of taking Lucia to see Breconridge Hall, and following her plea, he'd acted on it suddenly as well, making the impulsive decision to bring her to the house where he'd spent most of his time as a boy. Impulse or not, he'd time to reflect on the short drive, sitting with Lucia close and snug beneath his arm and the last of the rain splattering on the carriage's roof.

Even that wasn't enough to reassure him. If only he'd taken another moment to consider, he would never have suggested such harebrained foolishness. It wasn't that he was ashamed of the Hall, which was generally regarded as one of the most beautiful and impressive private houses in the country. The Hall had been the center of his childhood, the destination of school holidays when he'd been an adolescent, and remained the heart of his family's major celebrations. It was the gilded, luxurious symbol of the power and good fortune of generations of Fitzroys, which was much of the reason that he'd decided to take Lucia there. How could he not be proud of it? Even His Majesty had admitted a twinge of envy when he'd visited.

And it certainly wasn't that he was ashamed of Lucia. He would be proud to have her on his arm anywhere, and after her performance today and the grace and presence she'd shown, he doubted that anyone would question her right to be a guest of the Duke of Breconridge.

Nor could he be ashamed of his own family, who were, as families went, quite presentable and good-natured. Unlike most noble families, they harbored no feuds, dark secrets, or regrettable choices in their midst. His father was publicly proud of his three sons, and Rivers counted his two older brothers as his closest friends.

No, his unsettled feelings regarding Breconridge Hall were more complicated than that, and all of his own doing. He had the Lodge and the house in Cavendish Square for his own, and thanks to his mother's family, a handsome income. He was free to do what he wanted, when he wanted, without any obligations. His life was exactly as he ordered it, and most men would eagerly trade places with him.

But the inescapable fact of his existence was that he was a third son: necessary, but ultimately extraneous. From birth he'd known he was the third son, and the likelihood of him ever becoming the next Duke of Breconridge was remote. He wouldn't wish it otherwise, of course, because the cost would have been the deaths of his father and his brothers. But Breconridge Hall was the glittering, golden prize for every generation's duke. It would never belong to Rivers or his sons, and as welcome as they'd be to visit, it would never truly be their home, either.

It was no wonder, really, that he couldn't begin to explain this incoherent jumble of loyalties to Lucia, especially since he couldn't really sort it out to his satisfaction within his own head. Thus he did what he'd always done when confronted with similar puzzles: he turned pedantic and tedious.

"There was an old manor house on the site when the land was initially granted to the first duke a hundred years ago or so," he said, talking not so much to Lucia, who was still curled against him, but intoning to the air over her head. "Most of that was torn down in the 1690s when William Talman designed the south façade, with interiors overseen by Nicholas Hawkesmoor. Talman is not well-known today, but he was a pupil of Sir Christopher Wren, and his sense of proportion carried the master's gravity, evident in the Palladian influences of the window bays."

"Rivers," Lucia said. "Please."

"Please?" he repeated, though he could guess what she meant.

"I mean, please don't," she said softly, twisting about to face him. Her maid had brought her a short blue cape embroidered with silver flowers, and though it had covered her from the raindrops as she'd stepped into the carriage, the front kept parting as she moved, granting him tantalizing glimpses of her pale skin beneath. "You only become a schoolmaster like this when you're uneasy, and you needn't be with me."

He frowned, knowing she was right but not quite ready to admit it. "I am not being a schoolmaster."

"If any mere schoolmaster spoke of such lofty things as proportion and window bays, then yes, you are," she said. She ran her fingers lightly across the breast of his coat as if to smooth away any harshness from her criticism. "I am certain that these gentlemen you mention were most esteemed in their time, but I care far more about what the house means to you than to them."

He sighed, striving to think of things to tell her. "It was my home when I was a child," he said. "My mother believed that children should be raised in the country, not in London. While my parents remained in town, my brothers and I were kept here with a phalanx of nursery maids, governors, and tutors attempting to mold us into proper young gentlemen."

"That must have made for an enjoyable childhood,"

she said, and he didn't miss the wistfulness in her voice. Compared to her first years, his own had been positively idyllic.

"It was," he admitted. "My brothers and I were—are—close. Being older, they led the way in the mischief, and I happily followed. There was much potential for mayhem for three boys in a house of that size."

"*That* is what I wish to hear," she said, and for the first time that day she smiled with the eagerness that he loved so well. "Master Hawkesworth is well enough—"

"Hawkesmoor," he corrected from habit. "Nicholas Hawkesmoor."

She laughed, the merry sound like Heaven to him. "Oh, Rivers, you cannot help yourself, can you? Show me the places where you and your brothers were wicked, and I shall be a thousand times more content than if I learned what joiners put the windows in place."

He smiled sheepishly, realizing that he, too, had not smiled much today before now. Hawkesmoor had been a lofty and legendary architect, not a humble joiner, but Rivers would not give her the satisfaction of being a schoolmaster again by pointing out the difference. And she was right: it didn't matter. He still wasn't entirely sure why he was bringing her to Breconridge Hall, but he knew it wasn't for an architectural lecture.

"Then I shall show you the picture gallery where we ran races with our dogs when it rained," he said instead, "and the marble statue of a Roman goddess whose toe we knocked off with a cricket bat. We lived in fear that Father would notice, but I doubt he ever has."

She laughed again, and he laughed with her: not because the goddess's broken toe was that funny, but because laughing with her was one of the things he most liked doing with her.

"I promise *I* won't be the one to tell your father," she

said, "though I'd like very much to see the poor goddess."

"Father won't be there, in any event," he said. "No one will, not with Parliament in session and the Court in town until the end of the summer. The house will be empty except for the servants. We shall have the place to ourselves."

"Truly?" she asked curiously. "None of your family?"

"Not a one," he said. Their absence was so obvious to him that he hadn't considered that she might have wished to meet them. "I'm sorry to disappoint you."

"Oh, I am not disappointed," she exclaimed. "I am *relieved.* I do not think I could be presented to Mr. McGraw and His Grace the Duke of Breconridge in the same day. *Dio buono,* I would perish from too much magnificence."

She smiled, full of her old impish charm. Yet the fact that she'd fallen back into that little bit of Italian—she'd nearly abandoned it entirely along with her old accent for the sake of Mrs. Willow—proved that her true feelings were likely as unsettled as his own. Had she expected him to introduce her to his family?

He loved Lucia, loved her more than he'd ever loved any other woman. Yet to introduce her to his father, in his father's house, was so unthinkable that he hadn't even thought it, and he didn't like himself for doing—or not doing—so. In fact, as he looked at her lovely, trusting face as she smiled up at him, he felt shamefully unworthy, and a coward in the bargain.

"Perishing from magnificence is entirely possible where my father is concerned," he said, striving to continue the jest. "I suspect there have been more than a few people at Court who have felt that way in his presence. Here we are."

The carriage had stopped before the door on the West Front, the wheels crunching on the white stone that was raked daily. This wasn't the main entrance to the house—that would be the even more formal South Front—but this was the closest to the Lodge, and the door by which Rivers usually entered. It was a mark of just how large the house was that it even had three separate fronts and formal entrances, each added by a different generation of dukes, and each, too, calculated to be more imposing. The West Front had been built by the second duke, Rivers's great-uncle, and it was still sufficiently grand to leave most visitors awestruck.

It definitely had that affect on Lucia. He'd stepped out of the carriage as soon as the footman had opened the door, and now he stood waiting to hand her down, yet she remained half-standing in the door, her mouth open as she tipped her head back to stare up at the curving double staircase and the large house it led to.

"*Madre di Dio,*" she murmured faintly. "*Non ho parole.*"

I have no words. Perhaps Father should be here after all, thought Rivers, because he would have relished her reaction.

"I warned you," he said, thankful they hadn't gone around to the South Front. "The Hall can be daunting from the drive."

Still she didn't move. "It didn't seem nearly this big from the Lodge."

"No, it doesn't," he agreed. "But from the Lodge's roof, the Hall is a good two miles away."

"That's true." At last she recalled herself and took his hand to step down. She flipped the hood to her cloak over her hair, looked up at the skies, and then flipped it back. "And at least the rain has stopped."

"In your honor, madam," he said gallantly, leading her up the curving stairs. He usually took the steps two at a time, but on account of her shorter stride and because she was openly gaping up at the front of the house, he kept to a more leisurely pace with her on his arm. Besides, he liked having her beside him, with her little hand in the crook of his arm and her silk skirts blowing against his legs in the breeze. "I've arranged the weather entirely to your liking."

Skeptical, she glanced up at him from beneath her lashes, and found an appropriate quote from *Hamlet*. " *'How is it that the clouds still hang on you?'* "

He laughed as they reached the door. "Because I've taken them away from your head to hang over my own, entirely for your benefit."

The door was opened by a young footman that Rivers didn't recognize. This wasn't surprising; the butler, Mr. Maitland, usually stood guard at the primary door, and left the other entrances to lesser servants, especially when the family was not in residence.

"My—my lord, good day," the young man stammered, bowing repeatedly as he held the door wide.

"Good day to you, too," Rivers said, striving to sound as kind and unassuming as possible. "You're new, aren't you?"

"Since Michaelmas," the footman said. From his downy cheeks to the livery coat inherited from a much larger predecessor, he could not be more than fifteen. "I'm Tomlin, my lord."

"Welcome to Breconridge Hall, Tomlin," Rivers said as he ushered Lucia inside the house. "I trust you'll serve my father well for many years to come."

"Yes, my lord," Tomlin said, carefully closing and latching the door as he'd been trained. "Mr. Maitland didn't say you was expected."

"That's because I wasn't," Rivers said. "I'm here on a whim, for a brief ramble about the house, that is all."

The footman glanced at Lucia, flushed, and swallowed hard. "Will you be requiring tea, my lord, with the ah, the, ah—"

"My *friend*," Rivers said with gentle emphasis. "This is Mrs. Willow, Tomlin, and she is a dear friend of mine. And no, we shall not stay for tea. I would not dream of distressing the kitchen staff by appearing without any warning."

"Very well, my lord," the footman said, bowing one last time and to spare him further embarrassment Rivers hurried Lucia across the patterned marble floor, past a pair of gilded crouching lions, and up the staircase.

"Poor Tomlin," Lucia said when they were out of the footman's hearing. "You were very kind to him. Many gentlemen wouldn't be."

Her genuine sympathy reminded Rivers of how often she herself must have been treated rudely by gentlemen in the tiring room. She had changed so much in these last weeks that it was hard to realize she'd still been working there less than a month before.

"At least you've been spared being greeted by Mr. Maitland," he said as they turned down another grand hallway. Because his father was in London, the halls and rooms were all empty, and without the usual small army of servants bustling about and standing guard outside rooms. "He is the Hall's butler, and never was there a more fierce Cerberus to guard our doors than Mr. Maitland. He has the unique ability to approach without a sound, and catch small boys in the very act of willful misbehavior."

"I'm sure all three of you were quite willful," Lucia said, gazing around her. "Poor Mr. Maitland must have had his hands full when you were home. Rivers, I have never seen so many paintings!"

"We Fitzroys do seem to have a weakness for them," he admitted. She was right: every spare wall was hung with at least one large canvas, framed with a heavy gilded frame, something he took for granted. "I never gave it much thought, really. My cousin Hawk is the true connoisseur. He's advised Father on buying new pictures, as well as suggesting which other ones might be better retired to the attic."

She glanced at him curiously. "You have a cousin who's named Hawk? Like Hawkesmoor?"

He chuckled. "It's not his Christian name," he said. "Not that I can recall exactly what that is. Most likely John or George or somesuch. And it's not Hawkesmoor like the architect, but Hawkesworth for his ducal title, which we shorten to Hawk. The same applies to my older brother Harry, who isn't really a Henry or Harold, but Earl of Hargreave."

She paused, running her fingers lightly over the polished edge of a long satinwood sideboard while she considered. "So your true name isn't Rivers after all?"

"No, it is," he said, a little sheepishly. Most of the greater world went through life without any honorific whatsoever, but since his family was so riddled with titles of every degree, being a younger son had always been something just short of an embarrassment. "Being the third son, I have neither title nor name beyond Lord Rivers Fitzroy, and Rivers is what they poured over my forehead when I was baptized, or so goes the old family jest. Hah, here is wounded Juno, and still not mended."

He stopped before a nearly life-sized marble statue of the Roman goddess, standing on a black pedestal between two tall arched windows. Juno stood with her weight on one foot with the other coyly bent, and it was this foot that had suffered the long-ago loss of a toe to the Fitzroy brothers. And it *was* still broken, awkwardly snapped off where Harry's cricket bat had struck.

Rivers patted the statue familiarly on the knee. "I cannot believe no one has noticed it," he said. "Nor, apparently, has the lady herself complained over the last decade."

"She should have kicked you at the very least," Lucia said, coming to stand on the other side of the statue. "What became of her toe?"

Rivers tried to look solemn. "I regret to admit that I do not know. My dog—a wicked small terrier named Scrap—seized it as a prize and ran off, and for all I know it's now buried beside some prized mutton bone. So while it was Harry's bat that dealt the blow, it was my dog that completed the crime, and so I am every bit as much at fault."

She laughed, her head tipped to one side and the pale sun from one of the windows lightly gilding her cheek. Her beauty struck him once again, a kind of glorious enchantment that only she possessed, but this time there was something more, something amazing, that took him by stunned surprise.

Standing there with the arch over her head like a kind of halo, her blue flowered gown an extension of the now-blue sky through the window and her profile a twin to the marble goddess's, she looked as if she'd as much a place here as Juno herself. She looked as if she *belonged* here, as if she'd spent her entire life at a house such as this. The realization jolted him, and he swiftly tried to control it with reason: it was the dress, the sunlight, her smile, together conspiring to make the playhouse tiring-girl look at ease in the country house of the Duke of Breconridge.

"And thus I have seen the deity's toe, Rivers, or the absence of it," she said playfully, unaware of his thoughts. "Show me more of you as a boy, if you please."

Forcibly he pulled himself back to the present, the way she always wished him to be. He took her hand to lead her down the hall, trying to think of something else to show her in the vast house that was part of him. Absently he glanced at the large painting to his left, and smiled.

"Here's another," he said. "This is a portrait of me

with my brothers, though we're so young that you'd never recognize us from this now."

Frowning with concentration, she studied the painting. "I wouldn't know them anyway. I don't believe your brothers ever came with you back among the dancers, did they?"

"No, they wouldn't," he said absently. "They're both too occupied with their wives and children to bother with actresses or dancers now."

He'd forgotten all about this painting. He and his brothers had been very young, but at least Harry and Geoffrey had been old enough to have been breeched, both of them dressed like little gentlemen in miniature with their dark hair curled and clubbed to resemble wigs. He himself was still in a young child's long gown with a satin sash, and his pale blond hair in wispy ringlets to his shoulders. His brothers had teased him about those ringlets, he remembered that, just as he remembered posing for the artist in a makeshift studio in one of the guest bedchambers, and not beneath the shady tree shown in the finished picture.

"You don't look as if you belong with them," Lucia said. "You look different."

"That's because I was added in afterward, by a different artist," he said. "I suppose I was considered too young when my brothers were first painted."

It made sense to him, but not to her. "Why are you waving your arms about like that? Are you trying to get their attention?"

"I'm holding my hands out because I was still unsteady on my feet," he explained patiently, but clearly she wasn't going to believe him. "Here, I'll show you a place where we used to dare one another to go."

"A dare?" she asked, intrigued and perking up with interest as they turned down another hall. "Is it a frightening place?"

"No, but it was strictly forbidden," he said, trying to sound mysterious. "We were never to go inside, let alone touch anything. No one was permitted there, yet still we did, and never were caught."

He threw open the last door with a flourish and she hung back in the doorway, uncertain of what she'd see.

"It's the King's Bedchamber," he said with family pride. To have a bedchamber reserved for royalty meant that a family was important enough to have the king visit their home. "Only to be used by His Majesty when he comes calling, and never anyone else."

Tentatively she stepped inside the shadowy room. The curtains were drawn against fading from the sun, and the furniture was shrouded in drop cloths, but still the state bed rose in all its gilded glory, with a towering canopy and carved mahogany unicorns and lions supporting the bedposts.

"Does His Majesty visit often?" she asked in a respectful whisper.

"He has been here three times in my memory," he said, tugging one of the curtains open to let in a splash of sunlight across the patterned carpet. It also lit the portrait on the wall of his father, sternly imposing in the red velvet and white ermine of his Garter robes.

"That must be your father," Lucia asked, following his gaze. "You're fair where he is dark, but I can see your face in his."

"Then you're seeing a resemblance that few others find," Rivers said, considering the picture beside her. "You see how he's glowering, reminding you that it's treasonous for anyone other than royalty to be in this room. Why, if it were up to him, you'd be locked away in the Tower."

Her eyes widened even as she laughed. "It is not treason to be here!"

"High treason." He folded his arms over his chest and

scowled ominously, trying to emulate his father. "The highest. Should you care to test me, madam?"

She grinned, then crossed the room and hopped up squarely into the middle of the enormous state bed.

"Test me, my lord," she said, patting the coverlet beside her in invitation. "I dare you."

Her audacity shocked him. Not even his brothers would have taken that dare as boys. For all his teasing, the state bed was sacrosanct and untouchable, and always had been.

Until now. Until Lucia.

"Dare accepted," he said, jumping onto the bed beside her. Delighted, she turned her head and kissed him, and he thought of how this was the best possible dare in his entire life.

"Before, with the footman, you called me your friend," she said, her voice a husky whisper. "Your dear friend. You didn't have to do that, but you did."

"Because it was the truth," he said, brushing a stray curl back from her forehead. "I said the same to McGraw today, before you joined us."

Her smiled tightened, and she glanced down. "He believes I'm your whore."

"I told him you were my dearest friend," he said firmly, "and that I hold you in the highest respect and regard."

Her eyes fluttered up. "You did?"

"I did," he said, leaving no doubt, "because it is God's own truth. I also informed him that if he ever dares treat you in any fashion unworthy of you, he shall answer to me."

"Oh, Rivers," she murmured, the slight catch in her voice betraying her emotion. "That is why you were so— so short with Mr. McGraw this morning, wasn't it? You were challenging him on my behalf?"

"I was defending you, sweetheart," he said, leaning

closer to kiss her again. "Because you deserve defending. Because—"

"Rivers?" said a woman behind him. "Heavens, Rivers, that is you."

Instantly he whipped about, shielding Lucia with his body. The woman behind him wasn't just a woman, but a duchess: Her Grace the Duchess of Breconridge, his stepmother, Celia.

Nor was she alone. In the doorway with her were not only Mr. Maitland the butler and Tomlin the callow footman, but his two sisters-in-law, Harry's wife, Gus, Countess of Hargreave, and Geoffrey's wife, Serena, Lady Geoffrey Fitzroy. They were staring with various reactions—dismay, horror, amusement, and most of all, surprise—but none of that could match the mortification he felt there with Lucia beside him. Damnation, why hadn't anyone *told* him the ladies were here?

But all his ever-gracious stepmother did was smile warmly, a smile that included Lucia as well.

"How happy we are to see you, Rivers," she said. "Will you and your friend join us for tea?"

When this day had begun, Lucia had expected to play her part for Mr. McGraw. She'd never thought her performance would continue in the late afternoon, sitting on the edge of a silk-covered gold chair in a parrot-green parlor in Breconridge Hall, before an audience that consisted of a duchess, a countess, another lady, and, of course, Rivers.

Rivers had assured her she'd been prepared for that earlier performance, but he'd said nothing of this one, and since they'd been discovered, they'd had no time alone together to discuss it. She had no lines to recite, no well-practiced and considered gestures to fall back upon—especially not after having made her entrance and first impression tumbled like the lowest, most wanton chambermaid on the forbidden state bed. Now she'd only herself to rely upon, and she'd never been more unsettled or uncertain in her life.

She didn't know anything about ladies like these, the true versions of what Rivers had been trying to teach her to be. She'd seen plenty of gentlemen in the tiring room, but never ladies. And these women awed her: their grace, their jewels, their gentle voices, the way they smiled and held their teacups and laughed together.

Thanks to Rivers, she would not shame herself entirely, knowing important small things like how to curtsey when introduced and not to wipe her fingers on the tablecloth. Thanks to him, too, her flowered silk gown and blue short cape were entirely appropriate. But among these ladies, her accent sounded like a third-rate echo, her posture wrong, and her laughter strained and anxious. She felt ungainly and clumsy, as if she were back in *corps de ballet* rehearsal with her uncle Lorenzo critically noting every misstep and awkwardness. It was one thing for her to play at being Mrs. Willow before Mr. McGraw or Mrs. Currie, the mantua-maker, but another entirely to do so with these ladies.

"How long have you known Rivers, Mrs. Willow?" the duchess asked as soon as all the niceties of serving the tea had been accomplished. "I cannot recall Rivers bringing any other lady here to us at Breconridge Hall, so you must be a very fond friend indeed."

Her Grace smiled pleasantly, full of encouragement as any good hostess would do. The pale late sun caught the diamonds that she wore in her hair, around her throat, and at her wrists; given the rest of the house, Lucia was certain they were real, and not paste, and of a value inconceivable to her. The duchess was an exceptionally beautiful older lady, with masses of pale gold hair and a serene smile, and while Lucia believed her question was intended to show genteel interest and not to pry, it still terrified her, and she took another sip of her tea to stall, and think.

Was she still to be Mrs. Willow, or should she confess her role in the wager? What had Rivers told his family? How much did they know of who she truly was?

"Yes, Your Grace, Lord Fitzroy has been an excellent friend to me," she said cautiously. She'd succeeded as mad Ophelia; she could succeed again as Mrs. Willow, if that was what he wanted. "In fact sometimes it does seem as if we've known each other all our lives."

"An excellent . . . *friend*," the duchess repeated, delicately making it clear that she understood their true relationship, but that she didn't care. "How fortunate that you have found each other."

Lucia flushed. So the duchess had guessed she was Rivers's lover. What of it? She was, wasn't she? And if Her Grace was going to continue pouring her tea as if she truly were Mrs. Willow, then who was Lucia to disappoint her?

The younger ladies made happy sighs and coos of appreciation, a sign that she hadn't entirely faltered yet. Still, she glanced pointedly at Rivers, praying he'd understand that she needed his guidance. "Isn't that so, my lord?"

Rivers smiled and ladled more sugar into his tea, clearly enjoying himself much more than she.

"Indeed it is, my dear," he said. "We met long ago on the Continent, Celia. Her late husband was an acquaintance of mine. A military gentleman."

"Oh, sweet heavens, how very sorry I am for your loss," the duchess said, reaching out to pat Lucia's sleeve. "So young to be a widow! I, too, was scarcely a bride when my first husband was taken from me. How generous of Rivers to offer you solace in your grief."

"The Fitzroys are most accomplished at offering support and comfort," Lady Geoffrey said, smiling in sympathy. She was the most elegantly exotic woman that Lucia had ever seen in England, with golden skin and pale amber eyes and the merest hint of a foreign accent to her words that made Lucia wonder where she'd been born. "Before our marriage, I suffered through some difficult times, and I doubt I would have survived if not for Geoffrey's strength to lean upon."

"How fortunate for you, Lady Geoffrey," Lucia said softly, turning toward the other woman. The mention of marriage to a Fitzroy brother made her uneasy, for there was no question that she and Rivers would never be linked in that way. "Such devotion is a marvelous thing in a husband."

"My Harry has that quality as well," Lady Augusta said, her hand resting protectively over the swell of her pregnant belly. Lucia recalled Rivers saying how these two young women had so far produced only daughters, to the disappointment of his father, and how the entire family was anxiously awaiting the birth of this baby, and praying it was male. To Lucia, that had seemed an unfair judgment on both the mothers, and the infant girls, and she felt even more sympathy for Lady Augusta now that they'd met. Lady Augusta, or Gus, as Rivers called her, was the least daunting of the ladies, her round freckled face and coppery hair cheerfully engaging, if not fashionable.

"No gentleman could be more loyal to me and our little girls than Harry," Gus continued, "no matter what the rest of the world says."

The duchess leaned forward with concern. "Hush, hush, Gus, please don't vex yourself," she said. "Pray remember why we've come here, to remove you from the stresses of town, for the sake of the babe."

But Gus didn't seem to hear her, or chose not to. "Have you any children of your own, Mrs. Willow?"

"No, my lady," Lucia said. This was another awkward question that struck too close to her heart, and she was unable to keep the sadness from her voice. Because she'd had neither brothers nor sisters, she had always dreamed of having a large family of her own, and more than once she'd had to stop herself from including Rivers as the father in that dream. "Mr. Willow and I were not blessed."

"Children *are* a blessing, the greatest blessing in life," Gus said. "My three daughters are my little angels, a constant joy to Harry and to me."

Rivers laughed. "Your daughters are little hellions, Gus, and you know it," he teased. "Not that it makes them any less delightful."

Gus didn't deny it. "They are still a blessing," she said firmly. "I'd wish nothing less for your friend Mrs. Willow."

"Mrs. Willow and I have had other exciting events to occupy us at present," he said, smiling at Lucia. "Isn't that so, my dear?"

Lucia blushed with confusion at that endearment. What was he doing anyway? How did he wish her to answer?

"Forgive me, my lord, but perhaps we should not speak of that now," she said. "It might not be, ah, suitable."

"Now you intrigue us, Mrs. Willow," Serena said. "Surely these events that Rivers mentioned cannot be unsuitable for discussion here."

Gus nodded eagerly. "Yes, yes, you must tell us the truth, Mrs. Willow. One never can know with Rivers."

"Don't badger her, Gus," Rivers said. "She won't tell, and neither will I. It wouldn't be a secret if we did."

"His lordship is quite right," Lucia said. She set her saucer down on the table beside her, fearing it would rattle in her hands. "This—this secret is still not ripe for telling. Suffice to say that in my present situation in life, I owe his lordship everything."

"Everything?" repeated the duchess, clearly astonished.

"Everything," Lucia repeated, her gaze locked with Rivers's.

"Everything," he echoed softly. "That's very generous of you, Mrs. Willow."

There was no mistaking how blatantly he was letting his admiration for her show in his eyes. Part of her—a sizable part—wanted to gaze back at him in exactly the same way, and even to rush across to his chair and fling her arms around his shoulders and kiss him for being so ridiculously important and perfect to her.

"It's not generosity, my lord, but the truth," she said, forgetting being nervous and uncertain as well as the ladies, and seeing only him. He had that power over her, or perhaps it was she who could focus so completely on him. "You have given me more than ever I deserved."

He swept his hand grandly through the air. "You exaggerate, madam."

"Not at all," she said, raising her chin. "You gave me hope where I thought I had none, and made opportunity from the most insubstantial of dreams."

"'A dream itself is but a shadow,'" he said, quoting Hamlet. "You know that as well as I."

She smiled, for the next line of the play was strangely apt, as likely he'd already known. "'Truly, and I hold ambition of so airy and light a quality that it is but a shadow's shadow.'"

He didn't answer, but smiled, letting her words float there in the air, meant for him, meant for her. She was only vaguely aware of the two other young women beside her, listening rapt, their tea forgotten.

"Puzzles within puzzles, Rivers!" exclaimed the duchess, perplexed. "What is the meaning of these lovely words that you and Mrs. Willow are tossing back and forth like a golden ball?"

He grinned, still not looking away from Lucia. "No puzzles, Celia," he said. "These lovely words belong to the playwright Mr. Shakespeare, and Mrs. Willow and I often recite scraps of his plays back and forth to amuse ourselves."

"Will you please recite more, Mrs. Willow?" Gus begged. "I vow you are more magical than any London actress."

"Perhaps another day," Rivers said, setting aside his cup as he stood. He bent down and kissed Gus's cheek with genuine fondness. "Mrs. Willow and I have imposed upon you long enough, Gus. You must be weary if you came down from London this morning, and I wouldn't want to risk my brother's wrath by tiring you with my nonsense."

"Then you must promise to bring her back while we are here in the country," Gus said. "I'm not permitted to do *anything,* and you've no notion of how tedious idleness can be."

Serena rose, gliding over to rest her hand on Gus's shoulder. "Yes, Mrs. Willow, I hope you'll return," she said, smiling warmly. "No matter how close a friend you are to Rivers, he cannot keep you entirely to himself."

"Yes, oh, yes," the duchess said. "Fresh company is so hard to come by in the country, and you are a rare delight. You must bring her back to us, Rivers, and soon."

"You are too kind, Your Grace," Lucia said, overwhelmed by their kindness. Her head was still spinning when Rivers handed her into the carriage for the drive back to the Lodge.

"Well, now, that worked out well enough, didn't it?" he said as soon as the door latched behind them. He reached out and pulled her close, his arm familiarly around her shoulder. "I didn't expect Celia and the others to be there, but you, my darling Mrs. Willow, could not have made a better impression upon them."

He tried to kiss her, but she twisted around to look him squarely in the eye. "You truly didn't know they'd be there, Rivers?" she asked. "It wasn't another of your tests or trials for me?"

"Not at all," he said, and with such forthright indignation that she believed him. "Why in blazes would I have contrived to have you first meet my stepmother lying in the middle of the state bed?"

Her cheeks warmed at the memory, yet she laughed, too, because it had been so mortifyingly preposterous.

"No, you wouldn't," she agreed. "They all know now that I'm your mistress. A blind man could have seen that. And yet those ladies were so kind to me, Rivers. Such grand noble ladies! They needn't have been kind, not at all, and yet they were."

"There are plenty of noble ladies who believe themselves grander than God, but not those three," he said. "None of them would ever judge you for what you were, but only on what you are."

"Is that what you wished me to say, then?" she asked uncertainly. "Did you want me to tell them who and what I truly am?"

"I wanted you to tell whatever would put you at your ease in their company," he said with maddening logic. "You chose to say nothing, and that is well enough, too. I told you, it was your decision."

"But I couldn't tell them, Rivers," she protested. She understood perfectly well; why couldn't he? "They are *ladies,* and they would not be pleased to have either a playhouse tiring-girl or your mistress sitting as their equal."

"You are no longer a tiring-girl, nor will you ever be one again," he said firmly. "Besides, you misjudge those good ladies. The duchess does look for good company wherever she finds it. She truly doesn't care about a person's station or past, nor do the younger women, either. It's not my place to tell their stories, but each one of those ladies has suffered from life's unfairness, one way or another, and they would never fault you for not being of their rank."

"But you cannot deny that rank makes them different from me, Rivers, just as it makes you different," she said slowly, remembering the richly appointed rooms, one after another, that she'd seen earlier in his family's house. "It's part of you, and you cannot escape it. That's why you took me there in the first place, isn't it? For me to see where you lived as a boy?"

He grunted, noncommittal. "In a way, yes," he admitted. "I thought you'd enjoy seeing it. Quite the gilded pile, isn't it?"

She shook her head a fraction, unwilling to dismiss the afternoon with a jest. "I have not met your father, Rivers, but from what you have told me of him, I can see that the Hall is his, grand and formal and stiff, while the Lodge is all yours."

"To be sure, Father's left his mark on the Hall," he said, "but the estate more rightly belongs to all the dukes of Breconridge, past, present, and future, with father only the current example of the species."

He was in a good humor, expansive and relaxed, and she hated to ruin it, but she still had questions.

"Breconridge Hall is undeniably beautiful," she said carefully, "and yet while it was your home when you were a child, it can never be yours again."

"It belongs to the dukes of Breconridge," he repeated patiently. "I've explained that before. When Father dies, it shall go to Harry, who will become the fifth duke."

She linked her hand into his, toying with his fingers. "And after that? What if he and Lady Augusta never do have a son? What then?"

"Then the estate goes to Geoffrey and his sons," he explained. "Lucia, I've already told you this."

"But now that I've met them, I want to be sure I understand," she said. "What if Lord and Lady Geoffrey have no sons?"

"You are the pessimist today, aren't you?" he said, only half-teasing. "Then the estate would pass to me, and my sons. But that is not going to happen. Both Harry and Geoffrey and their wives are young and clearly capable of producing a half-dozen sturdy boys among them. Now, if you please, Lucia, I would rather we not discuss this any further. Regardless of what you or I say, Breconridge Hall will always be inherited by some young Fitzroy fellow or another. That cannot be changed, and never will."

The carriage bumped over a rut in the road, a jarring shake that gave extra emphasis to the finality of his words.

But it all made sense now to Lucia. He had promised to trust her with his past, and he had in fact trusted her with more than perhaps he'd intended, or realized.

"That is why you took me there," she said softly. "You must remain who you were born. You cannot change your life, or your lot in it, but you have changed mine."

He frowned. "You have changed yourself, Lucia," he said, pointedly ignoring her observation about him. "I've only made it possible with a bit of advice and a few fripperies along the way. You did all the work. Look at how much you've accomplished, too. I cannot wait to see the look on Everett's face. You must admit the transformation has been quite a success."

"I suppose it is," she said slowly, for this was hardly the conclusion she'd expected from him. "You will win your wager."

"Oh, hang the wager," he said. "I've never been more proud of you today, Lucia, first with McGraw, and then with the ladies. When I saw you sitting in the green parlor with a porcelain cup in your hand, taking tea between Gus and Serena, you looked as if you could have been their sister. You *belonged* there."

But she didn't. Not in that house, not among the welcoming ladies of his family. It was, in a way, a complement to her acting ability, her skill at imitating noblewomen as she sat in their midst. But she wasn't one of them, and all the lessons in the world wouldn't change that. She knew the truth, even if he pretended not to. Breconridge Hall was not her place, and all his wishful thinking could never make it otherwise.

"You mean Mrs. Willow belonged," she said finally. Mrs. Willow: the lady he'd made her over into, the one he'd wanted, his creation, not the tiring-girl who'd first bluffed her way into his house to see him. "Not Lucia di Rossi."

"I mean the woman I love," he said, gently cradling her jaw in the palm of his hand.

"Doubt thou the stars are fire;
Doubt that the sun doth move;
Doubt truth to be a liar;
But never doubt I love."

Her heart melted: how could it not? Such sweet words, such perfect words of love and devotion! He kissed her, and she kissed him in return, deeply, fervently, with all the love that she possessed. She would do as she'd told him to do, and love him and this moment as if no others would follow.

But never doubt I love . . .

It was only later, much later, as she lay beside him in his bed and the new moon rose high outside his bedchamber window that she remembered that those beautiful words of promise and fidelity had belonged to the doomed, disloyal Hamlet.

CHAPTER
15

After the excitement of the day before, Rivers and Lucia were in no hurry to rise the next morning. The rain had left their retreat on the roof too wet to use, and they had spent the night in the large, old-fashioned bed in Rivers's rooms. She had been quiet, even subdued, but she also had been so passionate during their lovemaking that he'd put aside any worries that she might be unwell. She loved him, loved him as he loved her, and that had been all that mattered.

It was nearly noon when they finally wandered downstairs for a late breakfast, still in their dressing gowns, and going no farther than the small parlor Rivers had converted into a library. He hadn't bothered to have Rooke shave him, and she hadn't called to have her hair dressed, letting it tumble luxuriantly around her shoulders, the way he liked best.

There was no talk of any further lessons. After Lucia's successful audition the day before, there seemed no point. Whatever additional instruction she might require could come later, once she'd rehearsed with the other players for the benefit. He didn't suggest returning to Breconridge Hall, either, despite the urgings of his stepmother and sisters-in-law. Although that surprising visit had gone better—infinitely better—than he ever would have expected, he wanted to keep Lucia to himself as their days together dwindled.

Nor did either of them speak of their imminent departure from the Lodge to London. They had this day left to enjoy and another besides, and then they would return to town, and this part of their lives together would be done. Everything would change, and they both knew it. It seemed that they tacitly agreed that they would savor these last two days in the country and not talk yet of the future, as Lucia had always begged Rivers to do.

But silence on the subject did not mean that Rivers was not considering their shared future. Far from it. He had no intention of giving Lucia up simply because the wager would be done, and they'd have a change of scenery. He loved her too much for that. In these short weeks, she'd become the best part of his life, and he easily envisioned a pleasurable and overlapping existence for them in London.

After her audition with McGraw, he was certain the manager would offer Lucia a permanent place in his company, as she deserved and as she wanted. He regretted having to share her with so many others, with the other actors and people of the playhouse as well as with the audiences who would surely adore her, but he would not dream of denying her the success that she'd wanted for so long. As much as he loved her, he couldn't selfishly expect her to give up that dream to dote upon him, nor did he want the guilt of her squandered talent upon his conscience, either.

He would simply occupy himself as usual with his own affairs during the day, and then she would again be his by night and on days when the playhouse was shut. He had already instructed his agent to find a small but elegant furnished house for her, one that was convenient to both the playhouse and his own home in Cavendish Square, and where he could visit her whenever he pleased.

True, she claimed not to want anything else from him, but a house would be different. Because of his wager, she'd been forced to quit her last lodgings, and in a way he felt he owed her a new residence. Besides, the dream of gathering her up from the playhouse each night after yet another brilliant performance was very sweet indeed, and he was already imagining endless cozy suppers and intimate evenings together in the delightful little house.

He smiled fondly at her. They were sitting together on the sofa, or rather he was sitting, and she was lying curled upon it with her head resting against his thigh. Her hair was loose and tumbled around her shoulders, and her rose-colored silk sultana draped sensuously over her naked body, falling open to reveal her bare, pale calves and ankles and feet in green beaded heeled mules, all of her a sight that he'd never tire of.

He was pretending to read the newspaper that had come with the morning mail, while she was intent upon the small, fat book in her hand: *The History of Tom Jones, A Foundling* by Sir Henry Fielding. Given the freedom of his library, she'd surprised him by becoming a voracious reader; he intended to surprise her with a subscription to one of the lady's lending libraries in town so she'd never be without books again. It pleased him that they shared this, too, and he loved watching her as she read, with one finger pressed to her lips and her brows scowling in fierce concentration.

"It's a novel, sweetheart," he said mildly. "It does not merit that much agony from you."

Her brows unknitted, and she looked up at him. "But it does, Rivers," she said. "Once again Tom nearly finds Sophie, and yet again they miss each other."

He brushed an unruly lock of her hair back from her forehead. His hand trailed down her cheek to her shoulder, and slowly eased the silk away from her collarbone.

"If they found each other as easily as you wish, then the book would be only fifty pages instead of six hundred."

"I know," she said, "but still I wish to know how it ends, so I need to finish the book before we leave."

"No, you don't," he said, thinking more about the softness of her skin than the book. "Take it with you. I would never deprive you of the unbridled bliss of Tom and his Sophie."

"It *will* be bliss." She wrinkled her nose, but smiled at the same time to show she wasn't truly upset with him. "You shouldn't treat their love so lightly, Rivers."

He slid his hand lower, to find and cup her breast. "I wouldn't dare," he said, leaning down to kiss her.

She let the book drop from her hands to the floor and reached up to slip her fingers into his hair, cradling his jaw with her palm. She made a contented purr deep in her throat as his mouth moved over hers, deepening the kiss. Perhaps they should go back upstairs again, or perhaps he should just join with her here on the sofa.

He didn't hear the front door open, and at first the voices didn't register, either. But as those voices—a man and a woman—came closer, and grew louder, he realized he'd no choice but to pull away from Lucia.

"Hell," he muttered, as she sat upright beside him, modestly pulling the sultana back over her breast. "This is twice in two days I've had my privacy interrupted. If this is more of my infernal family, I mean to send them on their way before they—"

"Rivers, you dog," exclaimed Sir Edward Everett, throwing the door to the library open himself and striding boldly into the room. "Your man told me you were not at home, but I know you too well to believe that nonsense. At home, my foot! You're at home, oh, yes, home with this divine little creature."

He leered at Lucia, clearly not remembering her, nor recognizing her.

"Blast you, Everett, you can't come barging in here without warning," Rivers said, standing and putting himself between his friend and Lucia. "At least no gentleman does such a thing."

But Everett ignored him, trying to get a better look at Lucia. "Sir Edward Everett, my darling, your ardent admirer and a friend of this dry old philosopher."

"*Asino sciocco!*" exclaimed the woman, a few steps behind Everett. "Foolish donkey! Cannot you see who she is?"

The rustle of too many silk ruffles and too much perfume entered the room as well, and even without looking Rivers knew who it was.

"Magdalena!" cried Lucia, and not happily, either. She scrambled swiftly to her feet, clutching her sultana more tightly about her body. "Why have you come? Why have you followed me here?"

Everett drew back uneasily. "You know her, Magdalena? Do *I* know her?"

"Of course you do, Everett," Rivers said, unable to keep the disgust from his voice. How in blazes had the earlier blissful peace of being with Lucia in his library turned into this farcical circus? "Or you should anyway, considering she is going to be the reason you have lost a hundred guineas to me."

"And a sorry business it is, too, my lord," Magdalena said with an unconvincing show of indignation, the oversized plumes on her hat twitching with it. "The proof is here, yes? You have ruined my little cousin, haven't you, made her your *giocattolo,* your plaything?"

"Hah, I see it now," Everett said uneasily, shoving his hands into his coat pockets. "The chit's the serving-girl from the playhouse after all. But what the devil is this game, Rivers? When we made the wager, she was as plain as they come. Now she's—"

"Ruined," Magdalena said succinctly, stepping so close

to Rivers that it felt as if she were swaying against him. "You will be made to pay my family in return for my poor cousin's maidenhead, my lord."

Rivers stepped back, wanting none of the intimacy that her nearness suggested. Without looking, he felt Lucia beside him instead, tucking her hand into the crook of his arm. At least she didn't believe herself to be ruined, and he covered her fingers protectively with his own.

"You should not be here, Everett," he said, ignoring Magdalena's accusation. "By the rules of our wager, you were not to interfere with my instruction or with Miss di Rossi—"

"'*Miss* di Rossi' my lord!" exclaimed Magdalena, dramatically pressing a hand to her bosom. "Did she dare call herself that to you, my lord? A tiring-girl who has never so much as danced a single step on a stage with the company!"

"No, I haven't, Magdalena," Lucia said, each word as clipped and well-bred as Rivers's own. "That is the reason I no longer go by that name, but by Mrs. Willow."

"You've duped me, Rivers," Everett said indignantly. "Listen to the girl! She's no more a serving wench than I am. She's an utter sham, that's what she is."

Rivers smiled. He couldn't help it. "I thank you for the compliment, Everett, and your concession with it. Mrs. Willow's accomplished speech is the winning proof of my lessons, and her diligence."

"Aye, 'tis that, Sir Edward," Lucia said, instantly slipping back into her old accent. She huddled her shoulders, clutched her hands together, and ducked her head; even dressed in the luxurious silk sultana, she once again became the shrinking tiring-girl. "No one's a better schoolroom gov'nor than his lordship."

Rivers's smile widened to a fully fledged grin. How could it not, when she showed Everett up as neatly as this?

Everett jabbed his finger in the air, encompassing both Lucia and Rivers. "I still say it's a trick, a low and dirty trick, and the two of you have somehow contrived to make me look the fool. It's a good thing I came down here to see for myself, Rivers, before you made me the laughingstock of the entire town."

"I would never do that to you," Rivers said evenly. "No one will laugh at you, so long as you admit that you've lost the wager fairly."

"Blast you, Rivers, it's not right," Everett said, his outrage spilling over into petulant anger. "McGraw has already been boasting how he's to have this Mrs. Willow in his playhouse. Who is she? Where did you find her?"

"*Stupido,* she is my *cousin*!" Magdalena grabbed Everett by the sleeve to claim his attention, her voice turning shrill. "Do you not see what his lordship has done? He has made my innocent cousin *prigioniera del suo desiderio*—a prisoner of his desire! He has seduced her, debauched her, ruined her. You must help me, Sir Edward, help me to save her and our family's honor and pride, and to rescue her from—"

"Magdalena." Lucia deftly removed her cousin's hand from Sir Edward's arm and drew her away; she'd years of managing Magdalena, and it showed. "Let us leave the gentlemen to speak together alone, while we shall walk in the garden. Come, this way."

Glaring, Magdalena jerked away from Lucia. But though she pointedly pulled back, making a faint hissing sound between her teeth, she still sailed from the room in the direction that Lucia had suggested. As she followed her, Lucia smiled over her shoulder—a smile that was both warmly reassuring and conspiratorial, and reminded Rivers all over again of why he loved her so.

Magdalena was already through the door to the garden when Lucia hurried after her. Without a hat, she grabbed the cream-colored silk parasol she kept furled in the stand by the doorway, and followed her cousin into the garden.

"Magdalena, wait, please," she called, opening the parasol against the midday sun and tipping it back against her shoulder. She fell into the familiar Italian that was always used among the Di Rossis. "Wait for me."

But Magdalena didn't wait, rushing ahead toward the rose garden. From vanity, she'd always worn her skirts short enough to display her ankles and feet, and the high, white heels of her fuchsia-colored shoes crunched briskly across the stone path. Lucia could tell her cousin hoped the gentlemen were watching from the window: not only did she twitch her skirts higher with one hand while she walked, but she also made her hoops bounce and sway invitingly over her backside with each step.

"Magdalena, please," Lucia said breathlessly, finally catching up with her.

Her cousin turned to face her, swirling her skirts as she studied Lucia up and down.

"A parasol, Lucia?" she asked, her black painted brows arching with scorn. "With a silk dressing gown, too? So you mimic the manners of a fine lady as well as the speech. How amusing to see you like a chattering little ape, trying to copy the airs of your betters."

Lucia raised her chin, determined not to falter and sink beneath Magdalena's hateful words. Her cousin had always done that, used mean-spirited criticism and little untruths that were sharp as knives to make Lucia bow to her wishes, but Lucia refused to do it any longer. Rivers's lessons—and his love—had done more than change her speech and her clothing. He'd given her confidence in herself, and this might well be the greatest test of it.

"The parasol protects my complexion against the sun," she said, purposefully mild instead of defensive. "As they say, my face will be my fortune on the stage, and I cannot let it be ruddy and coarse."

Magdalena's eyes narrowed beneath the curving brim of her hat.

"Lah, if your face is your fortune, Lucia, then you must have no more than a farthing or two in your pocket," she said. "I cannot believe that a gentleman like Lord Rivers would ever take notice of you. Look at how slatternly you are dressed, with hair trailing down like a rat's nest. It only proves how tedious life in the country can be, that he would seek amusement with you."

"We have amused each other, yes," Lucia said, striving to keep her composure and not to wince in the face of Magdalena's casual cruelty. "But that does not answer why you have come here, too. If the country is so tedious, then why did you come with Sir Edward?"

Magdalena smiled smugly. "Because he invited me, of course. He is a gentleman of wealth and rank, and such gentlemen are not to be ignored. But then, you have already learned that with Lord Rivers."

Lucia had learned many things from Rivers, none of which she intended to share with Magdalena—who of course took Lucia's silence as agreement.

"Yes, once I confessed my concern for your welfare, Sir Edward was most kind to offer to bring me here," she said. "Very kind."

"You didn't care at all when I left the company," Lucia said, twisting the ivory handle of the parasol in her fingers. "How did you even know where I was?"

"Because all the town knows you are here," Magdalena said airily. "His lordship has as much as announced it."

Lucia frowned, thinking how very unlike Rivers such an announcement would be. "I doubt that."

"You shouldn't." Magdalena stopped before one of the rosebushes, idly cupping a blossom in her hand. "His lordship has assumed all the costs for your benefit, including the use of the Russell Street Theatre and the company. McGraw has told everyone. He is, of course, putting a brave face on the benefit by saying you will be his next great actress, but everyone knows his puffery comes from his lordship's purse, and not through any talent of yours."

"He has paid Mr. McGraw?" Lucia asked, stunned.

"Oh, yes," Magdalena said, breathing deeply of the rose's fragrance. "I cannot guess what it must cost to hire a playhouse for a night. Far more than the wager, that's certain."

"But I auditioned for Mr. McGraw," Lucia protested. "He would not have agreed to the benefit if he did not judge me acceptable."

"He would put a donkey on his stage if a rich man paid for it," Magdalena said. "You know you've no talent. If you did, you'd already be with our own company."

"I never could dance, because I cannot hear the music," Lucia said. "But I'm not dancing now. I'm acting."

Magdalena gave her wrist a dismissive little twist. "It is all performing. Either one has the gift for pleasing an audience, or one does not. You, Lucia, do not. Doubtless your precious benefit has cost his lordship a pretty penny, especially considering you are no one."

No one: for the first time Lucia was unable to brush away her cousin's gibe. Rivers had invited the manager to watch her audition, yes, but he'd also let her believe that it had been her talent alone that had won her the offer of the benefit. She had wanted it so badly to be so that she hadn't questioned the unlikelihood of McGraw's offer. Rivers had made everything else happen for her, so she'd simply accepted this, too.

She could feel her newfound confidence crumbling away beneath her. It wasn't that he didn't trust her; he didn't trust her talent, her gift, which somehow seemed infinitely worse. It *hurt.* She'd believed she'd accomplished so much, but perhaps she hadn't after all. McGraw had been so quick to praise her performance, and she'd been just as quick to accept his praise as her due. Of course he could pretend she was the most marvelous actress he'd ever witnessed. He was an actor himself, wasn't he? Oh, how easily she'd been gulled!

"Yet that is what a gentleman does when he is beguiled with a woman, isn't it?" Magdalena continued. She snapped the rose's stem, and began to walk slowly with it, tearing out the velvety red petals one by one and letting them flutter to the ground behind her. "He will do anything to find his way between her legs. His lordship is simply rewarding you for what you have granted him, and the more he gives you now, the easier it will be for him to justify casting you off when he is done with you. New clothes, a silk parasol, a playhouse benefit. You must have pleased him very much, cousin."

"It—it is not like that between us," Lucia stammered, denying what now seemed painfully obvious. "Not at all."

"No?" Magdalena paused, and ripped another petal from the rose. "You do not please him?"

"His lordship and I please each other," Lucia said, her voice small. "There are many things we enjoy in common."

"Things *in common*?" Magdalena repeated with scathing incredulity. "As I recall, his lordship was exceptionally ardent as a lover."

"You didn't love him," Lucia blurted out, unable to help herself.

"No, I didn't, any more than he loved me," Magdalena admitted with a careless shrug. Now that she'd found Lucia's weakness, she was clearly enjoying herself. "There was an excitement between us, an allurement, but when I said we were lovers I meant—"

"I know what you meant," Lucia said quickly. "It's different for Rivers and me."

"What, all sighs and Cupid's arrow, bleeding hearts and cooing doves?" Magdalena teased. "If that is what you believe you have with him, then you *are* a fool."

"I know what I have," Lucia said. What she had with Rivers was deeper, richer, more perfect than anything her cousin could ever understand, nor would she try to explain it.

But Magdalena didn't expect her to. "Most likely any attraction he has felt for you came simply because you were here in this wretched place, away from all other opportunity, and you made yourself available."

She tugged out several more of the rose's petals at once, carelessly tossing them aside. "If you wish to stay in his lordship's favor once you return to London, you must do better than—"

"Stop," Lucia said, snatching the battered rose from her cousin's hands. "Those roses belonged to his lordship's mother. All the flowers here are hers."

Magdalena's laugh was harsh and mocking. "If you are as sentimental as that, then he will weary of you even faster than I thought. I vow you will be forgotten in a month, Lucia. You are a passing amusement for his lordship, nothing more. But he does have a conscience, rare for a gentleman. You must make the most of that, and take all you can from him before he tires of you."

Lucia shook her head, clutching the rose protectively in her hands. The pieces all fit together too neatly to ignore.

"I'm not you, Magdalena," she insisted doggedly. "I won't do that with his lordship."

"You're an imbecile if you don't," her cousin said bluntly. "You may think you're better because he's taught you to sound like a lady, but it's a false parrot's trick. You're no different than before, not in the ways that matter most to him."

"He says I am," Lucia said defensively. In her heart, she didn't believe it herself, but she would never admit that to her cousin. "Yesterday we had tea with the ladies of his family at Breconridge Hall, and they all treated me as if I were Mrs. Willow."

"But his lordship himself doesn't believe that you are, does he?" Magdalena said shrewdly. "If you truly were a lady in his eyes, then you would not be here alone with him in his house, and you would still be a virgin. Gentlemen like him do not spend their lives with women like us."

Lucia flushed, for what her cousin said was painfully true. Again. She knew it herself. No matter how many times Rivers said he loved her, it would never be enough to make her his equal, like Lady Augusta and Lady Geoffrey.

Magdalena leaned close, her expression turning uncharacteristically earnest.

"Do not waste this opportunity, Lucia," she said. "His lordship is the son of a duke, with an income beyond our imagining. You must seize what you can, for yourself, for your family. You are by blood a Di Rossi, yes?"

"Yes," Lucia said, reluctantly. By birth she still was a Di Rossi and always would be, but that was in spite of the way the rest of her family had treated her after her father had died, not because of it.

Magdalena nodded, her dark eyes glittering like flint beneath the brim of her hat.

"Then you know what you must do," she said. "Di Rossis look after themselves first."

"Magdalena, I can't do that," Lucia said. "I won't."

"You will," Magdalena said, "or you are even more useless than I've ever thought before. Take every farthing, every jewel, every silk gown that his lordship offers you, because you will not be in his bed for long."

Here in the bright sun, Lucia saw tiny lines around her cousin's eyes and mouth, lines that might not show beneath the theater's paint and lights, but were inescapable anywhere else. She was still beautiful, but there was a desperation to her beauty that had not been noticeable before.

Lucia knew it was this way for all the women who danced in the company: their faces hardened and their jumps grew shorter, their knees gave way and their waists thickened, and before long they were relegated to character parts and dowdy costumes, and the rich gentlemen ceased to send them flowers or invite them to dine. Not so long ago, Magdalena would have scorned a lowly baronet like Sir Edward. Now, at twenty-eight, she was doing exactly as she advised Lucia to do: taking what she could before it was too late.

"Magdalena!" Sir Edward stood beckoning from the garden steps, Rivers behind him. They were once again smiling, as friends should; at least they hadn't come to blows, which is what Lucia had feared would happen.

"I must go," Magdalena said, waving gaily to the men. "But consider what I've said, Lucia, and if you've any wits at all, you will follow my advice."

She didn't wait for Lucia to answer, but hurried back to rejoin Sir Edward, greeting him as fondly as if they'd been parted a week instead of a quarter hour. Lucia followed more slowly, the parasol on her shoulder. Rivers was waiting for her, his smile every bit as happy as Sir Edward's was for Magdalena, and she'd no doubt his welcoming kiss would be equally warm.

But after her conversation with Magdalena, her thoughts were in turmoil. She knew that her cousin often said things simply to torment her, and she wasn't above invention and outright lies, either. Yet much of what Magdalena had said this time held the ring of unfortunate truth, so much that she couldn't put it from her mind. The world of rich gentlemen dabbling among actresses and dancers was a familiar world to Magdalena, and she spoke from experience that Lucia herself did not have. She couldn't deny that, as much as she wished to.

And one of Magdalena's barbs had struck her to the quick. To learn that Rivers had paid Mr. McGraw to praise her and agree to the benefit had wounded her pride and shaken her confidence, but most of all it had hurt to learn that Rivers had so little faith in her and her talent. His praise, his compliments, had meant the world to her, and had helped to bind them closer as friends as well as lovers. Yesterday she'd wanted so badly for him to trust her, but if what Magdalena had said was true, then she was the one who'd lost all trust in him.

She slowed her steps further. Magdalena and Sir Edward had already disappeared into the house, while Rivers continued to stand on the top step, waiting for her with his legs slightly apart and his hands clasped behind his back, a quintessential Rivers pose if ever there was one. Because they hadn't been expecting guests, his hair was loose and untied, as bright as gold in the sunlight, and his jaw unshaven. His dressing gown had loosened, the front gaping enough to allow the breeze to ripple it over his bare chest. He was smiling still, smiling at her, and the entire sight of him made her chest tighten and her heart grow heavy.

Because she *did* love him, and likely always would. Nothing Magdalena or anyone else said could change that. Yet she needed to ask him about McGraw, no matter how difficult it would be to find the words. She had to *know*.

"What is that in your hand?" he asked curiously as she climbed the steps to join him.

She stopped one step below him, the difference in their heights exaggerated all the more. She looked down into her hand, realizing she'd forgotten she held the mangled rose, half the petals torn away and the yellow stamen crushed in the center.

"It's a rose," she said softly, opening her fingers so he could see.

"Or what's left of one," he said. "My God, what happened to it?"

"Magdalena." She sighed ruefully, thinking how her cousin had scorned her for being too sentimental. "She was tearing it apart, and I couldn't bear to see her do so, because it's one of your mother's flowers. So I took it from her."

"How very like Magdalena," he said. "And how very like you as well."

Even earlier today, she would have accepted that as a compliment. After what Magdalena had said, however, she wasn't as sure, and all she did was smile uncertainly.

He didn't give her any clues, either, just held his hand out to her. "Come, let's see them off before she finds something else to destroy."

She closed the parasol and took his offered hand, and together they joined the others in the front hall. The farewells were brief and a little strained, yet for Lucia the discomfort did not end when Sir Edward's carriage drew away from the house.

"Clearly I've forgotten how Magdalena can be," Rivers said, watching the carriage. "When I see you side by side with her, I can scarcely believe you're cousins."

Neither could Lucia, especially not when she recalled how fashionably her cousin had been dressed. Perhaps she *had* become a slattern, as Magdalena had accused her of being, and self-consciously she smoothed the silk over her breast and tightened the sash around her waist.

"But then, some might wonder why I am friends with Everett," Rivers continued as they walked back inside the house, back to the library where they'd been earlier, back to the same sofa as if nothing had changed, when everything had. "He really can be quite an ass."

"You are not much alike that I can see," Lucia said

carefully, believing that was safe enough. There was nothing controversial there, for it was true, too. She'd never understood how the two men could be friends, thoughtful Rivers with boorish, bullying Sir Edward.

"No, we are not," Rivers agreed, dropping back down onto the sofa. "But he was the very first boy who befriended me at school, and we've remained friends ever since. We've always made foolish wagers, too, over everything and nothing, and this one's no different. Do you know he remains convinced that you will falter during the benefit, and he will win?"

"Truly?" It was all she could think to say. She didn't sit with him, but remained standing, her arms folded and her hands tucked inside the full sleeves of her sultana. "Sir Edward did not seem convinced of that earlier."

"He is now," Rivers said, smiling as he remembered. He patted the cushion beside him as a hint for her to join him on the sofa. "While you were walking with your cousin, I made sure of it by dropping a few choice words and hints to let him think he still has a chance to win. None of it was true, of course, but the last thing I wish is for him to withdraw from the wager altogether, and end the sport before it has begun."

None of this felt like sport to her, and she remained standing, her back stiff and her hands hidden in her sleeves. "What did you tell him?"

"Only enough for him to forget whatever nonsense McGraw has begun braying about the town," he said blithely. "Everett is easily distracted, you know. He certainly was by your pretty face. But then, so am I."

She turned away and went to stand at the garden window, ostensibly gazing at the flowers. She didn't want to hear about having a pretty face, not now. She wanted to know that she'd talent enough to earn an honest role on the London stage, and not have it bought for her like a sugary, iced sweet at the confectionery. It was inevitable that she'd lose Rivers, but she'd consoled herself by knowing she'd be able to support herself on the stage. Without that, she'd be left with nothing, absolutely nothing.

Unaware of her thoughts, Rivers came to stand behind her at the window. He slipped his arm around her waist to pull her close, and she couldn't keep from tensing.

"You'll prove to him and the rest how fine an actress you've become," he said softly, sweeping aside her hair to whisper in her ear. "No, how fine an actress you've always been. You'll show them your mettle, sweetheart, and let them see your magic."

"You're very certain," she said, her voice sounding brittle. The heat of his chest against her back, the warmth of his breath on her ear only served to muddle her more. "How do you know I won't turn mute with stage fright, and forget my lines before an audience, exactly as Sir Edward predicts?"

"Where has this worry come from, eh?" he asked. "What of not looking too far into the future?"

She didn't answer that, because she had no answer. She closed her eyes, trying to lose herself in the rightness of him behind her.

"I cannot help it," she said. "I think of all the other actresses who've come to London, and how most have failed. Why should I be different?"

"Because they're not you, Lucia," he said, feathering a kiss along the side of her throat. "That's the reason."

She longed to believe him, yet her doubts remained. What would she do if he admitted he'd paid McGraw? What would she do if he didn't?

"I'm not sure that's reason enough," she said. "All those other actresses thought the same of themselves."

"But without your merit, Lucia," he said. He'd shifted his hand over her breast, gently cupping it in his palm and teasing her nipple through the silk with his thumb.

"Once the world sees you in *Hamlet,* I guarantee you'll be the toast of the town.

> *"Soft you now! The fair Ophelia!*
> *Nymph, in thy orisons*
> *Be all my sins remember'd."*

She closed her eyes, the pleasure of his caress turned bittersweet by his words. If he hadn't quoted from the play again, she might have been able to put aside her doubts and give herself over to his lovemaking.

But having him fall back into quoting the play made that impossible. Only Rivers could transform a random line from *Hamlet* into something that was both intensely personal and seductive. What had started out as a lesson had become a kind of game between them, like a secret lovers' language, flirtatious banter that they'd made their own.

It had made her feel clever and witty, but also made her realize how special Rivers had become to her. She thought of the first time they'd worked together on that particular scene, of how patient he'd been with her, of how he'd explained that "orisons" was simply an old-fashioned word for prayers, and how they'd laughed together over the funny sound of it. He'd treated her with respect and regard, and in these last short weeks, she'd come to love and trust him as she'd never done anyone else. He was her lover, but he was also her friend, and the thought that she might soon be neither to him was unbearable.

"I . . . I must go," she said, pushing away from him.

"Go?" he repeated, surprised. "Where are you going?"

"To my room," she said, already at the doorway. "I . . . I need to begin packing my things for London."

"No, you don't," he said. "That's for Sally to do, not you. Please, Lucia. Come back."

But she was running up the stairs, her eyes awash with

tears. She heard him call her name again, yet still she ran, straight to her bedchamber. The door was open, and the young chambermaid was sweeping out the grate. She curtseyed to Lucia as all the servants had been instructed by Rivers to do, but even that simple gesture of unearned deference seemed like a mockery to Lucia.

"Go, please, at once," she said, her voice breaking. "Leave me alone."

The chambermaid scurried to obey, gathering up her brushes and bucket, but before she could close the door, Rivers stormed into the room, slamming the door shut after him.

"What in blazes is wrong with you, Lucia?" he demanded. His blue eyes were flashing, managing to look both angry and wounded at the same time. "Why did you run from me?"

"Nothing is wrong," she lied, backing away from him until she bumped into the bed, the mahogany rail pressing against her calf. "And I didn't run."

"Oh, yes, you did," he said, following her. "Clearly something has upset you, and I don't want you pretending otherwise. You were fine this morning. Was it Magdalena? Did she say something to distress you?"

She looked down, unable to meet his gaze, and realized she was still holding the battered rose. "Is it true that you paid McGraw to tell me I could act?"

"My God, is that what she told you?" He raked his fingers back through his hair, but he didn't answer her question, nor did he deny it; she wasn't surprised, for he was far too honorable to lie, even to save himself.

She raised her eyes to his. Now that she'd begun, she was determined not to back down until she knew everything. "Is it true?"

"What, that I paid McGraw to praise you?" He shook his head, again not in denial, but incredulity. "You would take that woman's word over mine?"

"I would take her word because it's the only one I have," she said, her own anger beginning to rise. "Until you tell me otherwise, I have no choice but to believe it's the truth."

His face flushed. "We both know that Magdalena will say whatever the hell she pleases."

"While you have said nothing," she shot back. "Tell me otherwise, Rivers. Tell me the truth."

He didn't answer, his jaw tight.

"The truth," she repeated. "Just—just tell me."

He took a deep breath, and let it burst out in an oath.

"Very well, then, I did pay McGraw," he said, biting off each word. "I've paid him for the use of his theater for a night, for rehearsals and other actors. I've paid for the playbills, and I've paid for the musicians, and yes, I paid for the carriage to bring him here for your audition. Is that enough truth for you?"

She gasped, her fury fueled by disappointment, and by fear, too, for a future that had abruptly lost all its bright possibilities.

"Why did you lie to me, Rivers?" she exclaimed. "Why did you tell me I had talent and a gift, when you didn't trust me enough to win my own praise, but instead had to *buy* it, like one more foolish bonnet I didn't want or need?"

"Because, damnation, Lucia, I love you," he said, his voice raised and his anger a match for hers. "I did it all for you, and I'd do it again."

"*Love!*" she cried in frustration. "How can you say you love me? How can you claim to do these things for me, for my sake, when you did not tell the truth to me about the one thing that mattered most?"

She hurled the crumpled rose at his chest and spun around, unable to face him. The last thing she wished now was for him to see the anguish and despair that she knew must show on her face.

But he caught her by the arm and yanked her back around, trapping her close against his chest with one arm. With his free hand, he caught her jaw and tipped it up so she was forced to look at him.

"I never lied to you," he said, his voice rough, more a command than a confession. "Not once. I never flattered you with empty praise. I never told McGraw how to judge you. It was up to you to impress him or not, and you did, exactly as I knew you would."

"But you *paid* him," she said, her breath coming so short and fast she was almost panting. "When you paid for the theater and the playbill and God knows what else, you bought his opinion of me, too."

"I never intended it to be like that, Lucia, I swear to you!"

"Then what was it like?" she demanded. "You didn't trust my talent enough to let it stand on its own, or to let me earn McGraw's praise. You cheated me, Rivers, and I can't see it any other way."

"But *why* would I do that?" he asked, his voice rough with urgency. "Why would I do that to you, Lucia, when from the beginning I've believed in you, praised you, been in awe of everything that your talent and gifts have driven you to achieve? Why would I undermine all that now?"

She didn't answer, her thoughts so confused that she didn't know what to say. But she *felt*: she was acutely aware of his fingers gripping her jaw and the strength of his grip and his will. She'd never seen him like this before, and it excited her, and frightened her a bit as well. She'd never been so aware of the difference in their size, of the raw strength he usually kept carefully hidden away beneath his scholarly gentility. Her breasts crushed to his chest with only two thin layers of silk between them, and there was no mistaking how aroused he was with the thickness of his cock pressing against her belly.

Beyond their own ragged breathing, she heard a bored dog barking in the distance as well as the house sparrows chattering from beneath the eaves outside her open window, ordinary sounds that somehow served to exaggerate the tension between her and Rivers. She tried to push free, and he jerked her back.

"Listen to me, Lucia," he said sharply. "I could have done what Magdalena said, and forced McGraw to take you whether you deserved it or not. I could have done just enough to win the wager. I could even have paid McGraw to make certain you failed. But I didn't. I kept my part of our bargain, and gave you the opportunity you wanted."

She sighed, a deep, shuddering gulp of a sigh that was halfway to a sob as her anger slipped away. She could feel it go, fading beneath the bright truth of his words. She knew he was right. She knew she'd been wrong. But far worse was knowing that she had wronged him, and she didn't know how to begin to apologize.

"Oh, Rivers," she whispered haltingly, regret and remorse sweeping over her as she shook her head back and forth. "I never meant—"

"No more, Lucia," he said roughly. "No more *words*."

He bent to kiss her, still holding her jaw captive as he slanted his mouth over hers, his tongue plunging and searching and marking her as his. His unshaven face scraped against her lips, burning them. His anger hadn't lessened: his kiss was demanding and possessive, and just short of punishing. If his words had failed to make her understand, then he clearly intended to do so this way.

But she could do that, too, and she reached up to hold the back of his head, her fingers tangling into his hair as she held him as steady as he'd done her. She freely gave herself up to the kiss and to him as well. She should never have doubted him, never have questioned his trust, and she kissed him in hungry abandon to prove that she was completely his. Off-balance, she clung to him, and together they toppled backward onto the bed.

Still joined to her by the kiss, Rivers shoved open the bodice of her sultana, not bothering to untie the sash as he exposed her from the waist. Immediately he bent to lick her bared breast, drawing her nipple into his mouth and rolling his tongue against it, a pleasure that was velvety-deep and streaked straight to her core. He ran his hands along the sides of her rib cage, caressing her but also holding her in a way that was every bit as possessive as the kiss had been. Lucia arched into him to seek more, and blindly tried to unfasten the silk frogs on his dressing gown.

He pushed her hand aside and impatiently tore at the fastenings himself. She'd a fleeting impression of Rivers in all his perfection, of focused power and hard muscles and a lion's mane of blond hair. His eyes were dark with lust, his entire body taut with it, and she could tell he'd crossed the point of self-control. Not that she cared; she'd crossed it, too.

"Hurry," she said breathlessly, whispering her legs apart in invitation. She felt heavy and full from wanting him, already wet with desire and longing. "Please."

There was too much tension in his face to answer as he settled between her legs, and she sighed as he eased his cock into her passage. She always loved the moment of joining with him, of becoming truly his, and she caught her breath as he sank deeper and filled her all the way. He hooked his arms beneath her bent knees to open her even farther, and began to thrust in steady, forceful strokes that pushed her back across the bedcover. She reached up to hold his shoulders, the rose-colored silk sleeves slipping back and pooling around her arms, and crossed her legs over his back. Their bellies struck together with each thrust, and she loved that, too, arching her hips from the bed to meet him.

"Open your eyes," he ordered. "Damnation, Lucia, look at me. Don't hide. Don't run away again."

She hadn't even realized that her eyes had been closed, but she opened them now, wide, her gaze locking with his and her lips parted. With each plunging stroke she felt the tension building inside her and growing in shimmering, heated waves that melted away the last of her doubts. He was relentless, giving her everything she needed and more, and she writhed beneath him, doing the same for him.

It was always like this between them when they made love. Here there were no doubts, no suspicions, no secrets, no difference of ranks. Here everything was reduced to the essence of love, and the two of them bound together.

"I love you," she said raggedly, her words punctuated by the rhythm of his thrusts. "Oh, Rivers, yes!"

"Yes," he repeated, a single raspy, guttural syllable as he bowed his head against her shoulder. *"Yes."*

She came before he did, clawing at his shoulders, with her cries of release echoing in the bedchamber. Still she shook beneath him as he joined her, tensing as at last he spent in waves that shook them both.

Afterward they lay close together, their arms and legs entwined. She held him, and he held her, neither wishing to relinquish the other. It had as much to do with peace as with love: peace, and love, and trust, and contentment, all woven together so perfectly that it was impossible to tell where one ended and the next began.

She shifted just enough to pull the coverlet over their bodies, and then curled against his body. She smiled down at him, lightly tracing the bow of his lips with her fingertip.

Without opening his eyes, he caught her finger to stop its roaming.

"You're tickling me," he protested mildly. He turned

her finger to kiss the tip, then swiped it wetly with his tongue.

She laughed, thinking of how impossibly dear he had become to her. It wasn't just their bodies that were joined, but their souls as well.

"What you said about McGraw and the audition and the rest," she said softly. "Why did you do that for me?"

He opened his eyes, as blue and clear as truth itself.

"Because I love you, Lucia," he said. "Because I love you, I will give you whatever makes you happy."

"*You* make me happy, Rivers," she whispered, bending down to press her lips to his. "You make me, oh, so, so happy, and you must know I'd give the world for you to feel the same."

He smiled. "You already have."

She smiled, too, and bent to kiss him. So it was as simple, and as complicated, as that. It was love, and she felt the tears well up clear from her heart.

CHAPTER
16

Rivers slowed his horse as he came within sight of the Lodge. This was his favorite time of the day in summer, early in the morning when the dew glistened on the grass and the still-rising sun hadn't yet found its midday heat. He smiled fondly at the Lodge and its imposingly homely façade, wanting to remember it like this when they returned to London this afternoon. He'd been happier here these last weeks than at any other time in his life: so blissfully, joyfully happy that he'd sound like a complete love-struck fool if he ever tried to describe it aloud.

His smile turned into a grin. He *was* a love-struck fool, and he'd make no apologies for being so. He glanced up at the corner window that belonged to Lucia's bedchamber, imagining her as he'd left her earlier to go riding. She'd been sleeping, curled on her side with one little hand tucked beneath her cheek, and she'd scarcely stirred when he'd smoothed her hair back from her face to kiss her.

But sleepy or not, she *was* happy again. He was certain of that, and the certainty was what made him so happy now as well. He supposed they'd had a quarrel last night—he wasn't entirely sure—but he did know that he'd managed to say the proper words to make things right between them once again. No, he hadn't just said the proper words, calculated to please her. He'd spoken the truth, straight from his heart, and that was how she'd heard it, too. Love and truth and Lucia: what better combination could there be?

She'd be awake by now, and likely reading. She was desperate to finish *Tom Jones* before they left, even though he'd told her she could have the book to take with her. He imagined her now, lying naked beneath the sheets that still smelled of sex, a little frown on her face as she raced through the book. He could already predict they'd spend most of breakfast discussing Tom and Sophie, and that made him smile, too.

He whistled for Spot, and turned his tired horse toward the small stable yard. He could hear voices from the other side of the tall stone wall, though he couldn't yet quite make out who it was. The hour was too early for any tradesmen; most likely it was simply stable boys or one of the footmen from the house.

But as soon as he turned the corner, he saw it wasn't a servant at all. It was his father, watering his large bay gelding as he addressed Rivers's groom. He'd thought Father would remain in London at least another fortnight, but apparently he'd decided to follow the ladies to the country early.

Even at this hour of the morning, Father cut an impeccably imposing figure. Although he was past sixty now, he still sat straight and tall in the saddle, his crimson riding coat perfectly tailored over his shoulders and the long row of engraved silver buttons glinting in the sun. His queue was tied back with a black silk ribbon, and his boots were polished to a mirrorlike gleam. Even the silver spurs on his heels shone.

And from the clipped way in which he was speaking to the way his black cocked hat was jammed low on his head, it was also abundantly clear that His Grace the Duke of Breconridge was not in an agreeable humor.

"Good day, Father," Rivers called, striving to remain cheerful in the face of his father's grimness. "How fine it is to see you here this morning. I didn't expect you to leave town this early."

"I came because of Gus." Father's expression did not change. "If she has come down to Breconridge Hall to birth my grandson, then I wish to be here as well. And you needn't ladle out the pleasantries, Rivers. Under the circumstances, they are unnecessary, even distasteful."

"Ahh," Rivers said as he dismounted, handing his reins to one of the grooms. "Then at least let me offer you a bit of refreshment."

"Thank you, no," Father said curtly. "We shall walk amongst your mother's wildflowers. It will not take me long to say what needs saying."

Immediately he turned on his heel, expecting Rivers to follow. For a moment Rivers considered not doing so. He wasn't a child, but a grown man, and it irritated him to be treated this way. On the other hand, he'd no wish to make a scene before his own stable men, and so in the end he did follow, catching up to Father in several long strides so that they were walking together.

"Are you certain you would not prefer to go inside, Father?" he asked. "The sun—"

"The sun does not offend me," Father said, pointedly looking Rivers up and down. "If you were dressed like a Christian gentleman with a hat on your head and a coat on your back, then it would not affect you, either."

Self-consciously Rivers raked his fingers back through his hair. Beside his father, he did look like a ruffian: he hadn't bothered to shave or tie back his hair, his most comfortable boots were scuffed with muddy heels, and he wore a well-worn and grimy pair of buckskin breeches, a shirt with the sleeves rolled to his elbows, and an old waistcoat.

"If I'd known you were coming, Father, I would have dressed with more formality," he said, trying to make a jest of it and not sound defensive. "My guests at the Lodge are infrequent."

Father made a dismissive grumble deep in his throat. "A gentleman of your rank should always take care of his appearance, no matter the hour or expectation."

Rivers didn't answer, letting his father have his rebuke. Arguing wouldn't solve anything, not with Father. It never did. Besides, he doubted that his attire was the reason Father had come here today, and it would be better to marshal his defenses for whatever the real reason was for this visit.

"I'm glad to see you've kept up the flowers," Father said with brusque approval as they entered the garden behind the house. "They always gave your mother great pleasure."

"They do to me as well," Rivers said, thinking of Lucia bending over the blossoms to relish their fragrance. "They've flourished this summer, thanks to my gardener, and I—"

"I haven't come here to discuss your servants," Father said, wheeling about to face Rivers. "What I wish to know is your reason for foisting that impudent little baggage on Celia and the other ladies yesterday afternoon."

Rivers stared, aghast. He had not expected that, not at all. "You mean Lu—that is, Mrs. Willow?"

"Her name does not matter to me," Father said sharply. "What matters is that you had neither the right nor the decency to present such a creature to those ladies as if she were their equal."

"Mrs. Willow is not a creature," Rivers said, "nor did the ladies themselves appear insulted by her company. In fact, Celia herself welcomed her most cordially, enjoying her company, and invited her to return."

"That is because they did not know who or what she is," Father said, his voice rising. "You know I don't give a fig about the low women that you choose for sport and amusement. I do, however, expect you to have the decency to keep your tawdry misadventures apart from the ladies of your family, as a gentleman should. For you to bring her into my home, to parade her about as if she'd a right to be there, is despicable. Utterly despicable."

"You are wrong, Father," Rivers said firmly. "If you were to put aside your pride and permit me to present Mrs. Willow to you, then you would see what a wonderful woman she is. You would understand."

Father stared, appalled, his face mottled with outrage above his snowy linen shirt.

"*Present* her to me, Rivers?" he demanded. "Have you lost your wits entirely? Do you truly believe I am ignorant of who this person is? She is a foreign-born dancer from a family infamous for rascals and harlots. She has agreed to be a part of some outlandish theatrical wager between you and Sir Edward Everett that is the talk of London, and she has spent the last month sequestered alone with you here as your mistress. What else need I know of her?"

"That I love her," Rivers said. He couldn't help glancing up at the Lodge, thinking of her in her bedchamber on the other side of the house. He almost wished she could overhear this conversation so she'd know exactly how he felt, though it was just as well she couldn't hear Father's side of it. "That is the truth, Father. I love her as I have never loved any other woman, and I am happier in her company than I have ever been in my entire life."

"Then you are mad, Rivers, as mad as any happy lunatic in Bedlam!" Unable to contain his disgust, Father stalked away from Rivers, his boots crunching on the gravel, and then stalked back again. "You are in lust, not love. The damned chit has beguiled you, that is all, and will no doubt try to take as much money from you as she can. A woman like that is a born mercenary. Consider who you are, and who she is. There is nothing to sustain an impulsive infatuation such as this."

"There is everything," Rivers insisted. "She is beautiful

and intelligent, and she loves to read as much as I. She is quick and amusing, and she makes me laugh."

"Oh, yes, and I'll wager since she's an Italian dancer, she can put her ankle behind her neck, too," Father said, his words full of sarcasm. "That would certainly amuse most men."

"What of Serena?" Rivers shot back. Geoffrey's wife had been born in India, the illegitimate daughter of an Englishman and his Hindu mistress—a fact that Serena had kept to herself from shame until Geoffrey had discovered it, long after they'd been wed. "Certainly her heritage was more challenging than Lucia's."

"Serena's situation is entirely different," Father answered without hesitation. "Her grandfather is the Marquis of Allwyn, her father was a gentleman, and she was raised as a lady. Besides, she had a large fortune of her own. There was never a question of her making a fool of your brother."

"Lucia's parents were married."

"What else would she tell you?" Father said with a disdainful flick of his hand. "You know how those people can be, living indiscriminately together. They might as well be Romani living in wagons."

"Father, I am serious," Rivers said, and he was. He hadn't realized exactly how serious until the words were spoken, but there they were, more truth, more honesty. "I love Lucia, and nothing you say will change that."

"There is no reasoning with you when you insist on being stubborn like this." Father shook his head, his mouth tight. "Go, indulge in your little frolic for the sake of this wager. But there must be an end to this, Rivers, and soon. I don't want you to suffer. It's past time you married, and I have already begun considering suitable ladies on your behalf."

"Damnation, Father, we have already been over this bridge, again and again and again," Rivers said, exasperated. "I am not of a mind to wed some sow-faced lady of your choosing. I know you long for an heir, but that's a task for Harry and Geoffrey, not for me."

Father raised his chin. "It becomes yours since your brothers have failed me in that regard."

Rivers sighed, feeling his father's impatience closing in around him. "Harry and Geoffrey are both still young, as are Gus and Serena. There's no reason they won't give you that grandson. Why, the babe Gus is carrying now might well be your precious heir, and then all of this will be moot."

"You know as well as I that Gus's child is more likely to be another girl," Father insisted. "That's the way it is with women. Your dear mother gave me only sons, while Celia, as admirable a lady as can be, produced only daughters for her first husband, and lost his title because of it. I won't have that happen to this family. I will not have it."

Father could bluster all he wanted, but Rivers could see the undeniable desperation in his faded blue eyes. He had devoted his entire life to improving the dukedom he'd inherited, increasing the properties that supported it and gathering more power in the family name. The notion that it could all disappear for the want of a grandson plagued him day and night, and Rivers had witnessed how mercilessly he hounded poor Gus about disappointing him three times with daughters. Rivers understood it all, and yet he had no wish to bend his own life to secure his father's ambitions.

"Father, please," Rivers said wearily. "I wish to continue as I am, with Lucia."

"Lucia," Father repeated with palpable disgust. "Be reasonable, Rivers. I'm sure you'd find Lord Stanhope's daughter Anne to be thoroughly charming. She is quite the beauty—not 'sow-faced' in the least—and she is one of the most accomplished young ladies at Court at present. They say she's a bit of a bluestocking, which should appeal to you, and because she speaks German as well as French, she's already made herself a favorite of Her Majesty."

Rivers sighed again. Lucia spoke French and Italian, not that that would matter to Father.

"Lady Anne may be a paragon in beauty and accomplishment, Father," he said, "but I am not interested in marrying her."

"But you should be, Rivers, you should," Father urged, leaning closer, his voice turning confidential. "Consider how a lady like that could improve your life. She'd bring you true happiness, the kind that lasts. She would make your household run like a top, welcome your guests, even support your causes at Court. She's been raised since birth to do so, you know. She would be your equal, a loyal companion and dutiful helpmate for life. She might even be the mother of the sixth Duke of Breconridge."

What Father described were the two ladies he'd married himself, elegant and flawlessly bred women who'd made excellent partners for him. Rivers didn't doubt Lady Anne was exactly the kind of wife he himself was expected to marry, and doubtless, too, she'd be every bit the excellent spouse to him that Father predicted. Likely her parents were urging her to be agreeable to him as well, for even the third son of the Duke of Breconridge would be considered a first-rate match. But no matter how Lady Anne or others like her tried to please him, she'd never be Lucia.

"No, Father," Rivers said as decisively as he could. "No."

"All I ask is that you consider the lady, Rivers." Lightly Father patted Rivers's chest with his palm. It was the same familiar sign of fond concern that he'd shown to his sons since they'd been boys, and Rivers couldn't help but feel a rush of affection and empathy. "She is a prize, and some other gentleman is bound to carry her off if you don't."

"Father, I do not—"

"Consider it," Father said. He turned toward the stable, marking the end of their conversation. "That is all I ask. Consider it, and the lady. Lasting love and true happiness, Rivers. That's all I want for you."

Lasting love and true happiness . . .

The words burned into Lucia's heart as she stood by the open window of Rivers's library. She hadn't intended to overhear. She'd finished *Tom Jones,* and had come downstairs to replace it in the tall shelves that stood against the wall between the windows, and there Rivers and his father had been, not a dozen feet away, in the garden outside. She'd frozen where she stood, not wanting them to know she was there, while unable to not hear their conversation.

She'd never seen Rivers's father before, but she'd known at once that the other gentleman must be the duke. The resemblance between the two of them, young and old, was striking, and the older gentleman exactly fit the way Rivers had described his father, down to the polished silver spurs on his boots.

But it was what he said that made her sure he was Rivers's father, every word piercing the contentment and joy she'd felt since last night.

His Grace had contemptuously called her an impudent baggage, and ridiculed Rivers when he'd come to her defense. She'd listened, stricken, and though she'd longed to cover her ears and hear no more, she hadn't. She'd heard every word, and when His Grace was done and they'd moved from the open window, she'd sunk down to the carpet, her heart beating with painful haste and her face buried in her hands, yet too distraught for tears.

Because His Grace was right.

She wasn't worthy of Rivers, and never would be. She

couldn't begin to compete with Lady Anne Stanhope. She didn't have a drop of noble blood in her, while he was descended from royalty. She could no more run a huge household like the one at Breconridge Hall than she could sprout wings and fly among the clouds. She couldn't even give proper orders to the servants here at the Lodge, let alone arrange grand meals or welcome Rivers's guests. The elegant airs that she'd learned from Rivers were a falsehood that would serve on the stage but were empty at the core, and useless in the real world of Breconridge Hall, or even the Court.

Separately these were little things, but together they tallied to one very large fact: that she would never be able to make Rivers happy, exactly as his father said. She'd done rapturously well this month, true, but when they returned to London and his friends and family, everything would change, and slowly, over time, he'd come to see all her flaws. What once had made him smile would make him weary, bored, or resentful, and the love they'd both declared to be so strong would wither and fade away, and what remained would not be worthy of either of them.

Rivers would deny the truth, of course. He would fight it, just as he'd done with his father, and swear he loved her more each day. He was loyal to a fault, her dear Rivers, which was one of the things she most admired about him, but in this case his devotion would be misplaced.

Last night they'd promised to do whatever was necessary to make the other happy, the kind of vows that lovers make to each other in bed. Only now did she understand the truth of it: that if she truly wished Rivers to be happy, she must set him free. She would have to do it gently, over time, so he would not suspect her, but she must do it. She loved him too much not to.

With a shuddering sigh, she slowly rose. Rivers could

return inside at any minute, and she couldn't let him find her here.

Instead she must be upstairs in her bedchamber, packing her belongings, preparing for their journey back to town. She must smile and laugh and kiss him, as he expected, and ask him about his ride. Even if he told her about his father's visit, she must pretend she hadn't known, hadn't heard a word. She must speak of the audition, her excitement, the traffic on the road, and the book she'd just read. She couldn't ever let him guess the truth, that every word must be the beginning of good-bye.

She'd thought her performance as Ophelia was going to be the test of her talent as an actress, but that would be nothing compared to the role she'd now set for herself. Because she loved him, she would give him his freedom and his happiness.

Because she loved him, and would never stop loving him, she would do this for him.

For love. All for love.

"*Here's Russell* Street now, sweetheart," Rivers said, bending his head to one side to see the front of the playhouse from the carriage window. "Do you find it acceptable for your debut?"

"Oh, Rivers, do not tease me now," Lucia protested breathlessly. He'd never seen her so nervous, her hands working in her lap, and the little wired flowers on her hat trembling along with her. "Of course it will do. You know that as well as I."

"Well, then, shall we go inside, so you may present yourself to McGraw?" Rivers rapped on the roof of the carriage for the driver to stop. "He said rehearsal would begin at eleven, and it's ten-fifty now."

"No!" wailed Lucia. "He didn't mean that literally, Rivers. He meant in theater time, which is not the same at all as your minute-by-minute counting. Please, please, do not make me go in just yet, I beg you!"

"There's never harm in being prompt," he said as the footman opened the carriage door directly before the front of the theater. Rivers stepped down to the pavement first, holding his hand out to her. "Come, Mrs. Willow. Your glory awaits."

"Hush, Rivers, that is purest rubbish," she said, hanging back. "Don't say such things aloud. It's the worst luck."

Yet he could already see how she was working to control her anxiety, visibly gathering herself for her entrance. He'd seen such transformation before with her, but he never tired of watching it take place. Her back straightened, her features relaxed, and she held her head as high as any crowned queen. When she spoke, the nervous squeak had left her voice entirely, and in its place were the carefully practiced vowels of refinement.

"Thank you, my lord," she said, stepping down with such grace that the passersby paused to ogle her. She ignored them, giving only a glance at the imposing front of the playhouse before them. He caught a flicker of uncertainty as she did—an uncertainty that endeared her all the more to him—before she once again steeled herself for what would come next.

Russell Street was around the corner from its rival playhouse in Drury Lane, and the two of them were the grandest of all the theaters in London. Compared to the ramshackle quarters of the old King's Theatre, home to the Di Rossi Company, Russell Street must seem to Lucia to be as grand as a palace, with its looming brick façade, arched windows, and oversized iron lanterns across the front. There were no attendants out front, given the hour, and one of Rivers's own footmen hurried to open the theater's main door for them.

"Have courage," Rivers whispered as he led her forward, squeezing Lucia's hand. "You are not only the bravest woman I know, but the most talented as well."

She flashed him a quick smile of gratitude as they entered, the heavy door thumping shut behind them. The empty lobby echoed with the cavernous stillness of places that were usually bustling with crowds, and with the weariness, too, of such places seen by the watery light of day.

"You'd think someone would be here to greet you," Rivers said, his voice unconsciously hearty to fill the silence. "The door was unlocked, so they must be expecting you."

"I told you we were too early," Lucia whispered, her fingers tightening around his. "I'd wager a guinea that all the players are still in their beds."

"Not all of them," Rivers said. "You're here, aren't you?"

The inner doors flew open and a bleary-eyed McGraw himself came bustling through them, making a hasty yet practiced bow over one leg. He was wearing a worn fustian old coat whose pockets bristled with scraps and scrolls of paper and in place of his wig he had a crushed velvet cap over his close-cropped scalp. He might not still have been in his bed as Lucia had predicted, but he was clearly not far removed from it.

"My lord, Mrs. Willow, your servant," he said brusquely, dabbing at his nose with a spotted handkerchief. "Good day to you both."

"Good day, Mr. McGraw," Lucia said, her smile warm enough to thaw any man. "I am here for the rehearsal, as you requested."

"Yes, yes, Mrs. Willow, of course you are," he said. "I should prefer to have a complete reading of the play, but it would seem that certain members of the company have been unavoidably detained. I do, however, have Mr. Lambert in attendance, and as he will be playing our Danish prince, I see no reason why we cannot proceed through your scenes together. This way to the stage, ma'am, if you please."

He held the inner door open with the flat of his arm, leaving just enough space for Lucia to enter. Rivers reached up to push the door more widely open for himself, and McGraw frowned, his bristling brows coming together in a single thatch.

"Forgive me, my lord, but it is not, ah, the custom for anyone other than the players to attend rehearsals," he said. "I'm sure you would find it tedious beyond bearing. Now you may take your ease here in the lobby, or return later to collect Mrs. Willow, as you please."

"What I please is to accompany her," Rivers said sharply. "To send her unattended in there—"

"It is the custom, my lord," Lucia said quickly, placing a restraining hand on his shoulder. "None but the company is permitted in rehearsals."

Rivers glowered. It wasn't just that he wished to accompany her for safety's sake. After all the hours they'd put in perfecting her lines together, he felt he was entitled to watch her practicing through these last steps before her performance, and even offer a few last suggestions as well.

"I do not see the harm in my presence, McGraw," he said, appealing to the manager. "The entire performance is coming from my pocket."

"All the more reason that you should not witness it in its imperfect state, my lord," McGraw said, giving his fingers a little flourish as he tucked the handkerchief back into his pocket. "I promise you to look after this good lady as if she were my own daughter, and see no harm comes to her. Our rehearsals are all business, my lord, and I tolerate no flirtations or beguilements among my players. Love is the very devil for a company's peace."

"I shall be well enough, my lord," Lucia said softly.

"You must trust me. Recall that I was raised in such a place, and know all the tricks to guard myself in it."

Rivers grumbled wordlessly, not liking anything about the situation. He'd pictured himself sitting in the box nearest the stage, helpfully calling out to her in the same manner as he had these last weeks, and the thought of parting from her now, even for a few hours, seemed unbearable.

She was so lovely, gazing up at him like this through her thick dark lashes, her eyes so meltingly soft that he found himself smiling back at her almost against his will. She ran her gloved fingers lightly along his jaw, hovering for a tantalizing second longer on his chin.

"There, my lord," she said, her lips curving upward. "I knew you would understand. Spend the day at your club, amongst your friends, and when it is time to dine, return here for me."

"You would trust me?" he asked, prolonging the moment and daring her at the same time.

She tipped her head teasingly to one side. "What, to be amongst your friends, or to return for me?"

"Both," he said. "Or either."

"I will always trust you, my lord," she said, "just as I know you trust me."

His smile faded. How neatly she'd turned that against him!

"*'Farewell, Ophelia,'*" he said, falling into their old game of borrowing from the play. "*'And remember well what I have said to you.'*"

"*''Tis in my memory lock'd,'*" she answered. "*'And you yourself shall keep the key of it.'*"

She reached up to kiss him quickly, so quickly that he'd no chance to kiss her back. Then she was gone, off with McGraw and into the gaudy world of the theater, leaving him behind on the other side of the gently closing door.

CHAPTER
17

⁓

The hours had stretched like an interminable void before Rivers, the better part of a day to be spent without Lucia by his side. He hadn't realized how accustomed he'd grown to having her always there, and her absence felt like an indispensable part of himself had somehow been removed.

When he left the theater, he had his driver take him past the little house that he'd had his agent lease for Lucia. It was on a small, quiet street, the kind of street made for discretion.

He'd never taken this step with any other woman, and he was excited and a little awed by the momentousness of it. But then, he'd never known any other woman like Lucia, either. From what she'd told him of her life, she hadn't once lived in a proper house of her own, and it pleased him no end to be able to put this one in her name. It was a perfect Lucia house, a rosy brick with a white marble door case, and bright yellow shutters. He'd never seen another London house with yellow shutters like these, and they only made the house seem more Lucia-like. The brass knocker was in the shape of a basket of flowers, which reminded him of how she'd delighted in his mother's flower garden.

He hadn't a key, so he couldn't see the inside of the house or the furnishings, but he still could imagine her waving to him from one of the arched windows above the street. At one time, he'd thought that after the wager she would go off on her own as an actress. But as she'd become more and more a part of his life, he'd realized he wasn't ready to see her go, and instead he imagined her not as an actress independent of him, but here, waiting for him to return.

Satisfied, he next went to his favorite jeweler in Bond Street. Lucia always said she didn't want jewels, but he'd something small, something special, in mind that she couldn't refuse, that he'd give her tonight when they dined. He found it, too: a little brooch in the shape of a bouquet of flowers, bright enameled petals studded with dewdrop-shaped diamonds and tied with a curling bow of sapphires. It was quite a modest jewel compared to what he usually offered as gifts, but he thought it best for Lucia. He'd tell her that the flowers represented the ones that Ophelia carried, as well as those in the garden at the Lodge.

All he wished was to make her happy, in whatever way he could. A diamond brooch was easy. Leaving her behind at the theater today had been much more difficult. He'd seen the eagerness in her eyes when McGraw had held open the door, just as he knew how satisfying it must be for her to see all her work realized in a real performance. She had always wanted with all her heart to be an actress, and he'd been the one to make it possible.

Yet while most gifts offered as much pleasure in the giving as the receiving, this one didn't. Her growth as an actress and her interpretation of Ophelia had been a shared creation, and now it no longer was. His opinion had ceased to matter, and he felt it more than he would ever have expected.

Perhaps once he saw her on the stage, he'd feel better. She'd be his again. He meant to give her the key to the yellow-shuttered house then, a reward for her performance and a symbol of their new life together here in London. That cheered him, and at last he ordered his driver to take him to White's. He had been in the country for over a month; it would be good to see friends, especially if he could include a bit of good-natured gloating at Everett's expense.

He didn't have long to wait. He walked up the stairs to the coffee room and was greeted by Everett himself, loudly enough that several of the older gentlemen glared at him with disapproval.

"So you're finally come back to town, you old rogue," Everett said, clapping Rivers on the back. "You dallied there long enough, though I can't fault you, considering the delightful Mrs. Willow was your only company."

Two other men who'd been talking to Everett made appropriately male noises of interest and approval, so male that Everett must have been regaling them with descriptions of Lucia's charms. Rivers didn't care for that, but since he hadn't heard what Everett had said, he couldn't exactly take offense. But though he smiled genially, he was on his guard now, ready to defend Lucia if necessary.

"Mrs. Willow is presently in her rehearsals at Russell Street," he said. "You know I will be collecting that wager from you directly after the final curtain."

Everett's eyes gleamed. "I wouldn't be so certain of that. You've said yourself that Mrs. Willow is prone to fits of stage fright. You might have played your cards too grandly, Fitzroy. I've heard every seat in the house is sold. What will happen when your miss steps out onto the stage and sees all those eyes watching her, eh? What will she make of that?"

"She'll do well enough," Rivers said, purposefully bland. To keep Everett's interest keen on the wager, he had hinted that Lucia suffered from stage fright, but it wasn't true. She liked performing too much to be afraid of an audience, a true Di Rossi after all. "I could make you pay up now, considering how you've broken the wager again by braying about it to anyone who'd listen. That was one of my stipulations."

"I did no such thing," Everett said soundly. "That is, not beyond a word or two, here or there, when people asked why you'd fled to the country so suddenly."

One of the other men laughed. "A word or two or a thousand, Everett," he said. "The entire world knows of the wager. Have you seen the betting book downstairs, my lord? There's a score of other wagers about the lady and her, ah, talents."

Rivers could guess the nature of those other bets all too well, no doubt fueled by Everett. If Lucia wanted fame, it seemed she already had it.

"I'll leave it to Mrs. Willow's performance to settle everything," he said as evenly as he could. "I expect there will be a great many people who will be surprised by her performance."

"I'll bet she does perform," Everett said, openly leering. "Who'd have guessed that little mongrel bitch could become such a delectable morsel? I couldn't believe how agreeably she'd plumped in your care, Fitzroy. There's nothing quite like a grateful wench for doing whatever a man—"

"That's enough, Everett," Rivers warned sharply.

But Everett only pulled a face that made the others laugh. "No need to defend her, Fitzroy. We all know she's your whore."

Rivers drew in his breath sharply, his temper rising. "I'll thank you not to call her that."

Everett shrugged. "Why shouldn't I, when it's the truth?"

"Because it's not," Rivers said, abruptly shoving Everett back against the wall. He curled his hands into fists at his sides. One more word about Lucia, and he'd pound Everett senseless. "Not her."

Surprised, Everett tensed, ready to retaliate.

"Damnation, Fitzroy," he said indignantly. "What's this between friends? A spade's a spade, and a whore's a whore. When has that ever changed?"

"Not her," Rivers growled furiously, and drew his fist back to strike. "Not *her*."

But before he could hit Everett, someone grabbed his wrist from behind to stop him. He whipped around, now angry at whoever had interrupted him.

"No brawling in White's, Rivers," said his brother Harry. "Ever."

Rivers fought against him, struggling to jerk his arm free. "Blast you, Harry, let me go!"

"What, and let you shame us all?" Harry said mildly. "Come, this way, until that temper cools."

It wasn't enough that Harry was the oldest brother; he'd always been stronger than Rivers, too, even after the accident that had left him lame. Although Rivers was fueled by his anger, Harry was still able to haul him away from Everett and the entire coffee room of gaping gentlemen and into the dining room, which was fortunately empty at this time of the afternoon. A footman hastily closed the door after them, giving them privacy, and at last Harry released his arm.

Still fuming, Rivers said nothing, turning away to smooth his rumpled clothing as well as his temper and his pride. He knew he'd just committed an unpardonable sin in the club—or actually, several of them. He'd raised his voice, and then his fist against a fellow member. He'd challenged one of his oldest friends openly, and if Everett weren't such an unrepentant coward, they'd likely now both be sending their seconds to make the arrangements for a duel. Worst of all, he'd made a scene in the middle of White's coffee room and disturbed all the other members, who'd come there for a bit of peace.

Like a stone tossed into the still waters of society, the effects of what he'd done would ripple endlessly outward. It would become the talk of every polite gathering tonight in London and every unsavory one as well, and by morning there'd be scarcely a soul left who would not know that Lucia had been the reason for it.

He'd wanted to defend her, and instead all he'd managed to do was put her squarely in the center of today's tattle and scandal. He groaned, and put his hands over his eyes, as if not seeing the rather mundane landscape painting on the wall before him would also magically blot out the awfulness of what he'd just done.

"So," Harry said behind him. "Are you ready to tell me exactly what demon took possession of you?"

"If I knew, I would have cast him off directly," Rivers said. He took a deep breath before he turned to face his brother. "I should go back and offer my apologies to Everett."

"Not yet," Harry said. He pulled out two of the chairs from beneath the dining table, pointedly directing Rivers to one while he took the other. "First I'd like to hear more of this demon."

"There isn't more to tell," Rivers said, hedging. Harry would never understand about Lucia; he had fallen in love and married a well-bred young lady that everyone adored, even Father. "I lost my temper, that is all. It does happen."

"But not to my bookish younger brother." Harry rested one hand on the table beside him, lightly drumming his fingers on the cloth. He resembled Father more and more each day, not just in their shared features, but also in their mannerisms, like this finger-drumming that Rivers had always in the past associated with their father. "I believe the last time you lost your temper you were twelve, when Geoffrey spilled a glass of cider over some journal or another you'd been laboriously keeping. You were like a wild beast, flailing away at him until old Hartnell pulled you off."

"Hah, I'd forgotten Hartnell." Rivers smiled ruefully, and dropped into the chair. "He was an indifferent tutor, but he kept the peace amongst the three of us, which was all Father cared about. And that journal contained a summer's worth of lunar observations, which Geoffrey destroyed in a single moment of willful oafishness."

"I hope he has moved beyond willful oafishness, for poor Serena's sake." Harry chuckled at Geoffrey's expense, but Rivers wasn't fooled. He knew what would come next, and it did. "Am I right in guessing that your own oafishness just now had more to do with the young woman you brought with you to the Lodge last month than with anything Everett himself did?"

Rivers sighed, and with resignation leaned back in the chair, staring up at the ceiling to avoid meeting his brother's eye.

"Of course it was about Lucia," he said. "Or rather, Mrs. Willow. That's the name she will go by in the theater. Everett called her a whore, which she is not, and I lost my temper."

"But she is your mistress, yes?"

"To the world, I suppose she is, yes," Rivers admitted, and he'd a shockingly vivid memory of her lying in his bed this morning in Cavendish Square, naked except for her little cameo necklace on the coral beads and an emerald silk ribbon tying back her hair. "But to me she is far more than that. She has been my partner in contriving his wager, my student, my friend, and my lover. Very much my lover. Although I expect you've already heard that from Father."

"Actually, I heard it from Gus," Harry said. "I had a

long letter from her this morning, and she told me everything."

Rivers grimaced. "That didn't take long, did it?" he said. "Is she as offended as Father claims?"

"You know Gus," Harry said. "She never stands on ceremony. She'd make conversation with a fishwife, given the chance. It was Father who took offense, not the ladies. Besides, they all guessed exactly who your, ah, companion was before you introduced her. They're not fools, Rivers, and they've also heard the talk and read the papers."

Rivers should have guessed. Everett, and likely McGraw, had made short work of his great secret.

"At least they hid it well," he said. "They were kind to Lucia. They asked her to stay to tea, and you know what stock ladies put in that."

"They liked her, Rivers," Harry said. "Gus thought Mrs. Willow was beautiful, clever, and talented. But most of all, she said it was the first time she's seen you in love."

"I am in love with her, Harry," Rivers said, and just saying the words aloud made him feel better.

Harry smiled. "I'll have to tell Gus she's right. She's always imagining little winged Cupids flying over the heads of—"

"I am serious," Rivers insisted. He'd known Harry wouldn't understand, and that indulgent smile was the proof of it. "I have never loved any other woman the way I love Lucia, and I am certain she loves me the same."

"Of course she'll tell you that, Rivers," Harry said, too patiently. "It's in her favor to do so. Consider who you are, and who she is."

There it was, the inevitable conclusion, and Rivers was unable to keep the bitterness from his words. "I suppose next you'll begin to describe the virtues of a match with Lady Anne Stanhope, too, just as Father did."

"If I did, then I'd be marking myself as a failure, the

gentleman who can father only daughters," Harry said, his voice suddenly tight. "No, I won't say that. Even though you could do much worse for yourself than Lady Anne."

"I'd be happier with Lucia di Rossi." He wasn't being stubborn or obstinate. He was simply telling the truth.

Harry sighed, and the finger-drumming began again, a muted thump on the white linen cloth. "What I am saying, Rivers, is not to let this woman make a public fool of you."

"I won't," Rivers said, striving to sound confident, not stubborn. "And she won't."

"You already have, just now with Everett." Harry leaned forward, his expression earnest. "Soon she'll make this benefit performance, and you'll win this ridiculous wager. You'll both have gotten what you sought from the arrangement. It would be the perfect time to make a break with her, before things become any more sordid."

"They won't, I won't, she won't." Rivers had had enough lecturing, and he pushed back the chair and stood. "What else would you have me say, Harry?"

Harry rose, too, albeit more slowly on account of his leg. "All I ask is that you take care, Rivers. Don't let yourself be blinded by love, or at least not by a love like this. Things can only end badly if you do."

But to Rivers the flaw in that reasoning was that he'd no intention of letting things end at all. He didn't say it to Harry, for there'd be no use, and instead went to drink a conciliatory brandy with him. He apologized to Everett, who seemed more gratefully relieved than anything, and then he tried to be as agreeable to everyone else as he could. Harry was right in that he and Lucia had become something of a public spectacle, and for her sake, he'd have to watch what he said and did.

Yet as he rode back to the theater for Lucia, his thoughts kept returning to his conversation with Harry.

He knew his family well enough to understand that they'd all been talking about him and "this woman," as Lucia had clearly become in their minds. They were worried for him, as if he were some lost soul drifting through Hades with Lucia as his guide, and they were desperately hoping for something to draw him away from her and back into their comfortable fold.

Of course, behind all this worry and hope, there was a larger concern that not even Harry had dared raise. They were all terrified that he'd marry Lucia, the most unsuitable bride imaginable for one of the sons of the Duke of Breconridge. As long as neither Harry nor Geoffrey had a son, Rivers was the heir to the dukedom, and no one could stomach the possibility of a foreign-born actress from a troupe of dancers as the next Duchess of Breconridge.

But the real question for Rivers was not whether he'd one day be the duke or Lucia his duchess, but whether he could picture her as his wife. His *wife*. There, he'd forced himself to think the one thing he'd been avoiding, even in his head. He loved her more than any other woman he'd ever known. Did he love her enough to ask her to marry him?

And if he did, would she say yes?

He'd promised to do whatever was necessary to make her happy. He had always considered marriage a necessary state for happiness, confirmed by an extended family of successful unions amongst his brothers and cousins, and even Father and Celia. He'd never doubted that one day he, too, would wed. But he had an uneasy feeling that his view of marriage—of much lovemaking and companionship, of his house and the Lodge filled with laughter and children and a few more dogs, of entertainments with friends and shared dinners with his family, of silverware engraved with an interlaced cipher, and being known jointly as Lord and Lady Rivers Fitzroy—might not be the same as Lucia's.

In fact, now that he considered it, he'd never once heard Lucia speak of marriage. Most young women her age could speak of little else, dreaming of wedding days and bridal gowns in such detail that it terrified bachelors. But Lucia's dreams had always seemed to involve becoming an actress, and those dreams had been so fiercely all-encompassing that she hadn't seemed to have included anything beyond it. He wondered now if that was why she'd been so determined to live in the present, that she wanted no pleasant thoughts of children or a husband to distract her from her goal.

And yet he knew she loved him. He'd only to think of how she looked at him, kissed him, touched him, made love to him. He took the velvet box with the little flowered brooch from his coat pocket and opened it, making the diamond dewdrops catch the light and sparkle. Flowers would always remind him of Lucia, and he prayed these flowers would make her think of him.

He smiled, remembering as he turned the brooch in his fingers, and then his smile faded. It was strange to think that all those lines from *Hamlet* that had become their own intimate language would now be said before a theater full of others. They'd be given away, shared freely with people for whom the words would be no more than a passing entertainment, soon forgotten. For him they'd always be in Lucia's voice for him alone, and always remembered.

> *"There's rosemary, that's for remembrance;*
> *Pray, Love, remember:*
> *And there is pansies, that's for thoughts."*

Because he loved her, he'd promised to do whatever he could to make her as happy as she made him. But what if her notion of happiness wasn't the same as his?

The carriage stopped before the theater, taking him by surprise, and hastily he thrust the jeweler's box back into his pocket. He climbed down from the carriage to go inside for Lucia, as they'd agreed, when the door opened and Lucia herself came hurrying out. He felt an inordinate pleasure in realizing that she'd been waiting there for him, a pleasure that was lessened when he saw that there were two other men and a woman with her.

"Oh, Rivers, here you are!" she cried, flinging her arms around his shoulders to kiss him quickly. "Now you must meet my fellow players. Mrs. Painter, Mr. Lambert, Mr. Audley, Lord Rivers Fitzroy."

The three bowed and curtseyed there on the pavement as Lucia continued her introducing.

"Mrs. Painter plays Queen Gertrude," she said, "and Mr. Lambert is of course Prince Hamlet, and Mr. Audley is my brother, Laertes. That is, he's Ophelia's brother. They've all been so helpful to me today that everyone is certain you shall win your wager."

"Then you have my thanks," Rivers said, feeling extremely awkward. "All of you."

In the past he'd always felt at ease going backstage after performances and mingling with actors and actresses and, of course, with dancers. He'd enjoyed being part of their bantering and raillery, and visiting a make-believe existence that was so different from his own.

But because of Lucia, he now felt as if he were oddly straddling the two worlds and feeling equally uneasy in both, especially here on the street. By the early evening light, without the benefit of costumes or paint, they seemed very ordinary, even tawdry. They'd lost all their customary bravado, and kept stealing awestruck glances at his liveried footmen and his carriage with the Fitzroy crest painted on the door. The only one who was oblivious was Lucia, like a bright, beautiful butterfly darting back and forth.

Finally she parted with her new friends and she and Rivers left in the carriage; at last he again had her to himself.

"Did you enjoy yourself?" he asked. It was a moot question; she was glowing with excitement and happiness beside him.

"It couldn't have been any better," she said. "Truly. I think they were all amazed by how well I knew my role and performed it. It was obvious they were expecting me to be a silly little hussy who'd need to be cosseted and carried along, but I wasn't. Because of you and your lessons, Rivers, I was as good as—no, better!—than any of them."

Impulsively she kissed him, a wonderfully ardent kiss that didn't have a whit of gratitude to it, and banished the dark misgivings he'd had earlier. She was still his Lucia, and he let himself relax and share her joy in the day.

"So you are pleased with the production?" he asked, leaving his arm familiarly around her waist. "McGraw hasn't scrimped on anything because it's only a benefit, has he?"

"Not in the least," she said, twisting about to face him. "Everything is even better than I ever dared hope. The stage seemed so big at first, but then I became accustomed to it, and it seemed exactly right. Mr. McGraw made everything easy for me. He even told Mr. Lambert that I was the kind of actress that the people want now, and that I'd draw them to Russell Street and away from Mr. Garrick. From Mr. Garrick! Can you fancy such a thing, Rivers?"

"I can, and quite easily, too," he said, smiling. "So he didn't try to change what we'd devised for Ophelia?"

"Not so much as a word," she said. "He praised you, too, and jested that he should send the rest of the players to you for lessons."

Rivers had a brief, hideous image of his front parlor

filled with aspiring actors. "That's generous praise from him," he said. "I only wish he'd let me stay for the rehearsal so I might have heard it for myself."

"Oh, but it's better this way," she said. "Truly. This way you'll be *amazed* by the play, without having seen all the grubby work behind it."

"Have you forgotten how much of the 'grubby work' we did together, sweetheart?" he said, a little wistfully.

"Of course I haven't," she said. "But I meant the truly grubby work, like the seamstress fitting my costumes, or seeing how they make the ghost of Hamlet's father glow. It's a special paint on his robe that catches the light, if you care. And did you know that they've sold every single ticket? Mr. McGraw said he could have sold another hundred, there's been that much demand."

"That's because of you," he said, thinking uneasily of how many of those tickets had been sold in the eager expectation of watching a laughable performance by a nobleman's mistress. "I hope the crowd will be kind to you."

"They'll have no choice but to be kind," she said confidently. "I intend to be the best Ophelia that they've ever seen. I will *amaze* them."

He laughed softly. "I don't doubt that you shall."

"I will," she said again, her eyes narrowing a fraction with determination. "You'll see. I'll make them weep when I go mad. But what did you do today, Rivers? Did you go to your club? Did you see Sir Edward?"

"I did, and yes, I saw him," he said, purposefully omitting his near-fight with his friend. "He still believes he might win the wager."

"He won't," she said. "His money might as well be in your pocket already."

"Tomorrow night will be soon enough," he said. That time *would* come soon enough, in so many ways. "He and I will be sitting in the royal box, front and center, where I will expect him to admit defeat and pay the wager the moment the play is done."

She nodded vigorously. "Mr. McGraw said we could all come back on the stage to watch. He said that that will be the real point of the entire play. Not Hamlet's death, but Sir Edward conceding defeat."

She said it with such relish that he smiled. Really, Lucia's triumph and Everett's defeat were as good as guaranteed. It was everything following the end of the play that was so uncertain, and he wondered if she felt it, too.

"But I went somewhere else today, too," he said, belatedly remembering the brooch. He pulled the box from his pocket and set it in her hand. "A small token to remember your first real day as an actress."

She smiled at his compliment, not the box.

"You know you're not to give me jewels," she said, faintly scolding, even as she slowly opened the lid. "Oh, Rivers. *Oh.*"

"Do you like it?" he asked, not quite sure she did.

She pressed her free hand to her chest with emotion, and when she looked up from the brooch to him, he saw tears sparkling in her eyes to match the diamonds.

"It's a modest little thing," he said, regretting that he hadn't bought her a more lavish jewel. "It's not—"

"It's perfect," she whispered. "More than perfect."

She lifted the brooch from its velvet nest and began to pin it to the front of her bodice. Her fingers were trembling—he guessed from excitement—and that combined with the carriage's movement made her unable to fasten the little clasp. He reached down and did it for her, her breast pressing warm against the back of his fingers.

" '*There's rosemary,*' " he began to quote, " '*that's for remembrance.*' "

" '*Pray, Love, remember,*' " she said, finishing the couplet. " '*And there is pansies, that's for thoughts.*' You will not forget me, Rivers, will you?"

"Wherever did that come from?" he asked, surprised. He supposed that behind her bravado, she must be more anxious about the benefit than she wanted him to know, which he found endlessly endearing. "You know I won't forget you, Lucia. How could I?"

She didn't answer, but rested her cheek wearily against his chest, her fingers curled around the jeweled bouquet of flowers. He didn't say anything more, either, but put his arms around her and held her close, the way he wanted to do forever.

For remembrance . . .

CHAPTER
18

Lucia had been a part of enough theatrical benefits in her life to realize that the one here tonight at Russell Street was different. Unless the featured performers were especially popular with the public, single-night benefits were a risk; audiences often stayed away from what they perceived as an untried production or an inferior offering. She'd seen benefits that had been out-and-out failures, performed halfheartedly before a near-empty house.

This performance of *Hamlet* would not be like that. The house was already sold out, and Mr. McGraw had gleefully announced to the company that he'd managed to squeeze in a few more spaces for those who wished to stand. There had also been a lively business in tickets being resold, and sales for other plays later in the week had been brisk because of rumors that Lucia might appear in those as well.

Yet Lucia understood all too well that the crowds had come from curiosity, and that they were not here to see her act, but to witness her failure. She was determined to amaze them instead, exactly as she'd told Rivers, but as she stood in the wings, waiting for her cue, the task seemed infinitely more daunting. Beyond the orchestra sat rows and rows of pale faces, nearly every one of them belonging to a man or woman who wished her ill. They wouldn't be quietly polite about it, either, for most theatergoers believed their tickets entitled them to call out their displeasure during a performance. No wonder her heart hammered painfully in her chest and her stomach twisted with nervousness. She'd been too excited to eat more than a few pieces of toast since morning, and now even that seemed too much.

She couldn't fail, she couldn't. Rivers had given her this single, shining opportunity to prove herself, to be the actress she'd always claimed she wanted to be. She'd never have another chance to become independent, even wealthy, and if she failed, she hadn't the faintest notion of where she would turn next.

For last night Rivers had made it abundantly clear that once the play was done and the wager was settled, their liaison was over. She'd thought she would be the one to ease away from him, but he'd beaten her to it, and taken the first step. Oh, he'd been every bit the perfect lover, as charming as ever over their dinner together and then later, in bed, as passionate as a man could be.

But before that, in the carriage, he had given her the diamond brooch, and she'd understood. She'd seen it often enough with Magdalena and other dancers in the company. When a gentleman wished to break with one of them, he gave them a gift of costly jewelry; hadn't Rivers done exactly that when he'd parted with Magdalena last year?

She'd tried to tell herself that she'd expected this moment, that it was inevitable no matter how much she'd wished otherwise. But the little brooch had been so beautiful and perfect there in her hand, with flowers that held such significance to their time together, that she'd felt the shock of its other meaning like a blow straight to her heart. He'd said he'd give her what would make her happy, and this benefit was proof of that. He'd said he'd always remember her, and that was all she'd be left with as well: memories, a diamond brooch, and a broken heart.

She'd pinned the brooch to the front of her costume tonight, for luck and remembrance, just like Ophelia's spray of rosemary. She hoped Rivers would see it, too, and she leaned a little farther to one side in the wings, trying to see the royal box where he would be sitting with Sir Edward.

"Here now, none of that," whispered Mr. Audley sharply, tugging her back. "Don't want to show yourself before you make your entrance."

She gulped and tried to smile, and from the look on his face she didn't succeed.

"You're not going faint, either, missy," he said crossly. Beneath the heavy stage paint, his expression was irritated and worried. "For tonight, you're one of this company on this stage, and I'll be damned if I'm going to let you turn coward and spoil everything for the rest of us."

Instead of calming her, his words made her panic. What was she doing anyway? Who did she think she was, ready to go out and make an utter fool of herself before hundreds of people?

Her fear rising by the second, she stared down at her gauzy, gaudy, spangled costume, so unlike any of her ordinary clothes, and suddenly she thought of the long-ago pink gown she'd worn as a girl to recite poetry before the country folk. She'd discovered her talent then, how she'd the power to take words and turn them into magic that could make others laugh or weep.

That gift was still hers, and always would be. Acting couldn't mend her broken heart, but it could take that pain and turn the hurt into something else. That had been one of Rivers's first lessons for her; she didn't want to consider the irony of how he was the cause of her suffering now. Ophelia, too, had been pushed away by the man she'd loved, and if Lucia could bring her own pain to her performance, then she would succeed.

Mr. Lambert as Hamlet rushed from the stage, and a

single trumpet sounded to mark the end of one scene and the beginning of another. Lucia raised her head, took a deep breath, and linked her hand through the crook of Mr. Audley's arm, the way they'd rehearsed their entrance. He nodded, satisfied, and together they walked from the wings into the bright light of the stage.

She was aware of the murmur that greeted her, the rush of not-so-quiet remarks that had nothing to do with Ophelia. She ignored them all, and focused entirely on the play. For the beginning of this scene, Ophelia had only a handful of lines to speak, all simple replies to her brother and father. But finally came the first lines that rang true for both her and Ophelia:

"He hath, my lord, of late made many tenders
Of his affection for me."

The audience's interest rose, acutely aware of the double meaning of her words as she continued.

"My lord, he hath importuned me with love
In honorable fashion . . .
And hath given countenance to his speech, my lord,
With almost all the holy vows of heaven."

"Don't believe him, dearie!" called a woman's voice from the highest seats. "All rogues say the same false rubbish, and believe naught of it."

Some people laughed at the woman, others shushed her, but far more murmured with agreement, and Lucia knew she was swaying them her way. Her confidence grew, and as Ophelia's confusion and misery became more poignant with each scene, the audience's support grew, too. Not only did they begin to cheer Ophelia and openly call their encouragement, they also began to boo and hiss at Hamlet, much to Mr. Lambert's displeasure.

"It's not right, you know, not right at all," he fumed to Mr. McGraw between acts, and pointedly in Lucia's hearing. "The prince is the hero of the play, not that damned chit Ophelia."

But Lucia didn't care. She continued to pour herself and her heart into the role, and by the time she'd reached her final scene, playing the mad Ophelia with her hair loose and tangled over her shoulders, she had lost herself so completely in the role that as she handed out her flowers, her tears of sorrow and bewilderment were so genuine that the audience was completely silent, suffering with her. When she exited, she stood in the wings with the tears streaming down her face, overwhelmed with emotion and oblivious to the congratulations of the other players.

"Here, here, dry your eyes," Mr. McGraw said, hurrying toward her with a handkerchief. "They're calling for you."

She took the handkerchief and wiped her eyes, not understanding. "But they can't," she said. "It's the middle of the play."

"They can, because tonight the play belongs to you," he said, all smiles. "They know the story well enough to realize you'll die offstage and the only time you'll be back is as a corpse, so they want you now. Come along, ma'am, take what's due."

She composed herself as best she could and let Mr. Lambert lead her back out to the stage. The applause stunned her, and small bouquets of flowers were thrown onto the stage around her. She smiled through her tears and curtseyed her thanks, and the cheers grew louder. Not in her headiest dreams had she expected such a response, yet all she could think of was what Rivers thought of her performance. Somewhere in the crowd, he'd been watching her. Did he approve? Had she moved him, too? Did he recognize how much of her own sorrow had fueled Ophelia's?

Finally she left the stage, her arms full of the flowers that had been tossed to her, and the play was able to continue on. But McGraw wasn't done.

"A word with you, Mrs. Willow," he said, taking her aside. "You are a triumph, ma'am, a triumph, and the people adore you."

"Am I?" she asked, startled by this praise from him. "Do they?"

"Yes, and yes," he said firmly. "You have a rare talent, ma'am, but before we can proceed any further, I must know your understanding with his lordship. I'm all too aware of how gentlemen can be under the circumstances."

She frowned. "I'm not sure I understand, Mr. McGraw."

"Then let me be blunt, Mrs. Willow," he said. "He has paid for tonight's performance, and thus it will be his right to determine if it is to be repeated. Most gentlemen do not permit their mistresses to continue on the stage. The attention makes them jealous, and they don't like other men ogling what's theirs. So tell me, ma'am. Was this benefit to be a single event for the sake of his wager, or will he permit you to return to the stage for other performances?"

She flushed, chagrined that she hadn't understood his meaning. "I have no such obligations to his lordship, Mr. McGraw," she said as firmly as she could. "On the contrary, it is his express wish that I continue on the stage, and earn my living by acting if that is possible."

"Oh, it's certainly possible," McGraw said, smiling warmly. "Especially since his lordship has stipulated that the return from tonight's benefit is to go to you, not him."

Her flush deepened as she considered the significance of Rivers's generosity. He knew she wouldn't take money directly from him, but that she couldn't object to this, the money having been earned through acting rather than in his bed. It was a clever, thoughtful arrangement, and an honorable one, too, and entirely in keeping with Rivers's personality. He had said that he would do whatever was necessary to make her happy, and he had. It was also as sure a sign as the diamond brooch that he was done with her.

"Then I will consider whatever offers you make to me, Mr. McGraw," she said, striving to sound businesslike. "Another performance of *Hamlet*?"

"Another, and another after that," he said. "I should say six nights to begin, and after that, if we continue to suit each other, we might discuss a more permanent role for you in the Russell Street company."

She nodded, her head spinning with possibilities. She had acclaim, she had a future as an actress, and she had money in her pocket. What more could she want?

Rivers, her heart whispered. *You don't have Rivers, and most likely you never did.*

Swiftly she shoved aside the thought. "One more question, Mr. McGraw," she said. "Can you suggest respectable lodgings near to Russell Street that would be suitable for me?"

"I can recommend a half dozen without hesitation that would be perfectly agreeable for a lady," he said, studying her shrewdly. Despite clearly realizing the truth about her background, it was in his favor to perpetuate the myth of Mrs. Willow as a gently born lady driven to the stage by personal misfortune, even though most of London would know otherwise by now. "But if you're looking for a place for this night, Mrs. McGraw and I would welcome you as our guest until you find yourself a, ah, new situation."

Lucia raised her chin with determination. She might play Ophelia, but she'd no intention of withering away or going mad for the sake of Rivers. Part of her would never recover from losing him, yes, but she would be strong, and she would survive.

"Thank you, Mr. McGraw, on all accounts," she said, holding out her hand to the manager. "It would seem I've found my new situation already."

Impatiently Rivers shifted in his chair in the royal box, praying for the play to be done. Although Ophelia had already died and made her final appearance as a corpse, there was still the rest of the act to complete, and nearly all the other remaining characters to kill. Shakespeare was a bloodthirsty playwright like that, and it was a shame he hadn't kept Ophelia lingering a little longer to make things more interesting.

He couldn't wait to see Lucia, to congratulate her and kiss her and tell her how very fine she'd been. That was what mattered now, not the infernal bet that was keeping him here in this uncomfortable chair. Although he was surely the one person in the entire theater to know what Lucia was capable of as an actress, even he had been stunned by the depth of her performance and the emotions she'd brought to poor doomed Ophelia. All around him ladies and more than a few gentlemen, too, were shamelessly sniffing and blotting their eyes with their handkerchiefs, and he remembered how making the audience weep had been her goal as a dramatic actress. She'd done that, and more. Much, much more, and he was eager to tell her how proud he was of her.

"I say, Fitzroy, is this nearly done?" Everett whispered, leaning over to Rivers. "We all know your little filly has won the wager for you, and since her character's gone and drowned herself, there's really no use in wallowing through the rest of this, is there?"

"It's nearly done," Fitzroy said. "There's still a couple of poisonings and a sword fight to finish off the rest of the Danish royal court. Then you and I will shake hands, everyone cheers, and we're free to go to the tiring rooms."

"A good thing, too." Everett's attention wandered from the stage to the ladies in the other boxes. On account of the wager, they'd agreed to sit by themselves and not include any other guests in their box tonight, and Everett was clearly bored without a nearby female to toy with. "What I still don't understand is how you could have looked at your Mrs. Willow when she was whoever-she-was amongst the Di Rossis, and predicted she could turn into this. A worm into a butterfly."

"She's hardly a worm," Rivers protested.

"I said she *was*," Everett said. "She isn't now. But that's what I mean. How did you know then that she'd blossom like this?"

"I didn't," Rivers said, remembering back to that night in the dancers' tiring room. Lucia had been completely unnoticeable, until she'd spoken. Then he'd seen the spark that had nearly been driven from her, the same spark and spirit that he'd come to love so well.

"Whatever you saw in her then, she's become a tasty small morsel of beauteous womanhood, ripe for amorous indulgence," Everett was saying. "If ever you tire of her, Fitzroy, then I'd be happy to—"

"No, Everett," Rivers said sharply, unwilling to consider such an eventuality. "Speak of her again, and I swear you'll be meeting me with pistols at dawn. Content yourself with Magdalena."

"Magdalena," Everett said fondly, musing philosophically. "That is true. I can safely call my darling Magdalena my own. I do like a lady with spirit and fire, and she has that in spades. But then, I don't have to tell you that, do I?"

"It was so long ago, I scarce remember," Rivers said. "Besides, Magdalena suits you far better than she ever did me, and I wish you well of her. Look, the queen has finally died, and there goes the king. Hah, now we're well rid of Hamlet, too. One more speech, and then we'll be done."

That last speech ended, and the players came out together to bow, holding hands as they strung across the stage. In the middle was Lucia, still dressed in her madwoman's costume, with her hair loose and her eyes ringed with black paint. McGraw led her out to stand on the edge of the stage by herself, and she curtseyed as the crowd cheered and clapped.

She grinned, and flipped her hair back over her shoulders. There, pinned to her bodice, was the brooch Rivers had given to her, the jeweled flowers a bright spot on her white costume. For luck and for love, he hoped, and it pleased him no end to see it there at her breast.

She was peering up at the box, shading her eyes against the candlelit stage. Not only were all the other players doing the same, but the rest of the audience had turned to look as well.

"Stand, Everett," Rivers ordered. "They're all hunting for us, so make a show of it for Lucia's sake. Shake my hand, there, to show we've no hard feelings between us."

Reluctantly Everett rose and did as he'd been told.

"Damnation, I didn't know I'd be part of the show," he said, handing Rivers the small pouch heavy with the coins from the wager. "Though these guineas should all be going to Mrs. Willow. She's the one who won them."

"That she did," Rivers said, tucking the pouch into his coat. "I'll tell her you said so."

He'd already decided to give Lucia the wager, and hoped she'd accept it, though he suspected she wouldn't. Roses were safer, and he bent down to retrieve the enormous bouquet that he'd bought earlier. At once he plunged into the crowds thronging the passageway outside the box, determined to make his way down the stairs and back to the tiring rooms where Lucia would be waiting. He knew he wouldn't have her to himself—tiring rooms were always very public places—but he still intended to congratulate her, and give her both the roses and the key to her new house. He could already imagine her little gasp of pleasure when he explained about the house, and how warmly she'd thank him later in private.

But it seemed that nearly every person he'd ever met had come to Russell Street that night, and every one of them wanted him to stop to be congratulated about how he'd won the wager, slowing his progress to an interminable crawl. By the time he reached the backstage area and the tiring room, the celebration had clearly been in progress for a while. The narrow space was packed with well-wishers in addition to the actors and actresses, musicians, stagehands, and anyone else who wished a glass of the wine and ale that seemed to be flowing freely. Voices and laughter grew to a near-deafening level as each person raised his or her voice to be heard over the din, and if that wasn't enough, a fiddler stood on a table in the corner playing jigs.

All Rivers cared about was finding Lucia, which wasn't easy given her small size. He held the roses high, not wanting them to be crushed, and that must have been what caught her eye.

"Rivers!" she called, and stupidly he thought of how well she'd learned to raise her voice to be heard over a crowd. "Rivers, here!"

He turned to see her climbing on a stool or box, suddenly tall enough to rise above the crowd and wave to him. She looked happier than he'd ever seen her, her smile wide and her eyes dancing, and he felt a little catch in his chest at how much he loved her. She still hadn't changed from her costume, a cheap, tawdry version of Ophelia's burial dress that made the brooch he'd given her sparkle even more by comparison. She'd hurriedly braided her hair in a thick plait down her back and she'd missed one curling lock that hung free beside her cheek, and yet somehow all of it made her even more endearing.

"For you, love," he said when he reached her, handing her the flowers. Her smile warmed, clear to her eyes. "You were magnificent."

He kissed her quickly, self-conscious of the others around them. He hadn't realized earlier how much paint she was wearing, with her face covered with white to show that she was dead, and black lines around her eyes. It had an odd, greasy scent that didn't smell like her, and he recoiled from it.

"I'm so glad you are here, Rivers," she said, her voice breathless with excitement. "I want to make a speech, you see."

"One moment," he said, and handed her the pouch full of Everett's guineas. "This is for you, too."

She looked warily from him to the pouch, guessing from the weight of the coins what it was.

"Yes, it's Everett's stake," he said before she could protest. "He agreed that you earned it far more than I did. I'm sure you can put it to use."

She paused, considering, then nodded crisply. "I can," she said. "Thank you, and thank Sir Edward for me, too. Now I must make my speech."

He had wanted to give her the key to her new house now, not listen to her make a speech. But others had overheard and suddenly the moment had passed, and then it was too late.

"Speech, speech!" called one of the other players nearby, and the cry was quickly picked up around them until Lucia raised her hand to silence them.

"Friends, dear friends," she began, the roses cradled in the crook of her arm and the pouch in her hand. "Thank you all for joining me on this special night, a night that would not have been possible without this gentleman, Lord Rivers Fitzroy."

She beamed at him as the others cheered, and Rivers nodded and smiled, thoroughly uncomfortable with being lauded like this. She was the one who loved the attention, not he, and he was relieved when she began to speak again.

"You all know how last month his lordship and I made a certain partnership for the sake of a wager," she continued, her speech so polished and practiced that she might well have rehearsed it along with her lines in the play. "He promised to instruct me in the finer arts of being an actress, and I promised to quit my old place, do my best to learn what he could teach me, and mind his wisdom in all matters pertaining to acting."

"Sounds like a good recipe for a wife," a man called from the back of the room, and the others laughed in raucous appreciation. Lucia made a sour face, but she laughed, too, and didn't correct the man.

Rivers didn't laugh, because he didn't find it amusing. In fact he found it both uncomfortable and disrespectful, but he didn't see a way that he could correct the fellow's impudence without appearing to be a prig. He tried to remind himself that this was how theater people often were, and that any other time, in any other circumstances, he likely would have been laughing, too. Instead he merely stood beside Lucia, feeling deuced awkward, until she once again held up her hand for quiet.

"His lordship and I have shared common goals for nearly six weeks," she continued. "His lordship would win his wager with Sir Everett, and I would become sufficiently accomplished to take my place on the stage. His lordship gave me his confidence, and assured me that I wouldn't be permitted to fail. He believed in my talent, and he told me I'd have no choice but to succeed."

Her voice soared, and he heard the faint tremble that always betrayed her emotion. He was surprised she remembered that conversation in such detail. That morning when he'd been suffering badly from too much wine the night before seemed very long ago, but he knew he'd said all those things. He'd said them then, and he believed them still, just as he still believed in her. More, because he loved her, and he longed to pull her into his arms and tell her exactly that.

But she wasn't done with her speech just yet. "Although our time together is done," she was saying, "his lordship has kept his word, as I have kept mine. Now he has won his wager, and I've played on the stage here at Russell Street."

She held up his bag of guineas as proof, and more cheers and huzzahs greeted her. Rivers continued to smile, but a few of her words caught his ear and stayed there unpleasantly.

What the devil did she mean by "our time together is done"? If she meant the time stipulated by the wager, then yes, that was finished. But their time together certainly wasn't over—in fact, he believed it had only begun.

The key to the house with the yellow shutters was feeling very heavy in his pocket.

McGraw pushed his way through the crowd to stand on Lucia's other side. He, too, was clearly in a celebratory mood, his face nearly as ruddy as the gaudy red waistcoat he wore in honor of the occasion.

"Tonight may have been this splendid lady's first appearance on the boards here at Russell Street," he said in a booming voice, "but I rejoice to inform you all that it will not be the last. Mrs. Willow has accepted my offer to reprise her role of Ophelia in a special engagement of *Hamlet*, to play exclusively for the next week, which I pray will be only the first of many roles with our esteemed company. To Mrs. Willow, the newest member of our company!"

The cheers and applause erupted again, the congratulations warm and genuine. They'd every right to be, since

Lucia's performances would bring extra revenue to the entire company. There was no doubt that Lucia herself was delighted, too, making tiny hops of excitement up and down on the stool. She turned toward McGraw and said something that Rivers couldn't hear. Whatever it was, it made McGraw laugh, and he planted a swift kiss on Lucia's cheek.

That was enough for Rivers. Gently but firmly he took Lucia by the arm, and turned her so she had no choice but to look at him.

"Why in blazes didn't you tell me you were joining this company?" he asked. "Why am I the last to hear of it?"

"You're not the last, Rivers," she said defensively. "Mr. McGraw only asked me a short time ago, during the play, after I'd finished my lines. I couldn't have told you."

"Why not?" He wished she weren't standing on the stool. It felt odd, having her nearly eye to eye with him. "You could have told me first, before you announced it to the world."

"I thought you'd be pleased for me, Rivers," she said, more wistfully than he'd expected. "I thought you'd be happy, too. You got what you wanted, and now I have, too. We both should be happy."

He grumbled, and shook his head to show that he wasn't happy at all.

"This is not the place for this conversation, Lucia," he said. "Why don't you change your clothes, and we'll go to dine."

She hopped down from the stool and set the bouquet on a nearby table. She took him by the arm, not by the hand the way she usually did, and led him to the far corner of the room. It wasn't the most private of places, but at least it was out of hearing of the rest of the crowd, who were noisily continuing their merrymaking.

She turned and faced him squarely, staring at his chest

instead of meeting his eyes, and clasped her hands before her.

"I am sorry, Rivers," she said softly, "but I'm not going with you. I'm dining with the rest of the company to celebrate."

If she'd struck him with her fists he wouldn't have been more surprised.

"Damnation, Lucia," he growled. "You're supposed to celebrate with me."

"This is what I must do if I wish to make my way as an actress," she said. "You know that's what I want, above all things."

His immediate response was that this wasn't what *he* wanted, not at all, but with a manful effort he shoved aside his own wishes for her sake. This was her special night, and he did not want to deny her anything.

"Very well, then," he said. "Where will you be dining? I'll have my carriage waiting to fetch you home when you are done."

"No," she said, her hands twisting restlessly, betraying her. "I'm not coming back to your house, Rivers."

He noted the subtle yet devastating difference between *home* and *your house*. What nonsense was this?

"Of course you'll be coming back to Cavendish Square, Lucia," he said firmly, willing it to be so. "Where else would you go?"

"I'm arranging for lodgings of my own," she said. "I can't be your guest any longer."

He thought again of the house with the yellow shutters.

"I understand entirely," he said with hearty relief, reaching for the key in his pocket. "You should have your own home, to arrange however you please."

She nodded quickly. "I will be taking lodgings not far from here, close to the theater," she said. "Mr. McGraw is paying me fairly, and I can afford it now."

His hand fell away from the key. "There's no need for that, Lucia. I can—"

"Please understand, Rivers," she said, her voice flat and the words coming as if by rote. "Tonight I will be staying with Mr. and Mrs. McGraw, and then I shall be in rooms of my own. This is my decision. This is what I want. Please."

He did not want to understand. He wanted her with him.

"No, Lucia," he said, refusing, denying. "No."

Still she did not look at him, her fingers knotted together. "You said you would do anything to make me happy. This makes me happy."

"Lucia, don't—"

"This makes me happy, Rivers," she said again, so deliberately that only her hands betrayed her. "*You* have made me happy, happier than I'd ever dreamed possible, and I thank you for it."

He reached for her, desperate for any way to make her stop this madness, but she quickly backed away.

"You will be happy, too," she said, a breathless rush of words. "You may not believe it now, but in time you will. Be happy, my lord. That is all I wish for you, as you did for me. Be happy."

"Lucia, please," he said, reaching for her again, but this time she ran and didn't look back, darting away to rejoin the others.

It couldn't end like this, he thought. She loved him, and he loved her. He couldn't be mistaken about something like that. He had promised to give her whatever she wanted to be happy, but how could she truly be happier without him? He couldn't believe it, not after these last six weeks that they'd had together. He didn't want to believe it, because it couldn't be possible.

Yet as she ran away from him, he let her go, and did not follow.

CHAPTER
19

Lucia sat at her dressing table, leaning close to the looking glass as she carefully drew a fine line of the lampblack around her eyes. Her face and shoulders were already covered with pale paint, smelling faintly of the vinegar used to mix the white lead, and her cheeks were artificially flushed with red vermillion. It looked gaudy and false here before the glass, but beneath the stage's candles, she'd become the fresh-faced maiden Juliet, ripe for love, that the audience had come to see.

In the two weeks since she'd made her debut as Ophelia, she'd learned to outline each eye with two strokes of the brush, above and below, with one more artful curve to lift her brows in permanent surprise. She held her breath to steady her hand, a little trick she'd learned from one of the other actresses. She sat back and blinked at her reflection, then smiled. Beneath the gold-edged cap, she was the very picture of Juliet, without a trace of Lucia, exactly as she was supposed to be.

But then, wasn't that the way this entire fortnight had been? Everything in her life had changed. Her Ophelia had become the talk of London, and instead of being a mere curiosity, she now was praised for the sensitivity and sentiment of her portrayal.

In honor of her success, McGraw had given her a dressing room of her own, as much for receiving her admirers as for any real dressing. The playhouse was filled every night, and paeans to her talent were written in newspapers and magazines. She received amorous letters from men she'd never met, and she was recognized by strangers on the streets and in shops. She had become a *bona fide* celebrity, and one night even the king and queen and a great party of courtiers had come to watch her from the royal box, and had offered their compliments afterward.

But the backstage visitor who had astonished her the most had been the great Mr. Garrick himself from the Theatre Royal. He had praised her performance to the skies as he'd kissed her hand while McGraw hovered nearby, fearing that his rival would try to lure her to his own playhouse.

To counter Garrick's attention, McGraw had staged a revival of another of Shakespeare's plays, *Romeo and Juliet,* with Lucia as Juliet. They'd rehearsed the new production during the day and played *Hamlet* at night, until Lucia had fallen into her bed in her new lodgings each night so exhausted she'd no notion of how she'd rise to do it again the next day.

Yet she did. She learned this new part in a matter of days rather than the six weeks she'd had for Ophelia, and when they closed *Hamlet* one night and opened *Romeo and Juliet* the next, she'd been ready. Once again, the crowds came, and again she made them weep.

It came easily to her now, making them cry. Critics called this her special gift, but only she knew the real reason. She could wring the anguish from every word of Juliet's tragedy as if it were her own, because in a way it was. Rivers had been her Hamlet, her Romeo, and on the stage, through Shakespeare's words, she could set free all the pain and sorrow of her own broken heart.

Ending her attachment with Rivers had been the proper thing to do, the noble thing, but not a minute went by that she didn't think of him with regret and loss. That last glimpse of his face and the pain she'd caused him were the worst memories to have, and no matter how often she reminded herself that he never could have found lasting happiness with her, she still couldn't stop wishing it had been otherwise.

She hadn't realized how empty her success would feel without him to share it. They truly had been partners in creating Mrs. Willow, and she never imagined how much she'd long for his suggestions and challenges, and even how he'd suddenly charge off to retrieve a book from his library to read her a particular passage that he felt she needed to hear. She missed how seriously he'd taken her, never once making fun of her questions or missteps. All during rehearsals, she'd yearned to discuss her new role with him, and she wondered constantly what he'd make of her performance.

It only got worse, not better. Each evening before the curtain, she stood in the wings and scanned the first tier boxes, searching for him. Considering how she'd broken off with him before he could do the same to her, she knew rationally that he wouldn't be there, and he wasn't. Yet still she searched for him, her heart refusing to give up hope.

And late at night, when she lay alone in her bed in the dark, she longed for him to be there with her. She ached for the warmth of his big body beside her, for the passion they'd shared, for the love he'd given her that had taken away the loneliness that was once again her constant companion.

No one else around her understood. Of course her new friends knew that she'd parted with Lord Fitzroy—that was unavoidable, given that she'd done it in the tiring room—but they believed her to be like Magdalena, effortlessly shedding a gentleman when he no longer proved useful. They teased her about who her next lover would be, and when bouquets of flowers arrived for her from men she neither knew nor wished to, her new friends read aloud the cards with bad poetry, and made bawdy suggestions about the authors. Even Mr. McGraw had praised her for leaving Rivers, telling her that he would only have complicated her career and brought her trouble in the end.

In return, Lucia merely smiled, and let them think what they wanted. She alone knew the bitter truth, and the aching loneliness that went with it.

She touched the flowered brooch Rivers had given her, pinned for safekeeping to her stays, beneath her costume and over her heart. She always wore it now, a talisman and a reminder. It was all she had left of him.

"Scene three, ladies, scene three," announced the stage boy from the hall. "Make ready for your entrance."

Lucia gave a final pat to her cap and turned away from the looking glass. In the dressing room across the narrow hall from hers sat another actress, Martha, who would play Lucia's mother in the next scene.

"We should go, Martha," Lucia said, already up and closing her door behind her. "You know how angry Mr. McGraw was last night when Ned was late coming back from the privy and the whole scene had to wait."

"Oh, McGraw can wait, the old cow," Martha said, engrossed in the scandal sheet she'd spread across the table before her. "This will interest you, Lucia. It's about that lordling what made the wager with you. He is to wed, or leastways he's as good as betrothed."

Lucia caught her breath. "You cannot mean Lord Rivers."

"I can, and I do," Martha said, pointing to the page. "Here it is, clear as day, even with the proper names left out. Read it for yourself."

Reluctantly Lucia took the paper from Martha, and forced herself to read the item.

Lord R****s F*****y, son of the Duke of B*********e is said to have formed an attachment to the beauteous daughter of the Marquess of S*******e. The two are seen often in one another's Company, & since LOVE & HAPPINESS will not be denied, a nuptial Announcement by the Lady's father is regarded as Imminent.

" 'Tis fortunate you left the rogue when you did," Martha said as she rose, straightening her wig. "You're spared all the teeth-gnashing of him mending his ways for his new bride. Men being men, he'd likely been planning to marry her all the time he was with you, the lying rascal. Come along now, or McGraw will come yipping after us himself."

Yet Lucia lingered, unable to look away from the small item of gossip. Even this was enough to make her heart ache with loss, and long for all she'd never have. For two weeks now, he'd stayed away from her, accepting her rejection as final. Here was the last proof that he'd rejected her in return.

Because of course it was Rivers. Of course he was going to marry the daughter of a marquess, who was of course beauteous.

And of course love and happiness would not be denied. Wasn't that exactly what she'd wished for him? Love and happiness, with another woman who was his equal, and would be welcomed warmly into his family as his wife, not his mistress.

Of course.

Rivers, however, was not happy, nor was he in love, at least not with Lady Anne Stanhope. He was standing at one of the long windows of his father's house with his back turned to the rest of his family, who were gaily blathering on about some nonsense or other while they waited for their guests to arrive.

He was in no humor for either gaiety or blather, and if he was honest, he wasn't overly interested in his family at this point, either. Nor did it help his mood knowing that he was being a fool, pining over a woman who had discarded him as easily as an old pair of gloves.

Yet he could not help it. Lucia di Rossi had done that to him, and he'd make no apologies for how thoroughly her rejection had wounded him. He felt like a dog with a broken leg, hopping gamely along on three legs but still in pain.

He hadn't even been able to manage that much for the first days after she'd told him she no longer wished to be with him. He missed her more than he'd believed possible. Countless times a day he'd been sure he heard her voice in the hall, or turned his head, certain he'd find her there at his side. With only Spot for company, he had stayed in his house and he hadn't left it, hoping that she'd return to her senses and come back to him.

Instead she had sent a man with a cart to collect her belongings, the same little trunk that she'd once carried herself, and the new clothes that had been made for her in Newbury. To make matters even more humiliating, she had also returned the bag of coins that had been Everett's wager. With it had been a note explaining that the money should be considered repayment for the clothes, and that he should now regard her debt to him paid in full.

Rivers had cursed and sworn that he'd consider no such thing, and had insisted the man take the money back to her. He had no use for it, not when the one thing he truly wanted was Lucia herself.

Yet even after this, he had kept his distance, the way she'd requested. He hadn't gone to the playhouse to watch her perform. He hadn't loitered outside after the play was done, hoping to see her leave. He hadn't made inquiries as to her new lodgings, or asked if she had taken up with another man. He read her reviews, because he would have read the papers anyway, and he felt ridiculously proud of her for them. Even though she had banished him from her life, he was not able to do the same with her.

After that first week alone, he had forced himself to go out, and to pretend that there was nothing amiss. He went to his club, where he was congratulated for winning the wager. He dined with his friends, and his refusal to discuss Lucia was only taken as a sign of worldly manhood. He visited his family, and tolerated their attempts to make a match with Lady Anne. He was polite to the lady, who would have been entirely agreeable under other circumstances, but he did nothing to encourage her. He couldn't. His heart and his love still belonged to Lucia, whether she wished it or not.

All of which had led him here, to this window, staring out at the green oval of Portman Square in the falling dusk. The lanterns were being lighted now, little pockets of brightness against the night. He had thought he'd been invited here for a family dinner, his father and Celia, Harry and Gus, Geoffrey and Serena, but Harry had let it slip that the Stanhopes had been invited as well. He did not want to dine with the Stanhopes, or to have to suffer through a long meal with Lady Anne gazing adoringly at him with her blank blue eyes.

To his relief, they were late, and he surreptitiously checked his watch. Perhaps he could plead some other engagement and escape before they arrived. Perhaps he could shift from this window to the door and slip away unnoticed, and make apologies tomorrow. Perhaps—

"Lost in your own thoughts, Rivers?" said Father as he came to stand beside him, and put an end to all hopes of escape. He motioned to a nearby footman to bring them wine. "I don't blame you, when all the ladies can speak of is infants and children. There was a time when the trials of the nursery were left there, but now it seems that every tantrum and rash is considered fit conversation for the drawing room as well."

Rivers took the wineglass and raised it toward his father before he drank.

"You're only unhappy because they speak of their daughters," he said. He knew he was tossing a spark into dry tinder with his father, but perversely he couldn't stop himself from spreading his own general misery. "If one of those tantrums belonged to a son, you'd be directly in the middle of the conversation, praising that tantrum as a rare sign of spirit."

But to his surprise, Father didn't rage, the way Rivers had expected. Instead he merely chuckled, as if Rivers hadn't goaded him, but told an amusing jest.

"True, true," Father said, looking back at Serena and Gus. "With luck I'll have that grandson soon enough."

"Gus looks well," Rivers said. "She must be near her time."

"It could be this week, or another three," Father said, narrowing his eyes a fraction as if he were able to see Gus's unborn child. "Ladies—and babes—can be unpredictable that way. But that is no affair of yours, is it? Your head is filled with the lovely Lady Anne."

He clapped Rivers on the back so hard that the wine splattered from his glass.

"No, Father." Rivers set his glass down on a nearby table and shook the spilled wine from his fingers. "If I am honest, the lady is not in my thoughts now, nor ever has been."

"Then she should be," Father declared. "You're not the only young buck that has an eye on her. Has she told you that she has five brothers? Five brothers, Rivers, and her the only girl in the family! That's the kind of lady who'll give you sons. But if you don't declare yourself soon, she'll slip away."

"Then let her slip," Rivers said wearily. "I've told you before, Father, I've no interest in marrying at present, and especially no interest in Lady Anne Stanhope."

"Don't say such rubbish," Father said, his voice rising and his face growing flushed. "I know you were infatuated with that little actress last month, but surely you must be recovered from her by now. If you lifted your nose from your books for once, you would see what a fine opportunity the lady—"

"Brecon, please." Suddenly Gus was standing there, too, her freckled face smiling as pleasantly as if Father were not on the verge of apoplexy. "If you do not object, I should like to borrow Rivers for a few moments."

She tucked her hand possessively into the crook of Rivers's arm, making it clear that she would not be denied.

"Ah, yes, by all means, Augusta," Father said, visibly controlling his temper for her sake. "Take the rogue away with you if you wish. But mind he does not vex you, for your own sake as well as the child's. Do you understand, Rivers? Do not torment Augusta, or you'll answer to me."

"Rivers will behave with me, I am sure of it," she said, leading him away and from the drawing room.

She was so large and close to her time that she seemed nearly as wide as she was tall, with endless peach-colored silk ruffles fluttering like waves from her person. Rivers hoped he hadn't distressed her, the way Father had accused him of doing. He'd never forgive himself if she went into labor early because of him, and neither would Harry.

"Please, be seated, Gus," he said gallantly, trying to steer her toward one of the chairs in the hall. "No need to tire yourself."

"Don't be like your father, Rivers," she said breathlessly. "I shall not break, and neither will my little one."

Purposefully she continued another ten steps to a nearby settee. She dropped into it with obvious relief, cradling her hands over her belly as her ruffled skirts spread and settled around her.

"Oh, my goodness," she said with a sigh. "This imp gives me no peace in my womb, kicking me night and day. I'm sure Brecon would say that's a sure sign of a boy, which is why I've not told him."

Rivers wasn't any more comfortable with talk of unborn kicking babies than Father, and when Gus rubbed her belly to calm the "kicking imp," he looked down with embarrassment. But that was no better: beneath the hem of her gown he saw that Gus wore not shoes, but backless slippers, and that her feet were so swollen that even those were snug. Horrified, he hastily looked to his own hands, resting on his own knees.

"Father has become entirely irrational on the question of his heir," he said. "I do not know how you bear it, Gus."

"I do because he means well," she said, "and because I have no choice, because he is your father. I also trust that in time he will indeed be blessed with the grandson he so desires. You're the scholar, not I, but I'm certain there must be some sort of reassuring mathematical law regarding the progeny of three healthy brothers."

Rivers looked up sharply. "*Three* brothers?" he repeated suspiciously. "Are you party to the Lady Anne scheme as well?"

She tipped back her head and laughed merrily, the candlelight from the nearby girandole casting a coppery glow on her hair. There was no denying that Gus could be pretty, very pretty, even as pregnant as she was now, and Rivers understood entirely why Harry had married her. Lucia had liked her, too, and before he could stop himself, he was imagining Lucia with Gus and Serena, the three of them laughing happily together with a roomful of tumbling children around them. He was surprised by how appealing a scene it was to him, even if it was impossible.

"No, goose, I have no schemes for you and Lady Anne," Gus said. "She seems a sweet enough lady, but she is not right for you. I cannot begin to picture her clambering up to your rooftop haunt at the Lodge."

"Neither can I," he agreed softly, and he couldn't. He suspected Lady Anne would be one of those overly dainty ladies who shrieked at heights and clutched at her skirts and cap from fear a breeze would carry her away. She definitely wouldn't see the beauty in a new moon, or beg to use his telescope, or curl close against his chest while he pointed out the stars. "Then I owe you my gratitude for rescuing me from Father and his matchmaking."

"No, you don't," Gus said. "Because I must warn you: I am also matchmaking."

He groaned. "Not you, too, Gus. Who have you found for me now? A cousin from the country? An old friend from school?"

"You know her already, Rivers," she said, smiling. "It's Mrs. Willow."

He shook his head, stunned that she'd dare say that.

"No, Gus," he said. "You must trust me when I say that is not possible."

"And I say it is," she insisted. "I have never seen two people more in love than you and Lucia. That is her proper name, isn't it? Lucia di Rossi?"

He frowned. "How did you learn that?"

"I have my ways," she said smugly. "Besides, it wasn't that difficult. But do not distract me. Watching you two together at Breconridge Hall was like—oh, like poetry. You belong together, Rivers. Serena and I both saw it, and it was beautiful to watch. Love like that should not be denied."

"Poetry isn't true to life, Gus," he said, and stood, too agitated to remain still. "There are so many things you don't know about Lucia, or about me, either."

"Then tell them to me," she said promptly. "Make me understand why you cannot be with the one woman who is meant to be yours."

He shook his head, not knowing where to begin. "She dismissed me, Gus," he said. "The night of the benefit. She told me she'd be happier without me, and sent me away like some dunning tradesman."

Gus fluttered her hand dismissively through the air. "I do not believe it," she said, "because it cannot be true. Did you tell her you loved her? Did you speak of your future together?"

"She didn't let me," he said mournfully. "I was going to tell her all about our future together. That night I even had in my pocket the key to a house I'd put in her name."

Gus gasped. "Oh, Rivers, you didn't! You were going to ask her to become your *mistress*?"

"Yes," he said, glancing around uneasily to make sure no one overheard, for mistresses were another topic that was not encouraged in his father's house. "After the time we'd spent together at the Lodge, I didn't want to give her up."

"But to keep her as your *mistress*," Gus said, appalled. "Rivers, that is so shameful and unworthy of you that it's beyond bearing. If you'd offered her a house, she'd think it meant she wasn't good enough to live in your home with you. How can you be so thickheaded? A woman like Lucia would never settle for being kept. If she had even a hint of what you'd planned, then I'm not surprised she asked you to leave. You're fortunate she didn't break a bottle over your head and shove you down the stairs as well."

"But what else was I to do, Gus?" he asked plaintively. "I didn't want to lose her."

She looked up at him pityingly. "Rivers, in many ways you are the most clever and learned gentleman I have ever met, but in love you are nothing but a thick-witted dunderhead. If you don't want to lose Lucia, you don't make her your mistress. You ask her to marry you."

He stared at her, too stunned to speak. To Gus it must seem so damnably obvious, and yet he had never let himself dare to consider it. To have Lucia with him always, to never be apart from her, to love her forever—it was everything he wanted.

Except she didn't want the same things.

"If I asked Lucia for her hand, she would not accept," he said, the certainty of it turning each word to lead. "She told me that the stage was the only thing that would make her happy, and that is why I let her go."

Now Gus was shaking her head. "She may have told you that, but it isn't true. Why couldn't she act *and* marry you? Why couldn't she do both? There's no law at present against married women on the stage, is there?"

He frowned, thinking of how eagerly she'd thrown herself in amongst the other actresses and actors, leaving him behind. Would she do the same if she were his wife?

"You are *thinking* too much, Rivers," Gus said with exasperation. "I can see it in your face. Did Harry tell you that I made him take me to see Lucia in *Romeo and Juliet*?"

"He did not," Rivers said, and somehow this felt oddly like some kind of fraternal betrayal. "Was she—Lucia—as fine in the role as everyone says?"

"Better," Gus said. "I cannot believe you haven't gone yourself. No, I can believe it, for if you had, you would know she still loves you."

He thought of what made Lucia so special as an actress. Oh, he had corrected her accent and her grammar, and helped burnish the rougher edges, but her talent was her own. She had always wanted to make people cry, but to do so she had had to draw that emotion from deep within herself and share it with her audience. She'd been fearless that way. She dared to think of what she could give rather than what she could take.

He thought again of that last farewell, and now he realized what she'd really been saying. She hadn't said she'd be happier without him; she'd said *he'd* be happier without her. She hadn't pushed him away. She'd tried to give him his freedom, and he'd been too caught up in his own pride and sorrow to see the difference. He had in fact been—what was it Gus had called him?—a thick-witted dunderhead.

"You are being entirely too quiet, Rivers," Gus said warily, "which means you *are* thinking too much. If you become like your father next and begin to protest that Lucia is foreign, or a theatrical person, or some other foolish obstacle as to why you cannot marry, then—"

"Lucia will sleep beneath the stars with me," he said, his mind made up. "Why should I care who her parents were?"

Gus smiled, her face full of joy.

"If that is true, then you must go to her now," she said eagerly. "Go watch her as Juliet, now, tonight, and you'll see how much she loves you still. You may have already missed the first act, but that's mostly sword-fighting and brawling anyway. Go, Rivers. I'll make excuses for you to the others."

He grinned, and bent to kiss her cheek. "Thank you, Gus, for everything. No wonder my brother loves you so much."

"Go, go!" she said, shooing him away. "It won't matter one bit unless you return with Lucia on your arm."

*   *   *

Lucia hurried off the stage, her thoughts on her final scene. She'd already taken the potion that had made Juliet appear lifeless, and she'd only the final scene, where she'd awaken to find Romeo dead and kill herself. She was glad the play was nearly done, too. Some nights were more exhausting than others, and tonight she'd given so much to her performance that she was completely drained, with little left.

"Mrs. Willow, a moment," said Mr. McGraw, catching her by her arm. His face was wreathed with concern, and he held her as if he feared she'd collapse. "What is wrong? Are you unwell?"

Wearily Lucia shook her head and shrugged. "Nothing is wrong," she said. "Some performances are more taxing than others. You know that as well as I."

"I do, but tonight seems different." He studied her face, skeptical. "It is a virtue to put much of yourself into your role, but you can go too far, and let the passion destroy you. I won't have you ill."

"You needn't fear for me," she said. "I'm well enough."

But she wasn't. She wouldn't explain it to Mr. McGraw, but the shock she'd felt seeing the news-sheet with the mention of Rivers and his impending betrothal had fueled her performance. Her Juliet tonight had been more desperately in love than any other, and felt the agony of being parted from Romeo more deeply. She had thrown herself into the play as if she were jumping overboard from a ship into the deepest sea, and she'd let the lines and her emotions dash and carry her like stormy waves. It was no wonder that she felt so battered and spent, or that it showed on her face.

"You are certain?" McGraw asked, not persuaded and watching her closely. "The way you are now, I'm going to make doubly certain that Romeo's dagger holds a false blade, or you truly will stab yourself."

She smiled, thinking of the harmless, rickety trick knife

with the spring-loaded blade. "Not for the sake of a play, I won't."

He smiled, too, with relief. "Then go change for your death scene," he said. "But mind that I'll be watching you."

She left, and quickly shifted into her last costume: Juliet's white linen burial-clothes. The other actors saw and understood her mood, and kept their distance, nor did they speak to her, leery of breaking her concentration and the spell of her performance. By the time she'd returned to the stage and climbed onto the painted wooden box that served as her marble tomb, she was once again firmly in the grip of her character.

She lay there as the scene played out around her, her eyes closed and her hands folded over her breasts. She heard the scrape of the mock swords, the deaths of Paris and Romeo, the bustling horror of Friar Laurence, and yet all she thought of was Rivers.

She'd tried to be so noble, giving him his freedom for true happiness, but she hadn't realized how painful it would be to watch him find that happiness with another woman. Now she realized that she'd never love another man the way she had—no, she still—loved Rivers, but all the regret in the world couldn't change what she'd done.

It was, quite simply, too late.

By the time Juliet awoke and saw the horror of her dead Romeo, Lucia's grief was raw and eloquent, her few lines achingly poignant. Frantically she kissed Mr. Lambert, her portly Romeo, found the false dagger and raised it high. She barely heard the gasps and alarm of the audience as she stabbed herself with heartrending anguish, and fell across Mr. Lambert's body.

That was the end of Juliet. All she'd need do now was lie still and pretend to be dead, the hardest part of the play. She was thankful that her hair had trailed over her face like a veil as she'd fallen, for tears were still sliding down her cheeks, her emotions so mixed that she could not stop them.

As soon as the curtain fell, Mr. Lambert immediately sat upright.

"Are you all right?" he asked anxiously. "Faith, I've never seen such a Juliet as that!"

She nodded, recovering with great, shuddering gulps of air and dashing away her tears with the heel of her hand.

"I—I am," she said. "It's done now, isn't it? It's done."

She meant not only the play, but what she'd had with Rivers, too. All of it was done.

"Indeed it is," Mr. Lambert said, helping her to stand. "Come, the audience is wild for you. Are you recovered sufficiently for your bows?"

She nodded, and forced herself to smile. No matter how she felt, the audience was expecting Mrs. Willow. They didn't know about Rivers and his soon-to-be wife, nor did they care, and now she must try to do the same. The cheers and applause were deafening, the loudest she could recall, and as she curtseyed yet again, she realized for the first time she hadn't looked to the first tier boxes for Rivers before the play.

Maybe it truly was done after all . . .

The tiring room was even more crowded than usual, with far too many people crushing into the small space. She was greeted with more applause as admirers pushed forward to congratulate her. She tried to smile, but tonight she had no patience with their slavering praise. Tonight it meant nothing to her. All she wished was to be left alone.

She was only half-aware of a scuffle near the door, of one more man pushing his way into the room.

"Lucia!" Rivers called. "Lucia, here!"

Shocked, she turned toward his voice, unsure whether she'd imagined it or not. "Rivers? Why are you here?"

"Lucia," he said, holding his arms out to clear his path.

The crowd recognized him and melted back to give him room. He was rumpled and mussed, his golden hair falling across his face and his clothing without its usual neatness, yet he was still impossibly handsome, impossibly perfect to her. She forgot the lady he was supposed to be marrying, the cruel things she'd overheard his father say, how she'd tried to be noble and failed. None of that mattered now. This time he'd brought no flowers, but he didn't need them. His smile was more than enough for her as he held out his hand to her.

"Lucia," he said again, and the din around him faded as the others listened and craned their necks. "You were—you are—magnificent."

She smiled, and realized she was crying again. That was what he always said to her, and she answered the way she always did, too.

"Truly, Rivers?" she asked, her voice squeaking upward. "Truly?"

"Yes, truly," he said. "And yes, you made them all cry, just as you're crying now."

"I cannot help it," she said, her smile wobbling. "It's seeing you here."

"Ahh," he said, that familiar, slightly-grumpy noise that he used to fill time while he thought of what to say next. Oh, how much she'd missed him, every part of him! "So you made your audience cry, and now I've done the same to you."

"Yes," she said, every bit as foolish as he. "That is, I am very glad that you came here tonight."

"I'd a reason for doing so," he said, and to her shock, he sank down on his knee before her. "An excellent reason. You see, I've found it's quite impossible for me to live without you. I love you that much. Mrs. Willow. Miss di Rossi. My own Lucia. Will you marry me?"

Now she was the one at a loss for words. She gasped, stunned, her heart beating so fast that it drummed out everything else. She had never imagined this, never expected this, and most certainly never wanted this—this *disaster*.

Everyone in the room seemed to be holding their collective breath, waiting for her reply. Rivers's smile widened, certain she was simply too overwhelmed to reply—which, of course, she was, though not for the reason he believed.

Oh, how much she loved him when he gazed up at her like this!

"Please say yes, Lucia." He took her hand and kissed it, not letting it go. "Please be my wife."

She gulped, her eyes brimming with fresh emotion. There was only one possible answer to give now, only one, and she gave it.

"No, Rivers," she said. "No."

CHAPTER
20

❧

"No?" Rivers repeated, the single word echoing as if in a cold and empty cave. How in blazes could she refuse him? He'd offered her his heart, his title, his world. He'd done the honorable thing, the only thing, and yet she'd rejected it all. "Lucia, I love you, and you love me, and I want nothing more than—"

"No," she said again, more firmly this time, and scattered tears as she shook her head. "No."

He only half-heard the low, collective groan of disappointment and commiseration from those watching, and a single woman clicking her tongue with dismay. Awkwardly he rose to his feet, still clutching Lucia's hand. He felt foolish and ashamed, confused and distraught and furious, too, but most of all he felt as wounded as if she'd taken a sword and cut him to the quick. Damnation, he loved her, and she loved him. They were *meant* to marry, and be together always.

Weren't they?

"I wish to speak to you alone," he said. "There must be some more private place than this."

"My dressing room," she said, reluctantly. "But there's nothing more that—"

"Come with me," he said tersely, pulling her through the crowd and down the narrow hall. "Which one's yours?"

"The last," she said. "Rivers, please, I—"

"Not until we're alone," he said, leading her into the tiny dressing room and slamming the door shut. No doubt the crowd was already rushing to follow them and listen shamelessly outside the door, but at least he wouldn't have to see their looks of pity. When he finally released her hand, she immediately pulled it back, rubbing her wrist. He hadn't intended to hurt her—he'd never wish to do that—and guilt and remorse jumped in to join the rest of his turbulent emotions.

"I won't change my mind," she said defiantly. Now she was angry, too, and in a way that was better. "You can't make me marry you, Rivers."

"I'd never force you to do anything," he said. "But you can't expect me to leave you without a decent explanation."

"Because it would be wrong for both of us," she said quickly, too quickly. "Because I could never make you happy, not the way you deserve."

"Shouldn't I be the judge of that, Lucia?" he demanded, his voice rising with urgency. "When we are together, you have made me happier than I've ever been before, and more miserable when we've been apart."

She took another step away from him, her back against the bare wall as she hugged her arms defensively to her body. Yet her eyes were dark and challenging, her earlier tears now dried to murky streaks on her face paint.

"You are a gentleman, the son of a duke," she said. "You could never have an actress for a wife."

"I'd be the most selfish bastard on earth if I tried to stop you from acting," he said, and he meant it. "I saw you tonight. How could I wish to put an end to your talent, your gifts? I'll gladly share you with your audiences for performances as Mrs. Willow, if the rest of the time I can have you to myself as my wife. Will that do? Will that be enough?"

He smiled, coaxing, and believing he'd won. But her expression only darkened, and he realized there was still more to come.

"On our last day at the Lodge," she said, "I heard what your father said to you outside in the garden. He called me a 'creature.' I heard how angry he was with you for taking me to the Hall, and having me drink tea with Her Grace and the others."

His hopes plummeted. So this was it. Blast, why hadn't she said something about this before now?

"I'm sorry you heard that," he said. "My father is accustomed to speaking directly, no matter how it might wound others."

She looked down and shook her head, her long, loose hair falling over her face. Her arms were still clutched defensively around her body, and he hated to think that she needed to protect herself against him.

"If you heard my father," he said more gently, "then you also heard how I countered every hateful thing he said about you."

"But your father was right, Rivers," she said sorrowfully. "I can't make you happy, not in the ways that would matter to you. I didn't belong at Breconridge Hall, and I don't belong with you."

"Yes, you do," he insisted. "*We* belong together, and nothing anyone says—"

"No, Rivers, please, I beg you," she interrupted. She finally looked up again, the pain in her dark eyes unmistakable. "This is exactly what your father meant. You are so honorable, so loyal, that you would stand by me against the entire world, and I love you all the more for it."

"I would indeed," he said. "Why wouldn't I do that for the woman I love, and wish to have as my wife?"

She shook her head again, her earlier anger gone and her misery palpable. "Because no matter how much you love me, you loved your family first, and I could never make you choose between us. Your father, your brothers, your sisters-in-law and their children—they're all a part of you that I could never replace by myself."

"That's foolishness, Lucia," he said. True, his father would be furious, but his brothers and their wives would happily share their joy. "I would never expect that of you."

"Wouldn't you?" She uncurled one hand and placed it on his chest as she tried to make him understand. "Your father thinks I'm no better than a slatternly gypsy. If we wed against his will, you'd lose him and the rest of your family, and no matter how hard you fought it, in time you'd come to resent and despise me for it."

Loving her as he did, he knew she believed what she said. It wasn't a dramatic exaggeration for her.

"I'm a grown man, Lucia," he said firmly, placing his hand over hers. "I make my own decisions, and I have an income and property, and a life and interests of my own as well. I do not need my father to choose my wife for me. As soon as either Gus or Serena bears a son, I'll cease to be of any interest to him whatsoever."

"That isn't true," she said wistfully. "He loves you too much for that. You are fortunate to have such a father, Rivers. He may have no use for me, but you'll always be his son, and he cares for you whether you're his heir or not. I'd never, ever wish to come between the two of you."

He looked down at his hand across hers, her small fingers resting on his breast. He found it difficult to agree with her regarding his father, but then he had to remember that she'd no parents or siblings of her own, and that she'd never had the security of his two older brothers. All she had now was him, and he was determined to do whatever he must for her sake.

He sighed, and linked his hand into hers. "Tell me," he

said softly. "Would you marry me if we had my father's blessing?"

"Yes," she said at once and with gratifying conviction. "Oh, Rivers, yes."

"Then we'll go to him now," he said. Unlike his older brothers, he could recall challenging his father outright only a handful of times in his life. He'd never once won, either. But this was different; for Lucia's sake, this time he was determined to come away with what he wanted.

She gasped, her eyes wide with surprise. "Now? It must be nearly midnight, Rivers."

"Now," he said firmly. He pulled his watch from his pocket to check the time. Father's habits were as punctually predictable as his own, and Rivers knew he wouldn't retire for the night for at least another hour. "I'd rather not have to rouse him from his bed."

She smiled, too, an endearingly wobbly smile. "You are certain?"

"I am certain of this, and everything else as well." He smiled and drew her close, her body warm and soft against his. He felt instantly better, and having a plan that would join them together forever made him feel better still, and when he kissed her, he could tell she shared both his eagerness, and his excitement.

Reluctantly he broke the kiss and smiled down at her. Dressed all in white with her dark hair trailing over her shoulders, she looked younger than she was, and impossibly beautiful. "We must go now, sweetheart," he said. "There will be time enough for this later."

She nodded. "Your father," she said, but that wasn't the reason.

"Not at all," he said, and kissed her lightly on the forehead. "It's that I don't wish to wait a moment longer than I must to make you my wife."

*   *   *

A half hour later, after a breakneck ride in a hackney, Lucia found herself hurrying through the front hall of Breconridge House with Rivers's hand firmly clasped around hers. He had only given her time to wash the paint from her face, and she still wore her loose-fitting Juliet costume, her hair unpinned.

Rivers was striding so purposefully that she had to trot to keep pace with him, bunching her long skirts with her free hand so she wouldn't trip as they began up the stairs. She'd only a passing impression of the hall, of a great many candles and gilding and a marble floor that was chilly beneath her slippered feet, the same extravagance that she remembered from Breconridge Hall.

"Almost there," Rivers said as they reached the first floor. "At this hour, they'll be in the Green Parlor, listening to Celia play."

"They?" she asked, surprised. She realized she'd been picturing the duke sitting alone, waiting for them like some sort of awful judge. "There will be others there, too?"

"Only family," Rivers said, smiling. "My stepmother, Celia, of course, and my brothers as well as Gus and Serena. We always dine together here *en famille* on Thursday evenings. Except I left early tonight to see you instead."

In return her smile was tight, a sorry attempt to hide her anxiety. She'd much rather they declared their love for each other before a full house at the theater than face his family like this.

"It will be fine, Lucia," Rivers said, sensing her uneasiness. "I'll make Father understand, and we're not leaving until he agrees."

She rolled her eyes. "*Santo cielo,* I should like to see that."

"You will," he promised. He stopped before a closed door, and raised her hand to kiss it with the gallantry that always made her heart flutter. "I swear to it."

From inside the room came the muffled notes of a harpsichord, jangling and discordant to her ears, and she sighed with dismay. Wasn't this evening difficult enough for her without adding music, too? The footman at the door murmured a greeting to Rivers, clearly expecting him to give Lucia's name so she might be announced.

"There's no need, Willis," Rivers said. "I'll present Miss di Rossi myself."

The footman nodded and opened the door for them, and before she could hang back Rivers was leading her into the room, forward to the bright ring of candles at the far end, before the tall windows. She recognized Celia, sitting at the harpsichord's bench, and Serena, sitting beside her to turn the pages. Standing nearby with a glass in his hand was a dark-haired gentleman who so strongly resembled Rivers that Lucia knew he must be his brother Geoffrey. Though obviously surprised, those three were smiling warmly in welcome.

But the last person in the room was not.

Lucia swallowed a small gasp as the Duke of Breconridge turned toward them. He was every bit as formidable as she'd imagined he'd be, and impeccably dressed in a dark velvet suit that gleamed with golden embroidery. There was lace at his wrist and throat, a large emerald on his finger, and an elegantly curled and powdered wig on his head. While he still possessed the same handsome features that he'd passed on to his sons, his were set and world-weary. He had the well-bred yet jaded face of a man who had spent the majority of his life having everything exactly as he wished, and his expression was confident that that would not change now.

She forced herself to keep her gaze level and not look away. She'd met him once before, though then she hadn't realized he was Rivers's father. Did he remember, too, or would he pretend he'd forgotten?

"So you have returned, Rivers," the duke said, rising

to his feet, ignoring Lucia entirely. "The Stanhopes were sorry to have missed you. Lady Anne was understandably upset that you weren't here. I fear you have missed supper, but I can send for a little refreshment from the kitchen if you wish."

Lucia didn't flinch. She'd expected this slight from the duke, and she refused to let it intimidate her. She wished Rivers had mentioned that his rumored fiancée, Lady Anne Stanhope, had been among the dinner guests, but what mattered now was that she was gone. Lucia raised her chin a little higher, squared her shoulders a little straighter, and smiled as warmly as if the duke had smiled at her first.

Rivers was mortified by his father's reception. She could tell by the way he squeezed her hand, a kind of wordless apology and support. He took a slight step forward, holding their clasped hands in front so his father couldn't miss them.

"Father," he said, "may I present Miss Lucia di Rossi? Lucia, my father, the Duke of Breconridge."

She slipped her hand free of his and sank into the curtsey that was expected of her. It was also the curtsey that she'd practiced so often under Rivers's instruction, and she bent with the grace that she'd made her own. She was the noble-born Ophelia, she was the cherished Juliet, she was the honored Mrs. Willow, but most of all she was Lucia di Rossi, who loved and was loved by Lord Rivers Fitzroy. All gave her strength, even as she remained bent low on the carpet with her white Juliet-skirts spread around her.

But the duke still did not acknowledge her or her curtsey, instead looking directly at Rivers and ignoring her. She didn't have to look up to sense Rivers's growing anger, and her heart went out to him. How difficult this must be for him! She didn't want him to take her side against his father, but rather wished his father would accept their love, and with it Rivers, too.

"You've noticed that we're a smaller group than when you left this evening," the duke was continuing as if Rivers hadn't made his introduction. "Poor Augusta wearied, and Harry took her home. Of course every care must be exercised with her these last days before she's brought to bed."

"Father," Rivers repeated. "May I present Miss Lucia di Rossi?"

"Good evening, Miss di Rossi," Geoffrey said, coming forward to take Lucia's hand and lift her up. He had the same warmth in his blue eyes that Rivers had, and she couldn't help smiling in return. "I have heard much about you from my brother and my wife, and I'm honored to at last make your acquaintance myself."

"This is my brother Geoffrey, Lucia," Rivers said quickly. "Serena's husband."

"He is Lord Geoffrey Fitzroy," the duke said sharply. "Do not slight him before an inferior, Rivers."

"It is you who are slighting Miss di Rossi, Father," Rivers said, his voice rising. "Why you cannot put aside your pride and—"

"There's no reason for a formal introduction, Rivers," Lucia said, placing a light restraining hand on his arm. "His Grace has met me before, you see."

Abruptly Rivers turned to face her. "He has?"

"Oh, yes," she said, smiling to reassure him—and perhaps herself, too. She was going to need to give the performance of her life if this was all to work as she prayed it would. "Last week your father came to Russell Street with His Highness to see *Romeo and Juliet*. All the primary players had the honor of being presented to the royal party at that time."

Rivers looked sharply at his father. "You didn't tell me you'd seen Lucia perform."

The duke gave the slightest of shrugs. "Since I believed you had wisely ended your liaison with this woman, Rivers, I did not judge the matter to be of any consequence. I suppose it slipped my mind."

"Forgive me, Your Grace," Lucia said gently, "but that was not what you told me then. Before all of us, you said that seeing my Juliet had been an honor and a privilege, and you agreed with His Majesty that I had brought tears to the eyes of the sturdiest gentlemen among you."

"Hyperbole," the duke said with disdain. "If you were familiar with the ways of Court, ma'am, you would know that much is said, but little believed."

That stung, but she didn't let it show, and it helped that Rivers protectively slipped his arm around her shoulders.

"Father, please," Rivers said. "I have not brought Miss di Rossi here for your critique of her performance. Rather, I intend to marry her, and I hope you will give us your blessing."

Serena and Celia made little cries of rejoicing and Geoffrey grinned, and Serena hurried forward to kiss Lucia on the cheek and link her hand loosely into Lucia's: a small gesture, but one that meant so much to Lucia.

But the duke's expression only darkened.

"You will not have my blessing," he said flatly. "How can you possibly expect me to condone so unsuitable a match as this one?"

"Because I love her," answered Rivers without hesitation, "and she loves me, and I can see no reason under Heaven for that to be unsuitable, even to you, Father."

"Because it *is*, Rivers," Father thundered. "Consider your station, and then consider hers. Her parents were *dancers*, kicking their feet in the air for the amusement of the crowds."

"As was my mother, Brecon," Serena said quietly. "She was also my father's mistress, not his wife, yet you forgave that for my sake, and for Geoffrey's."

"Your father was a gentleman," the duke said firmly, waving away her objection. "That made it easier to overlook your mother's other, ah, deficiencies."

"Perhaps my father wasn't a gentleman," Lucia said, "but he and my mother were married, and they loved each other very much."

"They were foreigners," the duke said. "French, and Italian, I believe. They were not English."

"But I am," Lucia said, undaunted. "I was born was brought to London when I was less than a month old, which makes me as English as anyone."

"As English as any of us are, in any event," Geoffrey said, coming to stand beside Rivers. "Pray recall, Father, that we have a good share of Italian and French blood in our veins as well, back to the de' Medici, and—"

"I do not require a lecture as to our ancestry, Geoffrey," the duke said. "It is our future, not our past, that concerns me at present, and how this woman from the stage deserves no place in it."

"That's not what Her Majesty believed, Brecon," Celia said. With her customary poise, she glided from the harpsichord's bench to stand beside her husband, placing her hand lightly on his shoulder. "Didn't you tell me that after Miss di Rossi's performance, Her Majesty wished aloud for the young ladies of her Court to possess even half the grace of Miss di Rossi's Juliet?"

Lucia gasped. "Her Majesty said that of me?"

"She did," Celia said, nodding so that the white plume in her hair nodded in agreement as well. "Or so Brecon told me that night. My husband may be a stubborn man, Miss di Rossi, but he is always truthful. If the queen herself judged you would be an ornament to her Court, how could we Fitzroys possibly believe otherwise?"

Overwhelmed with unexpected emotion, Lucia was speechless. She'd never expected to find such acceptance from Rivers's family, or such regard. She felt it like a force enveloping her, wrapping her in a kind of security that she'd never felt from her own family.

Except for the one person whose judgment would matter most to Rivers.

"I will not be hectored in my own house, Celia," the duke said, the edge in his voice unmistakable. "You compel me to speak plainly. For his own good, Rivers deserves a lady for a wife. A *lady*. We all do, considering what may be at stake."

He didn't have to say more. Everyone else in the room understood. He meant that much-wished-for future Duke of Breconridge, the unborn boy that hovered over every family gathering.

The little boy who, if the duke had his way, would never be born to Lucia.

"I will marry her, Father," Rivers said, his words filled with angry determination. "I wished for your blessing, but if you refuse to give it, then so be it. I'll never again bring my wife to this house, where she is not welcomed, nor will I come without her."

Lucia bowed her head with misery and regret. This was exactly what she'd feared would happen. She'd never wanted to come between Rivers and his father, and now she'd done precisely that.

The duke began to answer, but Celia stopped him.

"Brecon, please, don't speak in haste," she said, her voice beseeching yet firm. "Remember what it is to love, and be loved. If you cannot, then you will lose your son."

The duke's expression softened, his belligerence replaced by a genuine sadness that Lucia hadn't expected.

"There are cases, Celia, where love alone is not sufficient," he said. "If my son persists on this course then I fear I'll have no—what in blazes is that?"

The knocking at the drawing room door was frantic, and one of the footmen opened it. The butler quickly ushered in another servant, in different livery, and the two of them made short, bobbing bows.

"Forgive me, Your Grace," the butler said breathlessly. "But this man brings news that you—"

"It's Her Ladyship, Your Grace," the other servant interrupted excitedly, forgetting himself. "That is, Lord Hargreave sends his compliments, and requests that His Grace come at his earliest convenience, as her ladyship's been brought to the bed of her babe."

"The child!" At once the duke snapped to attention, Lucia and Rivers forgotten before the arrival of the latest grandchild. "We must go to them at once. At once!"

In the dashing flurry of activity, Lucia hung back, feeling thoroughly out of place.

"I should return to my lodgings, Rivers," she said. "But come to me tomorrow, and let me know whether Gus bears a boy or another girl."

"Nonsense," Rivers said. "You'll come with us."

Lucia shook her head. "I don't think your father would—"

"I'm asking you, not him," Rivers said, and smiled crookedly. "Harry and Gus will want you there. Especially Gus. To be sure, I cannot force you to come, but I hope you'll choose to be with me."

She smiled. "For you, Rivers," she said softly. "I'll stay with you."

It was one thing for Rivers's father to declare that they all must hurry to Gus's side, but quite another to see it done in the middle of the night. Hats, coats, and cloaks must be fetched. The grooms, coachman, and footmen needed to be roused from their beds, the horses harnessed and two carriages brought around from the stable. Celia and Father rode in the ducal carriage, while Lucia and Rivers rode with Geoffrey and Serena in theirs. There was little conversation among them, with everyone acutely aware of the importance of the coming birth.

Nearly an hour had passed by the time the two carriages drew up before Harry and Gus's home, the only house on the square still ablaze with candlelight, and almost another hour besides since Harry had sent one of his footmen to Breconridge House. Nearly two hours, then, and more than enough time for Gus to be delivered of her fourth child.

Father himself was the first in the house, rushing up the stairs to the countess's bedchamber, with Celia hurrying to keep up. No one thought to stop him; it was his place to be first to see his newest grandchild. Next came Geoffrey and Serena, and then Rivers and Lucia.

"Even tonight, we follow by rank," Rivers said wryly. They were several steps behind the others and out of their hearing, which was fine with him. "We can't help it, can we?"

"I feel sorry for Gus," Lucia said, "having so many people crowding into her bedchamber at such a time."

"After three children, she's probably accustomed to it by now," he said. "The price of marrying Harry, I'm afraid."

He tried to smile, but Lucia was well aware of the tension that seemed to fill the entire house. It wasn't just her own worry for what would become of her and Rivers, or even the very real concern for the much-loved Gus as she endured the hazards of childbirth. There was a sense that the fates and happiness of everyone in this family depended on the safe arrival—and gender—of this new, small person into the world.

And as she and Rivers reached the end of the hall and Gus's bedchamber, that small person let out a monumental wail over the excited voices of all the adults already there.

"Does that sound like a boy?" Rivers asked.

"It sounds like a baby," Lucia said, drawing him forward.

Hand in hand, they entered through the open doorway. The room *was* crowded. In addition to all the Fitzroys, there were also assorted midwives and nursery maids, plus a physician. The two elder sisters of the new baby were there, too, brought from their beds by their own nursery maids. Also in attendance were a couple of large spotted dogs with feathered tails, bustling back and forth around the bed. In the center of all this swirling confusion sat Gus, flushed and exhausted but already washed and tidied, and propped up against a mountain of pillows and wearing an extravagant silk organza cap, new for the occasion.

Beside the bed stood Harry, the proud new father once again, looking thoroughly harassed in his shirtsleeves with his oldest daughter, Lady Emily, clinging to his leg. Next to him stood the duke, and in his arms was the well-wrapped bundle of lace-trimmed linen and squalling newborn babyhood that had drawn them all here.

"It's a boy, Rivers," the duke announced over the general din of the others, his voice reverberating with joy and emotion. "At last, a fine, healthy son!"

"Well done, Gus, well done!" Rivers exclaimed. "You, too, Harry, you dog, though none of the hard work was yours."

Gus, however, wasn't looking at him, or her new son, either, but at Lucia.

"Mrs. Willow, isn't it?" she asked, excited despite her weariness. "Did Rivers propose? Did you accept?"

The others fell silent, leaving only the crying baby. Harry took him back from the duke, soothing him to a whimper, which only made the silence following Gus's questions more awkward still.

Rivers's fingers tightened around Lucia's. "I have proposed, yes," he said. "Exactly as you advised, Gus, and Lucia has almost accepted me."

Gus frowned beneath the ruffled cap. "How can she almost accept? She either has, or she hasn't. Mrs. Willow, can you explain? Do you not love him?"

"I do love him, with all my heart," Lucia said, hesitating. "But because of that, I know I will make him unhappy."

"That is not possible," Gus declared, holding her arms out for the fretful baby. "Not if you love him as you say."

Carefully Harry settled the baby back into her arms, and Gus put him to her breast. At once he quieted, peacefully suckling as she rocked him gently, and she smiled with contentment herself, especially after Harry rested his hand on her shoulder. When she looked back to Lucia, her expression was soft with love, yet determined, too.

"Without love, you'll never be happy," Gus said softly. "But with it, anything is possible. With love, you *will* be happy."

Lucia nodded, her heart so full she feared she might weep from the weight of it. All she had to do now was say yes to Rivers, yes to love, and yet as she gazed up at him, emotion had robbed her of her voice. She, who could make a theater full of people weep at her words, suddenly had none of her own.

"It's my fault," the duke said suddenly. "I said I wouldn't give my consent to Rivers marrying Mrs. Willow."

"Oh, Brecon," Gus said. "How could you? Look at them. How could you stand in the way of love like that?"

"I won't, not now," the duke said gruffly, gazing down at his new grandson. "Babies change things, don't they? Rivers, you have my blessing. As Gus says, if you love her and she loves you, then that will be enough. That will be everything."

"It *is* everything," Rivers said firmly. For the second time that night, he dropped down on one knee before Lucia. "Will you marry me, Lucia? Will you be mine forever?"

Lucia smiled, and let her tears slip. "Yes, Rivers," she said. "Yes, yes, yes."

One year later

The invitations had been written in French, and therefore sounded dauntingly formal: *Fête Solstice d'été avec la Famille.* But the truth of the Duke of Breconridge's annual Midsummer Party with the Family was that it was neither formal, nor daunting. Instead it was a country affair for all the members of the duke's extended family, including every nephew and cousin as well as their wives, sons, and daughters, gathered together beneath the summer sun at Breconridge House. Every child was welcome, no matter how young, and for this one week of the year, the large old house echoed with the children's laughter and excitement.

This was the first year that Lord and Lady Rivers Fitzroy attended the *fête,* not only as husband and wife, but also as a small family themselves. Two months earlier had brought the birth of their daughter, Juliet, who was herself making her first appearance before the extended family.

Juliet had been named for one of her mother's most famous roles, and had in fact performed it many times with her. London theatergoers had been willing to overlook their favorite actress's pregnancy, and the famous Mrs. Willow continued to perform nearly until Juliet's arrival. As a result, her father, Rivers, was jovially predicting that her first word would not be *Mama* or *Papa,* but *Romeo.*

But for now she was a charming, happy baby, with her father's blond hair and her mother's round cheeks, and there was nothing she liked more than being on her mother's lap and watching the water drops fly and scatter from the fountain in her grandfather's garden.

"She does like the fountain," Lucia said. "She's fascinated."

"Every child loves that fountain," Rivers said. "I know, for I was one of them once. Next step she'll want to put her hands in the water, then will come wading, and then finally she'll want to climb into the center to ride the lead horses that spurt the water."

"I'd like that," Lucia said. "Would your father be upset if I went wading, too?"

"Oh, I doubt it," Rivers said easily. "Nothing much upsets him these days."

Lucia smiled, for they both understood the reason for the change in the once-overbearing duke's temperament. Thanks to Gus and Harry, not only did he finally have his heir in their son, young George, but Serena and Geoffrey had also recently given him a second grandson, Charles. With his legacy secure, the formerly stern duke had learned to relax and enjoy all his grandchildren, boys and girls alike, and had even been observed giving the occasional pony ride on his shoulders.

"You realize it will be our turn for a boy next," Rivers continued. "It's the law of averages, you know. Mathematical observations would prove that after so many—"

"Hush," Lucia scolded gently. "No mathematical anything today. I am on holiday, and I mean to enjoy it. You should, too, if you've any sense."

Rivers grinned, and took Juliet from her, cradling her in the crook of his arm. "I would be a fool not to enjoy this day, here in the sunshine with my two favorite ladies."

"As it should be," Lucia said, her face softening as she gazed at the two people she loved best. "Gus was right. Love is enough."

"Not even Shakespeare could have written it better," Rivers said, leaning over the baby to kiss her. "With you, love is everything."

"Everything," repeated Lucia softly. "Everything."